Gentleman Thief

Gentleman Thief

Recollections of a Cat Burglar

PETER SCOTT

HarperCollins*Publishers*

HarperCollins*Publishers*
77−85 Fulham Palace Road,
Hammersmith, London W6 8JB

Published by HarperCollins*Publishers* 1995
1 3 5 7 9 8 6 4 2

Copyright © Peter Craig Gulston 1995

The Author asserts the moral right to
be identified as the author of this work

A catalogue record for this book
is available from the British Library

ISBN 0 00 255565 4

Set in Linotron Meridien

Printed in Great Britain by
HarperCollinsManufacturing Glasgow

CONTENTS

FOREWORD

by Martin Short

For over thirty years Peter Scott was Britain's most prolific pillager of the Great and Good. To him being a burglar was far more than a job; it was a vocation, as he sensed one rainy night in 1957 on his first country-house raid. Through the windows of Dropmore House, the home of Viscount Kemsley, Scott saw a 'magnificent table laden with silverware and a great array of aristocracy coming down to wine and dine. I felt like a missionary seeing his flock for the first time and I decided these people were my life's work.'

From 1953 to 1985 this latter-day Raffles stole jewels, furs and works of art worth over £30 million from the 'real, meaty jugular vein of society', as he charmingly describes the succession of duchesses, film stars, opera singers, shipping magnates and 'royals' who have been his victims. I first met him in 1978 when he was being investigated over allegations of corrupt involvement with three senior Scotland Yard detectives. As I had recently made several television programmes on police corruption and co-authored a book called *The Fall of Scotland Yard*, I was bursting to speak to Scott or, rather, to someone called Peter Gulston, which is his real name.

As soon as he ambled into the smart hotel behind Harrods which was our rendezvous, I could see Gulston a.k.a. Scott was no ordinary thief. I had met many underworld characters but none like this. I did not believe so urbane and witty a fellow could be a serious villain. I also thought him a bit old (at forty-eight) to be shinning up drainpipes and blowing safes. Yet at that very time, as I later discovered, he was right in the middle of a series of burglaries audacious even by his standards.

Soon after our encounter he was jailed for eight years, but within a year he was free again on the orders of the Court of Appeal. He spent the 1980s playing tennis, scaling walls, looting another £6 millions' worth, and doing penance back in jail. For him the decade of rampant free-enterprise capitalism (of which he was a prime practitioner) was dominated by three kinds of courts: sporting, criminal and matrimonial, where he went through a salacious divorce.

I did not meet Peter again until 1993 when I was co-producing a television documentary series on London's underworld called *Gangsters*. I tracked him down to a council flat in a grim, graffiti-clad tower block in Islington. No longer dining in smart restaurants, he offered me a huge bowl of excellent Irish stew he had made himself. He had no money. In the fifteen years since our last encounter, he had taken huge financial tumbles but, like one of Dickens's most indomitable characters, he was as cheery, fluent and fiery as ever. On film his presence and personality came over so strongly that we were able to devote one programme entirely to interviews with him and his eighty-one-year-old partner, George 'Taters' Chatham. After fifty years' thieving, Scott was at last going public on his extraordinary life and thieving times.

Peter Craig Gulston was born in Belfast in 1931 to middle-class parents who sent him to the city's prestigious Royal Academy School. Blessed with an acute brain, sharp wit, good looks, rich blue eyes and a height of six feet one inch, he could have chosen almost any profession, but he possessed a fatal flaw. From the age of twelve he had a compulsion to steal: 'I was "a wrong 'un". In police parlance I was "light-fingered", and I was reasonably bright at it, which compounded my destiny.' Fate also propelled him to break into the unoccupied home of an upper-class woman who had died some years before.

> Suddenly I entered a house just like Miss Havisham's in *Great Expectations* – all dust, drawn blinds and antimacassars – and I found myself in a world of plunder: the mouth drying, the pulse racing. First I took a few bottles of Scotch and a handbag. Then I got upstairs and I can never forget the excitement of opening the drawers and ruffling through silken underwear. Then this terrible conjunction between larceny and sexual drive came over me, a feeling which was to stay with me all my life.

Soon young Gulston embarked on 'a one-man pilgrimage' in upper-crust Belfast, sporting his college scarf and carrying a rugby bag to fill with spoils. 'I fitted in so perfectly with the background that I was never a suspect. I committed one hundred and fifty burglaries before they got on to me but, so as not to make themselves look stupid, the police only put twelve before the court.'

For a while his family's status protected him, but in 1952 he was sent to Crumlin Road jail for six months. The Governor said, 'We've been waiting for you for a long time. It's only your connections which have kept you out of here.' The Chief Officer added, 'Yes, Mr Gulston, you will spend your life going in and out of prison,' a prediction which came alarmingly true.

On his release in 1953 he moved to London. He became a pub bouncer and fell in with full-time villains. Rather than discreetly monopolise his skills, these early partners talked so glowingly about his talent for burglary that soon the cream of London's thieves wanted to work with him. They needed his agility, athleticism and muscle. He needed an apprenticeship.

Stealing's like any other profession. You've got to learn. You also have to use your brains. I soon realised there was no point breaking into prefabs in Catford because there'd be absolutely nothing there. There was rather more to steal from the Virginia Water belt, the penthouses in Belgravia and the fleshpots of Mayfair.

In 1957 Scott began a thirty-year relationship with George 'Taters' Chatham, who had been at the top of the cat-burglar tree for the previous thirty years. Taters tutored Scott in the mysteries of the craft. He also infected him with his own life-long obsession with the Victoria and Albert Museum from which, back in 1948, Taters had stolen two ceremonial swords, presented to the first Duke of Wellington, which were encrusted with emeralds and diamonds. Neither the swords nor the jewels were seen again: just one piece of the substantial chunk of Britain's national heritage which Taters has magicked away. Scott's admiration was unbounded.

The times I've seen newspapers describe Taters as a 'gang'! In recent years when he stole a Renoir and a Matisse in Mayfair I remember reading in *The Times* and *Telegraph* with amusement about an 'international art gang', when in fact it was just George with a bit of wire and a knowledge of how to bend glass doors.

Back in 1952 Taters had taken part in one of Britain's biggest unsolved robberies, the £287,000 Eastcastle Street mail-van raid, in league with Billy Hill, self-styled 'boss of London's underworld'. Taters received a £15,000 share – over £300,000 at today's prices – but he gambled it all away in a few weeks, mostly at Hill's gambling club where the games were rigged. He tried to get his money back by breaking into Hill's safe. He was caught but Hill did not punish him because he knew Taters would soon be back losing a lot more money. Taters eventually saw the folly of associating with gangsters – 'thieves' ponces' as they are known in the underworld – and reverted to the craft of specialist burglar, a lonely trade but one with less risk of betrayal. He was in jail when Scott first met him. The pair got on well and when Chatham was released in 1961 they went straight to work.

They were hugely successful, hitting dozens of well-stocked Mayfair jewel stores, furriers and private homes, but both were degenerate gamblers. Taters would rapidly lose his entire share from their crimes. This forced them back to work too quickly, on jobs that were far too risky or not properly researched. They were now gambling with their liberty, committing ever bolder burglaries even when they knew the police were 'on to' them. Taters kept getting 'banged up' and Scott too was given increasingly severe jail terms. In 1957 he had been sent down for a modest two years, but in 1961 he was imprisoned for three, and in 1964 he got a further five.

Scott was an exemplary prisoner, always earning maximum remission. Released in 1967, he stayed out of jail for twelve years, mixing spells of intense criminal activity with legitimate business as a haulier, demolitioner and property developer, but in 1977 everything fell apart. His latest wife divorced him and his business went into liquidation. To restore his fortunes he reverted to crime. In less than two years he netted £5 million from a succession of burglaries, but it wasn't only for money that he kept on thieving.

A stimulus came from it. It was sexual and even more potent than any woman could ever provide for me. As a husband I was a failure and as a lover indifferent, because my real passion was to be out on the roof, or creeping through the country or making a little tunnel through a wall. I'd found this private Walter Mitty world which yielded a sexual, antisocial excitement unobtainable by other means.

To locate his prize victims – 'the wealthy, the famous and the greedy' – Scott used to read the social columns of the *Daily Express* and *Daily Mail*. He says he was working out a semi-conscious scheme of social revenge. A century ago, the fictional Raffles justified his activities this way: 'Why should I work when I could steal? Of course it's very wrong, but we can't all be moralists, and the distribution of wealth is very wrong to begin with.' In contrast Scott portrays himself as something of a moralist.

> I have an inbuilt suspicion that I was sent by God to put back some of the wealth that the outrageously rich had taken from the rest of us. Of course, if I'd been really bright I'd have been with all those City slickers who were ripping off pensioners and everyone else. Their asset is not just that they are bright: they are also degenerate, immoral and uncaring – all that's required to be a very successful thief. I wasn't uncaring, I was generous to a fault. I suppose it was part of my Presbyterian upbringing to try to get a few plus points for being a persistent sinner. I've spent my whole life giving to the poor, perhaps to get a few plus points, should there be a Hereafter.

Scott identifies with the thieves crucified at Golgotha on either side of Christ, but which thief is he? The one who mockingly demanded that Christ save himself and them as well, or the one who accepted crucifixion as his due punishment, to whom Jesus said, 'today shalt thou be with me in paradise'? Either way, Scott is sure the rich are condemned to the fiery furnace. This has long added to his career satisfaction.

> God, the rich have a lot to answer for! That Nazarene fellow knew a bit when he talked about the eye of the needle. When they meet the other fellow, they've got a lot more to worry about than I have.

Conventional moralists may see nothing to admire in a man who has squandered his considerable 'straight' talents up ladders, on roof-tops and in jail, but in this book Scott's talents are not squandered. Indeed, he emerges as a brilliant writer. This is no ghosted autobiography. It is penned by the man himself. A utility crime reporter would be tempted to tell Scott's story chronologically, scrapping his device of writing in the third person. That person is the 'tennis bum' Scott became on his release from jail in 1980. As a racquet for hire at one of London's smartest clubs, he recalls his life of crime in unchronological bursts. Drifting in and out of the club bar, he also drifts in and out of the Victoria and Albert, scheming a safe route into the Jewel House.

As a literary device the third-person approach works well, but Scott says this wasn't an artistic choice: he was just not capable of writing in the first person. Perhaps he cannot face the fact that this bizarre but largely wasted life is indeed his own. Also, as a veteran of countless police interrogations, he must realise that anything in the first person would read like a confession. In fact Peter Gulston has never been charged with many of the crimes he attributes to his alter ego, Scott. An 'I' book might justifiably provoke a visit from Scotland Yard detectives but, as it stands, the Scott in this book might be dismissed as a creature of fiction, so Inspector Plod need not call.

And so we discover the fifty-year-old gentleman con knocking tennis balls back to rich 'prats', while he recalls his triumphs and disasters up Mayfair drainpipes and in England's stately homes: plundering peers and parvenus, aristocrats and *arrivistes*, nobs and *nouveaux riches*, film stars and princes, tycoons and magnates, heiresses and actresses. His greatest claim to infamy is his pursuit of the world's most glamorous females. He says he stole the gems of Lauren Bacall, Shirley MacLaine, Vivien Leigh, Natalie Wood, Pier Angeli, Zsa Zsa Gabor, Mrs Gregory Peck, Margaret Leighton, Lesley Caron, Valerie Hobson (Mrs John Profumo), Dawn Adams, and Nanette Newman. 'I burgled but failed to find anything worth stealing from Judy Garland, Bette Davis, Elizabeth Taylor, Anne Bancroft, Shirley Bassey, Deborah Kerr, Maria Callas, and Ginger Rogers. The list is endless, like the list of Huntingdonshire Cabmen that used to appear in the *Daily Express*.' Of all these onslaughts, the most notorious was on Sophia Loren in 1960, while she was in Britain filming at Elstree Studios.

> When her husband, Carlo Ponti, returned home one evening from abroad, Sophia left the downstairs window open. Not only that, but upstairs she advertised the whereabouts of the jewellery by having this massive padlock on top of a tallboy. Who in heaven's name ever puts a huge padlock on top of a tallboy? It was almost saying, 'Here are the gems.'

Not that Scott sensibly invested the £30,000 he made from selling Sophia's gems to a receiver.

> I remember she appeared on television and pointed at me saying, 'I come from a long line of gypsies. You will have no luck.' Well, if it helps you, Madame Sophia, I have had no luck, the gems did me very little good. *I lost every penny in the Palm Beach Casino in Cannes.*

This is perhaps the most infuriating thing about Scott's predatory progress: he has never held on to even a small portion of his criminal profits. It is easy to appreciate his vast expenditure on good living, fast cars and 'tarts', but not his addiction to gambling. By 1957 he had piled up £65,000 in a safety deposit box, equivalent to £1.5 million today, but he gambled it all away. That year his biggest one-day loss was £7,000 at Newmarket races (£150,000 today). 'I'd really no use for the money. I gambled for large sums that most people could have lived on for the rest of their lives. The passion of finding the victims was paramount.'

Scott's most celebrated pursuer was Albert Wickstead, in his last post as Commander of the Metropolitan Police Serious Crime Squad. Wickstead was a crime reporter's dream. His gangbusting exploits grabbed the headlines and earned him the sobriquet the 'Old Grey Fox'. At the start of the 1970s he smashed the east London gangs who, he claimed, were planning to seize power after the fall of the brothers Kray. Then he turned to the West End and destroyed the syndicate running Soho vice and pornography. His last crusade was to crush the corruption then rampant among senior Scotland Yard detectives. He believed Peter Scott could help nail three officers who had allegedly appropriated many of the valuables, worth millions of pounds, which had been left behind by thieves who tunnelled into Lloyds Bank, Baker Street in 1971 and broke open the safety deposit boxes. The chief suspect was an inspector named Alec Eist. Wickstead believed Eist had been corruptly involved with Scott, but Scott says the only thing he shared with Eist was a pub in St John's Wood with a 'very attractive landlady'.

At that time a man called Stanley used to chauffeur me to various criminal activities, and he'd also drop me off at this pub. He turned informer and told Wickstead's lot I was having corrupt chinwags with these coppers who had been in charge of the Baker Street job. It was all bollocks. I'd never done any deals with these men. In fact, one of them was determined to lock me up himself.

The informer Stanley implicated another burgling associate, an ex-SAS officer called George Alexander, who also said that Scott had been paying detectives. These men's statements were enough to give a zealous cop like Wickstead due cause to interrogate Scott. The Ulsterman was offered total immunity if he gave evidence against the suspect detectives. It was made equally clear that, if Scott refused to co-operate, he would be pursued for his own crimes. But he could not co-operate: if he had anything on the detectives, he was not prepared to discuss it.

After Wickstead retired in December 1977 police enthusiasm for nailing anyone for corruption in relation to the Baker Street job seemed to evaporate, but the case against Scott went ahead. In 1979 he was convicted of several major burglaries and jailed for eight years. A year later the Court of Appeal viewed this turn of events as oppressive. The contrast between the offer of total immunity to Scott and his swingeing sentence struck their Lordships as vindictive. They reduced it to three years. This meant that, with remission, he could be set free straightaway.

Had he now gone straight he already had enough material for an astonishing life story, but he could not resist bleeding the jugular vein of society yet again. By 1985 he had stolen another £6 millions' worth of gear, including £1.5 million in jewellery from one Bond Street job alone, but he was bound to get captured sooner or later. In 1985 he was jailed for four years and his fourth wife divorced him. On his release in 1988 he was completely broke, but Islington Council took pity and housed him. At this point he resumed his humbling existence as a tennis racquet for hire and completed this manuscript.

Today, seemingly brimming with health, cycling suntanned and tracksuited through London, Peter Scott might be mistaken for a man who has triumphed over all tribulations. Getting his story into print must also satisfy a long-felt craving, which in the old days he had to repel at all costs.

In the 1950s newspapers were running articles about the 'Human Fly': someone climbing all over Portland Place, Mayfair and Belgravia, carrying out acts of circus daring. In fact, they weren't so daring. I was using ladders and taking them away with me, so it looked very daring. *I* was the Human Fly! And I remember finding it very difficult standing in Paddy Kennedy's old pub in Belgravia when people were speculating on who this jewel thief was, and having to stay silent. I didn't want to be silent, I wanted to say, 'Yeah, well I'm the Human Fly – it's me!'

In all Peter Scott has been sentenced to twenty-two years in jail. He has served twelve of them during six separate incarcerations. He is deeply aware that he has not been much of a role model for his son, who is remarkably well adjusted despite having a delinquent dad. Today Peter has almost nothing. He lives on a bleak estate in one of inner London's most deprived zones, where the nights are sometimes enlivened by the sound of gunshots fired by warring gangs. The ageing ex-convict regards his descent into urban hell as divine retribution, or yet another self-inflicted penance for the wrong he has done to a few good folk, to his family and to himself.

What have I done with my money? I educated a couple of brats, I bought a few houses, I ran expensive motor cars, I ate in French restaurants, I gave a lot of money to hookers, I gave a lot of money to bookmakers. In the last six years I've lived on around a hundred quid a week. Forty years ago I used to get rid of a hundred quid at lunchtime. And what a Charlie people must have thought I was!

Sometimes when I go back and look at places I've owned, I have to desist because I get a nausea, but I don't feel sorry for myself. I got exactly what I deserved. I was a predator, and I suspect somewhere deep inside myself, I wanted to punish myself for my passion.

PROLOGUE

—————

We cannot be impartial, we can only be intellectually honest,
aware of our passions and on guard against them. Impartiality is
a dream, and honesty a duty.

Gaetano Salvemini

THIS is a degenerate tale, told with little or no embellishment: one
man's life and glimpses of another's. Both kept the pot boiling too
long; both paid the price.

Players, places, events appear with scant disguise. The tale is written
from a standpoint of ageing vanity, challenging retribution. Should
you read it with care, it is certain to keep you on the straight and
narrow. Peter Craig Gulston – alias Peter Scott – is a man who has
made all the mistakes that vanity, greed and envy create.

Readers may relish the idea of a 'master criminal'; alas, such people
don't exist. Raffles was the stuff of fiction. Thieves in the main get
caught. Persistent ones get caught more frequently. Few escape the
narrow aisles of pain. If you decide to be a 'career criminal', be prepared to suffer; the slammer beckons.

This is a cautionary tale. The soul is not bared in order to eulogise
but rather to warn. The arrogance and vanity that fuel professional
larceny can, and do, create a private excitement and a dream of gracious living. The reality is one of long, lonely years spent trudging
round prison exercise yards while mentally flagellating yourself. That
is the spectrum of the criminal calling.

This is a true tale, told in the author's own words, and is a privileged
insight into the souls of two men, skilled in their craft, who hung
about too long. No one gets killed. Few improbables will occur to
stretch the imagination. Little blood will be spilt, other than their
own.

This is a thief's tale: immoral, sad, amusing in parts. It is as truthfully
told as memory permits. The connoisseur may read it to avoid media
myths about 'crime'.

Acquaint yourself with degeneracy and dishonesty. Get an insight into the emotional alibis and vanities that propel them. Then – who knows? – you may confront the Walter Mitty concealed inside yourself.

1

The Conspirators

In the autumn of 1980, two ageing men perched on the low wall that skirts the steps of the Brompton Oratory. The steps and façade of the church reared up behind them, lit by the sun, a refuge for penitents anxious to make amends in time for the life hereafter. Nothing was further from the minds of this pair. They were in animated conversation, shouting against the roar of Knightsbridge traffic on its relentless way to the West End.

The older of the pair was doing most of the talking. This was George. He had never been tall but now, past seventy, he cut a shrunken figure, despite his fine eagle-like head. The other, some twenty years younger, wore a tracksuit and trainers. His weather-beaten face gleamed in the sunshine: that of a large, florid man capable of all the affability of well-balanced middle age, except for the paradox of his disturbing, grey-blue eyes. These eyes continually shifted from George's agitated face to appraise each pair of shapely legs that tottered past.

Taters, as George was known to his pals, warmed to his favourite theme – the pursuit, as we will discover, of a lifetime. Peter showed scant interest, but from time to time nodded his head tolerantly. He had heard it all before. A fresh-faced constable strolled by with barely a glance, for there was nothing about the pair to interest him. But then, Hendon Police College had not acquainted the young cozzer with every durable conspirator from history. For conspirators is what these men were; it was what they always had been.

'We won't get a better crack at it. The scaffolding gives us a real chance,' croaked Taters urgently, sensing the other's scepticism.

Peter, his companion, gazed at Taters, looking for a clue. Despite all the years he'd known the man, he still found it difficult to *warm* to him. Yet, once, he had idolised him. Now, though time and proximity had dulled the worship, respect lingered like expensive perfume. Deep in the recesses of Peter's arrogance lurked the suspicion that Taters was the better man. It irked Peter, but he'd learned to live with it.

How does a withered old man deploy such drive and enthusiasm? It was true – they wouldn't get a better crack at it. But in Christ's name, who in their right mind would want to have a crack at it?

Yet right minds are the preserve of the successful. Peter decided to play along.

'Yes,' he said patronisingly. 'The scaffolding is a bonus, but not of the essence. I see it as a complicated "hurry up". It's all down to the enemy's response and predicting what contingency plans they may have. The entry's never been a problem, providing nothing has changed since our last excursion to the roof. It's the departure that worries me.'

Through the roar of the traffic Taters caught the lack of conviction in Peter's voice. He half rose, bellowing a final ultimatum.

'Well, if you're bottly, I'll find someone else.'

Peter blushed under his tan, then chose his words carefully.

'Tell you what, George. I'll take a shufty this weekend. The scaffolding on the Polish Church will be there for some time, so I'll see if anything's changed.' He held up his hand to forestall George's objection. 'I know, I know. You were up there last year, but security could have been tightened. I'll have a final recce, and we'll go on from there.'

Peter knew what was coming next. It was always the same on a meet with George.

'Peter, could you let me have a pony? I've a lot of laundry to get out.' The old man's voice dropped a respectful octave.

When tapping, George had a singular lack of imagination. This particular parcel of laundry had apparently been waiting thirty years for George to collect it, though Peter himself must have subbed its redemption a hundred times. Still, the weather was warm and Peter didn't feel up to an argument. Taters wanted a few quid to have a bet – the need was as compelling as a junkie's fix. Spieling and *going on one* were the only passions in his lonely life.

'Anyhow, you've got plenty,' Taters wheezed anxiously. 'I've not forgotten those Chinese figurines from Grosvenor Square you fucked me for, either.'

'OK, George, but this is the last draw you're getting. I'm not really *at* it. I try to respect money now.'

Taters let the homily pass unchallenged. He folded the notes and binned them, satisfied that he was getting a draw.

'Ta.'

Without another word he ambled away, with his peculiar sailor's gait. It would have been difficult for a passer-by to recognise the ancient gladiator. But he *was* a gladiator, nonetheless. To the cozzer and the felon alike, he was a legend.

Peter remained seated on the warm stone – emotions mixed, sad to be one of 'yesterday's men', with little to show for a lifetime of pillage – until Taters had passed from view.

George was always not just cool, but *cold*. For the last half-century, the cockney rhyming slang for that complaint – Taters-in-the-Mould – was applied by the Element as a virtual synonym for the utmost in criminal daring.

> He was always cold
> But the land of gold
> Held him like a spell.

Robert Service's sketch of Sam McGee might have been meant for Taters – although Taters's gold was differently located. Sam's was in the frozen rock of the Yukon while, on the day of the rendezvous with Peter, Taters's was a quarter of a mile from the Oratory, on the first floor of a well-guarded museum.

No doubt the contemporary young lions of the criminal class would give his plan a wide berth. For men of these years it was pure madness. But that was what attracted Peter. A yesterday's man he might be, but he longed for a final audacious thrust at British society and its most sacred bastions. He and Taters were old, but they were subtle. They were specialists. Their expertise would see them through.

In frank arrogance, their lifelong calling had been to persecute the bastions of privilege and accumulated wealth. And the arrogance was mandatory. Now, as he scanned the windows of the long, solemn building with his mind's eye, he saw well that it was vulnerable. But had he still the measure of arrogance, of criminal self-belief, left in him? His passion for larceny had for some time hibernated. Switching courts – from the Bailey to the clay of Paddington Lawn Tennis and Bowling Club – he had deliberately put it to sleep in the exhausting discipline of daily tennis.

The club was a refuge to all sorts. Tennis is a drug, an opium derivative, capable of weaning you off the excesses of a lifetime, and here at the club social attributes and upmarket drawls were merely optional. So, at the club, he was among his own. It was a backwater, an elephant's graveyard – in criminal parlance, a good bake. All his adult life Peter had struggled with his passion for thieving. He had made every possible mistake several times over, but this was an oasis where thirsts were slaked in exhaustion and shared effort. And now he was considering another rash, long-past-optimum raid.

And yet a final glimpse of Taters pushing through the Knightsbridge shoppers stirred his former passion in its sleep. He told himself, 'The old bastard's challenging you.'

'I'd have been up for it at your age. Did, too,' Taters had wheezed, twisting the screw.

And he had. Thirty-odd years past he'd purloined the Duke of Wellington's jewel-encrusted swords from this same building. There was a hell of a row: questions in the House, security reviews, public outrage . . . (Well, maybe so. One cannot be confident that the public is always outraged by deeds of daring in which violence is absent and fleshpots are the victim.) Recalling those swords, Taters was saying *he* was the better man, and calling Peter 'Gunga Din'.

Get back to the clay, an inner voice dictated. *Who will know you never took the bait?*

But surely, no harm came from inspecting the target. He sauntered round the side of the Oratory, heading north towards the Anglican church of Holy Trinity. As he approached the church, a sharp turn to his left gave a clear view of the target roof. His pulse quickened, the saliva dried in his mouth. A frisson of excitement ran down his spine.

Even now, after thirty years, it was a sexual thrill. The anticipation of larceny was like an imminent orgasm, a joust so adjacent to sex with a tart that it was hard to say which he preferred. So now, standing this autumn day upon sacred ground, gazing at the roof, he was like a man whose pulse raced at the sight of the crotch on a pornographic centrefold. That roof, sighted through the line of shady trees at the rear of the Polish Chapel, protected the nation's treasures. Its dorsal-finned windows coaxed the eye. They were almost phallic.

But the eye is a fickle harlot, seeing what it wants to, especially at the prompting of greed or lust. On more than one occasion, Peter had looked over the Victoria and Albert Museum, and today everything, from ground level, looked the same. But he knew that a further recce would have to be undertaken.

The great, smug edifice slumbering resplendently in the autumn light was one of several dedicated by the widow of Windsor to the sanctified memory of her husband. It had long assumed the morality – the sanctity, even – of ownership, yet the treasures it housed were mostly pillaged from around the world by the most successful race of pirates in history. Peter's only intention was to repillage them.

The narrow private road bent right, past the vicarage of Holy Trinity and into a mews which shrank beneath the bulk of Imperial College. A left at the end, and he was in Exhibition Road where, heading west, he passed a short terrace of elegant houses occupied mostly by Arabs and their retainers. Then he came to the rear gate of the museum. A glance under its fine arch allowed him a glimpse of where a security guard crouched in his hutch, one of a string of external custodians which ringed the building.

There had been none of these when, years earlier, Taters had profitably trespassed. It had been quite an accomplishment nonetheless, if not one that would recommend itself to Victoria or her most moral great-great-granddaughter. But a fellow thief employs no such terms as vandalism and sacrilege. He feels only an admiration no different from that once given to the 'accomplishments' of Clive of India or Gordon of Khartoum.

The recce began to bore him. He had always worked on the basis that *every* new scrutiny of a target was good, bringing something fresh to the eye which, in emergency, might be decisive in securing the prize or the felon's liberty. But he now found himself looking for a reason to swerve, which was either good sense or meant that his bottle was dodgy. Take your choice.

Taters was right about one thing, though. The scaffolding was a plus too big to ignore and it would not be there for ever. Now was the time for Peter to make up his mind, or never.

Taters got no further than William Hill's betting shop in Knightsbridge, where he did the pony immediately. His concern now was to replace it and he thought Harvey Nichols might assist.

Taters felt scant respect for the elegant store which he now entered. Once or twice he'd cleared out the fur department, and a smile twitched across his haggard, geriatric face as he remembered himself and Scotty humping ocelot and mink over the roofs to Harriet Place. The smile developed into a chuckle as he slipped an expensive piece of bone china into his tatty mac pocket and headed for the exit. The chuckle was abbreviated shortly after he reached the street. He felt a strong hand on his shoulder and heard a none-too-polite voice issue its request. 'Will you step this way, please sir?'

Even in good fettle, the beak at West London was something of a savage. Today the stipe was at his choleric worst.

'You're on a suspended sentence,' he bellowed from the bench, in a voice calculated to turn the prisoner's blood to water. But Taters showed no emotion. He had been here before.

'Yet here you are, stealing again. You have an appalling record and I'm not going to waste my breath on you. You will go to prison for three months. The three-month suspended term will also be activated and run consecutively. Take him down.'

Taters, poker-faced, gazed straight ahead, probably lost in the nether world of his deafness. His young lady probation officer had said nothing in mitigation; she knew it would be pissing into the wind. Nevertheless she felt sorry. He looked like her granddad. The arresting officer, a young PC from Gerald Road, looked sheepish at the old boy getting six months. He avoided Taters's eye as he led him down. There was only the jailer to show a modicum of compassion.

'Get the old boy a cup of tea and put him in a box on his own,' he said, wearily.

Trundling towards the Ville in the prison service meat-wagon, Taters dozed off. He was too old for this lark, of course, and yet society had been entitled to, and claimed, its pound of flesh.

Peter learned of the mishap only when a letter arrived at the tennis club, stamped with the familiar postmark of HMP Pentonville.

Dear Peter

As you can see I've done it wrong again. I'll be here four months. Let me have a few quid for newspapers.

Let Amy know where I am, and will you go round to Goldhawk Road and check my stuff is OK?

The beak took a right liberty with me, I think he was pissed, ha, ha. Keep an eye on Victoria, I'll send you a VO presently.

George

The note depressed him. Someone was always taking a liberty with Taters. He was blind to the real culprit, his weakness for playing up every penny he got his hands on. It was odd, but he didn't actually care. His world was a fantasy world – but then so, in a way, was Peter's. And when they tried to convert the fantasy into reality, they paid the price.

He turned back to the letter. Newspaper money was a must. The room in Goldhawk Road he wouldn't want to lose – it was a tip made available to him through a solicitor who appreciated his plight. You don't find many of that ilk charitable.

Tell Amy where I am. This was Mrs B, a hard-working divorcee with a carpet warehouse in Hounslow and a superb detached house in Lampton Road. It was a difficult assignment. Amy was currently smarting from a discovery she'd made on returning from a cruise. Taters had pawned her jewellery with Sutton's in Victoria and was outers for keeps. When Peter challenged him, he'd fannied desperately. 'I only put it there for safe-keeping.'

He probably convinced himself it was true.

Peter's eye wandered to the bottom of the letter. *Keep an eye on Victoria.* He sighed, pulled out his diary and scratched Taters's prison number there before dispatching the crumpled letter into a bin. At this moment the V & A had no higher status than that of a chore, done for the sake of an old pal in jail. He glanced around him. The old mock-Tudor tennis pavilion – vintage 1927 – compounded his gloom. What the hell was he doing in this stagnant backwater? He was in a way a prisoner here, confined by his own choice. Was Taters any worse off?

> Three times a day my meals I get,
> Sufficient, wholesome, good.
> Drink, then, the British Public's health
> Who all our care relieves,
> For while they treat us as they do
> They'll never want for thieves.

2

Last Remains of a Master Criminal

ONE door shuts, another opens. Outside the post office in Clifton Road, fate played an ambiguous card when Peter was hailed by Benny, a jeweller of his acquaintance from the coast. Alongside him was a young man, whom Benny introduced as Roger. Shaking hands with the stranger, Peter was conscious of being shrewdly appraised from behind wire-rimmed glasses.

It was raining with a dull drizzle, so they ended up in Raoul's for coffee. Spooning sugar into his espresso, Benny gestured at his lank, gaunt, almost professor-like companion.

'Peter, you and Roger should have a rabbit.' Pausing, he leaned forward before going on *sotto voce*. 'Roger's a bit useful.'

They exchanged small-talk and drank the coffee, but soon Benny was on the move. He had never been one to let the grass grow. Now Peter was left alone with Roger.

'Fancy a walk in the park?'

Roger's voice was a soft burr. Peter knew Benny didn't waste time on dead wood. He said, 'Why not?'

As they traipsed up a deserted Primrose Hill, the rain ceased. Roger chose the moment to confide that he already knew Peter's reputation. Was this Benny, arranging a shiddock? Peter let the thought lapse as he listened to Roger's carefully picked words. He was mentioning mutual friends, a low-key way of establishing his *bona fides*, and, after a few minutes, Peter began to wonder if this could be the one to fill for Taters on the V & A. Peter didn't think they liked each other, but that was not of the essence. 'Roger's a bit useful' had been a gee.

'We should meet up again,' he said. 'Have a proper talk.'

The younger man nodded studiously. 'Where can I ring you?'

'The Paddington Tennis Club. It's in the book.'

Roger made no mention of where he could be contacted but, as they parted, he gave an assurance. 'I'll call you at the club.'

'I bet you will,' thought Peter, looking after him. Roger struck him as ambitious. Useful, maybe. But definitely an oddball.

*   *   *

The V & A was floodlit that night, as Peter approached from the direction of the Oratory. He saw additional lighting on a cage of secure wire mesh which builders had erected up the side of the building. It enclosed an external pulley to the roof.

He walked quickly along the west side of the museum until he reached the Polish Church. It, too, was scaffolded, but the scaffolding was climbable, unlit, inviting. At pavement level there would be a fair degree of shadow cover for the most dangerous move – up the first, ladderless section.

Sweat broke out on his brow as he pulled on the gloves. An old friend – fear – took a stroll across the stage. Peter had always been afraid; it had never been any other way. But once he had mastered the initial surge, he generally became ice-cold. Fear is useful: it alerts the senses. But only intellect – criminal nous – allows control.

Above the first stage of scaffolding, ladders and ropes led up in their familiar snakes-and-ladders pattern to the church roof. He hauled himself up from street level and weaved his way silently to the roof. Seconds later he was crouching on his haunches, balanced on the church parapet, panting, scanning for sighters on the well-illuminated street below. None caught his eye.

Moving along the parapet, he skirted the pitch roof and arrived adjacent to the parapet wall of the V & A. To a casual observer on the ground it would look like a mere step across. In reality it was some ten feet. And seventy feet below was a line of spiked protective railings. Peter shuddered at the thought of impaling himself. It had happened to him before and the pain, both mental and physical, had never quit haunting him.

He managed a smile – a grim one, but it killed the residue of his fear. The last time he'd stepped across here was more than a decade past. Tonight, older, heavier, more cautious, he was chuffed to find a scaffold board lying amongst a load of builder's tackle against the slates. It would bridge him across.

He drew the friendly board back to the crossing point, slid it into position, and checked the scene below. All clear.

Perspiration now soaked him, even trickling down his testes. He crept along the plank until he reached the V & A roof, with its blank, black, dirty dorsal-finned windows spearing into the night sky. A peep inside was not worth the risk of disturbing the grime so, cautiously, he moved along the gutter to the water tanks, whose supports allowed him to shin up to a flat part of the roof. Now he had a pigeon's view of a security box at the rear of the building. A solitary, oblivious custodian was engrossed in his newspaper. The thief on the roof looked about him and saw that he, too, could perhaps be observed from above, for the elevated windows of offices in the main building reared over him. They were dark, apparently unoccupied.

A central, outward-opening door and a short flight of steps allowed access from inside the building to the section of roof that protected the treasure-house itself. Creeping silently up the steps, he took two wooden wedges from his pocket and using his silver-steel cane tapped them firmly into place, one at the upper and the second at the lower end of the door's lintel jamb. It would delay any security wishing to access the roof should Peter be detected, giving him valuable seconds. He stood up, breathing more easily. The roof was now his domain.

He moved gingerly over flat aluminium, a surface different from before. But the massive, unpolished Georgian wine-glass window of the target room had not changed. It gleamed, catching the sodium lights that reared around the perimeter. He inspected the window frame minutely, finding the trembler at the top, just where he had last seen it ten years earlier. Good. No one had had a pop at this in the interim: same trembler, same security. Taters was right so far.

Destruction of the glass would activate the trembler and alert the enemy. Not an insurmountable problem. Shading his heavy-duty torch with his palm, he focused the beam downward through the glass and caught the vague outline of the next obstacle, an iron grille covering the well of the window. Awkward, even formidable if the bars were of silver steel, but passable nonetheless. Under the grille lay a false ceiling, and here was something new: sonic and cameras had been installed. Peter could see traces of wiring and fittings. But in spite of this, Taters's assurances that nothing had, in essence, changed in the last decade were confirmed. A new frisson of excitement ran down Peter's spine. The coup was on.

He turned and hunkered down in the shadow of the dorsal-finned window, reviewing his options. With Taters unavailable, could he handle it on his own? He thought not, but had no obvious accomplices at present. Roger? He still had to think that through. Perhaps he would invite him to have a crack at something more modest. Get the measure of the man.

He lingered for a few moments, listening to the buzz and hum of the city at night, a plethora of ideas bombarding his mind. Then, recovering his wedges, he retraced his route to the plank bridge, crossed, and slid without mishap down the scaffolding.

Cruising back in the BMW to his place in Maida Vale, he became ordinary again. There was little to look forward to in the sparsely furnished flat, on a third floor in Sutherland Avenue. Its only virtue was proximity to his newly acquired vice – the tennis club and its sanatorium atmosphere.

By the time he shut the door behind him, the euphoria of fear and escape had completely evaporated. He put on Mozart and sat on the bed, shivering, closing his eyes. The sudden feeling of cold prompted a thought of Taters and his inner eye drifted back to the first piece of work they'd done together. It had been thirty years since Taters, burly, determined, pushing forty, had met him for the first time in civvy street. Taters had just finished a ten PD* imposed in 1954, while Peter was fresh from a two-year stint for a thrust at St Leonard's Castle, the seat of Horace Dodge the car magnate. They were both itching to return to the trenches, never mind the risk.

Fixing Peter with those soft, owl-like brown eyes, Taters listened as Peter sketched the coup, a mansion in Sunningdale, home to Alexandrine, ex-wife of Sir Alexander Korda and now married to Major David 'Fruity' Metcalf. Fruity had been the friend and confidant of Edward, Duke of Windsor, during the abdication crisis.

It was a totally uncomplicated strike. They'd arrived at dusk and Peter had put the ladder up to an open first-floor window and danced up the rungs. There in the bedroom, considerably left out for him on the dresser, was a jewel box. But it wasn't till later, sorting through the jumble of gems and glitter, that he realised he'd landed the magnificent Craven earrings, diamonds that each spread twelve carats. And *she'd* left them out for him.

'Check my stuff.'

Peter was heading down the Gore to Goldhawk Road. Taters's plea was his ostensible reason for the visit, but far more compelling was the fact that his Stilsons were there. They were about to be needed.

So, standing at the street door beside a chemist, he pressed the bell of one of Taters's neighbours. A young woman opened the door warily, then relaxed as she recognised Peter.

'The police were here last week,' she told him. 'I think George is in some kind of trouble.'

'Yes, I'm afraid he is. Out of circulation for a couple of months. He's asked me to check his room. He wrote to me.' As an afterthought he added, 'From Pentonville.'

---

* Preventive Detention.

'Oh, poor old chap. I'm sorry.'

She let him in. Peter trudged up to the second floor and found Taters's door ajar. Not even the cardboard strip he used to jam it was in evidence. A burglar, and he never locked his own door – make of it what you will. The police had had no need of a sledgehammer, or even a shoulder, to effect entry.

A wave of sadness came over Peter as he stood on the threshold. A phrase, *the last remains of a master criminal*, came into his mind. The room had a solitary window, as filthy and opaque as those of the V & A. He walked towards it, rubbing a spyhole in the dirt. Outside was an alley, in frequent use as a tip or a toilet. Depressing. Pathetic. It was all so bloody pathetic.

The law, when they visited, had given the place a scant spin. It was clearly too dismal. Peter opened a wardrobe and was surprised by a couple of new suits and two pairs of smart suede shoes. Hung on a hook, a tatty mac concealed what he had come for, the thirty-six-inch Stilsons. Cutters this size make light work of iron bars. He brought them out and, leaning them against the wall, looked on top of the wardrobe. There stood two glass decanters, huddled together like refugees. Taters had had them for at least five years. Whenever Peter had suggested selling them, the old man would mumble, 'Nah. Expecting guests.'

Peter took down the decanters and, with a certain reverence, wrapped them in newspaper. They were last vestiges of the old man's self-respect. Finally, cuttered and decantered, he found a key on the mantelpiece and locked up.

Why did he feel so bloody?

3

Dr Fell

H E got to the club at ten in the morning. The bar staff had a message. A 'Roger' would call again at 11.30.

Peter had a fear of phones. As a villain, he considered them more dangerous than a jealous tart, which was why his flat was phoneless. No matter how cautious one is, it's never possible to control your caller's openers. Phones, friends and cars are the most likely things to get you nicked, yet to live a gregarious life one had to have them all. For the felon, the choices were all Hobson's.

He went through to the clubroom, where only the jangling of two fruit machines trespassed on the silence. Each year, members stuffed more than twenty grand of pure profit into them, apparently without complaint. Aptly named, these 'bandits'. Morality being the expendable, elasticised quality it is, they're just another form of legalised thieving.

Peter sat around, hoping to get a hit. Then Sid Kiki, the bookmaker, arrived. 'Care for a hit, Peter?'

Peter agreed at once. Ki was a pleasure to hit with – competitive, fair, and always providing new balls. They went out and played a couple of tight sets, with Ki ultimately proving a bit too slippery and making Peter suffer. The punishment was ended by the tannoy, calling Peter to the phone. It was Roger.

'Hello. Can I see you?'

'Yes,' said Peter. 'Today?'

'Back entrance at twelve noon.'

Roger rang off, not waiting for confirmation. Well, well. He'd never been at the club, but he already knew of the back door, a tunnel that ran under the flats in Delaware Road and came out opposite the BBC recording studios. The discreet passage was used mainly by a select band of thirsty staff at the Beeb who were in the know. Certainly not by the majority of club members.

There was something covert about this entrance. The club's main entrance was in Castellain Road, giving access to the clubhouse only once you had passed a couple of courts and a bowling green. But Roger would not necessarily want to be seen.

'Seems a thorough young man,' thought Peter. 'No flies on Roger.'

As he climbed the tunnel steps into daylight, a gleaming Triumph 2000 appeared at the kerb. Roger was grinning as he beckoned Peter into the passenger seat.

'Very handy, that back door. I didn't fancy parading up to the club-house from the car park. Anywhere we can get coffee? I haven't had breakfast.'

'What about Raoul's?'

'No, we've been there before. I don't want to be seen with you on your manor.' Roger gave Peter a sardonic look. 'I fancy you're a target.'

Peter was accommodating. He knew he was targeted from time to time. He was one of the CRO* faces on the plot.

'As you like. Head for Park Lane. We'll go to Richoux's in South Audley Street. They have an all-day breakfast.'

Richoux's, an agreeable, long-time haunt of Peter's, was pricey without costing an arm and a leg. It attracted a mixture of punters: Americans, Arab Mayfair types, well-heeled matrons of all ilks, and the odd upmarket tart – either resting from her labours or looking for more. It was also a good place for villains to relax, too dear for prying coppers from West End Central, and a place where a visit by the Flying Squad would not go without comment.

On the way, Roger awarded himself his first black mark in Peter's eyes. He drove too fast, throwing the Triumph into corners with the zest of youth. Peter noted the fault, but made no comment. They engaged in mainly monosyllabic conversation until, settled comfortably on one of the half-moon couches, they had ordered their food.

'I saw *He Who Rides the Tiger* at Blundestone,' Roger confided in his quiet voice. 'I rate it. I remember every detail.'

It had been over fifteen years since a film had been made of Peter's exploits as a cat burglar, but it was still occasionally screened on TV. He had been played by the actor Tom Bell.

'You're very like him, you know,' Roger remarked with a sly smile. 'Only you're more bloody arrogant.'

'What were you in Blundestone for?'

'I was doing a nevis for a couple of screwers.'

'How long have you been home?'

'Just over a year.'

'And are you up for a bit of work?'

---

* Criminal Record Office (thus 'CRO face' is a targeted criminal).

Roger made all the appearance of considering. His eyes hardened slightly, as if to underline the effect. Since first meeting Peter, he'd striven to show confidence, mastery even, all too predictable in the arrogance of youth. Now, having paid his compliments to the film, he proceeded to undermine them.

'Don't know,' he said after a moment. 'Couple of people gave you a bad blow down in Blundestone.' Half closing his eyes, he waved his hand. 'Not that I would pay much attention to idle chatter. One listens objectively.' He smirked, complimenting and deriding in the course of a few sentences.

Peter had been around too long to worry about the fishwife gossip of the nick. True enough, in the early days his aloof attitudes – his posh, articulate background – had caused some ill-feeling. Now, though he liked to think his deeds carried their own justification, he felt the need to keep Roger on side. He said, 'You must have rubbed shoulders with George Alexander. He did a QE* on me for Bert Wickstead at St Albans Crown Court. I ended up with an eight penny-weight down to George.'

'Yes, I knew the prat. Some listened to him. But he spent the whole of seventy-eight down the block on protection. He was a jelly-baby. But then, most people are if they're put under enough pressure.'

This educated, bourgeois young man struck Peter as not unlike his younger self – in background at least. In appearance he was a contrast, the glasses thick and intellectual, the fingers long and slim, decidedly an oddball. Roger laced these concert pianist's fingers together and leaned forward.

'So, Peter. What did you have in mind?'

Whatever gossip he'd heard in the Suffolk slammer was apparently discounted. Peter replied in non-committal fashion.

'There are several bits to hand. Different risk factors, different rewards. There's one both rewarding and imaginative which I'd par-ticularly like to discuss. But I can't till I clear it with an old associate of mine. He's away at the moment.'

'Is it Taters?'

Roger had certainly been swotting.

'You know Taters?'

'Only by reputation. He's before my time, but commands a lot of respect. Is it him?'

* Queen's Evidence (giving evidence for the Crown).

'Yes. I shan't be able to talk to him till next week. There's a VO*
in the pipeline.'

'Isn't there anything we can discuss now?'

'Couple of furriers in Mayfair can be obliged, any time. You familiar
with Mayfair?'

'Mayfair? Not bloody likely. It's too fucking hot, man.'

This was the first time in Peter's company that Roger had sworn.
The idea of Mayfair had him in a sweat and Peter was pleased. The
young man was cocky but not foolhardy, not a blusterer. Underneath
the cockiness he was cautious, and this would serve him better than
bravado.

Peter also understood Roger's attitude to Mayfair, but the place
itself he understood even better. Mayfair was not unlike some great,
golden, uddered cow which always had milk to spare. He loved the
place like home.

Thirty years previously, when Taters first lured him there, he had
been nervous, just as Roger was now. It was early evening, gloomy
but not yet dark. Coolly, Taters indicated the Curzon Street furrier's,
whose alarm bell needed silencing. Past it swarmed Mayfair tarts and
office workers heading home. Worse, it stood right opposite the
rumoured MI5 building.

Taters, in his white smock coat with 'Brocks' stencilled on the back,
strode across the road, put a ladder up, and ran to the top. Seconds
later he was hacking at the exposed box. Holding the ladder-foot and
looking around, Peter began to relax. The old boy was right. The
promenaders took not a blind bit of notice. It was a matter of bottle.
The more blatant you are, the more lawful it looks.

The bell was duly cut and the tongue removed. They shimmied
over to the shop's front door where, masked from the street by Peter,
Taters expertly jemmied the lock. They went inside and immediately
began sacking up furs . . .

As Peter came back to the here and now, Roger was speaking again.

'Of course, I know *you* worked Mayfair. Everyone does.'

'Well, I never had a day's grief there. It's really quite simple. Do
your homework, know the plot, act decisively.'

He sought to fix Roger with his needle-sharp blue eyes. It was time
to assert primacy.

'Mayfair's the *pro's* ring, Roger. Amateurs and bullshitters better
give it a wide berth.'

* Visiting order.

But Peter felt he hadn't quite punched home. The trace of contempt in Roger's tone had irked him and he'd betrayed his irritation. He was on the defensive. His clutch was slipping.

To himself he acknowledged that Roger did look and talk like a pro. And he was bright enough to recognise the added hazard of working with someone of Peter's notoriety, a consideration he would have to adjust to, or pass. Yet there was something about the fellow which made Peter uneasy. He seemed to want to team up with him in the autumn of his career, but why? Some extravagances are irresistible: perhaps, for Roger, Peter was an extravagance he couldn't deny himself. As he looked at the man opposite, the ancient doggerel flitted into Peter's head:

> I love thee not, Dr Fell,
> The reason why I cannot tell,
> But this I know, and know full well,
> I love thee not, Dr Fell.

'About this *imaginative* job you mentioned. Go and see your friend and clear it with him. You can assume I'm interested.'

Roger got up. It was a second or two before Peter realised he was leaving.

'I'll be in touch at the weekend. You should know by then, yes?'

Peter nodded and Roger threaded his way between tables, stopping only to pick up the tab. He was one confident young man. So what? It wasn't until you had them on the roof that you got the strength of them. There were a hundred faces in their pews in Mayfair bars, heroes just so long as they had a large gin and tonic in their paws. Roger would have to prove himself an exception, simple as that.

4

The Great Fur Robbery

CROSSING Berkeley Square to Bruton Street revived pleasurable memories. True, that time he'd not been as fortunate as the angels in the Ritz, who heard the nightingale warble. He had to content himself with the strident bleat of burglar alarms that couldn't be silenced, and the police loudhailer bellowing up to the darkness of the roof.

'Give yourself up! You cannot escape, we have you surrounded. Best you come down.'

Come down? Not bloody likely. The roofs are the private domain of the cat burglar. Others forced to tread there found them alien, but to him they were a home from home.

We are talking about a couple of months before the Great Train Robbery, June 1963. The Great Fur Robbery took a little less time to gestate, and was less well publicised, but it would be worth a mention in any encyclopaedia of sophisticated larceny. The coup was both opportunist and a showpiece for the two hussars' criminal nous, with the vital added ingredient – a dash of luck.

The spring and early summer of 1963 had been disastrous for our pillagers' income, a comedy of errors. A lorryload of damask table-cloths were retrieved by the rightful owners when the thieves had the petrol tank run dry. Two modest safes they'd blown had jammed. Can *anyone* fuck up a John Tann*? They did, twice. Not a coin had been earned for three months. They were penniless.

'We're bang out of form,' Taters moaned. 'I need a few quid to go racing next week.'

Peter had equally pressing needs. An attractive young woman had appeared in his life and funds were essential to ensnare the lady's emotions.

'Tell you what,' Peter said in his growing frustration. 'I'll have a wander round Mayfair tomorrow morning, see if I can find something to break the bock.'

Sunday morning found him in Bruton Street. An observer would

* Make of safe.

have been intrigued by the stroller's preoccupation with roofs. Then Peter's eye caught sight of an elegant plaque: *Max Mitzman, Furrier, 5th Floor*.

Crossing to stand in front of Jack Barclay's Rolls-Royce showroom allowed him sight of Max's premises, a mansard-type attic with recessed windows. There was a crimson alarm box *in situ*, but it was accessible – the first of the plus points. When you're in form things fall into place. Fifty yards or so further along, on the same side as Mitzman's, there was an empty, which would later house the Allied Irish Bank. It would give easy access to the roof. More plus points. He had found a little bit of work.

At 9.30 the same evening, in sultry summer twilight, himself and Taters were on the roof of the empty, three premises away from Mitzman's. To get to the furrier's they would have to negotiate the parapet ledges. The street below was deserted, but should a passer-by glance up he would be able to watch the pair gingerly tiptoeing along the ledge, clutching bundles of mail bags to transport the anticipated booty. These same objects had given each of them years of soul-destroying toil in the slammer. 'Eight to the inch, lad!'

The alarm bell case offered little resistance to the shears. Peter twisted the striker tongue to render it impotent and then swiftly jemmied the light-framed window. They were on red alert now. The bell inside the premises would have to be silenced fast. As they jumped into what looked like a workroom, luck was on the intruders' side. The bell, screaming shrilly, was directly above them.

A firm clip with the jemmy dislodged it and an eerie silence prevailed. Then, barely audible, Peter heard the sound of a human voice. *'Intruders are on the premises! Intruders are on the premises!'* The automated device was relaying its fatal message to the nick. Dame Fortune smiled again as Peter found the machine on a rafter close to the ceiling. He ripped it down.

'Lively!' Taters rasped. 'Grab what we can, the law are on their way.'

The beam of his torch revealed a number of garments lying around, which were devoured in seconds, and the pair with a sack apiece were back on the parapet, heading for the relative safety of the empty.

'I think I caught it in time,' Peter panted. 'It hadn't time to connect.'

'I wouldn't bet on it,' said Taters, who was now peering out of the rebated window. He was watching and listening for the cavalry from West End Central to come screaming down Conduit Street. 'Don't know. We could be lucky, we'll know soon enough.'

They settled down to wait. Five, ten minutes ticked away then, just as they were becoming confident, a solitary copper appeared at the junction with Bond Street and strode confidently down Bruton Street.

'Bollocks. Looks like they've sent the Lone Ranger.' Peter couldn't conceal the disappointment in his voice but even now, with a ninety per cent malfunction rate on automatic alarms, the control room at West End Central would not be unduly anxious. It was standard procedure to send an officer on foot to inspect premises and look for signs of entry. Failing to find any, he would radio back and the keyholder would be contacted. Sometimes the constable would remain on guard outside the premises. As often as not he would return to base. It was a system full of holes.

'He don't know where it is,' offered Taters, beginning for the first time to sound elated. 'He'd be looking up by now if he did.'

You could have heard Peter's heart beating in the darkness as the solitary enemy strolled on, past Mitzman's building to Berkeley Square.

'We've cracked it!' crowed Taters in a hoarse whisper. 'Give it another ten minutes and we can be certain.'

They gave it only five, for greed overcame caution. Back in the workroom a padlocked door revealed itself to the shrouded torchbeam. It was quickly breached. Inside the windowless room they freed the beam and picked out row upon row of desirable garments. They had certainly broken their bock.

In high euphoria, they sacked up perhaps a hundred garments, mostly mink with a few others of shortly-to-be-protected species such as leopard and ocelot. The haul, unexpectedly plenteous, went into twenty-five sacks, all of which had to be transported along the parapet, still in full view of the street, to the empty. A sack with five full-length mink coats will weigh around forty pounds, so the operation took time. With elation double-burning their energy, they were quite exhausted as they hauled the spoils down to the empty's ground floor.

Already, suborning Mitzman's phone, Taters had alerted a former prizefighter friend who had access to a black cab. After a long twenty minutes the cab arrived and was packed up to the roof with furs.

'Drop them off at Biscay Road,' ordered Taters. 'We'll follow in the motor.'

At Biscay Road was an elderly pal, Jim Pointing, who lived alone and supplemented his pension with storage fees. A sort-out revealed that they had a hundred and twenty garments to divide between them, Mitzman having apparently been promoting a summer sale for the whole previous week in the evening papers. He probably had stock from half a dozen other furriers at his saleroom on sale or return. The luck element.

Max screamed for forty thousand — which would be fifteen times that sum today. Taters, anxious for play-up money, slaughtered his whack. Peter bought an E-type Jaguar and went to Cannes for the summer.

The Great Fur Robbery was planned and executed within the compass of twenty-four hours, while the Great *Train* Robbery took months to plan and two football teams to execute. The Train Robbers, admittedly, pulled in more pro rata, but at greater risk of detection. Not a reader will fail to have heard of them, while it's doubtful if a handful knew of the two hussars outside of the Element. And they got away with it.

The euphoria of his memories died and he was back at Paddington Tennis Club. He couldn't help dwelling on the contrast between now and then. The club may have been no more than a consolation prize for social misfits, but it was now probably all he had by way of a natural habitat.

What horrified him was the thought that he'd come to settle for it: it was barely a degree more civilised than Dartmoor. Meanwhile the easy decadence of the place was beginning to strangle him. Perhaps he was being unjust to the Sanatorium, unfairly judging it only on the merits of its 'live-in' members, who were found on its courts from morning to night. They were a sad lot as they pushed the ball about. The game was a substitute for the real game of life. Little seemed to matter to them other than how well they were playing. That is the opiate of tennis.

Helen's pleasant Cork lilt tannoyed him to the phone.

'Peter Scott here.'

'Mr Scott, my name's Prue Bolton-Smythe. I'm a welfare officer at Pentonville Prison. I'm ringing on behalf of a friend of yours, George Chatham. He *is* your friend?'

'He is indeed, Miss Bolton-Smythe.'

'I'm sorry to tell you he's not well. His heart's playing up and I've had him moved to the hospital wing. He's most anxious to see you. Could you possibly come tomorrow?'

Taters had had his dodgy ticker for thirty years, but it only ever played him up after the door banged. Only the tranquillity of the slammer produced palpitations. They never disrupted his frenetic pursuit of larceny.

'Yes. I think I can get up there. What about a VO?'

'I'll see that a visiting order is left for you at the gate. Ask for me and I'll come down and take you to the hospital. He's fortunate to have a friend like you. Bless you, Mr Scott.'

The line went dead. Ms Bolton-Smythe was not only a Christian, but a busy one. Alas, she was pure putty in Taters's hands, and yet what would we do without well-meaning, well-bred angels to help out behind bars?

Pentonville Prison was, in two words, a shite-hole. It was old, it was dirty, and it was the dumping ground for London's vagrants and petty criminals. Taters had cunningly contrived to avoid these eyesores by his admission to hospital. When you've done as much bird as him you know the moves.

Peter presented himself, smartly dressed, at the gate.

'This one's got no VO, he's a Bolton-Smythe special,' growled a paunched, middle-aged, bored man in a uniform one size too small. He was speaking to a colleague behind the bandit glass. Bolton-Smythe and her 'specials' found no favour with him.

'Right, hang on in the waiting room and we'll get her down to you . . .' He then added, in deference to Peter's Savile Row Prince of Wales check, 'Sir.'

Prison waiting rooms are the most depressing places in the world, and this one was packed to capacity. It made Peter's much-maligned tennis club seem a paradise. Stale tobacco smoke exuded everywhere. The door of a heavily frequented toilet swung open, wafting the stench of urine past his nostrils. Meanwhile the noise was a cacophony, as a score of small waifs screamed and their mothers, pale and silent except to rebuke their kids, dragged incessantly on their fags. Much older mothers, their heads bowed, wrung their hands, waiting to see the sons who didn't deserve them. You could cut the despair with a knife. Only a leather-coated tart, whose gleaming, dark court shoes supported long legs in tan stockings, provided anything to relieve the eye. Up to see her pimp?

Christ! What a price to pay for a twenty-minute tête-à-tête.

Forty minutes elapsed, and then a voice trilled, 'Mr Scott! Mr Scott, please!'

Taters's angel appeared and the thief could see at once that communication was not going to be a problem. She approved of him. She was slim and wore her hair swept back in a bun – a no-nonsense lady happy with her image and her job. Yes, a minor angel, though (just possibly) to a lost cause.

'Is this your first visit here, Mr Scott?'

Peter was tempted to betray his elegant, balanced image by saying, 'No, I was here overnight on transfer to Dartmoor Prison, eighteen years ago.'

Better let sleeping sins lie. He said instead, 'Afraid so. Have I missed much?'

'Sorry to say, not much. We're the Prison Department's poor relation. They keep putting off refurbishments by threatening to demolish the place altogether. If they go on packing in more prisoners every day, it'll fall down by itself. The Department is always the last to be budgeted for in Treasury Estimates, and we're last in line for what money there is.'

She unlocked a succession of doors and grilles and they arrived in a small yard, whose sparse greenery announced it as belonging to the hospital. They entered a half-empty ward on the second floor and Taters came into view. He was sitting on the end of a bed, staring into space. He looked bloody forlorn.

'Hello. So you got here.'

His almost child-like voice was barely audible. Prue made a gracious exit.

'Mr Scott, I'm afraid you can only stay twenty minutes – thirty at most. I'll come back for you then.'

As she left the ward, another head poked itself round the door of a small office. It belonged to one of the white-jacketed staff.

'No smoking, sir. I'm sorry.'

That was no penalty, since neither of them smoked. Peter slipped a bar of Cadbury's Fruit and Nut under the pillow.

'There's a score in the wrapper,' he mumbled. Taters, if he was grateful, showed no sign of it. He was anxious to talk about the V & A.

'Have you been up there yet?' he demanded in a croaking whisper.

Peter glanced cautiously round.

'Yes, I called in at the Old Vic. Pretty much as you described.'

Taters was staring at him tensely. Unreasonably irritated, Peter growled, louder than he meant to, 'It's a goer!'

Then, lowering his voice again, he added, 'It's the bars below that I'm worried about. They could be silver steel.'

'No, they're not. They been there for years. Stand on me, it's no problem.'

Taters's old head was trembling with excitement. He was alive again. 'You must ease the window pane out from the bottom. It gives access and won't upset the trembler.'

'Yes, I've thought of that,' interrupted Peter, finding the excitement infectious. 'But it may be possible to use a diamond-cutter and isolate the trembler.'

'No, no, you must take the window out. It'll take a bit of time. Are you *patient* enough?'

Peter smiled indulgently. Well, *was* he? But Taters was warming to the theme of a lifetime.

'Collect the tools from Goldhawk Road. Remember, it's best to be up there in November. It's dark at four-thirty and security's still on site. I was going to have a pop at it during a union meeting. You may be lucky early evening – sonics may be off.'

Peter didn't share the optimism. He swerved.

'Remember we once discussed flooding the basement from the hydrant, as a distraction?'

Taters nodded. 'Yes, I still fancy that, Peter, especially if it activates the alarm system. If they didn't put two and two together you could get lucky.'

The old hussar was in full spate. It was a long time since he'd called the thief 'Peter'.

'No,' said the thief. 'I fancy the Jewel House is on an independent system, and anyway I'm not sure I could handle a move like that on my own. I'm thinking of taking a new face with me. You're here till January, and we agree the best shot is November.'

Taters's owlish eyes narrowed in suspicion.

'Do I know him?'

'I don't think so. I've only just met him. Benny introduced us, gave him a strong gee.'

'Can you trust him?'

'How should I know? But I've had a couple of looks at him, and I like his style. He's a natural plotter and cautious too.'

'Not like Peter White,' remarked Taters, grinning weakly.

Peter White was a surgeon's son from Horsham who was nicknamed Peter the Plotter. He turned out to be a decided disappointment under pressure, getting his seven years with Chatham and a Lloyd's broker.

'Have you discussed it with the hoppo?' George wanted to know.

'Only the conception, nothing about what's the target.'

Taters lay back on his bed, seemingly satisfied but tired from the adrenalin he'd been pumping.

'I'll leave it to you.'

'George, listen carefully. I've been to your room and secured it. I've taken the decanters and Stilsons. Have you received your newspaper money?'

But Taters ignored the question. He'd been alerted by the mention of his decanters.

'Take care of the decanters. I want Amy to have them. Have you rung her?'

'I'll try tonight. If she wants them, I'll drop them off.'

He wasn't optimistic. Amy had a houseful of crystal, as became a pikey princess, and she wasn't about to let a couple of decanters purge Taters's trespass at Sutton's with her tom. Peter winced on recalling it.

Suddenly a sly, insipid smile crept over Taters's face. The angel had returned.

'Well, how's the patient today?' she chirped.

Taters replied in a coy whisper, 'I feel a bit better.'

'Well, I'm sorry, Mr Scott, we'll have to adjourn now. I am a servant of my masters.' As she spoke she indicated the stockade at the end of the ward. Yes, she was.

Being let out felt just as if he'd waited ten years for it. In the Caledonian Road the autumn haze struggled to penetrate the portals of impersonal Victorian stone. The mist conveyed a persistent gloom, as if the souls of the oppressed would have it no other way. The visit had left Peter with an attack of melancholy, a penal hangover.

As he reached his car, the tan-stockinged tart tripped past and before he could stop himself, he spoke to her.

'Need a lift?'

An arch smile appeared on the not unattractively rouged lips.

'I'm looking for a cab.'

'OK, let's pretend I'm a cabby, if it makes you feel better.'

He opened the passenger door invitingly and she slid in, exposing a slash of dull-gold thigh above the tautly suspendered stockings.

'You been visiting a friend? I heard the screw say you were to be taken to the hospital. Your friend poorly?'

The game had started, and he began to think about how to play it.

'Actually I've been in professionally. The SMO* called me in to look at a cardiac case, an inmate.'

'You a doctor?'

---

* Senior Medical Officer.

'Heart specialist. Up from Harley Street, slumming.'

He was enjoying himself now.

'You're having me on. Let's see your card.'

She sounded eager – status was what she was after. He glanced at her. Her enticingly pointed teats pressed through a semi-transparent silk blouse.

'My card? Are you ill? Do you need to consult me?'

Stopping at traffic lights, Peter reached out and tentatively fondled the adjacent breast. 'Nothing wrong with *your* heart.'

She pushed his hand away, without much conviction.

'You prats are all the same, ponces or doctors, all you want to do is get into my knickers.' There was boredom, resignation, in her voice. Almost disappointment.

'Well, I'd need notice to get into your knickers. But I would like to admire you. Is there a quiet spot we can park?'

Lust was thickening his voice. She said, lightly, 'Admire all you like for forty quid.'

Without speaking, Peter pulled out two banknotes and dropped them in her lap.

'Next left,' she said. 'There's a multi-storey car park. Drive to the top floor.'

In the half-light of the arched and cavernous space he pulled up the skirt of this new angel who had come his way, and pushed her sheened legs akimbo. His hand found his cock as his eyes fastened on her lovely contours.

'Take your tits out.'

She obliged and the thrust of her cones stiffened his shaft. His pulse was racing. Slowly she eased her head down to the helmet of his cock and her crimson lips encircled it. She pushed his hand away and moved the foreskin up and down over the glans. Her timing was superb. He caught a glimpse of his face in the driving mirror as she led him to ecstasy. He looked like the devil incarnate.

He ejaculated into her mouth and she sucked and swallowed with rare tenderness. He was embarrassed and surprised. He was also released. Looking into the mirror, he saw that his features had softened again. Satan was appeased and vanished. Peter stroked her chestnut mane and they both remained still.

He dropped her at Euston where, getting out, she had the last word, before strutting off into the station.

'Even if you haven't got a card, I've got one.'

She tossed a rectangular card at him. 'Maybe you'll ring me, Doctor.'

He looked at the card. *TRACY CAN HELP*, it said. Yes, he would ring her. He'd take her to the tennis club. And soon.

The club was packed. The Gang, as they were wont to refer to themselves, held court in the bar. The qualification for joining this gang was to have spending power. A Greek property developer, a couple of taxi-garage proprietors, a lady estate agent, and one who photographed fat cats. They worked and played hard.

Peter, in funds, could acquire temporary membership of the Gang, his largesse easing the way. But tonight he swerved. His little extravagance with Tracy precluded him doing another fifty buying rounds and talking bollocks at the bar. As he'd told Taters, he had to respect money now.

'Dry week,' he mouthed to the team, as they waved him over. He looked instead for a hit. He eventually went on court with a Mancunian who had turned up, but wouldn't be likely to get a hit himself if Peter hadn't volunteered. They played for an hour on court three, the furthest from the clubhouse, both playing well. Yet as the ball sat up to be struck, Peter kept on seeing Tracy's wonderful tits. He felt good.

Later, bedding down, Tracy came again to haunt him. 'I want to mother you,' she whispered in his fantasy. 'You need Mama. Everyone needs hugs. Didn't she say so?'

5

Roger Views the V & A

FRIDAY morning, Peter was back in South Audley Street. Roger was there, sitting at the same table as before. He looked relaxed, smart, in a hacking jacket and cavalry-twill strides, not unlike a young Guards officer in mufti. Greeting Peter, he grinned in his now familiar but still decidedly odd manner.

'I've ordered for you. I was certain you'd be prompt.'

'Not as prompt as you. You look smart. Where did you have the jacket made?'

Roger allowed himself a laugh. 'Marks and Spencer, in the sale.'

The exchange was casual and to some degree theatre for any ear-wiggers that might be present. The English breakfast arrived and they both ate hungrily.

Peter's eye was drawn to an attractive matron showing a lot of leg. She observed him and hastily arranged her skirt, giving him a calculated, quizzical stare. Roger wanted to go somewhere else to talk, so Peter paid the bill and they left.

'Shall we go to the gardens? It's quiet there and very peaceful.'

St George's Gardens, taking their name from the church in South Audley Street, were a favourite of Peter's. Passing Harry's Bar, the conspirators turned left past the library, and found a vacant bench under the spreading plane trees. In the crescent under the arbour, Roger asked, 'Seen your pal yet?'

'Yes. I saw him this week. I can discuss the work with you. Naturally, if anything comes of it, we have a sleeping partner.'

Roger nodded his assent. Taking a deep breath, Peter went on.

'We're going to have a pop at the Jewel House at the Victoria and Albert.'

Roger showed no emotion, though his eyes glinted behind his glasses. He was waiting for Peter to elaborate.

'Do you know it, Roger?'

'Yes. I was up there earlier this summer.'

Roger was full of surprises.

'Well, Taters and I have been working on it for years. Been on the books for a twenty stretch. We fucked up in the mid-sixties, and there have been one or two changes since, but the essential weakness still exists. We both feel, with a bit of luck, it could be had over.'

He waited for a reaction, but Roger gave not an inch. Peter persisted.

'I've been back over the course recently. The old attack plan still seems a goer, but naturally you'd want to familiarise yourself with it before deciding.'

Roger was ill at ease, staring negatively at his feet and shifting his body-weight from side to side. Then he spoke.

'First it's Mayfair, now the V & A. When do we get round to the Bank of England?' He gave a nervous laugh. 'You can't be serious, but, knowing what little I do of you, I expect you are. OK. Let's hear the worst.'

Peter outlined the history of the plot slowly and pedantically. He left nothing out, starting with Taters's successful foray against the swords in the forties. He was careful neither to enthuse nor depress, and spoke in a flat monotone. When he'd finished he looked at Roger. Behind the lenses, his eyes had begun to show faint interest.

'Yes,' the younger man murmured. 'As you say, I'll have to have a look at it myself. Let's shoot over there and have a butcher's.'

Parking on a meter in Exhibition Road, they strolled to the main entrance at Thurloe Place, only stopping to buy two mammoth ice-cream cones from a nervous fly-pitch vendor near the door. Security paid them scant attention as they passed the turnstiles: ladies were turning out their handbags for inspection; parcels and briefcases were treated with deep suspicion; ice-creams passed muster.

Roger strode ahead purposefully. Peter stopped to look out at the grass quadrangle that forms the heart of the building, leaning against the glass to get an oblique sighting of the Silver Gallery on the second storey. He had started to point out the former location of the showcase that had protected Wellington's swords – until Taters disturbed them in 1947 – but he thought better of it and followed Roger up the tapestry-hung stairs. Reaching the first floor, they met again at the turnstile to the Jewel House. They neither spoke nor acknowledged each other. Both knew that, from the point of entry, they were on video.

The Jewel House would take the devout aesthete's breath away. A veritable Pharaoh's vault, a monument to the sons of the British Empire, and their success at the game of worldwide pillage. The morality of these boys may have been that of James Bond, but their taste was impeccable. When it came to grand larceny, the British imperialists had been in a class of their own.

To the intended trespasser, this hoard was the fulfilment of his most greedy fantasies, but, of course, its custodians took considerable precautions to ensure that no trespass took place. Genuine tourists entering the one-way turnstile gate would probably be oblivious to video and sonics. Our trespassers logged every discernible electronic detail in the memory banks. Complementing these defences, two vigilant attendants paced the hundred feet or so of the gallery. The metal-framed glass showcases may have looked fragile, but anyone foolish enough to shatter one in order to snatch a bauble would be deterred by the one-at-a-time exit turnstile, manually operated by a guard from a booth outside the gallery. There was another exit to the Silver Gallery, but this was for emergencies and through a padlocked, heavy steel door. From here there could be no swift departure. During opening hours, the system was foolproof.

A false lowered ceiling about twelve feet up gave the gallery a claustrophobic atmosphere. It housed the internal lighting and, above that, some eight feet up, the steel bars that guarded the dorsal-finned window. From the inside, it all looked very formidable, but the reader has already visited the roof and appreciated the nocturnal game-plan. It was a security weakness that had, so far, escaped the attention of the V & A's advisers.

Twenty minutes elapsed as they browsed through the amassed pillage. Roger left first and, allowing a little time, Peter followed. Together again in the Silver Gallery, Peter beckoned Roger to come with him. Midway along the gallery they came to two flights of stairs leading up. They were marked *Staff Only*, though a conference room was also signposted. Unobserved, they slipped swiftly up the two flights.

The men shut themselves in a staff toilet. Peter hissed, 'If you look through the window and to the right, you can see the offices above the Silver Gallery. Straight ahead is the flat roof and the windows above the Jewel House. Offices obscure the actual windows, but those you can see are similar.'

'You mean those triangular dormers?'

'Yes. In the trade they're known as dorsal fins. You can see the slated pitched side from here. The other side of the pitch is a large glass pane. You'll get a better sighting from the church next door, when we leave.'

'How would the staff get to the roof?'

'See the offices? A door leads from there down a couple of steps. On the roof you can be observed from the offices. Seen enough?'

The recce had warmed Roger's interest in the work.

'Yes. Interesting. And I concur, it's vulnerable.'

Leaving the 'Staff Only' level with care, they weren't noticed, and Peter took the conspiracy a step further.

'I want to go up to the Ceramics Department in the main building. From there you can look down on the offices and get an overall idea of the layout.'

The magnificent marble staircase of the main building had windows at each turn of the stairs. Ascending the final flight, Roger nudged Peter to draw his attention to a window that was ajar. Inspection revealed the top of a twenty-foot ladder propped against the window ledge, standing on the catwalk that ran along the roof guttering below. The catwalk led in the direction of the Polish Church. Suddenly, without a word, Roger was out of the window and down the ladder.

'What in Christ's name is he up to, the prat?'

Peter quickly continued up the stairs to the Ceramics Department. There was nothing to do but dwell and see what transpired. Leastways, it showed some originality on Roger's part, and bottle too.

An anxious twenty minutes passed for Peter as he vainly tried to show interest in the pottery. He took up a watching post with a view of the stairs and the open window, and was very relieved as he saw Roger reappear, popping up at the window. He jumped back into the museum and disappeared down the stairs with panache. Chummy was a confident fellow.

When Peter found him, Roger was panting but in control.

'I've seen all I need. Let's leave.'

Peter didn't relax until they were back on Brompton Road. He was disappointed by his agitation, for it was a sign that he was growing too old for the game.

'For Christ's sake, Roger! What would you have done if you'd got a tug out on the roof?'

Roger gave a sly smile.

'Simple. Produce this.'

From his wallet he took out an embossed card in a plastic sheath. It read: *William Bates, Fire Prevention Officer, GLC*. It was Peter's turn to smile. Roger knew a move or two.

'Anyway, there are workmen all over the roofs,' Roger went on, pleased with himself. 'It was a piece of cake.'

'How did you come by your little pass?'

'Printed it a long time ago. Comes in bloody useful when you want to be where you shouldn't. The English love a bit of bumf, it's part of the system.'

Peter was reassured. Roger was cunning and daring, but his audacity was calculated, leaving as little as possible to chance. Peter was sure he was made for the work, even if he still disliked him.

They spent another hour inspecting the perimeter of the V & A and environs, viewing it from various angles and deciding on a general plan of action. Roger had been on the roof, seen the trembler-protected glass and the internal bars, so they now conferred as equals, Peter holding no master cards. In fact, he began to suspect that the younger man saw himself as the senior partner now, and there had been a time when Peter's vanity would not have countenanced this. Yet he was impressed by the oddball conspirator's ingenuity. He would let the sleeping dog of his resentment lie.

'I'm off to Spain for a month,' Roger told him. 'I shan't be back till early October. Meanwhile I'll creep about, see if I can't find any missed clues. I should tell you I never work till I've covered every contingency. You may find my caution boring, but that's where I'm at. Finally, I should add, I'm never committed to a bit of work till I go on it. I do my homework and if I don't fancy it I'll tell you. My style is to keep my options open, OK?'

Peter found no reason to carp.

'I understand. But we'll have to be ready in November. That's the positive optimum time.'

Roger nodded. 'I'll be off, then.'

Peter's eyes followed the angular figure as he crossed the road and disappeared into Alexander Square. Perhaps he should have a rabbit with Benny on Chummy's pedigree. Or was he becoming negative and indecisive in his old age? Meanwhile, funds were low: what could he find to boost them? Bobinet's in Mount Street caught the inner eye. He'd have a look at it again.

6

Bobinet's

A lifetime of crime teaches one lesson. You don't survive on the grandiose touches; it's the bread-and-butter work – such as the thief's intended foray at Bobinet's clock shop in Mayfair – which pays the bills and allows life to amble on. This is said to help the reader comprehend the sublime-to-ridiculous tactics of our heroes throughout this tale. All unhindered rewards are plus points. An easy monkey is just as attractive as a complicated ten thousand, from which follows the writer's contention that the exclusively big-time thief is a figment of media hype. A thief is a thief, when and where the opportunity presents itself.

Tuesday at the club was an anticlimax. He started on large brandies in the lunch-hour and suborned any friendly face to do likewise. By 3 p.m. he felt a confident, euphoric glow from the cognac, and decided to play cards that afternoon at Rousseau's. It would probably be Kaluki, which compounded his stupidity, for he was the world's worst card player and persistently refused to believe it. At Kaluki he couldn't hold a card.

The 'Bridge Club' was a large, far-from-salubrious first-floor room in the Edgware Road, and it was here that Bobinet's, an option before he sat down to play, became a must by early evening, the vain thief slaughtering seven hundred pounds to his betters. Imagine challenging McEnroe to play tennis for money and expecting to win. For Peter to sit down with the sharks at Rousseau's required the same blind optimism. With his options gone, Bobinet's became a reality. As a penance for his vanity on the green baize, the fifty-year-old Lone Ranger was taking on society again.

St George's Gardens off Mount Street, where we have been already, was the essential factor in his plan to escape with Bobinet's valuable stock. The Gardens were still open when he arrived, depressed after the mugging at Rousseau's. But the brightly lit interior of the clock shop, with all its spoils on view, revived his spirits.

The alley that leads from Mount Street into St George's Gardens was dark, save for a modestly lit phone box. He walked through the gate, which would presently be closed and padlocked. It was a simple plan. Nothing more than an audacious smash and grab, then a quick escape across the Gardens and out the other side into Farm Street, where he would have transport waiting. It looked a gift and it was. The best time would be Sunday night, during the changeover of shifts at West End Central.

As he strolled across the Gardens, the familiar sensuous excitement percolated through him. The alley leading out into Farm Street also had a gate, besides which a gardener's bogie was parked. This gate, too, would be padlocked, but it presented no problem. The little alley that led through to Farm Street was also in darkness, shadowed by high flats on one side and a tall school on the other.

He headed home, cutting an odd figure in the twilight as he hobbled stiffly back to Maida Vale. To any innocent observer he was nothing more than an ageing, tracksuited male confronting his flab. The imagined deception increased his pleasure. It was possibly just another symptom of the felon's madness.

'Didier, ça va? C'est Pierre à Londres.'

It was next morning, and Peter was in the tennis club office, using the affable secretary's private phone, Major Keith St Clair Pringle having obliged on receipt of a large Scotch.

Through this modern, crystal-clear phone line, Brussels sounded nearer than Ascot.

'Pierre, you are well? I know. You want to see me.'

'Yes. Fancy catching the hovercraft for a spot of lunch in Dover? Monday?'

'Mais oui! You have found what I wanted?'

'I think so.'

'Bon. I'll see you at our usual place, noon on Monday.'

'Merci, Didier. Au revoir.'

Peter replaced the receiver. He was pleased. At times phones must be used, but with Didier the discussion was invariably terse. Years of trades had made any protracted conversation between the two of them superfluous.

There was nothing for him at the club, so he returned to St George's Gardens and located the gardener's bogie. On the day, it would ferry the booty across the gardens. A scaffolding pole lay nearby. It would make short work of Bobinet's window. His brain was racing as it computed. Two minutes to move the clocks from the showroom to the bogie. A further thirty seconds to secure the gates behind him with a paddy. Another minute across the Gardens to the Farm Street alley. Thirty seconds again to secure the Farm Street gates. Allow a minute and a half to load the car boot with the booty. Another minute for the unforeseeable. Six and a half minutes, seven at the outside. The cavalry would have to be quick to locate him, and clever too.

Too optimistic? Response time to the alarm could be as little as four minutes. So what? He'd be out of sight and hearing by then, and there'd be two padlocked gates between them. No, by the time they got to Farm Street he'd be long gone. Everything was on his side. He felt it in his water.

His mouth was dry thinking about it; his heart pumped vigorously. He was ensnared by his old, irrational, private excitement – his personal 'Charlie'.

'I'll treat myself afterwards to a ten-day furlough at Forest Mere.'

Saturday and Sunday he hung around the club, vaguely remote and edgy, focused on the test to come. A solo assault in Mayfair was absurd. Kisses at fifty, maybe. Christ, the watering hole must be parched and weary of his attentions. Logic was against this, but logic cannot stem the flow of emotion. The work would be done. Impatient, he chased the ball in the swirling dust of the clay, waiting for Sunday, its darkness and the reward.

It went like a dream.

The padlocks cut, he swung the scaffolding pole just as a Porsche was roaring past. Bobinet's window yielded instantly. Securing eight superb bracket clocks, he propelled the bogie into the gardens and the comfort of their darkness, stopping only to secure the gate with his own padlock. No one saw him, apart from an irate observer in the Connaught Hotel opposite whom he heard – dimly through the alarm's shrill cries – yelling from an upper window, 'Come back! Come back!'

The plot was unfolding to perfection. He jogged with the loot-laden bogie to the Farm Street alley. After stopping to secure the second gate, he made a swift inspection of the street. Deserted. Earlier he'd parked his hatchback opposite the bottom of the alley, and now he transferred the stock to the car. Smoothly, slowly, he pulled away from the kerb, drove past the Farm Street church and, on doing a mandatory right at the end, stopped again. He got out of the car to remove the false number plates he'd lightly stuck over the existing ones. He was confidence itself now. He rounded Berkeley Square until he could turn into Mount Street and drive past the scene of the carnage. There was not a soul in sight.

He parked the car at the tennis club, covering its cargo with a blanket. Leaving it there till morning, he made for the flat to shower and take refuge in Mozart. But he was restless. The adrenalin refused to be reabsorbed. It was the early hours before he slept.

He rose at dawn, deciding on a bath. The hot water cooled as he catnapped until its tepidity alerted him to the fact that it was eight o'clock. Then he chose a herringbone jacket of pure wool, charcoal trousers he'd had from Savile Row, a dark blue Turnbull and Asser shirt, and a navy blue spotted tie. To all and sundry a successful tycoon in mufti. Another charade.

Traffic on the South Circular put him behind schedule but, reluctant to speed with the clocks on board, he disciplined himself to seventy on the motorway to Canterbury. He pulled into the private hotel in Marine Parade ten minutes late.

Didier was standing on the forecourt beaming, cigar in jaw. They hugged, as only the joint beneficiaries of the deceased can.

'Peter, you had a good journey? You look well.'

Didier's bonhomie put Peter on his guard. This was a sure sign it would be a tough trade.

'What have you got for me, Peter?'

'Finest English and French bracket clocks.' He held up eight fingers. 'Superb quality, I think. Anyhow, you'll know when you see them.'

Peter had neither inspected nor even glanced at their coded price tags. Bobinet's only handled best-quality stock. Didier was impatient to confirm Peter's opinion.

'Enough. Let's get them up to my room.'

Then it was Didier on his knees, in another world, paying homage to the exquisite clocks. Peter sat on the bed, a silent spectator as every segment of their movement was checked with a magnifying glass. Every so often Didier would set one to chime in the fashion of a bygone age. He worshipped beautiful things, desiring them first of all for his own private gratification. Many minutes passed before he spoke. When Didier did pronounce, he was coolly precise.

'I will not attempt to find fault with these goods. As you say, they are of superb quality. In effect, they are so outstanding that it will be difficult to let them see daylight. Of course, this is my problem, I only tell you so you too can know.'

He paused and cocked an eye at the thief.

'So what does Maître Pierre want for the parcel?'

The moment of truth had arrived. To sell anything one must have a good idea of its market value. To ask stupid money leaves you as vulnerable as one who would take a pittance. Peter had rehearsed his spiel.

'Didier, I won't play bidding games. I'm sure these chimers have a trade mark-up in excess of ten thousand – a couple probably considerably more. I think a fair ecret is fifteen hundred a lump.'

'Peter, what you say is true. That would be cheap, but I have hidden expenses. Will you take nine thousand for the goods?'

It was a sound offer, and Peter wasn't of a mind to haggle.

'Nine thousand it is. *Bonne chance!'*

Didier had an arrangement with a local bank. They drove there in silence and, returning to the hotel, Didier passed Peter nine bundles of banknotes, each in a wrapper. Peter felt elated as he shuffled them into the glove compartment of the BMW.

'Would you care for lunch, Didier?'

'*Merci, non.* You have done your work and now I must attend to mine.'

A quick embrace and they parted, Peter to London and Didier to – one could only surmise. They were two avaricious men, both very pleased with themselves.

Look at it this way. The insurers probably paid up, the clocks found a better home, and one bloody awful card player had more money to lose. It's an ill wind.

In the early evening, Peter rang Forest Mere Health Hydro.

'My name is Peter Scott. I wonder if I might come down Wednesday and perhaps stay for a week. I've been with you in the past.'

'Could you hold and I'll check . . . Yes, that will be all right.'

'If possible I'd like to be in one of the chalets.'

The refined voice thought that would be fine. Rates were quoted, the booking made, and he was wished a pleasant stay. All very civilised.

A new charade was beginning. One pitfall at the hydro was the other inmates, interminably asking, 'And what do *you* do?' It was necessary to have a fanny prepared and, having toiled in the construction industry from 1971 to 1976, he decided to be a retired contractor. He totally forgot that, at Forest Mere the previous year, he'd been a cattle importer. Liars and thieves need good memories, but no matter. He adored the light comedy of the place. It would be a dull mausoleum without that touch of theatre.

*   *   *

In the meantime Muggins returned to Rousseau's playing twenty-forty-eighty-pound Kaluki. It was not the worst of days. In the initial hour he was three hundred behind. Then, winning a game, he hit the front for small money and the rarity of such a happening elicited a round of applause in the smoke-polluted room. Summoned to the phone, he decided to call it a day.

The voice on the line was a gentle Welsh lilt.

'Do you know who this is, boyo?'

Peter was mystified. He kept it light-hearted.

'Will I get a prize if I guess right?'

'Well, boyo, you should.'

'Good God, is it Taffy Raymond?'

He'd collected the prize.

'Good man, Peter. Look, I'm round the corner. Could you give me five minutes downstairs? And don't fret, I'm not on the nip.'

It was twenty years since they'd met. That was shortly after Taff had escaped from the Ville in 1959 and got ambushed *en route* to Bournemouth by police officers Baldock and O'Connell at the level crossing in Sunningdale. After that he'd gone back to suffer.

Going down to meet him, Peter was surprised how well Taffy looked at seventy. They embraced warmly.

'Peter, I need a favour. I've got a newspaper interested in my memoirs. I'm going to say I was the coachman on Sophia Loren's lot. Would you mind?'

It wasn't much to ask and Peter answered at once.

'Not at all. Naturally I wouldn't want my name mentioned. Otherwise, be my guest.'

Banter followed. Old dreams were revived. Memory Lane. Peter was not certain how much he liked it. As they parted, he noted how brisk Taffy's step was for a septuagenarian. Prison, whilst fucking the mind, did tend to keep the body in good shape.

He probably owed Taffy the favour. The Welshman had been the first to introduce him to country-house work, and assisted his first touch in 1957. Tommy B., a localised Paddington pillager, had originally brought the two of them together, and Taffy had seemed delighted to make the younger man's acquaintance.

'Tommy tells me you're a bit of a screwsman, boyo, a goer, so I hear. Like to make one with Taff? Get a monkey a week, you will.'

A monkey a week? Chummy was talking! Peter had spent the last six months screwing Kensington to get six hundred into his post office book. Of course he'd like. He was also reasonably content that Taffy was the genuine article, effusive though he was, even boastful. So Peter needed little prompting. This represented a chance to up his game, to climb the ladder of criminal expertise.

Significantly, within five years of this meet, most (if not all) home counties police stations had a large embossed photo of Peter on display: 'THIS MAN IS A KNOWN COUNTRY HOUSE RAIDER.' All thanks to Taffy.

Viscount Kemsley was the patriarch of the Berry family, owners of the *Daily Telegraph*. The great newspaper magnate owned a magnificent mansion, Dropmore House, in Burnham Beeches. His socialite wife appeared in the glossies, much bejewelled, attracting Taff's ilk, and indeed, in the forties, the Welshman had made an abortive attempt on the lady. Neither time, nor Dartmoor, had diminished his desire to 'have her gear'.

Had Peter been less naive, he would have known that you're taking a liberty poaching the unsuccessful target of another. Nor had one of the oldest of criminal adages, 'Never graft with a face just out of the slammer', yet reached his ear. To the apprentice burglar, this target had glamour, and he was up for it.

A dour winter's afternoon found the pair of them prowling through the copse at Dropmore. 'Casing the joint' is unattractive as a phrase, but essential as a move. All well-planned theft is like a military assault. Taff was a bag of nerves, yet he immediately grasped the best way to strike.

'We'll come down at the weekend. There's certain to be a house party. We'll go in when they're at dinner, while all those bastards gorge themselves.'

The bitterness in the ex-Rhondda miner's voice recalled the tight belts of the thirties. Peter listened and learned.

They parked the hired Volkswagen about a mile from the house. It was cold, dark, and light rain was falling as they pressed on to the great house. Peter thought the noise of breaking twigs and undergrowth would waken the dead, but only a solitary owl spied the intruders, and hooted to warn its kin.

The house loomed up, a monstrous bit of Victoriana with a small zoo appended. The trespassers had arrived early and approached what they thought was an empty cage for cover, until Peter saw a large eye gleaming at him from the inner darkness. They hid instead in the shadow of a friendly conifer.

A butler was putting the last touches to a magnificently laid table, glittering with silverware. Almost as if he knew he was being watched, he immediately drew the shutters, but even this momentary glimpse into a world of elegance and extravagance had sent an envious shiver down Peter's spine. So far he'd preyed only on the moneyed professional classes. This was his first sight of how the British aristocracy lived.

He felt like a missionary who sees his heathen flock for the first time. He knew now that he had found his true vocation.

The rain started in earnest. The suit he was wearing – new from Charkam's – had been a foolish choice, the snob in Peter feeling he must dress up that night to deprive his betters. He was pissed off as he was pissed on.

At nine o'clock Peter stealthily ascended the steel girder that took him to the roof of the conservatory abutting the house. From there he edged his way around the lintels until he found an unshuttered, unlit window. He slipped his jemmy under the casing of the sash window and gently eased the catch off. But as soon as he tried to raise the window, dismay was instantaneous. There were burglar screws, a rarity in those days, on each window jamb.

Beckoning Taffy, who was watching points on the lawn, he hissed, 'Bloody burglar screws. I'll have to do the burnt to unscrew them.'

'Come on down, kid. I'm not with you if you break the window. It's too risky. Find another entry.'

Taffy's anxiety was at fever pitch, but not yet infectious. Peter hadn't destroyed one of Charkam's best to be deterred by burglar screws or a bottly companion. He quickly placed one of his gloves over the glass, punching it ruthlessly with the other gloved fist. The secret was to punch hard, no pussyfooting about. Give it your best shot. You rarely damaged your extremities and, better, you made little noise. A faint tinkling of glass ensued while Taff retired to the cover of a tree.

Removing the screws from the jamb, he gingerly raised the window and made entry. A mink coat carelessly strewn on the bed caught his eye and, expenses secured, he gathered it up and hurled it out of the window to the lawn below. A diligent search by torchlight produced no gems so, cautiously, he opened an adjoining door and found himself in another bedroom. Here he came across the prize: a jewel pouch. Holding the torch in his teeth, he opened it. It sparkled encouragingly.

From there he found a door to a corridor. He advanced along it towards what he suspected was the main bedroom but, creeping in, he was disappointed. Yes, it *was* the main bedroom. But, alas, Madam knew of his ilk and a massive safe was visibly *in situ*. A quick rummage through the dresser revealed a jewelled yacht-club badge and nothing else. He went back down the corridor to plunder the other guests' rooms and here his progress was checked. He found the unpredictable: a maid coming up the stairs. Before he had time to be inventive, she'd fled screaming. It was on top . . .

He went back in haste to the window of entry, and sixteen feet down a trellis to *terra firma*. Taff was at his side, panting.

'Lively, kiddo. I've had to chin someone out there.' He jerked his thumb at the lawn behind him. 'They jumped me.'

Chin someone? Bollocks.

'Taff, I aimed a mink coat out. It probably landed on you.'

Retreating, they found the mink where Taff had chinned it. They upped the coat and jogged back to the car. Taff was flagging.

'Come on, Ray,' Peter chivvied. 'If you knew what was in my pocket you'd get your second wind.'

Taff found oxygen.

'Have we had a touch?' he gasped.

'Yes, but get a move on. They'll be setting up roadblocks in no time.'

Back at the car they took the High Wycombe road in preference to the more dangerous route to London. Cotswold-bound, they found a guest house as their bake for the night. Once they'd examined the loot, the adrenalin pumped and sleep was an irrelevance.

Thirty-five years had passed, yet it was as if it were yesterday when Peter fondled the string of stomacher pearls, reputed once to have belonged to Marie Antoinette. With it were a pair of good diamond clips and a thirty-two-stone diamond bracelet from Van Cleef and Arples, with matching 2.2-carat baguettes.

The next evening in Highgate, Taff introduced him to the most valuable of contacts, Uncle Ben, and a trade was called at around six thousand pounds. Peter was certain that he had at last arrived.

The bracelet alone would have realised over two hundred thousand today. Such is the menace of inflation . . .

The thief's three thousand share was too meaty for his post office book. On advice from Uncle Ben, he opened a safety deposit box at the Pall Mall depository, and this became the first of many monies that were to rest there. Two years hence he would have in excess of fifty thousand pounds entombed.

His career as a thief, a compulsive big-time thief, took substance that night in Buckinghamshire. Sadly, he didn't fully comprehend just how wealthy he was to become in those years. Only the game mattered. Wilde's observation that 'youth is wasted on the young' is pertinent.

He was never again to look back – or, depending on the moral viewpoint, forward (for the consequences of his actions were all ahead of him). Converted by his brief contact with the opulence of Dropmore House, he was committed at last to the redistribution of serious wealth. The lives of the super-rich, dedicated to ostentation, are largely sheltered from demons. He became their demon, and he was never to lose a night's sleep over them either.

7

Nearly a Love Story

THE drill at Forest Mere was to arrive in the late afternoon, prior to the evening meal. After signing in at reception, a low-key ceremony, he was shown his chalet. It overlooked the pool and tennis court. The whole place had an austere luxury about it.

It was based around an attractive country house a couple of miles from Liphook in Hampshire. An annexe had been added and the Clock House, once a stableyard, had been converted as accommodation. It was the refuge for the famous, the well heeled, and the odd chancer like himself. Most mustered to lose weight, some to relax, and a few to play the field. Peter was there to switch off, relax, although fate was to decree otherwise.

Tennis, bridge and a jaunt to the theatre in Chichester were on the menu. Peter felt it was suitably ironical that the play was a piece about Oscar Wilde: *Feasting with Panthers*. He'd been doing just that all his life and was doing it here.

A mandatory medical and advice on diet were the following morning's appointments, and on each day after that (as on prison days) it was a dawn start. Lemon tea and toast arrived at 6.30. From eight, treatments, to include massage, consumed the morning – unless you were into facials. From midday, time was pretty much his own.

At lunch on the Thursday he took the opportunity to view those inmates not on a starvation diet. There was a surfeit of the female species, a tight-lipped, formidable array waffling on about fighting the flab. It was as if he'd stumbled on a Tory ladies' conference, a Daughters of the American Revolution sabbatical. Avoiding predatory ladies and bores might be a major problem.

That afternoon, while he was serving a couple of hundred balls alone on the solitary court, a slim, dark, intense lady passed him carrying a racquet.

'Would you care to play with me?' she called out. 'I used to play regularly, but I'm a little rusty now, I guess.'

The nasal New York accent grated a little, but she was attractive, sophisticated – middle-aged but in good nick.

'Sure. My name is Peter Scott.'

'Hi, Peter. I'm Irene. That an Irish accent? You can probably tell I'm from New York.'

'Yes, I was born in Ireland, and I did suspect New York.'

They knocked up for half an hour. She was a correct stylist. All her strokes were textbook but, as she said, rusty. A couple of competitive sets then revealed that, like any serious tennis freak, she didn't like losing.

'Christ, I'm out of shape. I should have butchered that lob.'

Mature and winsome, like so many of her American sisters, she wore the pants. For Peter, it detracted from her femininity.

'Are you going to the theatre tonight?' Irene asked. She had selected him as her beau.

A luxury coach ran the escapees to Chichester. They sat side by side, naturally and at ease.

'Peter Scott? You're not the famous wildlife painter?'

'Pass. My aesthetic talents lie elsewhere. I'm more or less a tennis bum since I retired from the construction industry.'

'Hell, a tennis bum? You can't support yourself on that.'

The elegantly groomed Irene had got to the heart of her sex's quest in one. *Are you well heeled?* But prepared by experience for this turn of the conversation, Peter parried.

'My needs are minimal. I survive.'

The sharpness in his voice betrayed him. Why the fuck was he on the defensive with this tough New Yorker? Had he *loser* written on his forehead? Changing tack, he lurched into Oscar Wilde. He felt he was on a safer wicket, having recently read Sheridan Morley's biography of Oscar.

'Are you familiar with the subject of the play?'

'Yeah, I was liberally educated.'

'Let me guess. Wealthy background. New York and I would guess Ann Arbor.'

He'd scored. Peter had devoured all the fables of John P. Marquand, an arch New England snob who only wrote of Vassar and Ann Arbor.

'Wow, how did you figure that out? There's more to you than meets the eye.'

So it was one bout apiece. Perhaps the rapiers could rest now. Leave the decider in limbo.

The play was turgid, an intellectual rehash of Wilde's Old Bailey trial. Peter, who knew some of the dialogue verbatim, impressed Irene, quoting before the actors. At half-time the (cheating) gin and tonics were superb. As they stood with their drinks, he caught sight of himself and Irene in the mirror behind the bar. A handsome couple. Pity it was a charade.

Serious cheating followed. Peter dragged Irene to the fish restaurant buffet nearby, where salmon escalopes and hock went down a treat. After the interval she linked arms with him as they sank into their seats. It was nice.

Oscar put himself to the sword. He and Peter shared the same trap: do something behind closed doors often enough and eventually you get careless and do it openly as by right. And neither of them *wanted* to avoid their destinies.

They were in the coach, driving back, when she returned him to the subject.

'He was a sad guy. He got his eras wrong.'

It was a glib assessment, but near enough to get Peter thinking.

'Oscar – sad? Never. It was the society he amused which was sad. Victoria's fifty years of grief was like a corset. His Celtic bravado didn't suit. He exposed the Empire-makers' hypocrisy. Then he foolishly challenged the obscene Queensberry and gave his enemies the chance to close ranks and destroy him.'

The venom in Peter's voice surprised Irene and she dropped the discussion, laying her head on his shoulder and feigning sleep. Peter continued to think about Oscar, drinking champagne on his deathbed, dying beyond his means.

Parting from Peter in the hall, a sleepy Irene blew him a kiss.

Next day they played tennis again. When they finished it was still early.

'Any ideas today?' she prompted.

'Yes. Fancy going over to Petworth House? The Turners are fantastic. And if we can cheat again, they do a lovely high tea.'

He failed to mention the Petworth silver, which he'd hoped to purloin the previous year until, sadly, he discovered that they vaulted it at night.

'Gosh, that'd be swell. Did I tell you my former husband has an art gallery?'

Irene went off to change. When she reappeared Peter had to admit she'd really made an effort. Petworth was to see a chic check suit and low-heeled Italian shoes. A discreet Dior scarf fluttered from a skin handbag. He enjoyed being with her.

The BMW growled along the winding road through Haslemere, like a bit-chewing thoroughbred needing to be held up in the first furlong. But time was not of the essence, so the Hun would have to be content with cantering up and down the dips. The journey gave Irene time to tax Peter's CV. She established he was divorced, unattached, his children grown up. Then, avidly, she gave him the headlines of her own life: divorced, five daughters, of whom three were still finishing their education in America.

'Peter, I want to be frank. I'm renting a country house in the Quorn country. I'm involved with the guy who owns it. He's very sweet but younger than I am. I've come away to get my head right. I wanted to tell you this . . .'

She ran out of words.

'No big deal, Irene. We're all scarpering from one spectre or another.'

'I'm trying to buy a house in London, see a little of my sister. She lives in Portman Square.'

They arrived at Petworth and Peter got immediate brownie points by enrolling Irene in the National Trust. It cost fifteen pounds, but it overwhelmed her.

'You're a very sweet man. There was really no need.'

They stood for a long time in front of the great Turner seascapes. Their dark and light ochre shades showed the master at his most imperious. They both found it stimulating. Later, tea in the great hall was fun but, just as he began to relax, Irene fired a salvo.

'Peter, come clean. What do you really do?'

His blue-grey eyes no doubt betrayed him as he searched for an answer. All his life they had done so, in confrontations with the truth.

'Irene, I'll be whatever you want me to be. How's that?'

'No. Not what I want you to be. Who are you? I can't figure you out. I'm out with a conjuror, that's the vibes I get. In Westchester County we like to know where we stand. With you I see a dozen different faces.'

Irene was coming on heavy. For God's sake, they'd only known one another two days. A conjuror? A dozen different faces? It annoyed him that she'd got on the trail of the truth; he'd no intention of confirming it. He decided to laugh it off.

'American women want everything in pigeon-holes. Take it out, dust it down, amuse yourself with it, put it back. I got out of that cage some years back. I'm not mindful of returning.'

The banter ran its course with Irene still seeking absolutes and Peter insisting there were none. It was like bidding to a slam in bridge without the requisite points in your hand.

Back at Forest Mere, Peter fancied making a night of it, a reward for his courage in Mount Street. Was Irene game?

'Fancy a bottle of wine at The Links tonight?'

The Links was a good-quality restaurant run by a Teutonic Brunnhilde some two miles from the hydro. It was absolute cheating.

'OK. But I mustn't eat or drink alcohol.'

She did both. And, by the third bottle of Tattinger Blanc et Blanc, she was back gnawing at the bone.

'Peter, how come a tennis bum can buy all this champagne?'

Peter cut the string instantly.

'Irene, since I *am* paying, you're not allowed to ask. Relax, be grateful!'

Back in his chalet with an unforgivable fourth bottle of Tattinger, they lay on the bed. Giggled. Fumbled not, save for their lips brushing once or twice. It was chaste in the extreme. Then, creeping out at dawn, he wondered. Should he have been more ardent? They hadn't divested a stitch of apparel. Maybe he couldn't screw. Maybe he didn't fancy her. All in all, he'd shaped up poorly.

It was so very déjà vu. Why did he play these charades?

Cruel fate was afoot earlier that night. Whilst the oddly matched couple were in their cups at The Links, an enterprising thief had come down his ladder with a million pounds' worth of gems from an Arab in nearby Rogate. The trespass was to embarrass the thief later.

It was now Saturday, and they spent the day together, though Irene often phoned her socially superior landlord. Peter may have been alluded to and, with her Sunday departure close at hand, he wondered if jealousy had been activated at his expense. It had.

On Sunday, the Laird arrived in style. Eton, Cambridge, the Guards, the Range Rover. Young, handsome, arrogant.

'Good of you to look after her, old man. Any chance of a bite to eat in this place?'

The scion of the aristocracy had found them in the dining room, where guests were strictly no-no. But panache won the day as Chummy filled a plate from the cold buffet. He was civil, even pleasant. He'd taken one look at Peter and was reassured. There was nothing to worry about with this old buffer. But after lunch, standing beside the Range Rover, he was not so sure. Wasn't it a shade too demonstrative of Peter to come out just to wave goodbye. Like all his class, he took refuge in breezy patronage.

'We must rush off. Lovely meeting you. Do lose a few pounds. Hahr! Hahr!'

His limp handshake compounded the insolence.

Irene managed a Queenie wave as they pulled away along the drive. The charade had come to a dismal conclusion. The knight errant had recovered his wealthy Yankee lady without so much as a lock of hair falling out of kilter.

The English upper class run the Maltese a close second in that island's finest pursuit – pimping. But naturally, they can't be incarcerated for it.

'Wish I had a hall and a family tree, been to Eton and Cambridge,' Peter muttered to himself morosely. Then he was laughing at himself.

'I've nearly met loads of important people. Well, that's a plus in the life of an antisocial social climber.'

It was a bloody Sunday. He stood at his chalet window staring at the tennis court. John, an inmate who (gossip had it) was on the Queen's Bench, was playing with an uptight, big-titted matron. Christ, she had a pair of udders. He remembered Maureen Connolly's advice: 'If I see my opponent has big tits I hit the ball straight at them.'

Irene phoned him at six the same evening.

'Hi, what are you doing? I suppose you have your eye on someone else?'

'Can I deal with those in reverse order? No. And I'm off to hear the local Schnabel playing Chopin soon.'

'What did you think of Robert?'

She was treading on dangerous ground.

'Charming, handsome, arrogant . . .'

'Too young for me?'

'Probably.'

'Yeah, I guess so. I told him you were a bum. He didn't approve.'

Peter grimaced at the receiver. No one approved of him; he didn't approve of himself. He managed to live with it.

'Understandable, Irene. He's from your Westchester County comparative. Pigeon-holes again. Likes to know what he's dealing with. If not, gun it from the butts . . .'

'Peter, I have a friend in London who knows you. Carole Harvey.'

She had omitted to say 'from your past'. Peter steeled himself.

'That's nice. How is the lovely Carole?'

'Peter, she says you're a no-no. Why?'

Irene had been busy. Lost for a reply, he let her go on.

'Aren't you a little old to be riding tigers?'

Irene had got the full SP. It was cards on the table time.

'I've been too old for the last decade. What I've lost in audacity I compensate for with guile.'

'Won't they catch you and lock you up?'

'Aren't we all under lock and key? No worse dungeon than conventional society. Lovelace had it four centuries ago: freedom's a state of mind.'

'Peter, I'd like to see you again. Is it mutual?'

'Yes, I'd like to see you.'

'Ring this London number Thursday around midday. I'll be at a house in Pavilion Road. Do you know Pavilion Road?'

Peter knew it. And every other inch of Belgravia. He scribbled the number down and agreed to ring on Thursday.

'Must go now, Peter. Young Lochinvar and I are hacking out.'

She blew a kiss into the receiver and rang off. Lingering in the phone booth, he realised he was pleased he would see her again.

Most men, if not all, masturbate frequently in the slammer. And, as the years pass, the fantasies become more and more bizarre in order to get the stimulus. The reality of a woman's love and flesh cease to be adequate and, more often than not, the recidivist is finally disqualified from normal relationships.

The Chopin prelude was sublime, but not enough. The judge's lady's superb bosoms caught his eye, encased in a transparent bra and chiffon. Then her strong leg intruded, in steel-grey nylon, dangling provocatively. She seemed to catch him looking.

Chopin drew Peter away from his degeneracy until gentle applause returned him to reality. Satan was afoot that night. He found the lady was in the next chalet.

The bench bedded early. Would he be bold and call? Light glowed through the net curtain of her boudoir as he approached, stealthy, undecided. He was about to give a gentle knock when, clearly beyond the net, she appeared in his line of vision. His mouth was parched, his pulse raced.

In the centre of the chalet, she stepped out of her dirndl skirt, revealing the long sturdy legs and a mist of grey silk tights superimposed over a pair of brief white panties. He was rooted to the spot.

Removing a necklace, she slowly undid her chiffon blouse. The flesh-coloured bra strained, full of the heavy orbs. A quick movement behind her back released them and Peter was powerless. Satan guided his hand to his stiffening member and, moving his foreskin over the glans, he had an orgasm within seconds. Sheepish, ashamed, stimulated, he tidied himself with his handkerchief. When he had crept like the thief he was into his own chalet, he was still trembling from the instant gratification.

He was mad as a hatter.

The time till he departed on Wednesday was empty in Irene's absence. He played tennis with M'Lord and she of the ample bosoms, a knowing smile from her from time to time causing him to speculate that the voyeur spectacle may have been a joint enterprise. He cracked the Maureen Connolly advice, which M'Lord found in bad taste. Grey Tights was amused. She knew the virtue of it.

Wednesday night he was back in London and – where else? – at the Sanatorium. There were no messages. No one was seeking him. He relaxed over cognac.

On Thursday he woke early. Irene day. Phone around midday. But first – the decanters! He must ring Amy.

'Hello?'

It was the deep-throated growl of an aggressive voice.

'Amy, Peter Scott. George is locked up. I have a pair of Georgian decanters he'd like you to have.'

He wanted to get it out in a rush before the invective started.

'Does he really? And did he tell you he pawned my jewellery while I was away?'

'I heard something about it. You got it back, didn't you?'

'Yes, but only because I found the ticket from Sutton's. He'd have sold that too. I ask you, who'd like to pay four thousand pounds to reclaim what's yours?'

It was a very irate Amy.

'I'm sorry, Amy.'

'You're not sorry. You're like him. No respect for other people's property. I don't want his bloody decanters. I don't want no begging letters either. Remember when he got fresh with the maid?'

Peter switched off. It was crucify George time, Amy's strident voice recalling all the sins of the past twenty years. He put the receiver down. When it comes to one's trespasses one can be sure a woman will have them on the tip of her tongue. No bloody magnanimity at all.

And she was right, Amy. He wasn't sorry at all. Why, for Christ's sake, do the hussars of the world give their hearts to dragons? It were better to play the St George.

He rang on the dot of noon, the dialling purr eating ten, then twenty seconds. Where was the bitch? At last a breathless Irene answered.

'Hi. I was in the bath.'

'Fancy a spot of dinner tonight?'

'Yes. That would be nice.'

'Fish or meat?'

'You decide. No, wait. Fish. Yes, fish.'

Irene gave him the address.

'Irene, will you be in your glad rags?'

'In what?'

'Tarted up.'

'No more than usual,' the tart reply bounced back.

He'd take her to Scott's in Mount Street, if only to put a few quid back in the street it had come from. He dialled their number.

'A table for Mr Scott at nine-thirty? *Oui, monsieur.*'

They were dating.

Irene was holed up in a modest block in Pavilion Road which, in more golden days, had been the servants' annexe to houses on Sloane Street. On being admitted, the first thing that caught the professional eye was the surfeit of burglar grilles. Idly he thought, what do you do if there's a fire at your door? Never mind.

In the solitary bedroom, Irene was on the phone. The nasal drawl was audible.

'What time does the meeting start? Have we voting rights? Yes, I know, gold was no good today. We'll wait for the Hong Kong market to open.'

It went on for ten minutes, Peter naively tempted to think the high-finance talk was for his ears. Later, as their friendship developed, he learned that Irene was into bonds, the dollar premium, property. Her high-powered acumen did nothing to lower the threshold of his impotence. This was a pimp's venue, and undignified ground for a thief.

At long last, she appeared.

'Peter, you look handsome. Help yourself to a drink. I house-hunted so long today I'm snow-blind.'

She nodded at the drink which was by now in his hand.

'Can you drink that in the lounge? I want to change.'

Brussels Man ushered them into the restaurant. He'd been in Scott's for yonks, shunting the unshuntable limos. He could tell a tale or two, but he didn't. Bobinet's glinted menacingly from across the road, as if it knew and resented that he'd dared return. There followed twenty minutes of Bloody Marys, a table wait. Then both had a half-lobster and a couple of bottles of house white to wash it down. Theirs seemed a natural, happy banter.

The maître d's eye sparkled as Peter produced two fifty-pound notes. Cash punters in Mayfair these days were rarer than a tuppenny blue. To appease the ominous shade of Bobinet's, he left a fifteen-pound tip. Irene winced at the extravagance. Ladies of loot distress easily in the face of unnecessary largesse. Peter had never known an exception.

The food was passable. When the Balcombe Street 'lads' gunned the place, it was rumoured that the chef lost his nerve. Stayed shell-shocked. He no longer wanted to seem anxious to please the Anglo-Saxons.

Car keys in hand, he and Irene linked arms as they sauntered to Park Lane.

'Gee, that's Purdey's on the corner. My pa waited three years for a pair of their guns. I use a little Spanish gun myself. Do you shoot?'

'No. Never had the desire to slaughter the defenceless. Breeding prey just to sate their bloodlust is an Anglo-Saxon sport. And arseholes like your Robert standing in the butts blasting away just adds incentive to my devil's advocacy.'

'Devil's advocacy? I don't follow.'

'Redistribution of wealth.'

Irene fell silent. Had he fucked up again?

'Irene, this will amuse you. See the Purdey shop annexe across the road? It once belonged to a furrier – Wolfe's, I think. Like to hear the quaint story?'

Irene wasn't sure she did. But it was Alice-in-Wonderland time.

'Shoot,' she said.

'Many years past I was into depriving furriers. I and my partner then, Taters, were giving the premises our best shot. I gained access to the flat above in order to deal with the alarm-bell boxes, the same as those there now. I was hanging by my knees over the wrought ironwork on the ledge, cutting the alarm casing.'

Irene was decidedly lacking in interest, but he ploughed on.

'Taters was standing here, where we are, watching points. I was struggling, knees cramping and the blood rushing into my head. It was an asbestos casing – they're bloody.'

By now he was talking to himself, guided by his inner eye.

'Suddenly, without warning, motorcycles rumbled and there was a clamouring din, like a crowd of people. Then two or three police motorcyclists took up position on the corner of South Audley Street.

I was too stunned to contemplate retreat. I just hung there. All I could think was, how the hell did they get here so quickly?'

Irene was looking agitated now.

'They paid no attention to me. The low rumble grew to a crescendo and suddenly a mob was streaming up South Audley Street heading towards Grosvenor Square. The cops sped off before them.'

Irene woke up. 'I get it. They were heading for our embassy to demonstrate, right?'

'Nearly right. Demonstrators, yes. But they were on their way to Claridge's to protest at Queen Fredericka's presence in London. The Colonels' firm had just ended the Greek democracy.'

'What did you do?'

'Cleared the furrier out, darling. Forty or fifty garments.'

Peter was preening and she reproved him primly.

'You think robbing people is clever?'

'Not really. There are degrees of skill in effecting it. One tends to take pride in work well done, if it's done without violence. Obviously, a lot of people are unhappy, but they live and breathe and fill in claims forms. I operate as kindly as the calling permits.'

'Christ, what would my family think if they knew who I'm with?'

'Just don't mention it. Westchester County will remain intact.'

Irene was mollified. She tried a jest.

'Don't let's talk shop. I'll pass on to you the houses I viewed.'

Back at her place, the phone lured her into the bedroom. The Hang Seng was on the move. Peter joined her, stretching out on the bed, a hand casually placed on Irene's sheened thigh. She accepted this but, when he loosened his tie, alarms bells rang.

'Peter, you can't stay here tonight. The porter's Robert's secret agent.'

His sheen-filled paw took up a more daring station. Irene moved to accommodate it. He took a firm grip on her pelvis. She looked like a celibate in knickers and tights. A little asexual. Maybe he should have kissed her first. Irene did not remove his hand; she showed neither pleasure nor dismay. He kissed her lightly, to excuse his impertinent grip.

'Take your skirt off. It'll crease.'

'You'll have to move your hand.'

She kissed him with tenderness but he could tell she was still undecided. Then she said it.

'Peter, are you impotent?'

He froze. Anger followed hard on his surprise.

'What the fuck kind of thing is that to bring up? If I wasn't, I am now. No wonder half of American males have their balls cut off.'

Irene remained grimly silent and, in his mortification, he rambled on. He felt embarrassed and inept as he filed the defence.

'Do you think at my age I'm into quickies? Cards on the table. Yes, I do have problems keeping my cock stiff. Doesn't mean I can't get it together with someone I feel for.'

Remorsefully, Irene appeased him.

'Peter, I'm so very sorry. It was crass of me.'

Sympathy he didn't want. He slid into his jacket, ready to leave, just as the phone rang to distract Madam. It was the young swain.

'Hi, Robert,' she was saying, 'I'm just bedding down.'

Blowing a demonstrably artificial kiss, he let himself out. The last thing he heard was Irene telling Chummy about a house she'd looked at in Gunter Grove. Fucking women.

As he drove much too fast up Park Lane, it struck him that maybe both Irene and the V & A were out of his reach. Later at the flat he cranked himself off.

> When I was young I heard a wise man say
> 'Give crowns and pounds and guineas –
> But never your heart away.'

Once a crank, always a crank.

8

Taters and Patsy

As he walked to the club on Saturday, his attention was seduced by loud music emanating from the ground-floor flat in Castellain Mansions. Twenty-five years past he called there frequently. It was then the home of Patsy and Shirley.

Patsy Murphy first made his acquaintance in Dorothy's Club in Knightsbridge, opposite the Green. The man was a quiet, thinking predator who idolised Taters. His Irish extraction helped him warm, also, to Peter. It was an association of less than a year but it had a lasting influence on the thief.

In 1955 Patsy was going through a bad patch. Possibly, in more affluent circumstances, Peter's extrovert habits would have disqualified him from Patsy's friendship, but mutual need made them partners. Patsy – apart from one short remand – never spent any time behind bars. By luck? More probably judgement. Arrogant, ill-tempered, but a shrewd gambler and a cautious thief, he had found some answers. He was also an astute observer of others and (reluctant as Peter was to admit it) had he taken his friend's advice much suffering would have been avoided.

Peter now had, wrongly, achieved what the Element call a 'lucky thief' tag. He preferred to stand beside Henry Ford on the subject of luck: 'the harder I work the luckier I get'. Anyway, as his reputation spread, he found many doors opening in the private world of the professional criminal classes. Patsy was one such door.

He had been dead some time now. All his life he suffered with arthritis and was in persistent pain. Latterly he became a successful businessman and, for the last twenty years of his life, Peter and he had not spoken – a silly dispute about credit at a chemmy game still festering. As it happened, this same dispute first brought him into proper contact with Taters. It was at Margot's Trojan Club in Phillimore Gardens. A fateful night for many.

Patsy set about acquainting Peter with the good life. He introduced him to Bertie Green's Astor Club in Berkeley Square and to Paddy Kennedy at the infamous Star Tavern in Belgrave Mews. The Star became a regular haunt of the thief, and he and Paddy became lifelong friends. Patsy also took the thief to Ascot races, awakening Peter's profound dislike of the prats who yearly trooped (and still troop) through the Royal Enclosure. Finally, he got through Patsy an introduction to old Mr Hanna the tailor, then in D'Arblay Street but later, and by right, on the fringes of Savile Row. Hanna was a gentleman and friend until death, a tailor's tailor, whose small workroom acted as surrogate for many of the big-name firms in Savile Row. When tailors sat down together, Hanna's name never failed to come up.

Luck is of the essence, and the Patsy connection was lucky. Cruising at dusk down Circus Road in Peter's Barker Special Sports Daimler – then a three-thousand-pound motor – an attractive house down a short lane caught the eye. Patsy knew it. Madam had plenty of jewellery but to date he'd been unable to crack it. As they passed, an elderly member of staff tottered down the drive.

Peter pulled up. Was there a chance the house was unprotected? Patsy doubted that, but fell in with his eager young companion's idea for investigating further. Peter strolled up the gravel path to the well-lit house. To the innocent onlooker it would seem to be occupied, but the intruder possessed a second sight which told him, maybe not. Maybe it was the 'moody lights' syndrome.

Boldly, he crashed on the knocker and fingered the audible bell. If there was an alarm he couldn't see it. He waited, and nothing happened. He crept to the rear, confident the place was empty, then forced a window, vaulted inside and swiftly ascended the stairs. At the top he scared the life out of himself. The figure of a man appeared out of the darkness in front of him, and he was sure he'd met the householder. It was his reflection in a full-length mirror. Nerves.

Collecting himself, he forced a secure drawer and the prize appeared: a fine skin jewel case. As he forced it open his eye was blinded by gemstone light. They'd cracked it.

As he crossed the road, he barely missed colliding with the elderly retainer on his way back to the house. Then the elated pair drove to Maida Vale, whooping with laughter as the jewel case revealed the details of its contents: a four-stone bracelet, each about five-carat. The evening papers told their readers, in the course of reporting the theft, that this had been the first time in ten years that the house had been left completely unattended. Unlucky old butler? Or a turn in the tide?

Whatever the truth, Patsy's barren spell had ended and a new, especially fruitful one had just commenced.

An introduction to another contact, Stuart Pulver, owner of Pulver et Cie, a furrier's in Davies Street, was to become a vital and rewarding association. Admittedly it was to come to grief at the Old Bailey in 1965, but that was far in the future. For the moment, Pulver became another member of Peter's cabal of specialised receivers and, without that valuable class of person, the thief's story would not have been worth telling.

Patsy had a bit of work for them, a top-floor premises in Princes Street, Mayfair, which was a manufacturing furrier's. The top floor of the adjacent property was no more than a façade, probably the victim of a Blitz fire, which meant that the gable-end wall of the furrier was exposed. They gained access from a language school below and attacked the two-foot-thick wall. It resisted all attempts at penetration and they were actually calling it a day when Peter, in frustration and anger, committed himself to one last frenzied assault with a steel point. A single brick was dislodged and suddenly they were through, the remaining masonry giving way without further obstinacy.

They ended up with a couple of thousand apiece, and the great pile of fur they accumulated on the roof in the gloom remains clearly in Peter's memory. It was the first of perhaps fifty fur thefts Peter went on to add to his CV.

An amusing incident occurred just before Patsy took him to see Mr Hanna. The thief's usual attire was sports coat and flannels, a throwback to his Belfast middle-class youth, where suits were for chapel and funerals. However, the Astor nightclub on his first visit expected better. Tieless and in his sports jacket, Peter was about to walk down the triple-section stairs when Bertie Green, sitting at the stairfoot with a carnation in his buttonhole, exploded.

'No, no, Patsy! He can't come in like that. No way.'

Even clubs in Berkeley Square had their standards, but of course they have their price too. Peter whipped out a roll of white fivers held firm with elastic – there was maybe five thousand pounds in all in the bundle. He stooped and rolled the money down the stairs towards the irate owner, who was joined at that moment by his manager, Sulky. They watched, mesmerised, as the boodle bounced towards them.

Picking it up at his feet, Bertie addressed Peter.

'You've dropped this, sir.' And to Sulky, 'Get the gentleman a tie and see Mr Pat has a good table.'

Peter at once became a member and, intrigued by the world of the club hostess, plagued the place for years.

In this period, the author was a six-nights-a-week cat burglar. What is a cat burglar? Simply one who, to secure his prize, shins up pipes and trellises, clambers over roofs and ledges. To the media and public at large it is a relatively romantic profession, whose daring dilutes the depravity of the theft itself. Peter's persistent attacks in Mayfair and Belgravia prompted the coppers to mark the press's card about the spate of rooftop jewel thefts, assumed to be the work of one man. Had Taters been at large, they'd have been looking for him but, alas, he had started a ten-stretch in 1954. The papers were interested enough to lavish on Peter a nickname all his own: the Human Fly.

Patsy would have no part in most of this campaign, though Peter and he still targeted fleshpots from time to time, and he was privy to the rest of Peter's activities. It was the talk of Paddy Kennedy's pub. Peter, stupidly bursting to tell, had his vanity kept on a tight rein by the wise old owl Patsy. Frustrating to be a star who never got a review.

When it suits, everyone is a thief's enemy. His infamy spread. Uncle Ben, having one of his regular spins from the élite Flying Squad, was asked by the then governor, Superintendent Frank Davis, if he knew the 'Irishman'.

'Irishmen are all over Camden Town,' Ben joshed.

'This bloody Paddy's not in Camden Town,' Davis growled, none too pleased. It may seem strange to find an Anglo attributing finesse to a Celt, but Davis did.

Peter's appetite for the game puzzled and worried the cautious Patsy. They were having a good run, but Patsy's enthusiasm was dying. Chronic rheumatism and persistent pain were factors, but the overriding one was that Peter was on borrowed time, and Patsy wanted no part of it. He'd used up all his best advice on the headstrong Ulsterman.

So when Peter turned up in Maida Vale one spring evening with the notion of having a pop at a house in Avenue Road, Patsy passed tersely.

'Not for me, boy.'

Thirty-five Avenue Road was an inspired guess-up. But in this inspired spell he felt London was his oyster.

Getting to the rear garden and crossing its rockery, he brought with him a ladder found next door. The house was occupied downstairs and the French window at bedroom level was open. Irrationally fearless, he put the ladder up and climbed in. He found nothing in the dresser. Pained, he searched cupboards – and there it was. A safe, fully rebated into the wall behind. Grasping the handle, he found he could manoeuvre it out of its hutch, though squeaking and protesting. He took a breather.

He'd already locked the bedroom door. Now he looked around. The mattress on the bed was a huge one but, yes, it would do. Forcing it out of the French windows, lowering it to rest at the foot of the ladder, he humped the two-hundredweight safe across the room and slid it down, holding on as long as he could before releasing it onto the muffling mattress. It landed with a thud and a clank before rolling into the rockery.

Out of the window and down to secure it, he was sure it must have been heard in the house. Nothing stirred. Struggling, he lifted it to chest height and, with superhuman effort, hoisted it over the dividing wall to the next garden. There was a row of dustbins and he concealed the safe in the largest one. There was a clamour now whence he'd come. Retreating another garden away, he found an overlooking tree and he climbed it. Crouched in the branches, he watched both the target house and his prize.

Two minutes later a distressed woman burst out onto the patio below the bedroom.

'My jewels! My jewels!' she screamed.

He was elated, fearful, his heart pumping like a turbine. It was out of his hands. All he could do, if he wanted that safe, was watch and wait. And that night his luck was at a premium.

The garden of 35 led to a smaller residence that fronted on Townshend Road. It too was unoccupied, and the police (having by now arrived) naturally concluded that the safe had been spirited away through it. Not a copper gave the wall or adjacent house as much as a glance while Peter clung to his perch in a lather of sweat and excited greed. He was even able to watch a police inspector sitting down in the losers' conservatory to compile a list of what was missing. Only when the police finally left did the thief descend.

With renewed panache, he backed his Daimler into the open-gated drive of the adjacent house, then manhandled the safe from its dustbin lair into the ample boot. Driving gingerly to his home – at that time in north London's Stamford Hill – he housed the prize overnight in his garage.

To open it the next day presented a problem. By the standards of 1957 it was a modern box, with bevelled corners to thwart the expedient of 'stripping' it from the rear. Eventually he had to resort to a silver-steel hacksaw blade to cut off two corners and punch the pierced outer casing back with a cold chisel and club hammer. It was a tedious job, peeling the steel an eighth of an inch at a time. When enough of this heavy outer skin was rolled back, he emptied the ballast and cut the light steel inner casing. It took three hours.

The hole he made was big enough to put his forearm through. His hand grasped a leather pouch which lay under a plethora of documents and packages. The jewels were superb – the insurance assessors later valued them at twenty-five thousand pounds. There was a flawless five-carat single stone, a ruby suite, bracelets and brooches. After he had gawped at these for a while, he pulled out the papers, to burn them. A solid brown paper parcel came out, looking like a bundle of tightly wrapped receipts. He was about to rubbish it along with the rest of the dross but, just to check, he ripped the wrapping off: four bundles of large white fivers spilled out – five thousand in each bundle.

The relative value of the gems and cash today would be half a million.

Some years later a governor of the Flying Squad, lecturing at Hendon Police College, specified the theft as an example of what the determined solo thief could accomplish. But Peter, having worked alone, couldn't keep it to himself. He showed the gems to Patsy who, piqued at having disqualified himself, growled, 'Good luck. You're too warm for me, kid. We'll call it a day.'

Peter was crestfallen at the rejection. He slunk away. God knows what would have been said if he'd declared the cash too.

9

An Awayday

THE autumn slipped by. Irene didn't phone. When he rang Pavilion Road, nobody answered. The only break in the monotonous gloom was the arrival of a long-time pal, Archie.

'Hello, mate, you look well. I've got to take this tennis up.' It sounded more like a threat than a promise as he eased his bulk out of the gleaming Rolls which stood in the club car park.

'Archie, it's saved my life. It could even save yours.'

Standing at the bar, Archie explained the purpose of his visit.

'You still got your private punters? If you have, I've a parcel they might like.' He passed Peter a cloth pouch.

Excusing himself, Peter recessed to the bog for an examination. Three superb diamond and pearl necklets. The stones were modern and the pearls beautiful. It could be that Benny would take them.

'Very nice indeed, Archie. What do they have to come to?'

'Twenty long ones. At that, there's a five-grand drink for you.'

Archie wasn't allowing him much room for manoeuvre. It was a pricey parcel, but he'd try anyway.

'I'll give it a whirl,' he promised.

Archie made a show of shaking hands and trundled out, back to his motorised status symbol. Peter slipped upstairs to the locker room. The lockers were old, almost defunct, and offered little security. Of course, when they were installed years ago, immorality didn't impose so much stress on the middle and upper classes. Today you fitted your own paddy.

Peter had two, both well shod, one visibly in his own name and a second in the ladies' changing room in a girl chum's name. Making sure the room was empty, he housed the parcel in the latter, a deceit that would make it difficult, if not impossible, for any searcher to detect the illegitimate treasure.

Later, having a hit on the show court, he felt prying eyes. A stranger on the verandah was surely paying more attention to him than his tennis skills warranted. Had Archie been tailed? Could Chummy be a copper?

With paranoia rising, he curtailed the hit and came off court.

Chummy had gone. But anxiety lingered and he gave Remy Martin a belting at the bar. Later, stumbling back to his garret in Sutherland Avenue, he suddenly felt very old. The feeling was to be confirmed later when, visiting Peter in the slammer, the young Regional Crime Squad officer who'd been watching him that day – suspecting him of a million-pound theft from an Arab at Rogate – told Peter that he'd looked like a lonely old man that evening.

In the afternoon, Benny turned up to view the parcel.

'Hello. Got up to any mischief with Roger yet?'

Benny was always working.

'Not as yet. He's away at the moment. Comes across as an oddball – is he reliable? I know he's capable, but I'm uneasy with him.'

'Sound as a bell, Roger. I don't mix with prats. He's certainly unusual, but very bright.'

Benny's voice brooked no further enquiry. He returned to the matter in hand.

'What's the parcel got to come to? Can I take it with me for a couple of hours?'

'I've got to return fifteen thousand. Anything in excess we share.'

Benny showed small enthusiasm when he heard the requirements, but he left to see what he could do. Later, Peter was in the club car park when Benny drove in.

'No good, son. Too pricey. Beautiful gear, but pearls are hard. Say hello to Roger for me.'

Passing the parcel back, Benny was, as ever, in a rush. He backed his car out and drove away. At this point, Peter committed a cardinal sin. Rather than take the time to put the parcel back in the locker, he elected to stuff it under the dashboard of the BMW, though he later moved it to the side pouch of his tennis bag, leaving it to languish there overnight.

At 6.30 the next morning his door buzzed. He knew it was probably the law and, in a flash, realised his stupidity. Panache was the one weapon left. He raised the sash window and saw five, perhaps six men on his porch.

'Police,' one shouted up, holding up his warrant card.

'Hang on.'

From the dresser he fetched his keys.

'Catch.'

He aimed them at his unwelcome guests below. A few seconds later, opening his door, they pounded in, aggressive, eager.

'Regional Crime Squad. We have a warrant to search these premises for stolen jewellery.'

The governor stepped forward, wasting no time.

'I'm Detective Chief Inspector Ryder. These officers will search the flat.'

'Please do. There's not a lot to search, as you see. I live frugally.'

A victim of many early morning spins, he noticed at once the desultory way they turned out drawers and cupboards. They know there's nothing here, he thought. Next question: do you have a car?

Ryder put it with studied politeness. 'Do you have a car, Mr Scott?'

'Yes, and I dare say you will know it's in the club car park.'

His panache was holding up.

'When we're finished here, I'd like to look it over, OK?'

Too, too polite. Peter remained flippant. The enormity of his carelessness flooded over him in nauseating waves. They knew the flat was clean and they fancied the car. Why?

The convoy of two cars drove to the club. Ryder, taking the keys, unlocked the BMW's boot, then the driver's door. He slipped into the driving seat.

'Give the boot a shufty,' he directed one of his fresh-faced minions, as he flipped open the glove compartment.

Fear in the pit of his stomach did not deter Peter from playing a minor trump. Beating the boy on the firm to the boot, he swiftly drew out the tennis bag from the plethora of tennis tonk that filled it. In one movement he turned it upside down and let the contents drop to the floor. They immediately attracted the prying sleuth's eye. Then, still holding the tennis bag, Peter invited the novice to run his hands over the innards of the upturned article. He did so.

Having satisfied the constable, Peter let the bag drop to the floor. Good fortune rewarded him; the bag fell face down, concealing the zippered side pocket that contained his liberty. An irritable Ryder emerged from the BMW having cannibalised the dashboard and its surround. Whoever had fired him at Peter knew of his penchant for concealment behind the dash. He hardly deserved it, but today the gods were smiling on him. As he glanced at the pile of tennis impedimenta, Ryder's politeness deserted him. He was disappointed and angry.

'Get that back in the car,' he growled.

Peter and the greenhorn flung the stuff back with alacrity, the tennis bag with its unopened pouch disappearing under the welter of tonk. Ryder locked the car boot and faced Peter.

'Mr Scott, you are under arrest. I propose to take you to a police station in Caterham.'

There it was in a nutshell. The search unrewarded, they were off to the tea-rooms for a couple of days to exchange bollocks.

'May I make a phone call?' Peter mock-naively jested.

'We'll see about that at Caterham.'

Silence reigned as they twisted their way across the South Circular, arriving not at Caterham but Bexley. Ryder went into the station, emerging only some two hours later. Still no one spoke as the ghost tour continued, until they arrived in Bognor Regis.

The shabby old town was to be home for the next two days. A smiling station sergeant patiently explained that he was to be kept there pending enquiries.

'May I make a phone call?' Peter reiterated. Judge's Rules made it his right, but professional policemen pay scant regard to Judge's Rules.

'When Mr Ryder okays it.'

It would be futile to ruck. Drifting with the ebb, he kept his mouth closed arsehole tight. That is easier said than done. Anyone who's been banged up will tell you. Silence under questioning in cell conditions can have a physiological effect, loosening most tongues and as many bowels. Grey cells are blocked as guilt and fear percolate.

Peter moved from silence to a tried and tested system. Answer the endless questions with as much bollocks as possible. Talk about the Arsenal, the ravage of AIDS, your dodgy ticker. I promise you, they'll get pissed off quicker than if confronted with a wall of silence, which (in spite of the so-called Right to Silence) can be commented on adversely by the prosecution in court.

A junior tec opened the batting in an interrogation room.

'There was a theft at Rogate recently. An Arab home was burgled and in excess of a million pounds' worth of gems was stolen. You answer the description of a man observed leaving the scene.'

'Really, I know nothing about it, but I don't suppose the Arab missed it much. They seem to have a surfeit of money.'

It was a walk along the beach with the Walrus and the Carpenter:

> 'The time has come,' the Walrus said,
> 'To talk of many things,
> Of shoes – and ships – and sealing wax –
> Of cabbages – and kings –
> Of why the sea is boiling hot –
> And whether pigs have wings.'

The Walrus had only one thing on his mind, the eating of the oysters, but he left this unmentioned. Peter did likewise, discussing anything other than what was on his mind.

It soon became clear that a number of people had been nicked in the swoop, including Taters. An attractive woman, whom he didn't know, was lodged in the cell beside Peter's. When they met at ablutions time, she confessed her fears of having said too much – but they'd threatened to place her children in care if she kept silent. There are no Queensberry Rules for the élite police squads.

She also told Peter she thought eleven people were arrested. Did he know anything about it?

'Nothing. Best we keep our heads down and let them sort it out. Don't fret over the children, it's a crude, cruel bluff.'

'Phone call, please. Phone call, please,' Peter harassed everyone he saw in parrot fashion. To no avail. It was day three now and he'd virtually disappeared off the street. No one but the arresting officers knew his whereabouts. He sat in his cell, brooding. He'd write to the *Daily Telegraph*. A touch right-wing it might be, but a fair-play rag. He did, too, on release, and they acknowledged but did not print. But some days later, they ran an editorial on the dangers of detention without access . . .

Ryder appeared.

'Mr Scott, we're going to release you. However, officers from another force are here to take you to Romsey, Hampshire.'

He was taken to Romsey. More bollocks. A bumptious tec related, 'A valuable diamond ring went missing at an auction preview. The auctioneer was suspicious of you and your companion and noted your car number.'

Arabs at Rogate, diamonds at Romsey. Would it never end?

'Yes, I was at the preview with a reputable dealer from Brighton. I can't speak for him, but I certainly know nothing about it.'

Benny had been his companion. Could *he* have flimped? Hardly.

'Who was this dealer?'

'I'm not prepared to say. What I will do is ask him to contact you as soon as I'm released.'

Not satisfactory. A fourth day's bang-up still elicited no phone call, even at rural Romsey. Then, on the Saturday morning, a compromise was reached. Peter would phone the dealer from the nick and ask him to make contact. Benny was not at home, but at least his wife was alerted.

It bucketed down as two young Romsey lads drove him back to London. It was done not so much out of courtesy as in the hope that he'd drop a clue. Some fucking chance.

Two thoughts polluted his mind. The first was to get the bloody parcel out of the car boot. He ought to be patient about it. They could be keeping an obs on him, though it was unlikely. The second preoccupation was, had Irene been looking for him? The depressing speculation was induced by the relentless rain.

Helen, the bar steward's wife, was waving a sheaf of messages as the drenched Peter paddled into the clubhouse.

'Where have you been? We thought you died. Here, these are for you. Dominic's written them all down in order of call. Where have you been, anyway?'

'In the slammer, Helen.'

'Get away with you. It's pulling a poor girl's leg, you are.'

She flashed him her lovely County Cork smile. Settling with a large Remy, he flipped through the messages. If he'd been running for President, he wouldn't be in much more demand.

Would you ring Irene at Pavilion Road? – Archie phoned twice, please phone him, it's urgent – Roger rang from Marbella. He'll phone again later – Your son Craig rang. He's bringing a friend for lunch, Sunday – Please ring Rousseau – Miss Bolton-Smythe would be obliged if you would ring her on extension 28 – Urgent, Diana wants you to ring her.

Better take Diana first. She was the nerve centre of Maida Vale and a loyal and affectionate pal.

'Diana? Peter. You called me.'

'Yes, you all right? Ginger heard from the law that you'd been spirited away last Wednesday. I phoned Raymond Davis and he made some enquiries, but nobody knew where you were.'

'I was at the seaside, paddling with the Regional CS for a day or three. Usual bollocks. I feel tired, dirty and shell-shocked. Don't let anyone tell you the air at Bognor's beneficial. Why did you ring?'

'Sheila and I are going to a funny do tonight in a church hall. Vicar's gay and the girls from Chesterton's are doing a review for him. It'll be booze, sarnies and a giggle. Relax you. Yes?'

'All right.'

'Meet you at Sheila's at nine. Take care, love.'

'Will do.'

'Oh, by the way, Carole got all busy when Sheila mentioned you might be nicked. Why was that?'

Diana was never far from the hub of scandal.

'Tell you when I see you,' he promised, and hung up. Carole concerned? That meant Irene would know too. He dialled Archie's Clerkenwell number.

'Hello, mate.'

'Peter, you ship-shape?'

'Archie, listen carefully. I'll see you tomorrow. Sunday, isn't it? God, I've lost track of time. Your mum's at three.'

The next call, the spieler.

'George about?'

'Who wants him?' a cultured voice enquired.

'Peter, from the tennis club.'

He made out voices and someone laughing. 'Bjorn Borg's on the trumpet for you, George.'

George came to the phone.

'Hello, mate, you sweet? Good, so can I see you Monday? Midday. I need a small favour.'

With Peter's OK and a quick ta-ta, Rousseau was gone. Peter was at a loss to imagine the favour needed. Something that money could not buy – for Rousseau had a surfeit of that.

He thought Bolton-Smythe could wait. Irene shouldn't have to, but he needed to construct what to say. More urgent, get rid of the pouch in the boot.

Ever since coming through the club door he had had an almost uncontrollable desire to make straight for the BMW in the car park. Control it he did. Despite the continuing downpour, he was terrified that the enemy might be in the vicinity. That is the type of paranoia imposed by guilt in the face of common sense. Common sense told him it was over, he'd had a miraculous escape. He merely had to wait until he'd access to the ladies' locker room for the parcel's reconcealment. He relaxed in a wash of cognac and waited.

The club emptied. At eight o'clock he commandeered the Major's brolly and slunk out to the car where, unlocking the boot, he refilled the gem-concealing tennis bag with its spillage. When he'd sauntered back to the clubhouse he slipped unobserved up to the ladies' locker room and housed the offending pouch. How very lucky he felt. A little sad, too. It was a distinct possibility that a pal had betrayed him to the unfortunate DCI Ryder.

Peter had been foolish all round. He deserved to fare much worse than he had.

10

These Foolish Things

THE Windsor Castle in Lanark Place was a better refuge. At 9.30, Diana, a very well-preserved fortyish ash-blonde, was holding court in the bar.

'Look who's here! Let Scotty in. All right, darling?'

A great hug completed his welcome and room was found for him in the midst of the assembled dragons.

Sheila Kelly, the landlady, was not down yet and – with the ring-mistress absent – the dragon ladies frolicked. Diana's strong arm was around his neck, an affectionate kiss firmly planted on his mouth. They were no longer a couple, but she was making it clear who was in charge. Peter nodded to the pack.

'Hello, Shirley, Val. Nice to see you, Mrs Chandler.'

Mickey, from the Walthamstow dog track, greeted him with a certain warmth. Both receiver and donor knew it was all on the surface, but it was part of the game.

'You going with the girls to the poof's do?'

Mickey, no respecter of persons, graded the vicar as if he were running at Walthamstow in the open race. Peter retaliated.

'The poof? Men of the cloth, gay they may be, but believe you me it's like that in eternity. Better you join the club now.'

Sheila made her entrance as he spoke, in her chic suede outfit. She knew more about public relations than the Saatchis. Peter was surplus to requirements for the moment. The ladies kissed and preened, not unlike prizefighters shaking hands before the bell. Duly fêted, Sheila pulled him aside.

'You OK? We were worried.'

'I went to Bognor for the week. The air does wonders for the libido.'

The entourage now donned mink to fend off the chill of the evening. The review was very camp indeed, amateur camp at that, and hilarious. The vicar had clearly missed his vocation. The evening had the precise effect Diana had predicted. Peter relaxed and got a little pissed. Afterwards, they were all going on to the West End, but Peter passed.

The tensions of the last four days had taken their toll and he drove back sedately to his gaff and slumbers.

The sun beat down on Sunday with such power it appeared to be trying to compensate for the deluge of the day before. But the clay courts were still flooded and the faithful were absent, as only the two hard courts played.

The bowlers, anathema to the tennis player, had a home match. Nevertheless, resplendent in their white flannels and blazers, they lifted the gloom around the clubhouse, where Peter was waiting fruitlessly for Craig. After two hours, he was tannoyed to the phone.

'Hello, Dad, I can't make it today. The band have a gig in Blackheath. I'm helping to hand out circulars. Do you mind?'

Disappointed, he did mind.

'That's fine, son. See you in the week for a steak, maybe the cinema.'

'Yeah, I'd like that. Ring you Wednesday. Got to go, Dad.'

The phone died. A gig at Blackheath? Hand out circulars? Rock 'n' roll was a fairly feckless trail, but better than the one he'd followed all his life. Yet Craig was perhaps the only catalyst for good in his life, and it was depressing that he treated his father so casually. God's ultimate punishment – no happy families.

'No fucking happy anything,' he muttered savagely to himself.

In his black mood, the next day he made the disappointment an excuse to exercise his degeneracy. He'd go and have a look at Zilli's in Bond Street. By tube and hoof he arrived.

Bloomfield Place is a cul-de-sac at the rear of Zilli's. There was a wrought-iron gate to the building's basement and it was unlocked. Conceal a ladder in the well, then come back later, raise it to the poorly barb-wired rail above, pull it up behind you, and so up to the next roof.

An initial bit of encouragement makes a target so much more attractive. Targets that present immediate problems are best left out, if choice exists. One of the cardinal principles of the journeyman thief is to have three, perhaps four, well-researched targets in view at all times. One of them will be ready when you are. Zilli's looked ready.

Archie's 'mother's place' was a coded location, referring to the Embankment tube. Peter walked down to Green Park. He'd be in good time for Archie.

He sat in Victoria Embankment Gardens nearby, ignoring but understanding the vagrants' umbrage. Archie's Roller purred up and he waved to locate himself. Archie joined him, making the hostiles even more resentful.

'Brought the parcel with you?' he gasped.

Shaking his head, Peter recounted the events of the four days' bang-up, missing out nothing, including his stupidity and possible betrayal. Archie listened impatiently.

'Can we pick the parcel up now?'

He didn't want post-mortems. He wanted to recover the gear, next case.

'Yes, listen carefully. I'm going to tube it back to the club. Let's think . . . I'll be at the back entrance in Delaware Road at nine-thirty on the dot. Drive by slowly, window my side down, and I'll throw the parcel in to you.'

Archie's little legs took off instantly. No recap necessary.

At the appointed time, Archie's Rolls puddled down Delaware. Peter slung the pouch through the open passenger window and the great phallic brute roared and accelerated away. A millstone was lifted from his shoulders.

At the club he rang Bolton-Smythe, but she wasn't in her office. Ring back.

The ageing tennis freak, musician, raconteur, journalist and some-times bore wanted a hit.

'Peter, give an old man a hit?'

Larry Adler's good-natured approach made it hard to refuse.

'Victor late again, Larry?'

Victor Lownes of *Playboy* infamy was Larry's usual mark. They played for money and Victor never won.

'Yes he is, but it's Victor I want the hit for. I arranged to play him, but I've got to review a restaurant for the press. I'm leaving now.'

Victor may have been the worst-mannered American ever to gradu-ate from Harvard. It was there he killed his best friend in a shooting accident. But he was also a heavy number, and righteous too. In short, he had little time for Peter, which Larry knew full well. It added additional spice to the shiddock.

'OK. I'll have a hit with Victor.'

His opponent arrived as Larry went away to shower. He showed little enthusiasm for the change of plan.

'Larry lunching again?' he mumbled. 'He can't pass on a freebie.'

On Court Six they knocked up for ten minutes. Victor, a leftie not without talent, stroked Peter's good-length ball about with confidence.

'Care to play a set?' he asked.

Victor won the first two games with a mixture of skill, luck and Peter's over-confidence. At this point Larry passed by on his way to the freebie meal.

'Larry,' Victor bellowed. 'Guess what? I'm two up.'

Larry gave him a 'you shouldn't have said that' smile as he continued on his way. Peter proved him right. They played two sets and, with Peter coming back decisively, Victor lost 6–2, 6–0. He left the court without a word.

Getting hold of Bolton-Smythe, he was told, 'George needs a radio. He'd like a Roberts Rambler. Can you help?'

Peter told her it would go off today. Eleven came and went and Rousseau didn't show. He thought again of ringing Irene. Any point now? Well, sleep on it . . .

Tuesday at the club, Roger was on the trumpet.

'Anyone looking for me?'

'Looking for you here? I shouldn't think anyone outside Benny would know we're acquainted.'

'Yes, but you never know. Old Bill get lucky sometimes.'

'You can say that again. I've just had four awaydays with the Regional Crime Squad.'

'What was all that about?' Roger's voice was not so flippant now, but anxious.

'An Arab lost a million pounds' worth of tom while I was staying at Forest Mere.'

'He lost it from the hydro?'

'No, Rogate, five miles up the road.'

'They have anything concrete?'

'Not really, a fishing expedition. What news of you?'

'Very little. Burnt a little. I was only checking you were OK. I'll phone next week.'

Bye-bye, Roger. Could he have second sight? Why ring now? He was a weirdo, all right . . . Charades within charades.

Leaving the booth, he was stopped by Dominic, the steward.

'Peter, there's a gentleman at the bar to see you.'

'What's he like?'

'Like? How would I know? Big, burly chap, looks like an undertaker maybe.'

Rousseau.

'Peter . . . Brandy? Large? Sorry, couldn't get here yesterday. When I phoned you were on court. Can we find a quiet table?'

They found one.

'You know Arlene, the bird I'm with? She's having a chavvy. I want to keep her sweet. Anyway, she's got this brother who plays a little tennis. A little retarded but not so's you'd notice. Arlene would like him to be a member here. You could keep an eye on him.'

In his tight-fitting black cashmere overcoat, Rousseau did look like an undertaker. There was a vague air of menace about him compared to the pallid sanatorium chic, and it amused Peter. Rousseau was a good head, he never talked bollocks, and his word was his bond.

'You say the boy plays tennis?'

'Yeah, every day.'

'Well, there should be no problem. If he can sustain a rally, the playing test will present no problem. I'll get a proposal form. Take it with you, give it to the boy to fill in, and when he comes round tell him to ask for me.'

George looked as grateful as if Peter had settled his tab in the spieler. He pulled out a wad of fifties.

'How much is it?'

'A hundred and twenty.'

Peter took the cash to the office, equipping himself on the way with a large Bell's for the Major. He tapped lightly on the door.

'Come in!' came the authoritative bark from one who'd soldiered in India for years. The Major was a very decent fellow.

'Keith, can I have a membership form, and perhaps you'd give me a receipt for this cash.'

Peter proffered the Bell's. 'You're spoiling me again,' the Major protested. 'I was adamant I'd not have a drink before lunch.'

At his interview, he'd told the committee he was teetotal, a claim they recalled when the time came to dispense with him. Things were like that at Paddington Lawn Tennis and Bowls Club.

'Hope it's one of your attractive fillies,' he continued. The Major had an eye for horseflesh, fillies in particular, but he was a gentleman, a real sport who never saw harm in anyone. A bloody good Englishman. Too good for this rabble.

Peter explained who the aspirant was.

'You'll have to play him in. Can you handle that?'

Strictly speaking, a committee member should give a playing-in test, but few were about and fresh members were always needed. The Major turned his Nelson's eye.

'The boy can play. Plays regularly.'

'Well, then, I'll propose him and you can second.'

The Bell's had done its work. Receipted and proposed, Peter returned to Rousseau.

'No problem, George. I may see you this afternoon. If I can escape I may play a few quid up.'

'Good, I like to see a strong player at the table.'

Rousseau might have been honest, but not *that* honest.

Hugging, they parted on the clubhouse steps, and Peter felt pleased. Rousseau owed him one, which was a useful situation to be in.

The phone at Pavilion Road bleated in vain. The bitch in the bath again? Or out after the Holy Grail in the shape of a luxury flat? Did it matter?

He got to Rousseau's at five and a seat was found for him at once. Never keep a mug waiting. At twenty-forty-eighty-pound Kaluki you could lose a grand very sharpish, and Peter probably would. The first game was a quickie and Peter fluked it. Moans and glares, blame apportioned, the wide-boys stunned.

The second game developed into a technical battle. Peter was still there with the other three when a call-up would win the game. The thirteen cards were dealt and Peter fanned his hand. He had three sets, a friendly joker, the king of hearts, a ten of hearts, and a rag two of clubs. A jack or the queen of hearts would give him Kaluki, the call-up and game, not to mention the thousand pounds in the pot. Peter concealed his elation poorly. The table knew he was buzzing. The player on the right – Rousseau – had to throw a card. He discarded the jack of hearts. Slowly, pedantically, Peter reached for the card.

'Kaluki,' he whispered, carefully laying his cards down in the sequence required by the rules.

Pandemonium broke out. The worst of Greek expletives rent the air and Peter knew Rousseau was suffering, just as if he'd double-faulted on match-point. He hadn't dispatched the jack to repay the thief for the favour over Arlene's brother: it was a fatal error. The invective went on unabated.

'How can a cunt like that win? He can't hold a card. He wouldn't know if it was up unless someone told him.'

A mug winning two in a row was a cardinal sin there was no forgiving. Euphoria tempted Peter to the phone, for Irene was on his mind in his moment of glory. The phone barely had time to ring.

'Hello?' the breathless voice said.

'Hello, Irene. Peter here.'

Silence was followed by an audible intake of breath, almost a gasp.

'Hi . . . I thought I might not see you again.'

Was she tearful? He couldn't be sure.

'I thought we might go to Mr Chow's tonight, have a drink in Jules's Bar before we eat. Could you cab there to meet at nine, say? I'm in town now. I want to go home and freshen up.'

'Yes, I'd love to. I'll get there at nine. I thought it was all over.'

'Nothing's ever over. I've learned that. Will you book a table for ten?'

'I'll do that. Where are you, darling? I can hear a race commentary.'

Emotional or not, Irene missed little.

'I've been playing cards at the club. See you at nine.'

He cradled the phone.

'You playing on, Peter?' The anxiety in Tony Q.'s voice betrayed him. Never let a mug out winning.

'Tomorrow, Tony. I'm in love. Apart from that, I'm punch-drunk after winning two on the trot.'

Was he in love? He'd like to be. It would have to go to a stewards' enquiry.

Someone was tugging at his sleeve and he turned. Two highly competent hoisters had something to sell the big winner. Have a look?

'What've you got?'

A handkerchief was produced and opened like a flower in the conjuror's hand. A superb black jet snake bracelet, its gold head set with emerald-chipped eyes and a ruby mouth.

'We just got it at Van Cleef and Arples. The ticket's still on it.'

Peter had been around too long to give credence to tickets. They manufacture easily. But the ticket marked the jet up at eighteen hundred, about right for Bond Street. It was what they said, a lovely piece.

'How much?'

'We'll take a monkey for it. It's for nothing.'

'I'll give you four hundred quid, take it or leave it.'

He moved briskly towards the door.

'Hold up, hold up!' The two hoisters conferred. 'You're a fucking hard man, Peter. When you go thieving you want to earn. You're stronging it. Four and a half.'

'Four hundred.'

Peter decided he *would* pay four and a half, if he had to, for suddenly he wanted the bracelet. But not yet. He pressed eight fifty-pound notes into the hand of the conjuror. The hoister demurred, then suddenly snatched the scratch and parted with the bracelet.

'Got a box for it?'

'Bollocks. The next thing you'll want is a receipt.'

The piano was tinkling *These Foolish Things* as he got to Jules's Bar. The place was busy but he got a stool at the bar. The keys flirted with the melody. *The airline ticket to romantic places . . .* Catching sight of himself in the mirror's octagonal glass, he was reassured. He looked well.

Suddenly Irene stood between himself and his image. They kissed lightly but affectionately. There were tears in her eyes. Conscience-stricken, he had a moment of panic. What the fuck am I doing to this nice lady?

Stool to stool, holding hands, indifferent to onlookers, they sat. The piano insisted . . . *remind me of you* . . . Peter was ill at ease, unable to rid himself of the suspicion that it was all just another charade.

'Did you get a table at Chow's?'

Nodding, Irene gripped his hand even more intensely. They were like two sophomores on their first date. The piano, hell-bent on romancing, had switched to 'A Nightingale Sang in Berkeley Square'. The piano was a conspirator.

Irene had gone to the powder room to repair the damage done by the lyric to her make-up and emotions. Peter was back among screeching alarm bells. They were his nightingales. Did the angels dining at the Ritz hear them? Never.

'Hey, you're a million miles away.' Irene was back.

'No, only a few hundred yards. It was the song, brings back memories.'

She mocked him. 'Probably of some dame.'

'No, my private passion. Roofs and ledges and an old hussar.'

'What the hell are you talking about?'

As he weaved the BMW down Piccadilly to Knightsbridge, she put an arm over his shoulder and he began to feel euphoric. The night promised well. But at dinner the euphoria proved short-lived. He was ordering the second bottle of *sake* when the grenade exploded.

'I can't have any more to drink, I've got to drive back to the Cots-wolds tonight.'

Peter was stunned. Irene saw she'd hurt him.

'I'm sorry. My young landlord carps about the time I spend in London, and we're riding out at seven in the morning.' Her mouth dipped. 'I'm in trouble being here already.'

Inwardly Peter winced. He'd planned to fuck her that night, for he'd not forgotten her 'impotent' jibe. The best-laid plans of mice and men . . .

'That pisses me off. Tonight was cuddles night. I need notice of action these days. Well, another time, Irene . . .'

Standing beside her Range Rover, he was still trying to make light of the disenchantment. Then he felt in his pocket.

'I nearly forgot. I've got a cadeau for you.'

He drew out the snake bracelet, which he'd wrapped in tissue, and peeled the paper back as the vendor had done to such good effect with his handkerchief.

'My God, it's *lovely* . . . But I can't accept an expensive gift from you.' It was Irene's turn to panic.

'Try,' he said, closing her hand gently over the snake. He wished it were its pulsating brother-in-flesh. A peck on the cheek merely intensified the gloom, as Irene and the Range Rover disappeared into Pont Street. It was a charade for her too. Now that he'd isolated the reality, it made him sad. Why? He knew only too well that he'd disqualified himself a long time ago.

Two weeks elapsed before she made contact. He could hardly ring her, he could only roast, get the Roberts Rambler off to Chatham, hit endless tennis balls. The only respite was the arrival of John, to claim the membership that his Uncle George had arranged.

Peter recognised John from playing in Regent's Park. It wasn't his skill which made him memorable, but a rather odd habit of gripping the racquet near the throat like a table-tennis bat. A quiet, introverted boy he seemed, as he passed the playing test well. But . . .

'Are there any girls I can hit with?' the innocent asked.

'Yes, there are a few around during the day.'

No red lights had been alerted by the enquiry, so John became a member. But the membership was short-lived.

Peter first got wind of the trouble when the Major called him in, all businesslike.

'The new member. You know him well?'

'Not really. I do know his sister.'

'He's been playing with a lady member. He passed some remark about her breasts on court.'

The Major was visibly ruffled. Peter wished he'd brought a large, ameliorating Bell's.

'Who was he hitting with?'

'Nickie.'

'Nickie's a prude at the best of times. Wrong lady to compliment.'

'Well, she's been to the office to complain.'

'What did he actually say?'

The Major allowed himself a shy grin. 'I think he said, "You have a nice pair of tits."'

'Oh, bollocks, I'll have a word with him.'

'Yes, will you do that? I'll overlook it this time.'

The Major was a man of his word and Peter was grateful for it, even if no one else at the club was. He went and found the sheepish John in the changing room. John avoided his glare.

'This is a tennis club, John, not Raymond's Revue Bar. Ladies don't like remarks about their tits.'

'I was only joking,' the boy muttered. 'Anyway, she kept sticking them out.'

'No more fucking jokes, OK? I'm responsible for you, so just play tennis. Come on, let's have a hit.'

Honour seemed appeased all round, but not for long. A day or two later angry voices from the Major's office alerted Peter, who was watering the show court. Through the window he caught a glimpse of John and, dropping the hose, he trotted into the clubhouse. He met John as he was leaving.

'I'll cut her hair off if she says things like that.'

'Whose hair are you going to cut off?' Peter asked.

'That bitch out there.'

Peter propelled John into the changing room.

'Calm down. Don't move from here. I'll sort it out.'

Back in the secretary's office, the Major was blood-red.

'He's just indicated to another lady member on court that he'd like to screw her. I'm returning his membership fee. Please get him off the premises. Bloody good job only you and I know. If Amal got wind of it, heads would roll.'

Amal Basu was club president. Poor John. Retreating down the path and into the unforgiving world, he bleated, 'I don't want to come back to this club anyway. All the bitches tell lies.'

John was sad, no different in his urges to others, but he didn't have the ability to keep them to himself.

'The bitches are all liars when it suits,' said Peter. 'No fucking magnanimity in them. Watch out, lad.'

Coming from a more sophisticated member, better couched, the words might have passed as complimentary. John, alas, didn't know the songlines. Life herself's a fickle bitch.

He had a fitting in Clifford Street at his tailor's. His miracle at Rousseau's allowed him the extravagance of a charcoal-grey, double-breasted hopsack. With Mr Hanna resting peacefully, his nephew Peter, the best trouser-maker in Savile Row, had assumed command after much family in-fighting. He would be supervising the fitting.

Walking down Bond Street, the thief stopped at Zilli's. Viewing their elegant window display, he was pleasantly startled at the mark-up on the fine garments. Jackets for four thousand; full-length coats as high as ten. A couple of snotty-nosed staff gazed aimlessly but superciliously out at the ageing, tracksuited duffer. Not a chance he'd stray in to buy one of their mink- or lynx-lined leathers.

They were right, but to compensate for any disappointment on their part, Peter proposed to himself the removal of the lot. The contempt in their eyes accelerated the desire for larceny.

'*Bonjour, messieurs!*' Peter bellowed at them as he moved off. '*A tout à l'heure.*'

They looked suitably startled.

The suit jacket hung perfectly.

'Perfection!' Peter the tailor eulogised, elated.

'Peter,' the thief asked him, 'do you remember the suit Mr Hanna made for my trial at Windsor in fifty-seven?'

The tailor had only heard of it.

'That was when he was in D'Arblay Street. I didn't join him until the early sixties.'

'Well, he made me a very similar charcoal. My first Waterloo.'

11
___

Go to Jail

Patsy murphy had been a harbinger of doom. His comment 'you're
too warm for me, kid' represented a warning Peter would have done
well to heed.

In the early spring of 1957 he was introduced to a man about town
called Roddy. He was a gentleman playboy and scallywag to boot,
who was tempted wrongly to see himself as something of a thinking
Raffles. However, his sophisticated, posh patter impressed the still-raw
youth from Belfast. Roddy's fashionable apartment in Belgravia, his
debby girl chums, bridged Peter into a new world – and it was in
some ways a bridge too far . . .

It certainly proved heady wine for the young thief. One glamorous
brunette, then reading history at Cambridge and later to become a
top model, was a particularly intoxicating draught.

His first meeting with Roddy seemed even then a shade theatrical,
and time hadn't shaken the opinion. There had been an interminable
drive at speed, following Chummy through squares and mews,
making certain they were not followed. However, the man about
town spoke with a certain seductive authority. A recent brush with
the law gave him a certain *locus standi* and, more to the point, he
knew the whereabouts of a visiting socialite's jewels.

'Peter, this is how it goes,' Chummy explained in clipped tones.
'Horace Dodge – you know, the Dodge motor car – and his lovely
wife Gregg follow the tennis circuit. They'll be in England for Wimbledon, at a house in Windsor called St Leonard's Castle. I have someone
in the house who is helpful. Naturally, I shall need you to meet him
– Jeffrey is absolutely pukka.'

Raffles he might not be, but this was surely a Raffles plot. Peter
was mesmerised.

'There's a safe in the house, a wall-safe. Pay no heed to it. Gregg
and Horace have a fragile relationship and both have access to the
safe. She conceals her jewellery elsewhere.'

'Where?' Peter queried.

'All in good time. Gregg has gems worth more than one hundred thousand. Horace keeps her on a tight rein financially, which is why she's so protective of them. But our sleeper, Jeffrey, is privy to their whereabouts.'

Looking back thirty odd years, Peter could smile. How artfully the buck had led him into enthusiasm. He still felt awkward in the Belgravia ambience, yet this was the status he wanted and was determined to achieve.

When he did, of course, he found it small beer. That is the folly of snob-bound youth.

The Dodge plot took flesh.

'Can we meet at Sloane Square tube tomorrow, on the dot of midday?'

The Land Rover swept into Sloane Square, Peter was beckoned in, and they were off, down the old London Airport road.

'We're off to Windsor. I'd like you to meet Jeffrey.'

Arriving below Ma'am's Norman keep, they skirted the town and ended up at the foot of the great lawn escarpment that sweeps so imperiously down from the castle walls. A solitary figure, perched on a public bench, gave them a wave.

'Good. Jeffrey's arrived. We'll park here. Must try not to draw attention to ourselves.'

That was baffling. With the exception of the traitor, there wasn't a soul in sight. The conspirators sat down together, and it occurred to Peter that nothing short of a zoom-lensed camera would be needed to detect them in secret. Jeffrey, an effete Anglo of a certain age, was nervous.

'Jeffrey, you know who this is?' Roddy barked.

'No, Roddy.'

'He's the finest burglar in the country. He's agreed to join us in our venture.'

If looks were a criterion, Peter still didn't pass muster. Jeffrey obliquely cast a jaundiced eye over his seen-better-days sports coat and shoddy brothel-creepers. He was not impressed.

'Jeffrey,' said Roddy, 'I'll leave you two to have a natter. Back in half an hour.'

Roddy strode briskly up the escarpment. Jeffrey's opening gambit was to the point.

'Where were you educated?'

Peter was taken aback.

'Royal Academy, Belfast,' he mumbled.

Could it be an essential ingredient of the venture that the players were all public school? A League of Gentlemen? If so, Peter's reply satisfied Jeffrey. Or he might simply have wanted to assure himself he wasn't dealing with a cretin. Anyway, he went on to spill the beans in true, pukka, clipped tones.

'Horace Dodge is dominated by his octogenarian mother, Anna May Dodge. She controls the purse-strings, regarding Horace as careless with the pennies. Significantly, she dislikes the current Mrs Dodge. There have been several predecessors. Gregg is a former showgirl.'

His mouth pursed. 'Gregg Sherwood, Miss Minnesota 1941. Horace, in his turn, keeps Gregg on a modest stipend, fearful that, in funds, she might leave him. Her jewellery's her independence. If Horace impounded them, he'd reduce her options. For that reason Madam's gems are not kept in the wall-safe, which he can access. Do you follow?'

Peter followed. A world of matriarchal power. Jeffrey went on with the tale.

'Gregg's friendly with a tennis player, Gardner Molloy, and so they do the circuit – Rome, Paris, and then Wimbledon in June. They're at the castle for two weeks. I hold a responsible position in the household . . .'

As traitors do. Recall the Corsican's advice? 'God protect me from my friends, my enemies I shall look after myself.' The diminutive Bonaparte knew a thing or two about traitors.

'And in this capacity I am aware of the location of the gems during their stay.'

Pausing, he studied Peter with a gimlet glare.

'Do you understand, burglar?'

Peter nodded, though irritated by the emphasis on the word *burglar*. He was coasting into strange waters. If Jeffrey betrays his employers, then why not me?

Almost as if reading his thoughts, the Judas put on a Uriah Heep voice to enquire, 'Are you interested, *sir*?'

'Naturally, otherwise I wouldn't be here. How do you value the baubles?'

'Insured for one hundred and fifty thousand pounds.'

Jeffrey preened while Peter, startled at the magnitude of the figure, thought he'd better get things ship-shape.

'And what do you expect for your corner if I'm successful?'

Jeffrey gave a genteel cough and lowered his eyes. Money matters were clearly an embarrassment to a scion of his ilk. He found a slip road.

'I'll leave that to Roddy.'

The weakness fired Peter up, and he decided to go on the offensive. The time for pussyfooting was over.

'Well, then, where *are* the gems kept?'

Jeffrey did not answer at once. He had his nut down, pondering. At last he sighed, 'I suppose you'll have to know sooner or later. They're in a hat-box beneath one of her Royal Ascot numbers. You may have to rummage two or three.'

'What about access to the castle?'

'Again, I'll leave that to Roddy nearer the time. Can I take it the matter is settled?'

Peter nodded. Jeffrey rose and extended a limp paw. It would be a gentlemen's agreement. The old school tie, even in larceny. Peter grasped and wrung the hand firmly. He had joined the League.

Speeding back with Roddy, Peter ventured, 'Sure we can trust Jeffrey?'

Roddy gave a scowl of disapproval.

'Jeffrey may be an odd cove, but he's a gentleman. He went to school with my brother. We can stake our lives on him.'

The plural 'we' set Peter thinking. There was only one party at risk in this plunder, and it was Peter. The gentleman duo made him feel ill at ease. Now Roddy introduced his trump card.

'Why don't you take Sascha out to dinner this evening? She's in London, just sitting around the flat.'

Peter was amused at this transparent ploy, but he was learning quick.

'Yes, that seems a good idea. Splendid. I'd love to.'

Later, at a fashionable watering-hole, the gauche thief struggled to make conversation with the glamorous Sascha, who was thoroughly bored with Roddy's protégé. Nietzsche of all people saved the evening, when Sascha discovered the yokel from Ulster was well read. Nevertheless, Peter's libido never got out of the starting gate.

Wimbledon was a month hence. He decided on a recce of St Leonard's Castle. At the time it was a necessary move, though in retrospect foolishly carried out.

Parking in St Leonard's Vale, he tramped up the pit-ridden shale road that led to a farm and then to the house. The house-castle was deserted as, in the dusk, he took stock of the target. He found the slipway that led into the garage and boiler house where, Roddy had revealed, there was a door and a staircase that would take him directly into the hall of the castle. He found everything as Roddy had told it. Peter was pleased.

Returning to the car, he thought he saw a face in a window watching him in the gloom. He hoped at least it was Jeffrey. But before regaining the car, his pleasure was rudely broken. A police car had drawn up beside him and from it a uniform enquired, 'Good evening, sir. Do you live locally?'

'No, London. I'm house-hunting – or rather looking for a plot to build on.'

He worked hard to fanny, exercising charm and panache to the maximum.

'You haven't been up to the big house, sir?' the uniform persisted.

'I think I got as far as the farm. Was I trespassing?'

'No, sir, but we've had a call. I wonder if you'd mind driving your vehicle down to the station. You can follow us.'

Alarm bells shrilled, then dimmed. They wouldn't let him drive his own car if they were anxious.

'Certainly,' he said.

Peter's elegant drophead Daimler was not the usual tool of the criminal classes, he had nothing on board and, he reckoned, nothing to fear. He was wrong. At the station, an astute DI, Gordon Speller, was eventually to best him, even though he was only there long enough to produce documents . . .

Not to call off the caper was madness even at the time, and harder still to explain thirty-five years later. Perhaps his three-year-long rampage, and the wealth accumulated, had brought Peter to see himself as a child of the gods. Untouchable. Or maybe it was his commitment to Roddy and his alluring world, the desire to prove himself in this new arena. Whatever the answer he was – not for the first time – a prize prat.

Royal Ascot was the week before the start of Wimbledon. He went racing every day of the meeting, having decided to attack on the Saturday night. Fate's an ironical bastard. In the Ring, he hit a golden patch, and with the inspired ticking-up of Jimmy the Spiv he slaughtered Victor Chandler daily for sums in excess of a thousand pounds. Untouchable, wasn't he? Prat.

By the start of Heath Day, the Saturday, he was six thousand in front, and he left with another two in his bin. In addition, Victor had left him over for twenty-one hundred, thanks to his bet in the last – four hundred pounds on Clouds at 7–2. R. J. Collings's horse hit Swinley Bottom in touch with the front pack. Coming into the straight, he went four lengths ahead and never stopped, making it another bloody day for Victor. Ever the gentleman, the bookie took it in his stride.

'All right if I leave the twenty-one hundred over till Monday?'

In five days Peter had won more than eight thousand pounds – worth a hundred grand or more today. And still he sought Gregg's gems later that night. Greedy prat.

Deserved to be caught, did I hear you say?

As dusk approached that evening he drove to Bracknell – then a village – and parked up the bottle-green 1.5-litre Riley he used for work. He took his cycle off the roof-rack and pedalled back to St Leonard's, impelled by God knows what, beginning to feel bloody. He would have given the thousand pounds in his pocket to have gone straight home. The vibes were lousy, and he'd never felt less like working. But hadn't he shaken on it? With others depending on him, he pressed on.

But how right his instincts had been. From the moment Ascot week started and the Dodges arrived, the ambush was laid. Two officers nightly drank endless cups of tea in Gregg's boudoir and there were others less fortunately posted around the grounds, with a dog. The snare baited, they bided their time.

But what of Jeffrey? Impossible that he was not aware of the police presence. He had a clear six days to alert Roddy. He didn't. The man had clearly attended a minor public school.

What quirk of misfortune allowed Peter to get into the castle undetected remains a mystery to this day. Perhaps it's a tribute to his stealth. Negotiating the stairs, he ever so softly eased the door of the master bedroom open and the first thing he saw in his torchbeam was the dresser, glittering with gems carelessly arrayed. Too late the alarm bells in his mind rang. This was not the scenario. A further flash from the torch revealed two startled faces peering out from behind the dresser.

Blood-red ruin. With instant presence of mind, he called out, 'It's all right. It's only me.'

He knew they'd pause for thought at that, giving him a valuable couple of seconds. He withdrew and closed the door, after slipping the key from the inside of the keyhole.

He locked the door, rendering the sleuths captive. He went pell-mell down the stairs and headed for the front door. A siren started up. People were appearing, startled, interested. Out the front door, more shadows. In the mêlée and confusion he made off across the estate, abandoning the bicycle. His luck, for the moment, held. The ageing police dog, normally reliable, sank his teeth into a pursuing constable's ankle.

He headed for Bracknell through copse and tangled undergrowth. Finally crossing a stream, he convinced himself he had, for the time being, lost the posse. But now he heard a bell ringing eerily in the night. Taking advantage of ancient rights, a copper was ringing the Tolst, warning the burghers of Windsor of a hostile presence.

At Winkfield he borrowed another cycle, pedalling steadily, conserving energy, to the Royal Foresters' Inn on the Ascot–Bracknell Road. Then Bracknell itself loomed and he dumped the cycle and approached the car on foot, having tidied himself up as best he could. A middle-aged, obese uniform stepped out of the shadows.

'This your car, sir?'

'Yes it is. Why?'

'Would you care to say where you've been, sir?'

'Yes, I've been to the races, ended up in the Royal Foresters'. As you can see by the state of me, I've been sleeping it off in a ditch.'

But yokel or not, Chummy was not having it, at once assuming a less polite tone.

'You *are* in a bit of a state, sir. I shall have to ask you to come to the station with me.'

It was the moment of truth. To chin or not to chin. Ponderous and nervous the copper might have been, but he had his truncheon drawn. And that wasn't the only reason Peter desisted. He'd gambled and lost. There was no mileage in bashing Berkshire coppers. He was also shattered from his flight. No, he'd try to bluff it out.

'If you insist.'

'I do, sir.'

At the unmanned police station, the custodian required Peter to empty his pockets. Fifteen hundred pounds' cash was disgorged, which of course convinced the copper that he had his man. He made them both tea and they waited, sipping, for the posse to get there from Windsor.

'There's been a break-in over at Windsor. We think you're involved.'

He was arrested, cautioned. He opted for silence. A smiling copper met him on arrival at the Windsor nick.

'Nice to see you again, Peter,' he said.

*   *   *

Banged up, he tormented himself with his stupidity. Sleep was distant.

Next day he agreed to an ID parade. Eight or nine immaculate guardsmen from the castle barracks made a line with the dishevelled Peter. The witness – it was a policeman – requested a side viewing.

'Right face!' barked the copper, and the guardsmen whipped round as one man, leaving Peter stranded. He knew the game was up then, and sure enough his shoulder was tapped.

Clothing to forensic and a remand in custody to Oxford Prison began the week. A phone call to a pal alerted London to his circumstances.

Odd science, forensic. An overcoat found in the grounds had a knuckleduster in the pocket. He was asked to try the garment on for size – yes, *that* coat, which he'd never set eyes on. The laboratory concluded that the overcoat had been consistently worn with the impounded suit . . . A dangerous old speciality, even then – never mind what it did to the Maguire family fifteen years later.

A friend obtained the services of a capable London solicitor, William Foux, of 6A Maddox Street, Mayfair. A competent, pragmatic man, he heard Peter's protest of innocence with professional blandness.

'Indeed, Mr Gulston, I take your point. But first things first. Can you obtain substantial securities – probably two in the sum of five hundred pounds?'

Peter said he could, so, in pursuit of the bail application, Foux recommended they enlist the help of one of the more colourful figures at the criminal bar, Mr James Burge.

'It will add weight to our application here, in the rural court,' Foux purred.

On his second appearance, two weeks later, bail was granted in two securities of five hundred pounds. Burge had bullied and charmed the bench by turns and Peter was free. The copper was sure he'd never see him again – probably the only thing he was ever wrong about.

Released, he travelled straight to Newmarket where, rather than collecting the two thousand from Victor, he ended the meeting five thousand down and owing the bookie a thousand. In the ensuing three months he dissipated the nest-egg he'd kept at the Pall Mall depository, gambling massive sums in his apprehension at the outcome of his trial in late September. Retrospect dictates that Peter would have been better languishing in Oxford.

He had a plethora of help preparing his case. Hanna made him the magnificent charcoal-grey worsted for the trial. Jocelyn Jasper Addis, who had recently been struck off, was kind, as were Addis's sidekick

'Sir' Sydney Patrick Rawlinson Cane, Bart, and the tough Irish nut Michael Neary. Long, gin-sodden sessions at his flat in Wymering Mansions, which he had from another fifties figure, Peter Rachman, would be entertained by Jasper's hilarious reconstructions of the ID parade.

The aforementioned had all been London players in the postwar period. Peter Rachman has been a grossly maligned player. In the thief's experience he was a kind and considerate man whose greatest crime was to exploit the useless housing regulations then prevailing. He never passed the needy but he put his hand in his pocket. A damned sight more charitable than the righteous of post-austerity Britain.

Foux prepared a splendid brief. Peter had found several witnesses who remembered him in the Royal Foresters', so Burge was not without ammunition. The trial began.

Most readers who have done jury service, and even more who have done bird, will know that trials are pure theatre. Limited degrees of guilt intrude, but on the thespian scale it depends on presentation. The bottom line is, who can abuse the truth most effectively? Same as life:

> To tell the truth with bad intent
> Beats all the lies you can invent.

Peter was resplendent in Hanna's charcoal worsted. Kenneth Jones, the prosecutor, was visibly dismayed at the handsome young man's appearance.

'He just doesn't look like a burglar,' he whispered to his junior.

Although it was Jones who had the surfeit of ammo, Burge was superb, reducing the ID evidence to farce, and berating the jury with, 'Can you believe a man who has won ten thousand pounds at Ascot is likely to be out burglarising the same night?'

It seemed a good argument until the learned judge – who didn't go on to become a Lord of Appeal by accident – summed up on the matter. He reminded the jury to bear in mind the magnitude of the prize the thief sought. Pausing significantly, he went on, 'One hundred and fifty thousand pounds of gems . . .'

The point found its mark. Horace Dodge appeared in court in a wheelchair, retainer Jeffrey steering him.

'I'm Horace Dodge, President of the Dodge Motor Company of

Canada. I did not give this man permission to enter my home. To my best knowledge, he does not know my wife.'

The latter piece of evidence was given to rebut a possible defence that Peter might have been in the castle on a tryst.

Peter was on bail during the trial, which returned for the final thrust. Courts then sat on Saturday mornings, and on this Saturday the judge delivered his summing-up, which forcefully diluted Burge's majestic thespian final address to the jury. He then sent them out at eleven o'clock.

The jury managed to deprive the bars that Saturday. They were expected back quickly, and social activities were being canvassed around court. By three o'clock in the afternoon, with Saturday spoiling, the Prosecution grew restless, then bottled out.

Peter was pacing the cell, awaiting his fate, when Burge appeared at the door.

'Ah, Mr Gulston. The jury are clearly having difficulties. I have spoken with my learned friend. I think, should you be mindful to plead to the lesser charge, His Lordship will not impose a sentence in excess of two years. It's a matter for you, Mr Gulston.'

Decision time . . . all duck and no dinner? It was too good an offer to miss and Peter agreed.

Here is the irony: no sooner had he agreed to plead than the jury returned to find him guilty on both counts. But the judge was a well-bred man and a deal was a deal. Peter got two years.

Travelling back to the gaslit Oxford Prison, his escort rasped, 'You're a lucky bugger. We expected you to get seven years.'

How did it all go wrong? A copper's hunch? Hardly. Jeffrey's duplicity? Probably. It didn't really matter now. His social aspirations would have to wait. Oxford, Leicester and Stafford in the next sixteen months did little to advance them. The truth was his time had been up. His judgement was flawed by the run of successes. Go to jail.

He was not to see Roddy for another fifteen years. Sascha? Only in the glossies. One lesson he did learn. 'Gentlemen' are as dangerous as lesser mortals, and a damned sight more cunning. Duplicity when it suits is Everyman's weapon.

And it was a lovely worsted suit.

12

A Large Diamond, a Horny Lady, and Some Visiting Cops

RELEASED in January 1959, barely grazed by the sentence from Windsor, Peter's passion for larceny trundled along in its feckless, predestined way. He was housed in Frank Clarence's 'judas hole' in Gloucester Walk, Kensington. The occasional chauffeur was portering at a block nearby.

His sixty-five-thousand-pound stash in the depository had been dissipated on bail but luckily, on the night before the jury retired, he'd gone to Wembley dogs for a last throw, and won three thousand. With no time to spend or gamble it, the money was still waiting for him. Meanwhile one of the few possessions that had survived the sixteen-month sabbatical in Oxford (still with its gaslit cells), Leicester (with the massive bell on its centre), and Stafford (a sallow, grey, crescent block of coops) was his Barker Special Sports drophead Daimler. The car had been garaged in the empty basement of a mews garage off Spring Street, Paddington, and a mere hundred pounds was required to release it.

There was another modest passion stirring, a slim redhead who hostessed at Churchill's Club – Jackie Whitehead. She warbled with the band at times and, being older and a thousand times more worldly than the thief, treated him as casually as befitted her calling.

Dorothy's Club in Knightsbridge was his refuge, where Dorothy Foxon, a vivacious South African, was in charge. Peter had a pal behind the bar, Molly Brennan, who'd loyally stood bail for him at Windsor. A long-time employee of Morrie Connolly, the club owner, and from (where else?) the west of Ireland, Molly was probably his only true friend, had he but known it. Like certain kings and boxing champs, the successful thief is first surrounded by sycophants and then sent to the dungeons to be forgotten. On his return, he stupidly forgives every arm that is draped across his shoulder in false bonhomie. He is like a stray dog wagging its tail to any friendly hand.

'Oh, you're out, darling!' Dorothy waffled, kissing him lightly before passing on to another to confide knowingly, 'He won't be out long.'

Dorothy's – an in place on Knightsbridge Green – was another east-meets-west venue, and a place of pilgrimage for successful herberts from the suburbs. It was also one watering-hole that no sensible thief should show his face in, full as it was of coppers' narks. No one with an ounce of true nous will consciously risk Golgotha, but 'sensible' and 'thief' are contradictory terms.

In time, Peter was to punish Dorothy appropriately, hoisting a ladder from the rear flat roof of the club to her apartment to nick her bit of tom and a magnificent mink which he himself had sold her.

'I know you stole my things the other night,' she told him, her eyes probing and glinting with venom. Peter laughed.

'I'd hate to disappoint you.'

The candour disarmed the harpy, or seemed to. She whispered, 'If you hear anything, let me know. I'd love my mink coat back.'

And so, with the Flying Squad waiting patiently in the wings, Peter, passion-bound, pillaged. The activity ranged from the Windsors at Great Westwood, through Aspinall and Lauren Bacall, to half a dozen furriers, half a dozen roofs, in Wilton Crescent and Chelsea. It was carnage such that it could only be him or Taters, and George was still two years away from freedom. The detective Jack Brodie put it in perspective, discussing the campaign with Bill Baldock.

'I feel sad for the boy. He's got bundles of arsehole but all those ponces put an arm around his shoulder one minute and get on the trumpet to mark our card the next. He'll not last long.'

The spring campaign of 1959 gave the thief the means to go to Johnny Tilley at Shepherd's Bush roundabout and trade in the handsome but unreliable Daimler for a silver drophead 1.2 Jaguar. The car paid for itself in a single jaunt to Manor Road, Chigwell, to relieve the ebullient slot-machine tycoon Sam Norman and his wife of money and other bits and pieces – amongst the booty a diamond-encrusted man's watch, a rarity in those days. Unknown to Peter, Superintendent Stephen Glandor had married into the family. He let Albert Dimes know that Sam must have his watch back and Albert, a bookmaker in Soho, passed the message on.

Peter returned the watch, leaving Sam to lick his lips over the hoot for his other effects. Essex Man knows the rules: every man to his own game. Superintendent Glandor was less magnanimous. To Bimbo, another chum of Peter's, he growled, 'Tell that flash Irish cunt I'm looking out for him.'

Peter took the warning blithely. Such was the arrogance of the boy from Belfast.

Jackie Whitehead had taken up with the bubblegum king, franchiser, and gangster's pal John Hoey. Such was the thief's passion for La Whitehead that a confrontation between Peter and Hoey at Jackie's pad resulted in John getting a scar on his forehead, though it should be said that Hoey acquitted himself well, was unafraid, and stayed on his feet. The incident brought another message from Albert Dimes, commanding Peter to appear at the latterly notorious Esmeralda's Barn in Knightsbridge for a meet. The gripe was that John Hoey was to have been a witness for one of the Firm but Peter's head-butt had reduced his credibility by scarring his boat race.

It was something of a court martial, with Bimbo accompanying the young thief as 'prisoner's friend'. A skulk of moody gangsters assembled there for the hearing – a bunch for whom Peter had scant respect at that time (he has none now), with the exception of Albert, who was a likeable, capable man. Dimes explained that Hoey was on the Firm and that Peter had taken a liberty. Then a sharp but friendly slap on the cheek came by way of chastisement and honour was satisfied. Many there thought a kicking would have been more appropriate.

Jackie, accompanying Peter to the chemmy parties, exchanged admiring glances with Peter Rachman. Peter was Jackie's shunt with the gaucheness of youth, an attraction that can appeal to even the most hardened female predator. But it made foolish, jealous, unwitting Peter suffer.

Then he learned that he too could play at that game. He moved a well-bred girl from the sticks into a flat in Gloucester Place. Her name was Andrea and they'd met at Roehampton swimming pool where, in those years, Billy Hill and Charlie Mitchell held court. Andrea was a horny handful but all the time his loving, or more accurately his *jealous*, heart belonged to Jackie.

The aftermath of a modest pillage in Avenue Road, Hampstead lost him his freedom for six more months. As he was parking carelessly in Little Venice to sling some crap jewels in the canal, two young coppers pounced on him and his silver Jaguar. Stupidly, he tried to leg it, was caught and held at Brixton. It was Derby week.

Though it was a minor charge, the Firm saw to it that there was no bail. A playboy brief, whom he knew slightly from Paddy Kennedy's, appeared for him. He was a Churchill's customer and, in taking instructions, he was interested to learn that Peter knew Jackie. He would probably, he thought, have to take a statement from her. Then Dave, a pal from Hoxton, came in to see him on a morning visit. He was uneasy.

'I'm not sure I should tell you this, but . . .'

The words were a sure portent that he would, and enjoy doing so. Peter growled, 'Get on with it.'

'Well, you know that cunt who's defending you? I went round to see Jackie last night and his RollsBentley was parked up outside.'

Peter for the moment put the best construction on this news.

'Yes, that's probably true. He has to take a statement from her on our relationship.'

'It must have taken him all night,' said Dave. 'His Roller was still there as I passed in the morning.'

In those distant days it was possible to organise a second visit on weekdays, for in Brixton staff were flexible. Jackie got in on the same afternoon, looking like she'd just got out of bed.

'Hello, darling. Had a late night. Stayed with Mum in Seven Kings.'

Peter's face did little to conceal his rage.

'Well, well. Did my brief go with you, you shit cunt whore?'

Jackie, her face pressed to the reinforced glass that separated them, was fortunate to draw back in shock as Peter butted the pane, shattering it and then trying to grab her through the jagged hole. A very lucky hostess withdrew as Peter was restrained and taken down to the tea-rooms for three days' punishment.

Chummy eventually showed up. Lack of courage was not one of his shortcomings. He'd flown in the RAF and boxed for his university.

'Sorry about the Jackie business, old boy. I was at Cleveland Place to take her statement and when I came out my Rolls packed up. I was unable to move it until the next day.'

Peter knew it was bollocks but said nothing.

'You're very badly wanted by the police,' Chummy went on. 'Top priority, in fact. Could very easily get a lagging again. But I've a chum at the London Sessions I can have a word with. I think you probably deserve a chance.'

Peter saw mileage in the situation and enquired with polite menace, 'Probation, perhaps?' He wanted to indicate just how seriously he regarded the brief's trespass at Cleveland Place, just how much Chummy owed him.

'Hardly, old man. But it could be a mere six months for receiving, which would be a result. Be assured, I'll do my best for you.'

He did, too. Peter appeared in front of Henry Elam and copped the predicted six months. An article in the *Daily Telegraph*, dated 15 July 1959, was the first of a number over the years to allude to his special skills and social aspirations. Either the Yard or the brief must have marked their card, for the receiving charge was hardly newsworthy.

Peter, when he came out at twenty-eight, would have already totted up three years behind bars, confirming Governor Lance Thompson's prediction in Belfast: 'You will spend your life in and out of prison.'

Out in a fist of months, not respecting the leniency of his sentence, he holed up in a room a pal had got him in Barkston Gardens, Earl's Court. He got a car on the book from Jimmy O'Connor's in Warren Street, thinking at the time he was lucky to do a sign-up with the convicted murderer turned playwright. He was later to have second thoughts for, when signing up for the police car look-alike Riley, he'd revealed his Earl's Court address . . .

A chance meeting with Bruce in Dorothy's led to a touch.

'Dr Janeiro's drum. He has the Society Restaurant and his old woman has a cotterell of tom. We've been fucking about with it for a couple of months, but we got the pox on it. Maybe you could have a shufty.'

'Love to. Where's the house?'

'Avenue Road. It's on the right as you leave the park heading for Swiss Cottage, immediately after St Edmund's Terrace. You can't mistake it. It's a postwar house well grilled, with floodlights on the lawn. Not easy, but is anything these days?'

Bruce grinned while Peter pulled a face. Avenue Road, again? It would be nearly opposite his 1957 tilt with the safe at 35. But grilled, floodlit? However, he was just home, skint, and his options were few. More important, he respected Bruce as not only reliable, but as a determined thief to boot.

'I'll look at it. If it comes to copping for her gear, I'll pull a few quid out for you.'

'No need. If you cop for her gear you'll deserve all you get.'

The orange floodlights accentuated the gleaming grilles as Peter poodled by the same evening and turned to park in St Edmund's Terrace. It was a hard coup. The house, though forty yards from the road, was so harshly lit up it was discernible down to the mortar between the bricks. The main bedroom-boudoir, under full lights at the front of the house, was the challenge. It would probably have to be backed.

The driveway was sheltered to a degree by a hedge. Peter crept up the drive to inspect the target at close range. There was, however, no easy route to the rear. The padlocks on the bedroom grilles were clearly visible. Could he hoist a ladder and cut them in full view of the traffic along Avenue Road?

Locating a ladder was the first step, he decided, creeping back hopefully unseen to the road. If he did succeed in finding a window ajar and cutting the grille padlocks, would the alarm activate? A host of doubtful thoughts passed through his head as he retreated, but once again in his water he felt lucky. A lifetime of larceny had allowed him to take this gift, the inner voice, the ESP, for granted. Peter is in no doubt that it exists. A handful of thieves swear by it, as sure as the faith that inspires religion. It's a question of finding the latent power, whether for good or evil. It will defy understanding in those who deny its existence.

He borrowed a ladder from a nearby building site, concealing it near the house. Then, back in his shabby room, he considered the logistics of the strike. The gas fire puttered as he wondered whether, with so much obvious external protection, it was just possible that the Janeiros felt safe inside. Would it lead them into carelessness within the keep? He dozed off uneasily. His master passion was at work again, defying common sense. Should he, just out of the slammer, take up a challenge that could return him to it? But the passion was cruel and the thief, feckless, was caught in its vice.

His second natural passion, lust, was as active as ever. He was quaffing a well-constructed Pimms at Ruby Lloyd's when a superb pair of silk-clad legs walked by. He knew the legs. They belonged to an ash blonde with whom he'd had a brief, fruitless liaison in 1957. It culminated in taking her and her younger brother to the races. Knickers off, not in the handicap, missing the starter's flag in homage to his prime passion, larceny.

'Hello.' The aggressive, deep voice gave a renewed twist to his libido. 'Let you out, have they?'

Carole's greeting had the additional effect of alerting the whole room to his sins. Peter ignored the bitchery to greet her with warmth.

'Fancy a drink, darling?'

'Not now,' she said firmly, 'I'm off to Harvey Nick's.' Then she relented, perhaps in pity, perhaps finding him more attractive second time around. 'I'll be here tonight.'

More likely she was bored and at a loose end. Carefully he watched the seams of Carole's stockings as she swirled out and unconsciously his hand went down to console his limp cock. He could well be back tonight, but first he had a skirmish to make into Avenue Road.

The house looked even less receptive, the orange floodlights if anything brighter, the grilles more daunting. But he pressed on, sidling up the drive with the firmly clutched ladder. From the shelter of the hedge he examined the grilles, staring at them like an aesthete in the Tate making sense of a Turner. Suddenly – Christ! – was he imagining it, or was there no padlock on the boudoir grille? He inched nearer. There fucking wasn't and the window stood ever so slightly ajar.

His prick twitched and began to swell in anticipation. Then, for some reason, an image of the seams of Carole's hose flitted across his mind as, reckless and by necessity fearless, he ducked under the blazing triangle of illumination that the great lamps created. He hoisted the ladder to the window and ascended. He was like an actor, coming onto the glare of the stage. 'Peter Gulston, THIS is your LIFE!'

The window swung open, the impotent grille slid quietly back. Then, ignoring any drivers on Avenue Road who might be observing him, he clambered into the heavily scented boudoir. The first drawer he opened revealed a circular chamois pouch. As he grasped it, the weight told him it was the prize. Only platinum-caressed gems could be so dense. The zipper arced back, and the reward for his determination glistened reassuringly. From the wardrobe, a mink coat compounded his fortune, and then he climbed out into the glare and . . . he knew not what.

He descended the ladder with only the hum of traffic to the West End breaking the silence. On the ground, no strong hands seized him, no voice was raised in alarm. He lowered the ladder and left it, making his exit like the matinee idol he imagined himself to be. Only the applause was absent.

Back at Barkston Gardens the gas fire now seemed friendly. He sat and examined the prize, all superb gear, carelessly tangled inside the pouch with little regard for what the carbon of the diamonds could do to the ruby corundum or to the beryls set in the magnificent, primarily emerald bracelet. One very large stone – sadly with light striations – could have been a diamond, though in the gaslight Peter convinced himself it was a white sapphire. No matter, there were a dozen or so superb pieces.

He mustn't leave them in his room. Where should he hide them? He returned in the Riley to an old haunt in Duchess of Bedford Walk, Jack Lyon's garden, and buried the pouch under a tree.

*   *   *

'Bottle of wine?'

Showered and primped, he appeared at Ruby's, the anticipated cash from the strike allowing him to be bold with his small tank. Carole sensed his renewed confidence. She slid onto a stool alongside the free-spending thief.

The bubbly was ice-cold but it did little to dowse the flames in his expectant loins. He offered Carole a lift and she agreed.

They ended up in the shabby room with the gas fire lit. Yet another role to play. Carole was stretched out, legs akimbo, on the floor in front of the gas, skirt hoisted to her thighs. Peter, perched on the edge of the bed with a bottle of Charlie Heisinck, was certain he was about to be rewarded again.

'What do you do for sex in prison?'

'Wank. Imagine you're fucking everybody from your wife to your mother, creating fantasies which afford relief.'

'When you weren't wanking over your mother, did you ever wank over me?'

'Of course I wanked over you.' His voice thickened, and the wanton sensed it, running her hand slowly up to her crotch.

'Let me watch you wank,' she whispered.

Peter fumbled to get his expectant, dully purple organ out for inspection. 'What a lovely prick,' was her comment. 'I hope I'm the first to kiss it welcome home.'

She reached out and drew his foreskin back roughly to run her nicotine-stained fingers over his knob. She clearly now wished to forestall his masturbation. They slid to the floor together in the glow of the gas jets, Carole soon entering another, private world, mumbling incoherently about an absent 'John Ireland's' cock and its dimensions, which had recently given her much pleasure.

The comparative reference didn't abate her passion as they clasped together, wriggling, biting, rutting on the floor.

'Don't you dare fucking come, you bastard!' she hissed in his ear, ecstatically. 'I'm going to cream your balls and arse.'

From nowhere she found a tube of cream and began roughly to apply the cold white ointment to his balls and buttocks, before slipping her finger into his bumhole. The thief was entering nirvana. Then a vice-like grip had him by the neck as she fumbled in her handbag under a chair. She kissed his lips with a violence that drew blood and then, without warning, plunged a small dildo up his butt.

'Ahh, you bitch!' he yelped. 'Christ! What're you fucking doing?'

Pain and pleasure were inseparable and, in the hissing, amber light, he found no will to resist her throat-hold, her preconceived plot, her vengeance. In fact, he surrendered.

'I want to fuck you all night, you arrogant, aggressive cunt,' she gasped.

He moaned and thrust, as if trying to penetrate her stocking-taut thigh below the pelvis. And then she eased the rubber phallus out from between his buttocks, and he shot his load.

'Now, darling,' she assuaged. 'That was not too terrible. Auntie Carole knows what's best.'

Maybe she did, too. The warm glow in his vacated arse was not the worst of sensations. Lighting a cigarette, Carole puffed contentedly. Peter the robber-beast was prostrated, tamed. She put out the cigarette and kissed him, then arranged her clothing and departed silently in triumph.

He crawled to bed and slept in fits, before being awoken by a heavy banging on the door of his room. He knew it had to be the law. He slipped on his dressing gown, reasoning it was most unlikely that they were calling about his touch in Avenue Road. Too early for that. Maybe Carole had reported he'd been raped.

He was grinning as he called out, 'Hang on, I'm getting dressed.'

That was not good enough. The impatient callers booted the door down.

'Police.' The dark-haired man was flashing his warrant card.

'Harry boy!' said Peter.

It was an old adversary, Sergeant Harry Challenor of the Flying Squad. He had an Inspector Dilley in tow.

'Got anything here you shouldn't have?' the ebullient Harry bellowed. He looked at Dilley, who nodded, and Harry turned out a couple of empty drawers. Turning to Peter's only suitcase, he found a torch battery and whooped.

'Where's the gelignite?'

Even by Challenor's imaginative standards, it was a long way from finding a torch battery to expecting to locate jelly. But Peter felt the rebuttal was forced.

'Not my forte, explosives. You know that.'

Dilley cleared his throat and spoke with quiet menace.

'You'd be surprised where we find gelignite.'

Peter would not be even mildly surprised. These were the years when certain officers on the Squad were finding the stuff where they chose, and there was more rogue jelly in lockers at the Yard than in all the stone quarries of Wales.

'The playwright fire you here?'

'What playwright would you be alluding to?' asked Harry with a grin. Dilley wore a straighter face.

'Jim-boy isn't your enemy, but believe me, you *do* have plenty. OK, we've found nothing here today. But we'll get lucky in the end. You're top priority at the Factory, so take a tip — take a holiday. There are big eyes on you.' Dilley was giving him the routine spiel, covering their presence. You have a lot of enemies, but today I'm your pal. Then a bellow from Harry-boy, looking under the bed, interrupted him.

'What the fuck's this?'

He was holding up the dildo. It had a forlorn look in the morning light which made Peter laugh.

'I'd a bird here last night, she forgot it. Gets her rocks off ramming that up aggressive boys' arseholes.'

'Then I better be careful, eh?' jossed Harry, dropping the soiled sex toy on the bed.

They left, looking not unlike a pair of protection gangsters who'd called to warn a client. The élitist squads were all like this. Peter sat for some time, pondering on the events of the last twelve hours. Gems, ash-blonde, artifacts, élite cops. Life in the fast lane, but for how long?

The same evening he travelled to Leicester where a contact wanted to brief him as to the possibility of spiriting Alderman Whitbread's safe away. Waiting at the hotel for the meet, Peter bought an evening paper. A headline caught his eye.

'TWELVE THOUSAND POUND DIAMOND STOLEN: A single diamond, part of a thirty thousand pound haul, was said by police . . .'

Lucky bastard, the thief thought. But then, reading on, he saw it had happened in London, in Avenue Road! He sat bolt upright, realising the pouch buried in Duchess of Bedford Walk contained a twelve-grand diamond. By the time Leslie showed up to brief him on the brewer's safe, he wasn't up for it.

'Leslie, something's come up. I must go back to London. Sorry for messing you about. We'll attend to it next week.'

Leslie was a worldly soul and knew the pressures of the game. He simply pumped Peter's hand and sent him on his way.

It was illogical, really, crashing back to London. But somehow the thought of an eight-carat diamond languishing in the soil was too much for a now extremely taut nervous system. The good alderman could wait.

Retrieving the pouch that night, he inspected the superb stone which had been so carelessly left to rub shoulders with its brothers and sisters. It had light striations on the table, easily buffed out. They would not affect the value. Today a diamond of such size and quality would weigh in at around a quarter of a million pounds. He sold it for five thousand and the other gems, with the emerald bracelet, for four thousand. It was a daring strike. As Bruce so pragmatically put it, 'You deserve all you got.'

The Janeiro house whence the gems came has long been demolished to make way for an awful block of flats. Harry Challenor was to retire, nutted off in disgrace. Believe it or not, this was a sad loss to society. In today's scum-bag world of criminals, he was a very necessary type of copper. Dave Dilley became a Commander and a respected figure on the sixth floor.

Carole? She went on to marry well and never came back for seconds – or for her not-so-little toy. Bruce masterminded a theft at Linkslade. Alderman Whitbread did have visitors, but never lost his safe.

And the thief? He was a couple of months away from doing the largest jewel theft ever. Again the master passion was in control, and Wandsworth jail waited patiently for him in Trinity Road, if only to ensure we know that the 'happy thief' is a myth.

13

Ferdie in Drag

LAWRENCE ran him round the court for an hour in the morning. Most of the time it was moonballs and topspin, drop and lob, drop and lob, and the occasional devastating forehand. Peter felt very fucking old and hostile towards the arrogance of youth. Exhausted at 6–1, 6–2 to the boy, he cried off.

The club was filling up, the Sunday autumn sun luring all but the most reluctant down to the fray.

'I can't cope,' he thought. 'I must have a drink. In my cups I either become more tolerant towards them or they to me.'

On his second large brandy, Helen remarked, 'Starting early today, Peter.'

She was right. Too early. But in his aimlessness (Rousseau's being closed on Sunday) the second half of the weekend took some getting through – unless the good club member in him blossomed and he played in the endless round of mixed doubles. Why didn't the bitch ring? Wasn't she saddle-sore by now?

He drank a third brandy in a single gulp and left the change from a twenty-pound note on the bar. An aggressive gesture of his intent of doing some serious drinking.

The force of a slap on his shoulder nearly drove him to his knees. Only Ferdie could give you a friendly pat of such violence.

'Hello, son. You're at it early.'

There he was, for all the world a cross between Charles Bronson and Emil Zapata. Macho and moustachioed, gleaming, wavy black hair, bulging biceps. He had a couple of Prince racquets tucked under his arm.

'Ferdie, thank God you've come. I'd got the feeling I might be nicked for loitering here this morning. Large glass of white wine for the bandit, please, Helen.'

'I want a hit,' Ferdie told him. 'Have you a court booked?'

Ferdie spent a lot of time in Florida, and was anxious to improve his tennis.

'Yes, we can get a court. Where's the lovely Rachel?'

'Back in bed. She's coming later. What time are we on at?'

'Twelve-thirty. Anything else you want?'

'Yes, I want a bit off the back.'

Peter had borrowed a thousand quid from Ferdie in the early summer and this was the first time he'd seen him since Bobinet's.

'Yes, I can let you have a couple of hundred.'

'That'll make it a bottle you owe me.'

'Ferdie, don't drive me mad. I'm old, impotent and rotting here, and all you can do is bully me.'

'Seen the Greek arsehole?'

'The gang don't come here on Sundays, you know that.'

'The gang?'

'You know – Ken, Carol, Avril, the Greek . . .'

'I'm taking my mother to the Greek's place on Tuesday night. I want you to come with us.'

The Greek's place was La Venture in Blenheim Terrace, St John's Wood, a middle-to-upper-range French restaurant.

'Will Katherine let us in? I thought you were outers.'

Katherine, the French manageress, got pissed off when Ferdie embraced and kissed her waiters, which he often did. But with his mum in tow, surely even Ferdie wouldn't do that.

'She's only sour because I don't screw her.'

'Ferdie, I think she's more concerned for her waiters' virtue . . .'

Ferdie smiled in a knowing fashion.

'No harm in having a few poof friends. You never know when they might come in handy.'

His great physique, from years of pumping iron, didn't give Ferdie the suppleness necessary to grasp the rudiments of tennis. He snatched at everything. On the credit side, he was very mobile, and ran his heart out, but his wicked temper and gangster attitude were not conducive to learning, and Peter settled for putting the ball where Ferdie could clout it. On the odd occasion he did, the ball flashed past Peter as Ferdie giggled delightedly.

Rachel turned up and they played a couple of sets of doubles until Peter, heavy with brandy, crept back to his pit in Sutherland Avenue. As he was retreating, Ferdie bellowed after him, 'You're coming to dinner tonight. The parrot misses you. Around nine, OK?'

'Yes, yes. Around nine,' Peter called back. He liked the parrot.

Ferdie had a lot of irons in the fire in Soho's sleazy underworld of peepshows and strippers. Though not quite of the criminal ilk, he was well respected in that cesspool of vice. And – if current gossip was right – a very rich boy. He was also a superb cook, so the invitation to mange did not weigh heavily on Peter's shoulders. Leastways, it got him out.

Ferdie had a flat in Hampstead. It was a top-floor penthouse in a converted property, where the main attraction was the parrot Ambrose. Ferdie, who got little response or affection from Ambrose, frequently gave him a clout – often too sharp a clout. But for some reason the bird took strongly to Peter. Were they fellow souls in pain?

When Peter arrived at 9.30, Ferdie was in the kitchen and Rachel swanning around looking very attractive, her ash-blonde hair swept up, her body swathed in a turquoise kimono trimmed with Chantilly lace. Ambrose let out a squawk of welcome. His pal had arrived.

'You're late, cunt!' shouted Ferdie.

'Sorry, Ferdie. Hello, beautiful lady.'

Rachel embraced him.

'Peter, good of you to come.'

'What do you mean, good of you to come?' thundered Ferdie. 'The arsehole's got nowhere else to go. Who'd have him? He's as fucked up as me.'

The aggressive banter went on as Ferdie grilled fillet steaks saturated in garlic.

'Ferdie, can I take Ambrose's chain off?' Peter asked.

'Up to you. The bastard'll nip you.'

But catching Ambrose's beady eye, Peter recognised a 'you're my kind of master' look. He unhooked the chain. Ambrose hopped onto his shoulder and rubbed his glossy-feathered head against Peter's ear. The only thing he nipped was the collar of Peter's jacket – and that in the most friendly manner.

'He shits all over the place. I'm going to get rid of him.'

Ferdie had a fetish that everything should be spotless. His desire somehow to gain Ambrose's affection had forced him to tolerate the bird's habits thus far. Or was the bird frightened into incontinence? Parrots, like ladies, need affection, not clouts.

'I'll buy him from you now, for cash,' said Peter boldly.

'No you bloody won't,' Rachel piped up. 'He's mine, and I love him. If Ferdie would stop playing the brute with him he'd settle and stop his poo-poos.'

'Parrots, birds, mad fucking burglars. Why do I have you all around me?'

'You know, darling,' Rachel said sweetly. 'Because you love us.'

'Do I bollocks!'

And so it went on. It was less trying after the food and the surfeit of wine on hand had been eaten and drunk. The brute was a marvellous host. The food, especially the garlic steaks and the side salad made predominantly with onions, was excellent. So were the Gevrey-Chambertin and the Brouilly.

Television now intruded and, as that didn't satisfy, the macho video. Peter, no lover of the box, had switched to brandy when, totally unexpectedly, the cabaret commenced. Ferdie had left the lounge and now, suddenly, he returned. His great muscled bulk was squeezed into a woman's dress, black tights, high heels. He didn't speak at first, and Rachel gave Peter a 'get this' glance. Peter, in a haze of wine and brandy, felt oddly at a loss for words as Ferdie minced around, taking the debris from the lounge to the kitchen and beginning to wash up as if nothing at all had happened. Rachel and Peter's eyes were now glued to the screen as to their salvation. Then Ferdie reappeared.

'I'm going to bed. You'd better fuck her.'

He was pointing at a not-so-astonished Rachel. Then the bedroom door slammed and the key turned. Peter poured a final four fingers of brandy and sloshed them down his throat. He found his jacket, kissed Rachel lightly on the forehead, and let himself out into the chilly autumn air.

14

Last Glimpses of Westchester County

'Hi, it's me.'

Back in the claustrophobic atmosphere of the booth under the stairs at the club, his head pounded.

'So, where have you been?'

Silence. Then, 'Are you angry?' The little-girl voice.

'Is your arse sore?'

'Why should my arse be sore?'

'All that fucking riding you've been doing since you disappeared.'

More silence.

'Peter, my sister Roberta and I want to take you to lunch in Soho today. Can you make it?'

'Yes, I suppose so.'

'Will you come to Portman Square? You know the block. Just ask the porter to ring up. Can you be there for one-thirty?'

'Will do.'

He quickly put the phone down. He couldn't be sure what he might say next. He loathed being treated casually.

He got to Portman Square at 1.20, unchanged in his tracksuit and trainers. When you don't feel like making an effort . . . don't. The porter was expecting him.

'Mr Scott?' he asked, picking up his phone. 'Mrs R, your guest is here.'

He replaced the phone. 'They're coming right down, Mr Scott.'

Irene materialised as if by a conjuring trick at the bend in the stairs. She came quickly down and took hold of Peter's arm. She led him beyond earshot of the porter.

'Peter, I didn't want to ask you up.'

He thought he was in for a bollocking about his casual appearance. He was wrong.

'Roberta's got a lot of valuable paintings in the flat. Picassos, Impressionists. If anything ever went missing, I wouldn't want your name to come up.'

If she had hit him with a fourteen-pound hammer he could not have been more astounded. He was speechless with anger and embarrassment. He counted to ten, and then went on to twenty. At last, he managed, 'Yes. Good thinking.'

Roberta appeared, a younger, blonde edition of Irene. Her eyes swept over him like an auction appraiser.

'Hello, Peter. Irene has told me how kind you've been to her.'

Peter hailed a cab in the square and was saved further embarrassment when the sisters embarked on a long discussion about money matters. He became a ghost. At the Chinese gaff, Roberta went to the powder room.

'Peter, can I tell you quickly that Roberta's having marital problems. She's married to a very stuffy banker and she's on a low.'

What the fuck am I doing here with this pair of harpies? Peter thought.

The subject of money – and, among other things, how *terribly* economical the restaurant was – dominated the lunch. Westchester County teaches a girl, no matter how rich she is, to find a bargain. Peter thought the place a pisshole but didn't resent paying a very small lunch bill.

They began to walk from Soho down Piccadilly, but Irene had to go to Swaine, Adeney's. Could she see him at nine that evening? He could and Irene peeled off. Roberta and Peter continued on to the Ritz, and she got down to the serious business of telling him how concerned she was for Irene. The tight grip on his arm made him aware he was being grilled.

'Roberta, Irene will come to no harm with me, I promise.'

Roberta looked reassured. Then she, too, had to fly, hailed a cab outside the Ritz and was gone. The depressing Chinese cuisine was already attacking Peter's bowels as he glided through the swing doors into the men's room. He was in no frame of mind to care what anyone thought of his appearance.

He left a pound for the surprised attendant and pressed on, down Piccadilly. Crossing the road, he momentarily caught a glimpse of himself in the plate-glass window of a car showroom. He looked like a hobo. Some front, going into the Ritz for a crap like that. He chuckled. He felt in better form.

He was back at the club as the bar opened and got on the brandy route. He felt his amazement at the Picasso incident begin to swamp him. His cheeks glowed, and not because of the brandy. How fucking silly could the lady be? Did she know what she'd said and what the connotation was? Women have nothing to offer; try to remember that, Peter.

He nonetheless made an effort for Pavilion Road. At Sutherland he dropped two Alka Seltzer and soaked in the bath while their magic took effect. Then on with the Prince of Wales and the two-tone Gucci shoes, a light pink Harrods shirt and a brown silk tie. He began to feel good.

The door on the second floor was open. He went in. Irene made a gesture of mock surprise on seeing how he was dressed. She hadn't made any effort and was simply dressed in a pair of velvet trousers, a fisherman's sweater and sneakers.

'God, you're all dressed up.'

Did she think he lived in a tracksuit?

'Look at me, I'm a wreck. I wish you'd let me know.'

'I presumed we were going boogying.'

Peter tried to be light-hearted. In his soul he knew the charade was in its death throes.

'Peter, I can't accept this present.'

In one jerky, hostile movement, Irene thrust the snake bracelet at him. Slowly he took it, casually slipping it into his pocket. The *coup de grâce.*

'Well, I'm sorry, Irene.'

'We come from different worlds, Peter. You're a very generous guy, but I've my family to think about.'

Peter was trying to move imperceptibly backwards in an uneasy exit. Cover arrived when the phone growled. Irene turned to answer it and he, in his ambivalent mood, retreated smartly and quietly closed the door. He was left with a last memory of her nasal New York twang telling someone how nice it was of them to call.

One door shuts, another opens. He got into the BMW and, there on the dash, was Tracy's card. Why not?

'Hello, Tracy here.'

'Tracy, it's Dr Scott.'

'Oh, hello, Doctor. How are you? Keeping out of Pentonville?'

'Listen, do you fancy a meal?'

'I'd love it. But it's such short notice. I'm working.'

'Fuck that. I'll look after you.'

'But I can earn a hundred and fifty pounds if I stay by the phone.'

'That seems reasonable. I'll pick you up in half an hour.'

'You're sure it's all right about the money?'

'Yes, sure as hell.'

'Are we going anywhere nice?'
'Anywhere you want.'

He got to Westbourne Grove at 9.30, after a couple of brandies in the Horse and Groom. Tracy had dressed up, and she looked knock-out.
'You're a very pretty girl, Tracy.'
They were speeding down to Holland Park when she said, 'Can I have my money now, Peter?'
A deal's a deal. At the lights, Peter drew three fifties from his inner pocket and gave them to her.
'I'm glad you think I look OK. You look very handsome.'
She was beginning to relax and, as they turned into Holland Park proper from Abbotsbury Road, she teased, 'Why're we going into the park – to feed the rabbits?'
'There's a very good restaurant here.'
She didn't believe him, until they'd parked in the drive outside the ancient orangery of Holland House.
'I never knew this existed.'
The maître d' knew Peter.
'Good evening, Mr Scott. You're very late and you haven't booked.'
But the grin on his face told Peter they would be accommodated.
'We want to sit upstairs if possible, John.'
'*Mon Dieu, vous êtes très difficile!* Go into the bar. A couple upstairs are just finishing. You are quite lucky. A large party has just arrived and will be sitting late, so you won't have to rush.'
'John, this is Tracy, my daughter.'
John gave a small bow.
'*Enchanté.*'
John had seen too many of Peter's daughters to comment further. Imperviously he led them to the bar, with all eyes on Tracy's wonderful legs, spectacularly displayed under the short hemline of her brown moleskin suit. In addition she wore a ruffled blouse, dark brown stockings, tasty slingback shoes and high suspenders detectable even under the moleskin.
As they sank into the great sofa couch at the bar her long legs were shown to even greater effect. Peter felt relaxed. For once this was not part of a charade, it was just a tart and a thief. The young Italian waiter, bringing Campari and sodas, couldn't take his eyes off the dark brown silken thighs. The more he stared, the more she showed. It amused Peter and she knew it would, the clever girl.
The Belvedere was the most beautiful restaurant building in London

in Peter's experience. If, occasionally, the food could be mediocre, the ambience more than compensated and, sitting at a corner table on the upper floor, overlooking the floodlit fountain, Tracy was enchanted. The large party was opposite them and Tracy's lovely legs, like an orchid in the heat, blossomed open from time to time. One of two middle-aged men seemed somewhat perturbed.

To his surprise, the food was excellent. Artichoke starters with a Pouilly Fouissé and later a Chateaubriand and a fine Béaune allowed them both to adopt an air of euphoria. The moleskin jacket now hung over the back of her chair and the near-transparent silk blouse displayed her heavy teats. As brandy arrived, Peter stuffed a Monte Cristo No. 2 into his mouth as Tracy lay back in her chair, to reveal the first light band of her stocking top. She was certainly being provocative. The large party across the room could hardly stop looking at the crossing of her legs and the large brown nipples vying with the silk of her blouse every time she stretched forward to sip her brandy. And the waiter, Peter was sure, was by now at torque. The bulge in his trousers betrayed him and so, shortly afterwards, did his foolishness. Serving Tracy a second cognac, he not too dexterously slipped a note into her hanging jacket.

Peter was in his element. It was for nothing at a hundred and fifty quid. Handsome Italian waiter slipping notes to his escort – well, he wasn't so sure about that. As Tracy shimmied across the floor to the powder room, turning the heads of the large party, his chance came. He took the note from her jacket.

'My name is Mario. Please phone me any day between 4 and 7. You are beautiful.' A phone number was attached.

Tracy returned and, sitting down, hitched her skirt up several inches to allow her legs total freedom. The second, darker ring of the stocking tops now appeared and even, as she crossed and uncrossed, the button of a tight pink suspender.

'Which one at the big table would you like to fuck?' whispered Peter.

'The way I feel now I'd like to fuck them all. Do you mind me saying that? When I'm like this I can imagine the whole table standing round me, tossing themselves off over me.'

'No, you can only have one.'

'Oh, the bald one at the top of the table, then. Spoilsport.'

'Why him?'

'Because he's rich and kind, and I can see from his eyes that he wants me.'

'Take a couple of your cards over.'

'Don't tease, you cunt. You know the only person I'm going to fuck tonight is you.'

'What if I can't fuck?'

'I'll make you fuck.'

She was in no doubt about it. Peter did not argue.

He called for the bill and Mario brought it. Peter slipped his note to Tracy into the folds of the account and Mario, thinking it was a credit card and cheque, removed it to the cash desk. Peter watched with a certain cruel glee as the boy's handsome face turned tomato-red. He came hurrying back.

'Sir, I am very stupid,' he whispered. 'If the maître d' sees this I am out.'

Enough was enough and Peter, relenting, put down two fifty-pound notes and took back the *billet doux*.

'At your age, I'd have done the same damn stupid thing,' he said, getting up to leave.

Tracy was at a loss and it was only in the car that he told her. She was excited, as he'd known she would be.

'Give me the note, it's mine. He's a lovely boy. Give it to me.'

A good sport to the end, Peter dropped the note into her handbag. Perhaps she and Mario had conspired. Was he growing so old that he'd missed it?

'Peter, let's go back to your place. At mine the phone and people will drive us mad.'

People? Punters and pimps, she meant.

'I've only a bed at my flat. I've just moved in,' Peter lied.

'Do we need anything else?'

Tracy was not impressed by the stairwell.

'Christ, you live here?'

'Wait till you see the flat. It's quite comfortable.'

This was true. Though not furnished, it had a Wrighton kitchen and a compact bathroom, and one expensive monster bed. In the kitchen, Tracy, still in her high heels and stockings but with her pert teats unencumbered, set about getting Peter at it.

'So,' she said. 'You can't screw?'

Peter opened the fridge where, apart from milk, the only tenants were a couple of bottles of Tattinger Blanc et Blanc.

'Most times. Let's finish these off and see how we go.'

'I don't think we'll have any problems.'

Tracy was grinning impishly. Peter was touched.

'Good. I was resigned to being the original Portnoy. But should you get me at it, I'll give you this.'

He pulled the rejected snake bracelet from his pocket and dangled it. Tracy's eager hands examined the jet snake.

'Oh my God, it's so lovely! Do you really mean, if I make you screw, I can have it?'

Peter nodded. It gave him pleasure to give her pleasure. She was in a hard lane.

By the time dawn pierced the makeshift curtain, the gift was installed firmly and permanently on the child's wrist. A deal was a deal. He went for a newspaper and, when he returned, she was up. Still enchanted with her gift, she was admiring it from every angle.

'Darling, can you run me home?'

As they puddled down Westbourne Grove, Tracy noticed the tennis bag on the rear seat.

'Do you play tennis?' she asked. 'I used to play a little. Can we play sometime?'

Peter nodded patronisingly. But he doubted it would happen. Outside her flat she got out of the BMW after kissing him lightly on the brow.

'You're a lovely man. Here, I can't take this.'

She made a movement with her hand and was gone. Can't take what? He looked at where she'd been sitting and there, on the bucket seat, were his three fifty-pound notes.

'And you're a darling too,' he mused, binning the notes.

He drove back under a dull November sky. The V & A had to be looked at again, he remembered. Deciding to leave the BMW at the club, he met Dominic in the car park.

'Hello, Peter. Hang on . . .'

From his pocket he fished out a slip of paper.

'I'd say someone was after you.'

The note read, 'Please ring Irene. Important.'

Just as he'd buried something it was trying to resurrect itself. Would he? Wouldn't he? Was there any bloody point in prolonging the agony? In the end he went to the cubbyhole under the stairs and dialled.

'Peter, is that you?'

'Yes. I thought we held the wake last night?'

'I wasn't myself last night.'

The home of Peter's aunt at Castle Cat, Bushmills, in County Antrim, where he spent many a happy summer holiday.

Belfast Royal Academy, where Peter was at school from the age of twelve to seventeen.

'A missionary seeing his flock for the first time' outside Viscount Kemsley's country-house in 1956: a fellow-convict's idea of the moment inspiration struck.

Peter at Crawford Scott's farm in Antrim, c. 1963. It was from Crawford Scott that Peter took his 'professional' name.

Left: Peter's girlfriend Coleen at the time he was on home leave from Crumlin Road prison, Christmas 1953.

Far left: Gaby, an aspiring actress, was with Peter one night in Sloane Street in 1960 when the Flying Squad searched his 150S Jaguar.

'Liz Taylor rarely let her tom out of her chubby paws.'

SOPHIE circa 1960

Recall this well, wish I had it now

NACK LACIS

'Sophia Loren committed a far greater crime than Peter. She was not insured.'

Tina Onassis, the Marchioness of Blandford. ' "You must be the man who's left his ladder in our compost heap," she gulped as Peter picked her up.'

Jackie Bowyer, the thief's second wife and probably the only one he was to care for.

Jackie and their son Craig in 1972.

Salad days at Bonchurch, Isle of
Wight, with son Craig, c.1974.

Peter with Emma and Craig at
Bishopsbourne, Kent, 1972.

Peter with 'jolly good pals together' on the Isle of Wight, 1974.

It was Marlena who encouraged Peter to take up tennis.

Peter's third wife Fay's home, Chamberhouse Mill in Thatcham, Berkshire.

A view of the mill leap; it was in the orchard (out of the picture on the left) that Peter learnt of Commander Albert Wickstead's burning interest in him.

Fay (and Peter), 1976.

He thought, as a sex, you are not yourself. You're simply what you want to be, when you want to be it.

He said, 'I thought you were about par for the course.'

'Peter, Roberta's had a bad night. I told you about her problem. I want to take her out and cheer her up today and we'd like you to come. Any suggestions? She really thought you were a sincere guy.'

'With or without her Picassos?'

A long pause.

'I only told you that thinking of your welfare.'

Let's just drop the bullshit, he thought.

'I'm going to the V & A at lunchtime. I'll be outside at one-thirty. We can have a snack there.'

'Peter, you're a genius. Just the very thing. We've been meaning to go and look at the Indian antiquities for weeks. Darling, we'll see you outside the main hall at one-thirty.'

Peter was not her darling and he'd not love her all the life's long day.

'See you then,' he said, and cradled the receiver.

You mug. They shat on you yesterday and today you're off on another excursion. Will you ever learn?

They debouched from the taxi at 1.27 – elegant, confident, garrulous – and hugged him ostentatiously. They must be feeling penitent; they'd even paid the cab. Peter, dressed in his charcoal jacket, cut a more impressive figure for Roberta than on the previous day.

'You do look handsome, Peter,' she pouted. 'I'll have to steal you from Irene.'

Tracy's more my style, he was thinking. At least she's grateful.

'We can't all be thieves,' he replied.

They went through the great mock-Gothic doors where security required the ladies to expose the contents of their handbags. That done, they were in, under the great dome. Peter was just about to move off towards the treasures when he saw him. Roger, smiling, standing in their path. It gave Peter quite a turn. He should be in Spain.

Clearly he wasn't, and if the load of bumf under his arm was anything to go by, he was researching.

'Roger! How odd to find you here. We just dropped in on the off-chance.'

He introduced the Daughters of the American Revolution. For their benefit, Roger cut an almost academic figure, smiling and saying he was delighted. It was all mildly theatrical, but didn't he know he was an oddball?

'Girls, you want to look at the Indian section. How about if Roger and I go up to the ceramics. We can meet in the tea-room in half an hour.'

They weren't best pleased but agreed and ambled off. Seeing them turn to look back at the miscreants, Peter waved, hoping they were reassured.

'I came back last week,' Roger murmured. 'I've been prowling around here for a few days. I'm beginning to like the idea.'

'Shall we pop up to the Jewel House?'

'Yes, why not.'

The Jewel House was crowded as they slipped from showcase to showcase, indicating with their eyes what they thought were interesting baubles. They went back and forth to the catalogues and, in total silence, checked out the gems' numbers, their origins and provenance. Time passed swiftly, assisted by the excitement of their quest. Then Roger tapped his watch-face – it was nearly a quarter to three.

'Where did you meet the bird?'

It was simpler to lie.

'At the club.'

'Well, I think I'll give the tea-room a miss. I want to look at the Polish Church. Can we meet tonight? I've a lot to tell you.'

Peter nodded. Roger, understandably not fancying any exposure, was anxious to escape.

'So I'll see you at eight, St John's Wood. Best we both come by tube. Don't want to be bottled off. Ta-ta.'

And Roger was gone. Curiouser and curiouser.

They'd got a table, and a high tea for four was spread.

'Where's Roger?' Irene wanted to know.

'He's doing a research paper on early Bow porcelain. He's gone off to a lecture at the British Museum. He lives for his work.'

'What exactly is that work he lives for?' Roberta followed up.

'He's one of the great porcelain restorers in London.' The trite lies were snowballing.

'Yeah, he looks an odd sort of guy. I figured he might be in something specialised.'

It sounded as if Irene might be taking the piss. He rode it on the ropes. All he needed now was for one of them to have a piece of porcelain in need of repair.

'Peter, we thought – and correct me if I'm wrong – we saw you coming out of the jewellery section.'

Can't these bitches leave the bone alone?

'You're not wrong. Roger wanted to look at some eighteenth-century porcelain ropes in the Jewel House.'

The game palled and, on his return from the men's room, they were discussing Roberta's previous evening at Annie's. Who was there, Princess this and Prince that, a famous playwright and Betty Bacall . . .

Peter's ears pricked up. Lauren Bacall in London? She was one of his favourite movie stars.

15

Bogie's Widow

It was in 1959 at Cadogan Place, the second-floor flat. From the cul-de-sac that ended Cadogan Lane, Peter had found an entry to the rear of the block. An amicable, solid Staveley drainpipe led up from the basement to the second floor. The Staveley is the cat burglar's friend. It is a reliable climb.

As in most ventures, information is of the essence. During the late fifties, Peter cultivated the friendship of one or two chauffeurs at Daimler Hire, then at the corner of Montpelier in the Gore. They used Dorothy's Club in Knightsbridge, as did Peter, and often knew the whereabouts of transient celebrities as they ferried them around London. Such knowledge is invaluable to the target thief – one who selects his victims beforehand, researches them, and strikes. Naturally, persons in the public eye are most vulnerable to his attentions. Persons like Lauren Bacall.

Press coverage announced her arrival and she became a target. Can you not trust chauffeurs, then? Not the one that put the thief up to this bit of work. Frank Clarence, not merely a chauffeur, but caretaker at the block of flats in Gloucester Walk where Peter had been offered lodgings on his release from Stafford. He was a weak, greedy man, the thief's worst foe.

In his *pied à terre* Peter was unaware of the jeopardy at hand, and a relatively simple climb had deprived Humphrey Bogart's handsome widow of her gems. Bacall hooted volumes and the press took the widow's plight to its bosom. The pressure was on Scotland Yard to get a result.

Frank wanted to place the gear. Peter agreed and let him take the parcel. But whether or not Frank ever tried to sell the jewels is speculative, for the next afternoon he returned them with a ludicrous offer of a thousand pounds. He doubtless knew Peter would refuse. Before he left, he aroused the thief's suspicions further.

'It's best you move the gear. I don't want it in the flat.'

Peter left almost at once, after putting the gems in an empty Cadbury's choc box and sealing it. The Daimler was parked outside the flats. Drawing away from the kerb towards Campden Hill Road, his worst fears were realised. A bull-nosed Wolseley pulled out into his path and it was not difficult to recognise the Flying Squad. It was on him.

Wrenching the steering wheel, Peter slung the Daimler up on the pavement and swerved past the Squad, whose startled driver had to take evasive action to avoid a collision. The Daimler got only as far as the corner where, turning at speed, it struck a stationary car in Hornton Street. Peter took off on foot in the direction of Holland Park, clutching the chocolate box with Bacall's gems inside.

The enemy was right behind, also now on foot. But the odds were stacked against the ironically named Flying Squad, the thief, a non-smoker and (then) non-drinker, easily out-distancing the middle-aged, overweight, drink-sodden, smoke-polluted posse. But radio they did have, and assistance was thundering down from Ladbroke Grove nick.

Get rid of the bloody chocolates. Where could he bury them? Panting heavily, he'd reached Duchess of Bedford Walk, a long, straight thoroughfare where he'd be sighted before he could reach the anonymity of Holland Park. He ducked into a student hall of residence, coming out opposite the back of a private garden. The baying hounds forced him over the fence into a shrubbery where he found a bush with freshly turned earth around its roots. He clawed back the earth and buried the box. Then, boldly and fortuitously, he rounded the house and left by the front gate. On past the secondary school and into Holland Park, where he took a breather on a bench and worked out a game-plan.

Twenty minutes later he walked into Ladbroke Grove police station.

'I've been attacked by chemmy thugs in Campden Hill Road. I abandoned my car and ran here.'

The affable station sergeant gave him a consoling smile.

'Chemmy thugs? What's that, sir? We hear of all kinds of thugs, but that's a new one on me.'

'I'm in debt to a chemmy-game heavy. That's gambling, French card game. Can you help me?'

The sergeant was sympathetic. We tend to forget that most policemen, even today, are kind and want to help.

'Where have you abandoned the car, sir? I've got a skipper and crew here. He'll take you back to the car and get it sorted.'

In the back of the Q car, Peter clutched the new box of Cadbury's he had bought *en route* to the nick. At Campden Hill Road there was a lot of activity, even a TV crew, and an awful lot of coppers. The skipper laughed.

'Looks like a film set.'

He pulled up near a knot of Flying Squad bods who, seeing their quarry, wrenched open the door and dragged him out. The young skipper explained, innocently, 'The gentleman's been attacked by chemmy thugs.'

'Has he indeed? Don't believe that kind of bollocks. *We* want a word with him.'

None too gently, Peter was thrust into the back of a Squad vehicle and left there, a frightened yet alert suspect, to view the scene. He was still clutching the chocolates. His luck was holding. They appeared to be searching the basement of Campden Hill Mansions, the opposite side of the road from the halls of residence.

'What've you done with the parcel you ran off with?' a raucous and angry burr from the Highlands growled as the rear door was opened with a jerk. Politely, Peter passed him the chocolate box. The burr flung the chocolates into the gutter with a grunt.

'OK, laddie, if that's how you want it. You bloody near killed us all, pulling round us like that. Are you mad?'

They were probably both mad. The thief's insanity had infected the stalker from the grouse moors.

'Not mad, Jock, just frightened. I owe a few quid at chemmy. I thought you might be their heavy mob. Sorry.'

The unhappy ghillie reluctantly smiled and slammed the door abruptly. Chemmy was a sport of the fleshpots and he had little more respect for his masters than Peter. A policeman's lot . . .

The sweat trickling down the thief's scrotum evaporated to a clammy clutch. The longer they searched the more confident he became. No gems, no jail, he thought. Then a friendly face indicated that he should lower his window. It was DCI Bob Anderson, the team leader, who was later to become head of racecourse security.

'We can do this the hard way, or you can make it better for yourself by telling us where you hid the parcel you ran off with. If you do, I'll do what I can for you.'

He spoke in soft, compelling tones. Peter, far from ready for another crucifixion only a month after his release, remained respectful but silent. Anderson studied him, then made up his mind.

'In that case, I'll have to conduct a thorough search of the area. Meanwhile, you'll be taken to Earl's Court police station and detained.'

Back to jail, but for how long? In fact, the longer they let him sweat in the cell the happier he was. If they couldn't find the prize, they couldn't keep him. In the late afternoon a mildly deflated Anderson opened the cell door.

'We're going to release you. Before we do, I want to give your room in Gloucester Walk a spin. You've got nothing there, have you?'

A friendly tone, almost. He went back with them and the room got a cursory spin. They'd even missed the racing bins he'd secreted in his waste basket to defy the local drummer thief. The game was far from over, but Peter had won the first round. Those, anyway, were his thoughts as the team trooped out, leaving him in his uncertain liberty. Were they going to prat up on him?

He spent a restless night, pondering on the absence of Frank Clarence. Next morning Frank turned up briefly, apologetic, effusively concerned. The police had CRO'd him and he too was a suspect, he said. Making his retreat, he forgot his chauffeur's cap. He knew that Peter knew.

The gems weighed heavily on Peter. They were in what turned out to be the garden of Jack Lyons who, thirty years later, was to be found guilty in the Guinness fraud trial. Two days later, he was walking along Campden Hill Road when he saw the army out with their mine detectors in the grounds of the student residence. The game was certainly not over.

For Peter, to dig or not to dig, that was the question.

Late the same evening, in the light of a full moon, Peter crept through the garden of the house next door to Lyons. Approaching the dividing hedge with stealth, his worst fears were compounded. An overcoat hung from a tree close to the lethal bush. They were waiting, he thought; they might have found it and were now hoping to catch the thief red-handed. Sweat coursed down him, generated by a mixture of fear and excitement, as he rested by the hedge to organise his thoughts. Then he heard voices mumbling in the dark. Conquering the desire to flee, he looked, his eyes growing accustomed to the gloom. Ensconced on canvas stools, sitting directly under the very bush that concealed Bacall's gems, were two men. From time to time they raised night-vision binoculars. They were watching the garden of the student residence!

It meant they were actually squatting on the booty while waiting for the retriever. He retreated, his fear dispelled by amusement at the irony of the situation. Back at 'Traitor's Gate' Peter did some more thinking. They must suspect he had buried the gems and concluded that they were somewhere in the student residence grounds. But they couldn't find them. So they'd be hoping Frank was privy to Peter's next move. Wrong. So how long would they keep up the twilight patrol? And would the army eventually sweep Lyons's garden? They might. The gems must be retrieved as soon as possible – and in daylight.

He didn't fancy it, but most nefarious enterprises come down to Hobson's choice. So, in private anguish, he steeled himself to retrieve Betty Bacall's gems the next morning. Hopefully unseen. And on from there. God, what a fuck-up.

At 10.30, thwarting any spies in the front road, he slipped out through the gardens at the rear of his Gloucester Road pad and got to Hornton Street. He strode purposefully across Campden Hill Road and into the drive of the Lyons house, wearing Frank's chauffeur's cap. God knows why.

Rounding the house, he crossed the patio and went down the sloping garden to the bush. A pair of unoccupied canvas stools still rested there: the night watch was still on. Thrusting them aside, he scooped the soil aside, retrieved the gems, and made off like a shot over the hedge and into the student home. He thought he heard a shout, 'STOP!' Not bloody likely.

Fifteen minutes away he found an empty house and concealed the offending parcel in its under-pavement coal bunker. Then, full of relief, he went to have coffee in Kensington High Street. His elation was short-lived. That afternoon, back at Gloucester Walk, there was a light tap on his door and Frank's voice, *sotto voce*, enquired, 'Can I have a word, Peter?'

He opened the door and Frank's face told the story. Judas time. As the Flying Squad team sprang from the stairwell to shuffle Peter back into his hutch, it looked like the bell was tolling for the last round.

Bob Anderson sat grim-faced opposite him, and spat it out.

'Peter, you've made a cunt of us again. You were seen in the grounds of a private house in Campden Hill Road. You picked up a parcel and scarpered.'

He gave a thin smile.

'Your luck helped, because my two lads were having tea in the house. They saw a man in a chauffeur's hat disappearing. That hat there.'

He indicated the peaked cap on the dresser. Lost for words, Peter reviewed the situation rapidly. They still didn't know where the gems were so it was effectively status quo.

'What do you want? The gear back? Or bodies? You can't have both.'

It was Peter's master card and he played it as authoritatively as he could.

'Is the parcel intact?' asked Anderson, almost too eagerly. 'How soon can we have it?'

So, he recognised the Mexican stand-off and had clearly opted to retrieve the broken-hearted widow's gems – including, no doubt, much loving memorabilia paid for by Bogie. Peter would come to hand another day . . .

'I'm going to let you go on your own. You must return with the gems in, say, half an hour. I'll be on the corner of Vicarage Gardens. You won't be nicked, OK?'

The team looked decidedly displeased, but then they were all only boys then. All incidentally went on to become high-ranking officers: their day would come.

You either accept the spoken word or you don't. Of course, he could have scarpered – but then he would be on time borrowed at a very high interest rate. Instead he chose to trust Anderson. He went out, collected the chocs and returned to pass them over in the appointed place. He was suddenly alarmed as one of the team grabbed his arm. He needn't have been. It was Peter Vibart, a heavy-handed sergeant, growling before he released his grip, 'We'll have you soon, sonny.'

Peter caught Anderson smiling. The pow-wow broke up and an item in the evening paper the next day reported that a man exercising his dog had found Lauren Bacall's jewels in a dustbin in Kensington.

Gossip had it that Bacall gave the Squad a good drink. And they deserved it. I wonder, did Frank Clarence get one?

16

Pussy Galore

Aт eight o'clock, Peter was at the bar in St John's Wood tube station for the meet with Roger. Smiling and effete, the oddball arrived five minutes later.

'Evening. Nip in the air. How's Ethel?' A typical bollocks opener to put off any earwiggers. 'Fancy a walk?'

'Why not?'

They strode down Wellington Road towards Lord's. Roger addressed the agenda immediately.

'You mentioned a furrier's you fancied. Could we go take a look at it? I've had a lot of expenses, what with Spain and moving house. The batteries need charging up. The V & A's excellent, but it still needs a bit of looking at. So something less demanding, eh?'

Peter stared hard straight at the myopic glasses. 'You gone off the V & A?'

'No, no, no. Not at all. I'm saying it needs a bit more researching, that's all. More especially, what we're going to do after we've had it. There'll be an awful hoot, and I fancy you'll be in the frame for it.'

Roger spoke deliberately. There was sense in what he said about the aftermath. Peter had not given this aspect a lot of thought, though he wasn't eager to admit it.

'The work's over-researched. It's a goer. Of course, I can envisage the furore, but I've learned to live with that all my life. My old pal and I decided late November, early December at the latest, was the optimum time. You don't sound like you see it that way.'

Roger blinked under Peter's hard glare but did not look away.

'You may have learned to live with your notoriety. I don't propose to try. Look, Peter, I told you my style. Unobtrusive, cautious, and only if I fancy it. OK? Well, sure, I do fancy it. But I want to be certain we can get offside and leave nothing to chance. Maybe we'll be able to attack in six weeks' time but, as I see it, we've a lot more work to do. We'll have to go up there again at night and find every possible route the cavalry could use to get to us. I'm not too struck with a rope escape. I think it's got to be via the Polish Church. And we've still got to investigate creating a diversion. Meanwhile, I need a few quid for Christmas. Don't you?'

Peter did. Recent evenings at Rousseau's had made serious inroads into his eight grand. The logic was not unappealing. So he said, 'Roger, you've only had this in your canister for a couple of months. I've been fucking around with it for years and I was hoping some young blood would accelerate the pace. Still, it might just be best to knock out a furrier's and have a look at each other. And yes, I've a couple in mind.'

'Good, that's settled, then. Where are we heading?'

'Oxford Street, near the Circus.'

'Let's walk, then. I've been taking very little exercise recently.'

Both aggressive long-striders, they reached D. H. Evans in thirty minutes. They hardly spoke, wary of each other, but leaving emotions to one side. It didn't matter that they found each other's personalities unattractive. Success was the name of the game.

'I've been here a couple of years back on the hurry-up,' said Peter. 'This scaffolding wasn't there then. It should help a great deal. I crashed directly into the fur department off the canopy at the back of the building. Got twelve full-length mink coats, pricey ones too – six, seven grand apiece. It was a nice touch. I knocked them out for a grand a lump.'

'What do you propose to do this time?'

'Much the same, only this time go through a window down that passage, whilst it's in darkness. Then we'll cross the floor to the fur department. We will of course climb up the scaffolding that's *in situ*.'

'How long will it take?'

'Let me explain. The trip from, say, that window there . . .' He indicated a leaded window in the gloom of the passage. 'It causes no problems. We won't encounter an alarm till we reach the fur department. If we're careful, the sonic won't pick us up till we crash the glass showcase.'

Roger was still mystified. He hadn't been in this area of work. It showed.

'And once we've bashed the showcases and start to load up, we're on borrowed time.'

'What about the security people in D & H?'

'Can't get to us quickly. Great fire doors have to be opened. What's more, they have to come from the basement.'

A glimmer of enthusiasm crossed the angular jawline.

'How many coats can we take?'

'I figure six sacks with six coats each. Thirty coats maximum. Now, be warned. A sack full of six full-length coats is very heavy. Two together take some dragging.'

'How long from when we set the alarm off to when we come out?'

'If we work quickly we can do it in three or four minutes. We'd be very unlucky if the law got to us by then.'

'Let's go round the block.'

Leisurely – and alas conspicuously – they trod the perimeter of the great store. Peter pointed out the whereabouts of the fur department on the north-east back corner of the building, and showed Roger where or how he had previously attacked. Roger nodded sagaciously but, maybe, anxiously. Was he thinking that this fifty-two-year-old associate was as mad as they come? Youngsters would have seconds about this work.

Something Herman Hesse had alluded to was Peter's talisman. 'Some old men, mainly intellectuals, are neither young nor old. When they want to be young, they are young, when they want to be old, they are old.' Anyway, Peter was (owing to his excesses) most times skint. He had to be young, there were no other options. At a time of life when most people were slowing down, he was still in top gear and secretly, as Roger suspected, he liked it. Even as he strode through the store the adrenalin was pumping, his mouth was dry, his bowels rumbling. There are few constipated cat burglars.

Roger broke what had become a long silence.

'If we've got six sacks out in the passage, where do we take them?'

'We're in alpaca coats, we look like workmen. So we drag them down this short stretch of passage as if leaving rubbish for the refuse men. Then we'll turn right down Oxford Street and round the corner to the Bank of Scotland, where we'll have the transport parked.'

'What if someone sees us?'

'Hundreds of people will see us. We're only cleaners from the store, dumping the rubbish.'

'Sounds chancy to me.'

Peter tried to keep his cool. What did this cunt want? Someone to put fifteen, twenty grand in his pocket? Nothing's easy, everything's chancy.

'Listen, pal, I've been at this game thirty years. I don't take stupid risks, only calculated ones. This isn't high up on that scale. Please be told.'

'Sorry. You obviously know. I've not grafted the West End.'

'Let's find a pub and have a brandy. There's not a lot more we can do tonight. Let's meet tomorrow and look at the set-up inside the store.'

The proposed retreat to an inn put Roger in good spirits.

'Where shall we go?'

'There's a pub in Davies Street.'

Settled in the pub, which should have been refurbished twenty years previously, the brandy diluted the apathy. They even chatted amiably. Peter could see that, beneath his arrogance, Roger was only a boy. So let's find out how good the boy is, he thought. We'll leave the V & A till he's had a trial. See how he is under fire.

'If we purchase the goods, can you sell them?'

'Good question, Roger. Yes, I can, but if we sell them in bulk we'll get murdered. I've got a girlfriend who can knock them out three or four a week for the right money. How much do you need for Christmas, anyhow?'

'Two grand.'

'No problem.'

'Two more large brandies, please.'

They caught the tube together at Oxford Circus, parting as Roger changed lines at Baker Street. Peter was left to stare at the reflection of his grey-haired, bulky figure in the darkened carriage window. A sadness came over him and, just for a moment, he was tempted to wallow in self-pity. He chose instead to sit up erect, squaring the image of his head, arrogance replacing his previous posture. The speeding image knew only too well that he was simply getting his just deserts for the conduct of a lifetime. You can't be in the business of creating sadness and expect to find happiness.

Next day they were united over tea and scones in the store restaurant.

'I've been up and had a look. I assume it's the line of cabinets on your right?'

Peter nodded.

'But what about the foxes and raccoons? Wouldn't it be better to have a mixed bag?'

Roger was learning fast, asking the right questions.

'If we weren't on such a short time-scale, of course it would be better. As it is, though, minks are by far the most reliable sellers. More important, they're in two cabinets in a line. The most difficult thing is to get the minks into the sacks quickly. The fur by its nature and sheen slips, and unless one man holds the mouth of the sack wide open they can be a bastard to load up. It's a question of dexterity.

We're fortunate here because the garments will come off their hangers without delay. Sometimes you encounter security hangers.'

Roger took the lecture like a student, anxious to do well.

'I've counted the full-length coats in the cabinet. There are over forty. Any preferences by way of colour?'

'Yes, definitely. We take the black Glammas first, then the wild minks, last of all the colours – blues, off-whites, canaries. I don't think it'll be a problem. The maximum we can carry is three sacks apiece – thirty to forty garments.'

'Let's wander over to the window you think we'll come through.'

They crossed the floor of the store, circumventing the main stairs and fire doors, which would be shut at night, and going by the probable route that would be followed during the attack. The window Peter wanted to come through was in a ladies' changing room. The sales staff must have thought that the two men lurking there were voyeurs. Finally it was empty of female strippers and Roger shot inside, checked the windows, and returned almost immediately.

'No problem with that. Knock one of the leaded panes out and open sesame. When do you fancy popping it?'

Roger was hotted up.

'Saturday night, if the store's empty. From time to time they work late. If that's the case, Sunday night. No one ever works Sunday.'

'What tools do we need?'

'A cane, half a dozen GPO sacks and a glim. I'll arrange the sacks. I'll plant them Friday night, behind the railings of the medical centre in the passage. Big odds against anyone touching them. So we'll pop it this Saturday. No point in hanging around.'

In practice, it was not to be as simple as that.

For two weekends running the store was permanently lit up and presumably occupied. Hanging about endlessly frayed the nerves and what had started as a simple screwer became less and less attractive to both of them. On the other side of the coin, they'd both come to rely on the work for their Christmas money.

No situation in thieving is worse than having to go to work. Whenever possible, options have to be kept open but now, with Christmas drawing near, the work was becoming a must. It hung like a millstone round their necks.

A third weekend passed. About to attack on the Sunday night, Roger was sure a window shopper was onto them. Certainly the lone male was hanging about, as they were, for an inordinate length of time. He kept looking in their direction with what seemed like more than a passing interest. They left for home, nothing accomplished.

Two weeks before Christmas, it was a now-or-never situation and they arrived at the store about eight. Lingering till nine again chafed the nerve-endings. All kinds of ghosts were manifesting themselves, and both Roger and he were on the brink of pissing off again when suddenly Peter, in anger or fear, slipped on his gloves and shinned up the first stage of the scaffolding to the canopy.

'Pass the sacks up. Is the cane in the sack?'

Peter's precipitate action galvanised Roger. He passed up the sack containing the cane, then the other five, before monkeying himself up to join Peter. In the gloom of the side passage, shrouded by scaffolding, confidence came seeping back. Cautiously, silently, they made their way along to the window chosen as their point of entry. They found that, even from the canopy, a small ladder was needed to reach the window and its broad ledge. Conveniently some prat had left one out on the canopy. Perhaps it was the window cleaners.

The noise of Oxford Street traffic drowned everything, and cracking the pane next to the handle went sweetly. Or did it? The handle wouldn't budge. Temper got the better of Peter and he called to Roger to bring him an offcut of scaffolding board.

'We'll smash our way through. The fucking windows are locked.'

Roger now showed the first true sign of his mettle and, as quietly as possible, pushed in a section of leaded panes to make a gap they could get through. Peter, clumsy as ever, cut himself doing so. But they were in.

A swift glance up and down the passage assured them nobody had heard anything. They moved discreetly across the floor, using hanging garments as cover, and approached the fur department.

'Right. Here we go.'

As Peter stepped into the fur department he heard a click. They were on borrowed time now, for certain.

CRASH! The first cabinet glass succumbed to a violent blow from the cane. Roger had a sack open, its mouth gaping hungrily. In went the black Glammas – five, ten, twenty. Three bags full.

CRASH! The second cabinet. Into the sacks went the wild and coloured minks. Two more sacks.

'Enough,' gasped Peter. 'You drag two, I'll handle three.'

Peter's strength had not deserted him in the autumn of his life. Back across the store they went, the lone alarm bell droning out its danger signal, and into the changing room, where they heaved the sacks out of the holed window and onto the canopy.

'Listen, Roger. I'm going down. Drop the sacks as I signal.'

In the passage, all was well.

'NOW!'

And down they came, one, two, three, four, five. All down.

'COME!'

Roger was beside him. They took a second to compose themselves, and went on with the plan.

Slowly and with a look of authority, they dragged the sacks out into the lights of Oxford Street. No one gave them a second glance. Along the shop fronts, past the window gazers, and around the corner to the Bank of Scotland. The station wagon seemed miles away. In fact it was parked eight or nine vehicles up the street, and at last they were there. As casually as possible they loaded the spoils.

Still no sighters. Jump in, start up, and gently pull away . . .

Job done.

Sweat lashed Peter. He caught a glimpse of his fiery red face in the driving mirror. His stomach churned. He wound down the window and, circling into Marylebone Lane, retched out of it.

'Getting too old,' he gasped. 'Either I spew or shit myself.'

Roger, barely perspiring, was grinning.

'You look pretty good to me. It went as sweet as a nut. Piece of the proverbial cake.'

'Piece of cake? You prat. Listen, son, it was only that because I've had thirty years' experience. I've had to learn the hard way. See that furrier's there?'

He indicated an elegant corner premises next to John Bell & Croyden.

'That's the House of Worth. Twenty-five years ago I fucked up that piece of cake.'

Roger was surprised by the savagery in Peter's voice. It was to him quite irrational in view of their successful night's work.

'And . . . ?'

'They used to be in Grosvenor Street. I was about your age at the time. The only difference was, I was tackling it on my own. Same system as tonight basically, challenging the alarm response-time. I got into the flats at Carlos Place and Grosvenor Street, up the fire escape and over the roofs of the Japanese Embassy and the Ladies Residential Club and into the Worth building. Down I go to the showroom and crash straight into the fur cupboard. I load up four sacks and lug them all the way back over the roofs to Carlos Place.'

He paused, thinking back.

'My outside man that night was a little younger than I am now, a Chelsea face who got dizzy on a first-floor sill. Anyway, he was supposed to be at the foot of the fire escape. I can tell you I'd taken quite some time getting all four sacks over there, so now I look down and I see someone. OK, I shout. OK, he responds. So I drop the sacks one after another and down the fire escape I go. When I get to the bottom I find my accomplice was, in fact, the caretaker of the flats. He's had the presence of mind to wave me on. Now he's disappeared with my furs into the flats, locked the door and rung the law. The arsehole that night hadn't played his part and, if I'd not had another out, I'd have lost my liberty. Still, I do recall cleaning out Worth's some time later.'

They were speeding up Gloucester Place by now, towards NW1.

'So nothing's a piece of cake. You're only as good as your plan, but you still need luck. It's taken me thirty years' trial and error to perfect the little stroke we pulled tonight. Would you be surprised if I told you the V & A isn't that much more difficult?'

Roger remained silent, probably thinking, 'Let the old cunt ramble on, if it makes him feel better. He needs me at his age a damn sight more than I need him. He should remember that. The V & A's another kettle of fish and has to be thought about.'

They backed into the garage in Circus Road and unloaded the booty. There were twenty-nine mink coats in all, not as many as Peter had hoped for, but a sufficiency. They checked through them, then Roger had his first shock. Peter put three of the coats to one side.

'What are you doing with those?'

'For friends of the firm. People who made the whole thing possible, who I owe my current liberty to. And of course, a few quid for the old man when he comes home. Don't be a cheapskate, Roger.'

Roger took the medicine.

'So in reality, we have thirteen each to knock out, right? I'm going to take five black Glammas with me. They're not as expensive as your last lot. These are ticketed at four and a half grand each. What do you think we should get for them?'

'Coming up to Christmas, I'd say a bargain-basement figure of seven and a half hundred apiece. But as I told you, they'll go at three or four a week if we want top money of say a grand a lump. I assume, though, you're going to knock those five out now.'

'Yes, I've got a pal who'll have them. Let's split.'

Peter shut and locked the slaughter.

'On you go, Roger. I'll walk home. Shall we meet say midday Wednesday, at the back door?'

'Will do. Ta-ta.'

Roger roared off in the station wagon. Peter was physically exhausted yet walked home to Sutherland Avenue elated, on a high. He stopped at a late-night Paki and rewarded himself with a score's worth of filth. It would help pass what was sure to be a restless night. He'd get in touch with Diana tomorrow, no need to hurry now. The Christmas money was assured.

Normally he was restless after a touch, but that morning he didn't wake until nine. Odd, very odd indeed. After collecting his papers he belled Diana. She was fine and would come to the club for lunch.

By the time he returned to his flat, the postman had visited. There was a tell-tale envelope from north London, and an elegant envelope addressed in a firm hand that he didn't recognise. The former was a note from Taters, enclosing a VO. The second disgorged a short note from Irene. Did Peter know where she could get her racquet strung? She'd still like to see him . . .

He binned it.

17

A Lady Fence

Diana, tall, chic in her mink coat, sauntered into the club at 1.30. All eyes followed her progress across the room.

'Hello, darling. How's it with the still-life mob?' she rasped in her attractive yet vulgar tones. She too had but little respect for the tennis club clique. 'Get me a large Teacher's. Got the lunch menu?'

She settled with her whisky and Mrs McGee's hotpot, fur draped over the cubicle, the gold thrashing against her throat, three-carat square-cut sparkling on her finger.

'So. Got anything for me?'

'Yes. I've a few coats. Usual black G's and wild.'

'Christ, you've left it a bit late. Everyone's cash is spoken for. How many coats have you got?'

Peter mentally deducted the freebies. 'Twenty-one.'

'Good-quality gear?'

'Best. Four-and-a-half-lump touches.'

Diana went silent, her fingers tapping. She was scheming.

'You'll need a few quid for Christmas, no doubt. I can let you have three grand in the morning. So stay out of that Greek ponce's spieler.'

Diana was, after all, a former lover turned surrogate foster mother. She knew his weaknesses.

'What do you want for them?' she asked softly.

'I fancy you'll get a grand a lump for them. I'll settle for eight hundred apiece from you.'

The hotpot was being twiddled with. Diana was calculating again.

'The price is right. Take a bit of time, so I don't want you driving me mad for readies. That OK?'

Peter nodded.

'Get me another Teacher's, then. Only a dash of water.'

Walking Diana back to the car park, he slipped the garage key to her.

'They're in the usual pitch. There's a sack tied up at the back. Leave it. Prezzies for loyal troops.'

'I didn't know you had any loyal troops. Drop round in the morning and I'll give you readies. Take care, darling.'

With a flash of her long legs, she was into her chariot and off. Peter wove his way back to the club.

Four enthusiasts were knocking up in the bitter cold on the hard courts, their hands blue. He shuddered and walked quickly back to the bar and the comforting warmth of brandy.

Maggie, the local cop, was at the bar, sweat-drenched after a hard squash session. Her companion, a pretty girl, had the look of a cop too. Pity.

'Hello, Maggie.'

'Peter. Who was the gorgeous lady you were lunching?'

Were they ever off duty? He swerved.

'You on Bell's, Maggie? Large Bell's, please. And for you, pretty lady?'

'Bell's for me too. I'm Ann. I work with Margaret.'

Peter's eyes dropped to the nipples nubbing the sweat-stained singlet. I'd like to fuck you, he was thinking. I'd like to fuck you in your uniform. Seeming to read his thoughts, Maggie butted in.

'You keep your eyes off Ann. Her young man's a DI on the Crime Squad. But me, I've always been a fan of yours.'

Peter grinned at her. Casual as the banter was, everything she said had to be carefully sifted. Maggie knew about him – how much, he wasn't sure, but she was the enemy.

Lady cops, give them their due, can drink. A very wet half-hour passed before the ladies departed to their locker room. Peter's eyes, ever attentive, fastened on their taut blue knickers as they ascended the stairs.

'How much do I owe you, Helen?' He had been running an after-noon account.

'Twenty-six pounds. God, that seems a lot, Peter. But then you only drink large ones.'

As he settled down recently to read the *Evening Standard*, an article caught the thief's eye. Casino owner John Aspinall was objecting to other casinos' gaming licences. It brought the thief back to his golden years.

They were the 'Human Fly' years, when his excesses on the roofs prompted the same evening paper to give the jewel thief this nick-name. Peter could not steal money fast enough to get to the chemmy tables of Aspinall's host of imitators, many from the underworld, which was then slowly but surely percolating into deb land. Aspinall himself was, as ever, keen to keep his games exclusive; he didn't want wide-boys. But games Peter attended threw up society types like Peter Rachman, Ruby Lloyd of the Maisonette Club, and Sir James Scott-Douglas, the racing driver. Scott-Douglas must have weighed twenty stone, and Paddy Kennedy, of the Star Tavern, would amuse his guests by telling them, 'Peter's training Jamie to be a cat burglar.'

The master thief, Jimmy Hunt, found time to look down from his exalted throne and downgrade Peter.

'He talks too much. He wants the glory and the readies.'

Perhaps, for Jim, the thief's unforgivable crime was to steal the limelight. Silent or garrulous, all villains need notoriety. At that particular time Peter had plenty to talk about, but others must have found his self-advertising galling.

At this time Paddy Kennedy was doing his best to throw the handsome Irish thief at Bobo Sigrist, heiress to an American dynasty. But Bobo found Peter gauche. She was trifling instead with Kevin McClory, a film-maker later to produce *Thunderball*, Irish too, who once in his cups threatened to chastise Peter if he continued to pay court to Bobo. In due course, he married and divorced Bobo: she was much too nice for the prat. Peter, anyway, was more at home with hostesses at the Astor and Churchill's.

Paddy's 'little shop' in Belgrave Mews was refuge to a cross-section of the aristocracy, thespians, and senior coppers, who mingled comfortably with the civilised upper echelons of the criminal classes. Admittance to the primitive upstairs sanctum was dependent on one's standing in one's chosen calling. Some achieved it by an accident of birth, some on account of their wit, a number by virtue of their seniority at the local nick. Finally, but not least, there were the 'chaps'. It was a bake for, among others, Eddie Chapman, Jimmy Hunt, and George Dawson and his beautiful wife Olga. Patsy Murphy smoothed membership for Peter. Paddy adored the shy George Chatham. Billy Hill held court there, and the Twins were sometimes his guests. Christine Keeler prattled there. The Aspinall team were often in evidence – Silent John Burke, Ian Maxwell-Scott, Johnny Bingham. One of the team was not as reliable as the 'gambler' thought. He pulled Peter aside one afternoon.

'John's having a chemmy party this week. You could do worse than have a look at it.'

For a moment Peter thought it was an obscure invitation to the game in the third-floor flat in Eaton Place, then the penny dropped.

It was an incitement to plunder. *Noblesse oblige* lured Peter to burgle the Aspinall fellow.

John Aspinall's costly legal objections to his competitors' gaming licences brings a wry smile to the author's face. After all, he was in the van of those pressing in the late fifties for legalised gambling. He jumped the gun frequently with his private chemmy parties, which at that time had become all the rage with the smart set. He was one of the heralds of the decadence of the swinging sixties.

His imitators were jealous of his success, many trying unsuccessfully to ingratiate themselves with him. But Aspinall was a shade too wide to rub shoulders with gangsters, well aware what tigers it was safe to stroke. Even in possession of privileged information, Peter was to discover that it was not such a simple gems theft.

Aspinall's flat backed onto the bijou mews, West Eaton Place, which, at that time, comprised only two private residences. He drove down one day to reconnoitre and found a helpful rooftop parapet running from the mews to abut Aspinall's place. From the roof of the mews houses he could climb onto the parapet and, with stealth, edge his way directly to the balcony window of Aspinall's.

As he reversed out of the mews, satisfied with the possibilities, the thief's exit was blocked by an incoming Rolls. Common sense dictated that the Rolls should reverse, but common sense is not so common and a Mexican stand-off resulted. The driver, small in stature, was in the mood to duel, and the thief had to shake him physically to persuade him to give way. If looks were lethal, the dwarf could have killed. A day or so later, the thief saw him in the *Evening Standard*: Roman Polanski. The angry dwarf was living in the bijou mews. He was a very talented man, an unattractive human being with a temper not in tandem with his size and a yen for child-flesh in later years, and one can only suppose he would have been even angrier if he'd known the Jaguar driver was to use his roof to access Aspinall's home.

Crossing the parapet on the night of the chemmy party was a delicate task for two reasons. First, it was only eighteen inches wide and forty feet up. Second, the people in the basement flat were having alfresco drinks. Should they have looked up in the dusk he would have been discernible and the game would have been up. Banco. However, he negotiated the parapet without mishap and found Aspinall's balcony window open. Why not? It was a warm night, and who would anticipate a trespasser from there?

It was the master bedroom, and the mistress had thoughtfully left her jewels on the dresser. Relishing his good fortune, he retraced his steps. A casual yet skilful cat burglary had been expedited.

Later that same night the thief was drinking in Kennedy's upstairs bar when a breathless Ian Maxwell-Scott arrived with news of the missing tom. Would Paddy pass the word around that John had a thousand available for its return? Was it the thief's imagination, or did Ian stare at him a little too long?

Peter chose to ignore the offer, feeling he could get more. And he did. The eventual buyer was an unusual one, Patsy Murphy, a chemmy party proprietor himself, who wanted to get into Aspinall's good books by giving him a present of the gems. But the word was Patsy had a knock-back from Aspinall, who knew that if you lie down with dogs you will get fleas. (He seems to have mellowed since those days. Hardly a month passes but he is seen frolicking with lions and tigers at his private zoo. It's nice to know that, even if he has no respect for friends in general, he makes an exception of wild beasts.)

A couple of years later another 'friend' alerted the thief to the possibilities of Aspinall's hoard of silver, pre-war florins and half-crowns, kept in his cellar in Kent. But the silver's bulk and attendant transport problems were unattractive.

'No,' he said. 'This time let sleeping tigers lie.'

18

Home Is the Sailor, Home from the Sea

CHRISTMAS 1983 was a difficult time for the thief. He was alienated from his family and his casual relationships – the only kind he had – quickly exposed their fragility. Even though in funds, loneliness and self-pity intruded. He'd never encouraged lasting friendships and his one or two intimate acquaintances had gone cold in view of his recent irrational behaviour.

On the run-up to the holiday, he made an excursion up to see Taters at the Ville. It was the one place where he was probably welcome, but even here the relentless questions about the V & A and Roger depressed him. There was no sheen-stockinged Tracy this time to distract him as he left. She'd gone off to an aunt in the Cotswolds (why do so many tarts shelter in the Cotswolds?). So he was on his own with his sins, which even the Messiah's birthday couldn't assuage. It was a bloody time.

The Sunday after Christmas found him aimlessly wandering around St James's. But, like the enemy, he was never off duty and he chanced on Pickering Place, a Georgian annexe and courtyard next to Overton's, a tourist gem. It was deserted today. Berry Bros & Rudd, having sated Christmas cheer, scowled behind their black façade in the corner. An architect's premises had invaded a Georgian house in the courtyard, where there was also one private residence. Then it caught his eye: a modest brass plate in a recessed corner, announcing How of Edinburgh.

He looked the premises up and down. The first-floor windows were grilled, while the ground made do with external bars. He peered between them. Silver objects glinted in the gloom. He'd found a silversmith's.

There's a small, inexplicable mystery about the way the prowler recognises a target. Gazing at the shop in the silence of the time-warped courtyard, he felt the old excitement beginning to percolate. Not unlike the effect of an attractive harlot outside the Hilton on a horny punter. It was a 'must'.

A friendly pipe gave him the idea of inspecting the upper grilled window. He shinned up, laboriously – he was not the cat of yesteryear – and a breathless glimpse inside confirmed it was a worthy target. A plethora of glinting showcases had come into his view.

He was barely back on *terra firma* when his isolation was interrupted.

'How quaint this is!' It was the easy drawl of a fox-coated woman from the Americas. She was looking shrewdly at the tracksuited, and only just grounded, cat. 'Do you know how old it might be?'

'The courtyard is early Georgian.' It was a guess.

'You out jogging? You're out of breath.'

'Yes, something like that,' Peter mumbled. He was taken off guard by the American's directness. She looked at his eyes. Attracted maybe by the handsome façade, yet her intellect told her she'd stumbled on something odd. She turned and shimmied from the courtyard.

A further look showed him a possible back entry to How's roof from parallel Crown Passage, to which an empty building site allowed access. Peter was cheered. Finding a bit of work was compensation for his loneliness. He returned to the flat on a high.

A note under the flat door greeted him: 'Will call at 10 a.m. tomorrow. Roger.'

It added another point to Roger's credit: resourcefulness. He knew where Peter lived and he'd got past the front door, God knows how. Peter was not sure whether he was pleased or not, but Roger certainly did his homework. The imponderables deflated a now-tired Peter.

A smiling, bouncy Roger was at his door at 9.50.

'You're early.'

Letting him in, Peter was tempted to ask how Roger knew where he lived, but thought better of it.

'I can get up when I have to,' grinned Roger. 'How are the coats going?'

'Six more sold. I've two grand here for you.'

Expressionless, Roger took the money. 'Only six sold? Would you mind if I pulled my corner out? I can do them myself.'

'Please yourself,' said Peter. 'You have four garments to come, right? And a half-share in another. I'll let you have three hundred and fifty quid for the half-share.'

Roger seemed almost pleased.

'That sounds OK. Give me a breakdown of how it went.'

'Five you took originally. If I give you three-fifty and four coats, that keeps us ship-shape.'

'Can I pick up the four now?'

Peter nodded. 'I'll take your car and fetch them. Meet me at the back of the club in fifteen minutes.'

When he returned from the slaughter, Roger was on the pavement in Delaware Road.

'The coats are in the boot,' Peter told him, getting out. 'By the way, I've found a bit of work in St James's.'

Roger was gunning the engine. He bellowed through the window, above the revs, 'OK. Let's look at St James's at the weekend.'

And he pulled noisily away. For the life of him, Peter couldn't rid himself of the idea that he was being hijacked. Roger was so incisive, and Peter was feeling his age . . .

Later, eating at the club, he caught Lena, the club caterer, staring intently over his shoulder.

'Peter, has that old boy come to see you?'

Peter turned. Taters stood in the doorway, blinking, forlorn, soaked by a drizzle that threatened to turn to sleet. The old man was adjusting his eyes to the dimly lit clubhouse.

'I'm right, aren't I?' asked Lena. 'He's the old fellow who used to come to see you in the autumn.'

Peter nodded and raised his arm.

'George! Over here.'

Startled, Taters focused in the direction of the familiar voice. He gave a shy smile.

'There you are! Funny old light in here. I couldn't see you.'

'It could have something to do with your minces. George, you remember Lena McGee? She has the catering franchise here.'

George narrowed his eyes, then blinked in his owlish fashion.

'Yes, I do recall her.' And he acknowledged Lena with a nod. 'All right?'

He shook out his shabby mac. You'd have to have been psychic to recognise in him the great man of yesteryear. He'd reached an age when he didn't care – perhaps he'd never cared.

'Want something to eat?' asked Peter. 'It's Lena's rest-hour, but if we ask her nicely . . .'

'Yes. That'd be nice.'

'George can have a plate of my *boeuf bourgignon*. It's lovely today.' Lena seemed to want to spoil the old man, sensing it was a special day. She went off to the kitchen.

'I thought you weren't out until Thursday. I was coming to pick you up. Why now?'

George shuffled into a pew.

'Got the dates wrong. They woke me up this morning and aimed me out. I didn't complain.'

He grinned. Everything was nice today. It was sure to change . . .

Lena emerged from the kitchen carrying a massive platter.

'Thanks. That's nice,' said Taters, getting straight down to it. He'd always had a lion's appetite.

As he was chewing away, he confided, 'I've been over to the Borough to see my probation officer. I came to your place after, then I came here. That Lena does a nice bit of grub.'

Peter was fumbling in the pouch of his tennis bag. 'You staying at Goldhawk? I've got the keys here.'

Peter was unsure about the continued goodwill of Taters's landlord.

'Yes, I'm going back there. Simmonds is all right. My decanters safe?'

Decanters? Decanters? Then Peter remembered.

'Yes, they're safe. Amy didn't want them.'

Or any begging letters! What a harridan.

Peter said, 'I'd like to buy them off you. How does a couple of hundred strike you?'

He knew he'd have to sub George anyhow. And Taters would probably merely knock the decanters out. They were fine pieces, better with Peter. Slightly to his surprise, Taters agreed, in his usual terms.

'Yes,' he said. 'That'd be nice.'

'Another plate, George?' It was Lena, returning to top up the old lag.

'Yes, that'd be . . .'

'And bring him the apple pie and cream. Do you want coffee?'

'That'd be nice.'

George wanted the lot. Later, he suddenly veered back to business.

'What about the V & A? A night like this, you'd have a chance.'

Peter felt his hands dampen with sweat. This old soldier was four hours out of jail, and he wasn't joking. He was even madder than Peter.

'The V & A's in hand. Roger's shaping up well. I'll tell you on the way to Goldhawk. Finish your grub.'

Taters wiped his mouth on the napkin and rose. Lena watched the pair of them from the service booth, puzzled. She liked to pigeon-hole her customers, but George she couldn't fathom. Peter said, 'Put it on my account, Lena. We're off.'

Shrugging into his tatty mac, Taters showed off his manners.

'That was a very nice meal, Mrs McGee. I could eat it all again.'

The sleet was blinding as they drove down Ladbroke Grove. Replete, and warmed by the car heater, Taters had dozed off, but when Peter had to brake to avoid a bus pulling out, he suddenly awoke.

'Yes, this is the perfect night for the V & A. Not as good as the night of the fog I had in '48, when I nicked the swords.'

'Swords? I thought you only took one – Wellington's.'

'No, I had three. The Duke's was a jewelled one. What a fuss there was over that. The nation nearly went into mourning!'

Childish pride had crept into George's voice. 'I was lucky, mind you. I was up a ladder in the quadrangle and one of the minders comes out. He walked right past me, right past the ladder. Never looked up.'

Taters was getting animated now. 'And then, when I was sheltering in the phone box in Exhibition Road, a law car shot by. Never saw me.' He paused, reflecting. 'Didn't do a lot of good, though.'

'Why was that, George?'

'You know. I did them spieling.'

'Oh, so Murphy's story's true? That you called a bet in a Baron's Court spieler by prising a stone from the hilt.'

Taters was gazing out at the sleet. He looked distracted, forlorn, wizened.

'Can't be sure, can't be sure,' he said after a long silence. 'It was so long ago. Wish I had them now. Cor, what they wouldn't sell for today.'

Turning into Holland Park Avenue, they sat in a line of stationary traffic. George nodded off again. The self-imposed bleakness of his life was awful to Peter. Neither of them had much other than memories, and perhaps the dream of a repeat performance. It was surely an exercise in vanity to contemplate burglarising the V & A. An act of revenge to compensate for their stupidity in the past. Yet if they failed they would only compound it and spend their last good years behind bars. The thought repelled the thief. In their empty lives they were still totally irresponsible. It was an incredible coincidence that they were in the same lifetime, let alone in the same car.

The light was on in Taters's room as they pulled up outside the house. Peter shook the old man gently to rouse him, pointing to the glow from the window.

'We here already? Oh good, Eva's got my letter. I wrote to her, asked if she could tidy up my room for my . . . my homecoming, you know.'

'Eva?'

'Eva's the black girl with the room next to mine. I always leave a key with her.'

Climbing the shabby stairs, Peter grew even more depressed. After a lifetime of pillage, they had settled into pissholes like this. Taters turned the handle and opened the door to a surprise: a spotless room, a glowing electric fire, clean sheets on the bed, a pristine sink, and a quantity of groceries on the draining board. Taters couldn't have been more shocked if he'd found himself transported inside the Jewel House itself. He sat down in the only chair to take it in. The handiwork of the black angel had silenced them both.

Peter was the first to speak. 'I hardly recognise the place, it's almost comfortable. Go find Eva, thank her. I'd like to give her a few quid.'

Taters shook his head. 'She's at work. She's a good girl, she don't want your few quid. She's religious, she enjoys helping.'

'Well, I book her as an angel and even they have to eat. A few quid won't go amiss. I'm going to give you the two hundred for the decanters now – put a tenner in an envelope for her, show you appreciate her.'

Taters didn't enthuse over this idea. It would be a tenner less to play up. Eva's kindness was taken for granted. Meanwhile he suddenly started to complain.

'Only *two* hundred? I thought it was two for the decanters and another two hundred from you. I've exes. I've forty quid's worth of laundry to get out. I've food to buy . . .'

And so it went on, the fannies of a lifetime feeding his spieling habit. His infantile philosophy was that he'd have more chance with four hundred than with two. But Peter wasn't playing.

'I'll give you two hundred today and another two this day week. I'm your bank manager.' He handed over four fifty-pound notes.

'Try and look after it, George. Not for my sake, but yours. And for God's sake, get that bloody laundry out.'

Driving back to the club through the sleet turning to snow, he felt better. Taters was warm, dry, victualled, and had a few quid to play up. He'd probably lose it very quickly, but if he got a buzz from doing his money, how bad could that be?

They were short of a fourth for bridge and Peter, *faut de mieux*, was pressed to sit down. He'd been a prison bridge player and knew his limitations. The other three arseholes hadn't discovered them yet.

They were playing Acol. The opposition had part-game and, on the fourth deal, Peter held five hearts and thirteen points. He opened one heart. A pass on his left, and his partner bid one no-trump. A further pass, and Peter was left considering.

'No bid,' he said.

All hell broke loose. His partner – who owned porn shops – threw a fit.

'How can you pass after my one no-trump response?'

'Quite easily,' said Peter, knowing he was probably at fault, playing it low-key. 'I'm not sure what the bid implies and I'm on a minimum. So where do you think we were going?'

'Rubbish. My one no-trump shows a strong opening hand. Any fool knows that!'

Peter's temper frayed at the public humiliation. When they'd played out the hand, he rose.

'I think I'm out of my depth. Find someone to take my place.'

He took solace in a large Remy at the bar. Perhaps he'd play a few quid up at Rousseau's later. Then a thought struck him, and he went to the cubbyhole and dialled.

'Club here!' a chirpy voice answered.

'Ask Taters to come to the phone,' he said, modulating his voice to disguise it.

'Who is it, please? He's at the table. Could you ring back later?'

'Just say his bank manager called.'

'His *bank* manager? Is this a wind-up? Taters hasn't got a fucking bank manager.'

Peter replaced the receiver. Taters had quickly found his most comfortable escape route from reality. Peter did not feel cross.

Bed, he thought, was his safest place. Alone. With the evening paper.

19

Nearly a King: a Windsor Tale

H E ambled, not unpleasantly, through flurries of snow to the tube at Maida Vale, where he bought the *Standard*. Mrs Thatcher's words brayed from the front page: BRITAIN'S NEW IMAGE. Further down the page, another child was missing, and, in Paris, the Duchess of Windsor's health was giving cause for alarm.

Newspapers, like himself, were in the lament business, designed to reassure us of our good fortune. If it weren't for the circulation war, we'd miss all the tragedies of the world. We wouldn't know how lucky we are.

Mrs Simpson, the Yankee divorcee, stared at him from an inner page, teeth and jewels in place. She'd perfected the duchess role over the past fifty years. As Peter well knew, if you play a charade long enough, you come to believe it. Wallis believed it.

Probably Peter's bitching thoughts were for no better reason than that she was one who escaped his larceny, twenty-five years past.

Tanfield had announced in the *Daily Mail* that the 'royal' pair were house guests at the Earl of Dudley's home in Buckinghamshire. It was a rare weekend visit to England. Dudley may then have still been Viscount Ednam. He'd married an attractive South African actress, Maureen Swanson, and Great Westwood, his estate at King's Langley, was known to Peter.

The thief respected the Royal Family; they worked bloody hard. It would take a hardy Jacobite to find fault with the Queen – then, as now, a gracious lady (your servant, ma'am). He regarded David and Wallis, on the other hand, as a pair of parasites, antisocial butterflies. So he could regard them as legitimate targets. Digesting the Rothermere snippet, Peter laid his plans. He would have to be quick; it was already Saturday.

Seven on Sunday morning saw him turning left off the Aylesbury Road at Kings Langley, towards Sarratt. The midnight-blue 1.5 Jaguar purred in the fresh morning air. A solitary Wolf Cub was at the corner, thumbing for an unlikely lift. Quick as a flash, Peter recognised good cover and the Cub got his lift. He was assembling early for a rally. He prattled on, as the innocent are wont to do.

A semi-private road led to Great Westwood, undulating and tree-shaded. Turning a corner carefully, a blind corner, he found a shooting party crossing the road in front of him. He slowed to a crawl. Instantly, he recognised David Windsor. Dudley was there too, with the toad Onassis in tow, and someone who looked suspiciously like Gary Cooper. To a man they waved in appreciation of Peter's courtesy. He took it as an omen. He would secure the prize.

Round the next bend, the gates of Great Westwood appeared. Half a mile on, he dropped the grateful Cub and parked up in Buck's Hill. The recce would begin with a closer view of the target so, boldly, he skirted the trees till he was almost at the house. A pair of U-boat captain's rubber-cased Zeiss binoculars made the inspection thorough.

The first necessity was to locate a ladder. Small chance of locating one at the house, with the probable police presence. The Windsors, though perhaps an embarrassment to the royals on site, would still warrant courtesy cops. There was a swimming pool at the corner of what looked like the banqueting room. A small, dully lit annexe protruded from beyond it, and this seemed to be the protection's lair. Such a problem is not always insurmountable, for this reason. Monitoring the police presence in order to effect entry, things can become considerably easier for the cat burglar or the ladder thief once he's inside. His main intent is to avoid meeting his victims in their bedrooms and boudoirs, and gatherings basking in the knowledge of external police protection are at times indecently sure nothing is going to happen.

Back at Buck's Hill he searched for a ladder. At the top of the hill, builders were in evidence, and Peter had a choice of three ladders from the site. Everything was falling into place. His pulse raced.

Back at Belgrave Mews North, where he was living at the time, he knew a decision had to be made. Did he need an outside man? Probably, but where would he find one at such short notice? It would have to be a solo sortie.

By six o'clock that Sunday evening he'd picked up all the necessary transport impedimenta from a slaughter in Pont Street – tax disc, plates, and a forged cover-note that would survive a tug from uniformed traffic police. Then he collected one of his two ringers, a 2.4 Jaguar garaged at World's End.

At seven o'clock he was at Buck's Hill, the Jag hidden in a field. It was dark, with the odd star visible as the clouds parted. Guests in the country generally come down to dinner at around 8.30, in any event not later than nine o'clock. That was the optimum time to make entry, so the thief had an hour to observe the house and the activities around it.

He was moving through the trees towards the house when dancing torchbeams ahead announced the police presence. There were two of them, making a circuit of the house. Their mumbled conversation reassured him as he waited patiently in the twilight. There were no alerts or alarums. Half an hour later, on the dot, they circled again, and this time Peter tailed them at a distance. Finally they returned to their lair in the annexe, where a light went on. The coppers were visible inside, making a cup of tea.

The ground-floor drapes of the banqueting room chinked and he looked through. The sight of an elegantly laid table, awaiting the privileged, steeled him. He stepped back and looked up at the main house. The first-floor windows were blinded but illuminated as the privileged prepared themselves for the feast. He stepped back into the shadows and waited silently for the minders to make their third half-hour pilgrimage. Lights on the first floor were being extinguished. Red alert.

The still night's silence was broken by the sound of a sash window being raised. It was almost above his head and immediately beside a drainpipe. He froze in expectation, hardly breathing. Could he get lucky? Would the sash be left open?

Confirming that the minders were tea'd up in their post, he returned in time to see the upstairs room light go out and the sash window six inches up. The conspiratorial Staveley pipe led up to the omission. He was on form.

The Staveley did its job and he raised the sash wide enough to admit him. He was in a guest bedroom, with a dull light coming from the en suite bathroom. He moved inside with caution and suddenly the silence was broken. Shouts, bushes rustling in the garden below. He looked down. Torchlight danced, a dog barked. Christ, was it on him? He went back through the window as the noise receded, lowered the sash, and swarmed down the pipe. Whatever was happening was on the other side of the annexe.

As he sprinted to the cover of the orchard, lights going on and angry voices told him the coup was over. No point dwelling, it was on top, but how? He could only speculate that someone *else* had been there in the night, and had been tumbled just as Peter was about to strike. Incredible!

Back at the car and breathing hard, he pulled the Jaguar into the road and puddled away with the sidelights on. He had been dealt a cruel card. Fuck it, he thought, as he gradually increased his speed towards London. Chances like this come once in a lifetime.

So the Duchess retained her gems and, on her death, they were auctioned, the proceeds going to the most worthy of the French research laboratories, the Pasteur Institute. In death, Wallis Windsor had achieved a status that often eludes the latter-day 'Royals'.

The *Daily Mail* had the bright idea of buying some of the Windsor jewellery to raffle to their snob readers. The thief didn't buy a ticket.

20

Chelsea Blossoms

DIANA found him at the club as the first signs of spring appeared – watery sunshine and a clear sky. He was hitting up on Court Nine with Larry Adler. It was a godsend that Diana arrived. Larry was spraying the ball everywhere except where Peter was feeding from.

'Hello, mate.' The gruff, sensuous voice seemed at odds with the mink-coated elegance of his visitor. 'Is that the harmonica player? I thought he died years ago.'

If Larry heard, he ignored it, raising his hand in a friendly wave.

'I've got your final draw from the pussy. Can we have a quick drink in the clubhouse? I want a favour.'

Settled with a large Teacher's, Diana confided, 'You know my son-in-law, Clyde? He's just come home. I wondered if you could put him in a bit of work. He's a live-wire, bright too, but skint. You met him once at Hendon when we were together.'

Peter remembered Clyde, a bright boy, as Diana said, maybe a bit too bright to be told.

'Yes. Aggressive, sharp kid. Tell you what, Taters has been home a couple of months. He's been driving me mad about the museum. I'm not up for it at the moment, but he did mention Bourne & Hollingsworth were winding down. Get Clyde to have a look at it and report back here to me. There's a fur department.'

'He's in Spain at the moment with Anne. I'll tell him when he comes home. Check those readies. There's three grand there – keeps us right.'

Diana downed the Teacher's in one gulp, pecked his cheek, and made her exit. Peter didn't need to check the bundle. Diana's arithmetic was always flawless.

'Who is that lovely lady? She reminds me of Veronica Lake.' It was Larry, creeping up with his showbiz memories. 'I was in cabaret with her in Vegas.'

Peter said, 'An ex-lady of mine. She wants me to find her son-in-law employment.'

'I'll keep it in mind,' called Larry, wandering off.

Reassuring, thought Peter, with a sigh.

The bar was filling up with, among others, parched BBC musicians. A very tall, willowy redhead stood out amid the motley crew, talking to an elderly man whom Peter vaguely knew. He was fairly certain Red was his daughter, even before the old fellow confirmed it.

'Peter, come and meet my daughter Chelsea.'

Peter shook the most beautiful, slender, pale hand. Superb green eyes, legs to the sky. A lovely image.

'Hello, Chelsea. I haven't see you here before. Do you play tennis? I know your dad from the bar.'

Her eye casually but shrewdly assessed the ageing tennis bum.

'Well, I have been here before and, yes, I do play a little. I was tennis captain at school. How do you keep your tan in winter? Under the lamp?'

Admire and deride: the emancipated female. He looked carefully at her. She was bloody lovely, but there was something about her he couldn't account for.

'No lamp,' he said. 'Born in the north-east of Ireland. The Armada perished on my coastline – lots of tall, dark-skinned men. Spanish heritage.'

Dad was amused. He decided to mark his offspring's card.

'Don't let this old man near you, Chelsea. He's always with attractive women. I just saw one leave him. And he's a scallywag too.' He added, for Peter's benefit, 'Chelsea's mother's Irish, you know. From Kerry.'

'That accounts for her good looks. Irish women have a special beauty. Kerry women are something else.'

The compliment was noted but now a younger voice beckoned from another part of the bar and Chelsea let the exchange die. Peter bought a round and went back to observe the scene. Vain old prat he was, chatting up the unobtainable. Or so he thought.

They met again minutes later in the car park. Chelsea was getting into her car and, gallantly, he opened the door.

'Will you give me a hit next week?' she asked sweetly. He nodded. Then, having remanded him in custody, she drove off, acknowledging his acceptance with a smile.

Roger was in the car park, lurking in his Triumph. A soft toot of the horn made his presence known.

'You're incredible,' he remarked enviously. 'She's beautiful. Not a day over thirty and *you* get hold of her. Have you had her back at your garret yet?'

Peter blushed but Roger was enjoying himself.

'Now if it was a penthouse in Mayfair and you were a millionaire, OK. But to be in that pisshole with a skint burglar, old enough to be her father . . . I'm impressed.'

'Roger, she only wants a hit. She'd smile at a toad if there was mileage in it for her. I don't kid myself, not about women anyhow. Cards, maybe. So, what's got you here? And in the car park. You throwing caution to the winds?'

He felt it was his turn to mock. But Roger turned serious, the steel-framed eyes glinting.

'Time to work again. You mentioned St James's.'

'Taters is out and about again. The V & A's on the agenda.'

'Not V & A time,' said Roger firmly. 'The autumn will come round. Wasn't there something you mentioned in Bond Street?'

Roger's memory served him well. The French leather and fur goods shop, Zilli's, was on the cards.

'Yes, there's a couple of bits and pieces. But Taters wants to go to the V & A. He's impatient.'

'Let him be. I'm not ready for it.' Roger's snarl was unattractive.

They left the chariots in the club car park and took the tube. Roger strode ahead as they crossed Oxford Circus but then, in Hanover Street, he pulled up abruptly. Something had caught his eye. He indicated an ornamental brass plate. 'Wittie & Co. Furriers.' Peter gave an indulgent nod.

'Yes, I done them in Bruton Street years ago. Never forget it. Ruptured a radiator going through the wall, flooded the stairwell.'

'What about here? It can go again.'

Roger wanted to take control.

'Not really. Taters had a hundred grand's worth here in '78. I got a tug over it at West End Central, but Taters was on his own – in his sixties, mind you.'

He smiled to himself at the youth's arrogance. He wasn't sure Taters *had* been on his own, but chances were he was. Anyhow, Roger was suitably impressed.

'In his *sixties*?'

'Age never occurred to Taters. He can't afford to be old. I may have told you before what Herman Hesse said on the subject. "Some men when they want to be young, are young . . ."'

Peter couldn't stop himself thinking about Chelsea. Roger did not tipple this, for his mind was elsewhere. Standing on the pavement at Sotheby's they perused the target opposite. The same supercilious staff

at Zilli's stared aimlessly at the passers-by. Did they ever lure a customer in? The fur-lined coats and jackets were priced at between four
to ten thousand pounds; it was hard to imagine who lived in their
catchment area.

Roger was full of enthusiasm.

'I'm going in to chat them up, maybe try on a coat.'

He went off to implement his unilateral decision. Good for you,
son, Peter mused. You won't get much civility from that mob. He
moved away down the street, where a fluttering flag on a pole caught
his attention. 'The Antique Porcelain Company.' Now why had he
never noticed that before? He prided himself on his knowledge of all
the high-value premises in Mayfair, but this one had eluded him.

In the first-floor showroom window a couple of Sèvres vases
preened themselves, a pair of Chelsea birds dancing attendance. Difficult to dispose of, but nonetheless another target, and approachable
by the same roof as Zilli's.

'What a load of arseholes!' Roger's voice boomed behind him. 'Like
vultures round you. God help the hoister that strays in there, he'd
not have a chance. But we will. There's a couple of hundred coats in
the rear semi-basement area. I've pinpointed the pricey ones, though
God knows they're all pricey.'

The enthusiasm in Roger's voice pleased Peter. He was up for it,
but could they sell them? He'd make enquiries.

'How many garments do you think we can take?' Roger was counting his chickens again.

'Enough, lad. Selling them *is* the problem, it's specialist gear.'

A quick recce round the back in Bloomfield Place established that
a ladder would be needed to get onto a first-floor roof. They found
one they might use in nearby Bourdon Street. There was no point
putting the attack off once a purchaser had been found.

A phone call to Brighton the same evening confirmed they were
desirable and would sell.

'No point in fucking about. Everything's in our favour,' Peter told
his assistant. 'Shall we oblige it at the weekend? Saturdays the law
are kept busy in Soho on vice.'

'Sounds good. Saturday, then. I'll ring you Friday evening.'

On Friday night Peter was back at the bridge table when Roger
phoned.

'Hello, mate. Can't be this weekend, I've got to go away for a few
days. Put it on hold, or do a Taters. 'Bye.'

Brief and explicit. Do a Taters? On his own? Strange face, this Roger, changeable. Was he trustworthy? Peter tried to concentrate on his cards, bidding three no-trumps as he dismissed the chameleon from his mind.

As two weeks passed, and not a dickey-bird from the elusive Roger, fate introduced a new player – but not before Taters turned up, sheepish and uncomfortable.

'I'm out on police bail. I hid in Bourne & Hollingsworth the other night. Then I was coming out under the canopy when a cozzer in Oxford Street saw me. I had to go back in and put back a sackful of furs. They searched the place. Dogs found me. I put the fanny up I went to sleep upstairs on the empty floor – I think they believed it.'

He shuffled nervously, awaiting Peter's reaction.

'Police bail? Looks like they do believe you. I think you wanted me to have a pop at it – was I wrong?' Peter eyed Taters kindly. He'd properly fucked up Bourne & Hollingsworth, but how can you get angry with such a trier?

'Yeah, I know. But I needed a few quid to do the V & A. I'm sorry, Bourne's will have to be left for a while now but it's still a goer. They don't know anything was touched because I put the smothers back . . .'

He tailed off, staring into space. Then woke up again.

'Can you let me have a few quid? I want to give my brief a few bob.'

Bollocks time, play-up time. Taters hadn't paid a solicitor since Mafeking Night. Peter delivered himself of the usual homily and Taters pretended to listen. In his head, he was already sitting down in Rousseau's.

The new player arrived quite deliberately. In the gloom of the club verandah, Peter was startled by a low voice.

'Hello, boss.'

It was Clyde, Diana's son-in-law. Compact, alert in his expensive leather jacket, his hair in a short back and sides, Clyde's smartness was marred only by the cigarette hanging from his lips.

'Hello, Clyde. Good you're home. Fancy a drink?'

Even the darkness could not conceal the grimace. Clyde was no respecter of the bourgeoisie or their haunts.

'Not with this shower of prats.'

Peter found he understood. 'Got time for a rabbit, anyway?'

Clyde nodded. They paced up and down the empty verandah. The diminutive tennis captain slid by with a hostile glance. Clyde waited till he'd passed into the clubhouse.

'You mentioned to Di I should look at Bourne & Hollingsworth. I've been up there. I think there's a move. The fur department has bundles of stock.'

Clyde waited for Peter's response. He had respect for the ageing thief, unusual in a young live-wire. Peter told him in detail about Taters's recent visit and its outcome. Clyde was visibly disappointed.

'Don't worry,' Peter told him. 'B & H can wait. It's still a goer, but something else has cropped up. I've a premises in Bond Street that's worth tackling. Fancy it?'

Clyde fancied it. A meet was arranged for early Saturday night.

'Oh, Clyde, one thing. I was to go on it with another guy, but he's disappeared. Should he turn up in the meantime, we'll have to parley again. But the business is mine, I have a free hand.'

Clyde grasped the inference and they shook hands, agreeing to meet. Peter was barely back in the club when the captain pounced.

'I wish you wouldn't bring people like that here. If you have business to do, make it outside the club grounds, please.'

A flash of anger swept over Peter, but he took in a deep breath.

'People like what?'

'People like *him*. You can see what he is. This is a members' club, not the stock exchange for funny business.'

Had the prat been listening? Peter said, 'The next time my friend comes, I'll let you tell him yourself.'

The implied threat found its target and the captain retreated. The club had been full of amateur, self-appointed sleuths, ever since he'd first arrived in company with John McVicar and Blond George. Fortunately these busybodies didn't know their arse from their elbow, but nonetheless it irked.

When they met again, Clyde had inspected Zilli's.

'Bream gear. What a rip-off the prices are. I wonder who buys it.' But, even though a boy, Clyde could read the portents. 'Can we sell it?'

Peter nodded. He left the meeting full of pleasant anticipation. Roger had still not surfaced. There was a ladder secured and housed in the basement area behind the shop, and the attack was on for Sunday.

As the two of them crept into the cul-de-sac in Bloomfield Place, Peter whispered, 'Stand on the corner and watch the passage to Bond Street. I'm going to put the ladder up to that flat roof with the barbed-wire rail. As soon as I'm up, join me and we'll draw the ladder up behind us. OK?'

It was done. Safe on the roof, the pair moved with care. The old tenement block overlooked the balconied front doors, giving a clear view. Eventually they got out of spotter range and haunched, assessing the position. Clyde was very cool.

The ladder was to be a godsend, for there was a central well in the Zilli building. Lowering the ladder to rest on a massive fuel tank – it just reached – they descended to a pair of sash windows that gave directly onto Zilli's stairs and from there to the showroom. The glass was barless and negotiable and either the windows or the carpeted stairs were certain to activate an alarm. Vulnerable windows are one thing. Making good your escape is another.

'Let's go back up and find a sweet out,' Clyde whispered. Peter approved. His philosophy had always been to begin by finding an out. The roof they were on, in varied undulations, reached Bruton Street with the Irish House at one end and Marie Claire at the other. More fortunately, it formed a T-junction with Bruton Mews. Here a top-floor office drew Clyde's attention.

'If we're able to get into these offices, we might find a key to the street door in the mews. If we did, it would be a bream out.'

It turned out to be an architect's studio. Inside, a key was found that gave them easy access to the roofs that led to, amongst others, Partridge's, London Fine Arts, Wildenstein's and the recently found Antique Porcelain Company. More important, it offered a sweet escape route to Bruton Place.

(This key is a mystery solved for Superintendent Stephenson, late of West End Central, should he ever read this.)

Clyde's find made the pillage very much simpler. He was all Diana had promised, a natural. Bad habits were to forestall his further progress, but on that night Clyde was to prove a very bright, game thief.

As they opened the sash window, the alarm bell trilled in Bond Street. The internal showroom bell was barely audible as they worked swiftly, loading fourteen sacks with around eighty garments by the time the solitary copper arrived in Bond Street to spray his torchlight through the door and into the visible parts of the showroom. Beyond his beam, it was time to leave.

Bruton Mews was dead. Peter stationed himself with the sacks at a sharp right-angled corner leading to Bruton Street while Clyde located the station wagon. Seconds later they had gone.

'You've cracked it again, Mr Scott. What a bream number that was!'

Dripping with the sweat of fear and effort, Peter accepted Clyde's accolade.

'Not bad at all,' he said. 'Give the lads at West End Central something to ponder on. It'll keep them pondering when we return with our key. We can work that roof again.'

At the garage in Circus Road it was lucky-dip time. They decided to divide the garments.

'Diana will do mine,' said Clyde. 'Have you an out?'

'I'd say these are unique. I may have to take my time. I've a pal on the coast that will place them, but I dare say we'll be slaughtered at these prices.'

Peter felt monkeys apiece was a good ecret – rather a bitter pill for the unknowledgeable, for this was less than one-tenth of the mark-up. But swag's only worth what you can get for it and Peter had no illusions about this parcel: it was distinctive goods.

Peter eventually took thirteen thou for his share, allotting one coat to Ferdie to clear the balance of his debt. Temporarily, at least, he was in funds again.

He'd also made a lot of people happy. One of the more rewarding by-products of the thief's forays into Mayfair was knowing that a number of folk with limited income were going to wear and enjoy garments or jewellery normally within the reach only of the mega-rich. Admittedly this was not his main motive – he was no Robin Hood – but it was a side-effect that accorded him some satisfaction. Even the smallest plus points had to be credited.

Finally, Zilli's were sensibly insured, it seems. They hooted for half a million. Peter and Clyde had probably done them a favour, too.

21

Fucked-up by the Snow Queen

THE buzzer rasped. Having no entry-phone, he went to the bedroom, raised the sash window, and hollered down.

'Hello?'

A head peered out from the shelter of the Victorian porch. Taters. Peter pitched the keys down, but Taters made a hash of gathering them, and had to retrieve them from the basement area below. When he let himself in, he was wringing his paw.

'Don't half sting, those keys,' he complained.

Peter was more impressed by the fact that five flights of stairs had not winded the seventy-year-old.

'Tea? Fancy a toasted banana sandwich?'

'Yes, that would be nice.'

Peter busied himself with his long-favourite snack.

'Well, what's been happening, George?'

'I should be asking you that.'

'Me? Why?'

Taters gave a knowing smile.

'You did Zilli's last week. Why didn't you put me in it?'

The question rattled Peter. Why *had* he not put Taters in it? He decided to be frank.

'Diana asked me to put her son-in-law in a bit of work. He researched it with me. I couldn't very well put another body in. He wouldn't have understood our arrangement.'

Peter had done his best, but it felt a little lame. Taters looked abashed.

'You know you can have a few quid if you need it,' Peter appeased.

The old man's kindly brown eyes blinked behind his shoddy glasses. But they gave a glint of defiance which told Peter this was not going to wash. Taters was not here for a hand-out; he'd come to tackle Zeus.

'I don't want no few quid. I'm going to have a pop at the V & A with or without you. This week. It's now or never and if you don't fancy it, I'll go it alone.'

Irritation swamped Peter. He knew the old boy meant it.

'Exactly when do you want to pop it?' Peter controlled and modulated his voice. He wanted to betray no anxiety, assert authority.

'Tomorrow night. Just you and me.'

'I should ask Roger. He's done some work on it, but he's on the missing list. You know it would mean you'd have to go up on the roof?'

'Don't worry about me.' Taters was staring into space as he spoke. 'I'll do what I have to.'

Peter knew that. But would it be irresponsible to let him? Almost as if reading Peter's thoughts, Taters went on.

'It's my decision, and I've made it.'

It looked as if the die was finally cast. Peter had no contact point for Roger, and only the chance of his getting in touch might revise the plans. Meanwhile, Taters continued, 'Better give me a couple of hundred quid. There's a few things I must get. We need a heavy-duty diamond-cutter and we'll have to tape the glass. It's a large pane, take a lot of tape. You got the bolt-cutters?'

Peter nodded as, mechanically, he pulled out four fifty-pound notes.

'I'll bring the pump-jack over. Just in case the bars don't cut, we can bend 'em.'

Peter smiled. 'George, those dorsal-fin windows don't open, so we can't be sure the bars aren't silver steel until we're inside. We'd be bringing the pump-jack anyway.'

Taters grinned sheepishly. 'I only said it because you needed pushing.'

Needed pushing. You're right there, old son. He certainly did, and Taters had pushed. Peter spent the next twenty-four hours hoping that oddball Roger would get in touch and perhaps allow him to abort. He didn't.

Late Thursday afternoon in the bitter cold he pushed the Stilsons into a mail bag, along with the pump-jack. Taking the strain, he judged them to weigh all of one hundred pounds. And they were to be humped up the scaffolding, a formidable task for a youngster and madness at fifty. Still, it had to be done.

He pulled the station wagon out of the lock-up and waited. He got a glimpse of Taters in the rear-view mirror, struggling to shut the garage door, and the folly of the raid struck home. He was dying to call it off, but vanity didn't allow. He closed his eyes.

'Looks like a bit of snow,' said Taters matter-of-factly as he joined him at last. 'Could come in our favour.'

In anger and fear, Peter snapped back, 'Could come in our favour? How? If it snows when we're up there it'll be a fuck-up. You remember that night when it happened in Chester Square? *I* was on the roof . . .'

Chastened, Taters stayed silent as they drove across the Park. They were in Exhibition Road when he found his voice.

'Foxwell, wasn't it? Lady Zena Foxwell. You nearly fell into the mews.'

In spite of his annoyance, Peter smiled, recalling the touch. The house was a stone's throw from the Gerald Road nick. But a lesson he'd learned that night was stark: give roofs a miss in black frosts and *never* have them on your mind when it's snowing.

As they planted the tools under a tree in the courtyard of the Polish Church, a flurry of light snowflakes brushed his face. The church was in darkness, the odd annexe light being no match for the pitch dark, as he humped the sack to the scaffolding. It felt more like two hundredweight now.

Taters ran up to take his share of the strain. 'Bit of weight here,' he whispered.

Peter's nerves were as taut as violin strings.

'Never mind. Follow me. We're going up now.'

The snow flurries had vanished but, in the autumn of his physical prime, the sack sapped his reserves. Reaching the first stage, he stopped to rest and glanced down at the old man climbing gingerly up behind him. He suddenly felt less the martyr. It was all too bloody ludicrous. He started to giggle.

Reaching the roof at last and depositing his burden, he extended an arm to help Taters up the final stage.

'You OK?'

'Sure. It's you that carried the sack.'

He grinned broadly. The banter calmed Peter, locking out the reality. Edging round the gutter of the roof, partly concealed by the coping stone, they arrived at where they must cross. Peter paused to give the security box down below a last look before slipping the scaffolding board across to the V & A roof. All had been quiet below. Only the gods knew they were on the roof, and the gods didn't tell tales. A renewed scattering of snowflakes blew into his face.

'I'm going over first. Push the tool-sack after me and keep a weather-eye below.'

Sweating freely, Peter was glad of the freezing air. Just before setting off, he looked at Taters. His sallow face was as dry as a bone. He didn't weigh eight stone, and he was humping fourteen!

When Peter was safely over, Taters slid the sacks and tools across, then followed with a nimbleness that must have amazed the watching gods. Together the two thieves haunched down and pulled the board across. Artificial light illuminated their kingdom. Above, the sky was hostile. If the gods were angry at this trespass, the men paid scant attention. They pressed on carefully to the flat roof of the target, with its dorsal fins catching the lights and gleaming like upraised swords. Peter spoke first.

'I've got to wedge the door leading to the roof. Watch points while I do it.'

Taters's face, as the fleeting cloud broke and a moonbeam hit it, was iron-set. He nodded encouragement. Then the gods announced their presence as great flakes of snow began to bombard the huddled pair. Taters grunted, 'It's only a shower. It'll pass.'

Peter couldn't share this optimism. In his heart he knew they were about to be thwarted. They sheltered behind the dorsal fin, which quickly became invisible as a fine, dry snow took hold. Over the next five minutes it became apparent that Peter's scepticism had been justified. The ageing intruders had best be off home.

'I knew once I mentioned Chester Square I'd bock it,' Peter hissed through clenched teeth. 'We'll be lucky to get back and not do ourselves a mischief.'

'Going to leave the tools here?' wheezed the now very old man, hopefully. Snow and extreme cold were gaining purchase on his ancient bones.

'Not fucking likely. If they find them, they'll tipple. They come back with us. You lead. Here.'

Peter pulled out a length of rope, lassoed his waist and passed the end to Taters. 'Link this round your waist. If we go, we go together.'

Getting back was bloody. The snowflakes danced around them in glee, like malicious ice fairies, aware of their plight. Every foothold had to be tested and the scaffolding board, as he slid it back across, looked instantly treacherous under the volume of pounding snow. Peter thought about his namesake, thwarted at the pole by Amundsen, dying on the journey home . . .

But they made it to the roof of the Polish Church and, looking back, Peter was delighted to see their tracks obliterated by the blizzard. They would live to fight another day.

Almost blinded as he descended the scaffolding, Peter chanced dropping the sack of tools to the ground. No one would see or hear them in this. He dropped the last few feet to stand beside them. Then, sheltering behind the churchyard's double doors, which gave on to Knightsbridge, he said, 'The Snow Queen fucked us.'

Taters wasn't familiar with the reference and didn't care, his teeth chattered so. Peter got the car, picked up Taters and the tools, and began a slow, cumbersome journey to Goldhawk Road. It was here that Taters had the last word.

'If the snow clears up, we can have a pop at it on Saturday night.'

He kidded not.

Peter churned away through the rapidly deepening snow. He was wondering what Freud, or some other shrink, would make of the pair of them. Accumulative ages one hundred and twenty, on the roof of the V & A in a blizzard. Attacking the Jewel House. Infantile? Irrational immaturity? They both might plead diminished responsibility, for all he knew, for the old guidelines on criminal insanity – the McNaughten Rules – still held good then. Well, was their responsibility diminished, or were they just a pair of old prats?

The snow was clogging the wheels of the station wagon. He'd better concentrate on his driving.

22

A Gypsy Curse

THE mausoleum took on a less hostile air, now that Peter was in funds for Christmas and the New Year. Everyone and everything became almost tolerable. A familiar skull appeared in the form of John McVicar. They were polite antagonists on the odd occasion on the court, enjoying their games rather as they each enjoyed the other's notoriety. With reservations.

'Peter, hello. Fancy a hit?'

John kept his best dialogue for the media. Since distancing himself from his youthful criminal carnage, he had not only taken a degree in prison but was making a fist as an investigative journalist in matters pertaining to the criminal ilk. He had survived the long years of confinement well, and was mentally and physically alert. The attitude scars were more persistent, the private trauma of a life at war with society being difficult to disguise. So the convict image lingered in John's intense dark eyes and air of heavy bonhomie. Peter wasn't sure if John *wanted* to disguise it. It was the calling-card of his new game.

'Love one. But be considerate to your elders,' Peter said. 'I don't want to have to run round the court like a blue-arsed fly.'

Peter was perhaps the more skilful player, but he didn't enjoy John's fleetness of foot. Run he had to, for there were no easy points with McVicar. The match ended in an honourable set each, with both egos still in place. In the changing room, the tennis player gave way to the journalist.

'Peter, I've been doing a series of profiles in the *New Statesman* about the more . . .' John searched for the inoffensive adjective. '. . . ebullient characters among the criminal classes.'

Pausing for a reaction, he allowed himself a rare smile. Peter was, if nothing else, one of the Element's characters. It was a difficult cross to bear at times.

'I read that Sophia Loren's gone to the slammer in Italy for tax evasion. It gave me the idea of profiling you. Lightly disguised, of course. What do you think?'

The idea appealed to Peter's vanity. Over a very wet lunch, with inhibitions gradually washed away in a good Sancerre, McVicar wrung the arrogant malefactor out. Peter told him he was going through an odd time, recklessly plundering and yet coming through unscathed. He was beginning to believe his good fortune was down to the deity's assistance.

John was an astute observer of criminal vanity, but he began to suspect Peter's line was a send-up. However, in his cups, he was unable to make one of his precise judgements. Indeed, leaving aside its ambiguity, it was a wonder the interview ever got into print. In due course it did appear in the *New Statesman*, McVicar being gracious in print to the lightly disguised 'Billy'. The law-abiding were predictably incensed at the portrayal of the thief's attitudes. But did he steal jewels and a pair of knickers from Sophia Loren? Well, he didn't wear the knickers at a party or flash his member inside them. As for the jewels . . .

In 1960 the press put the thief on to Sophia Loren and her father-figure husband, Carlo Ponti, telling readers how Miss Loren expected to be given a suite of gems after each completed film, and making them privy to all except the exact whereabouts of her residence. The clues were not hard to follow, however: the house was called the Norwegian Barn and it was near Elstree. This was the start of the thief's pilgrimage to what would be billed as Britain's biggest gems theft. Over the years, a number of villains have claimed they did it. The reader will make his or her own judgement.

Elstree is a small enclave so there was unlikely to be a profusion of Norwegian Barns. Someone would know of its whereabouts, he thought.

The post office didn't, nor the postmen. That was strange: how were the letters delivered? He tried some aged locals but they'd never heard of it. Even when he dangerously coupled it with the star's name it didn't help.

Frustration set in. Had the press laid a red herring? And why? Prowling about in one of his 2.4 'ringer' Jaguars in the Elstree area with a bogus press card on the windscreen, he struck lucky at a petrol station in Elstree Road. A movie buff was in attendance and his eye caught the press card.

'You going to interview her?'

Peter saw there might be more to come. He nodded.

'She's lovely. I went up to the Edgwarebury Country Club at the weekend, hoping to catch a look at her.'

Edgwarebury Country Club? I wonder . . .

'Is that where the Norwegian Barn is?'

'Yes, it's in the grounds. Off to the right on the bend of Elstree Lane. Think she'll see you? They say she's very shy. Good luck, anyhow, mate.'

A private excitement developed instantly. He was on form. He'd found her – by luck, too. Could it last? Looking back thirty years later, Peter is disposed to believe that fate was pre-ordained. It certainly was for the thief – and the actress. Sophia wept, Peter laughed. But her tears had dried before Peter's were to start.

Peter was in Elstree the following night for a routine recce. Parked cars at the Edgwarebury Country Club afforded his Jaguar anonymity as he slipped on his turtles equipped with a torch. Twinkling lights through the trees led him to the target, a low-slung wooden chalet.

The windowed and doored gable-end met the narrow road. A pointed pitched roof formed the upper storey, beneath a recessed area that housed the door, with windows on either side. Sidling up to one of them, Peter found it carelessly curtained. He viewed a long passage leading to what looked like a sunken lounge. He skirted the chalet. It was lit up, but he saw no signs of life. Returning to his starting point, he took refuge beside a rectangular hedge grown to conceal the dustbins. Suddenly a door opened and a flood of light illuminated his lair. He froze. Footsteps approached and there, literally six feet away from him, was a female, joining him in the coop. She was po-faced as she dumped a clutch of Chianti bottles in one of the bins.

She was a tall, hook-nosed Neapolitan girl in black trews and sweater. Peter assumed she was the maid, and if she'd chosen to look to her left, the world's largest jewel theft would not have taken place. She didn't. She was lost in her own private world.

She started to retrace her steps, still oblivious to the intruder, and only then did he realise that this was *her*. The actress herself. Time – and the knife? – have since been kind to the great beauty. That night she looked for all the world like a big, handsome peasant girl. Not quite what later admirers would have expected.

Peter read his close shave as a portent. He'd found so often, after something like this, that the prize was secured. His loins tingled with sensuous excitement. Poor Sophia.

Peter was back the following night. Now Carlo Ponti had arrived – *just* arrived, judging from the luggage he could see dumped in the hall. His suspicions were confirmed as he saw the film-maker hug his young Neapolitan bride in the lounge beyond the hall. He looked around. A ground-floor window to the left of the door had been left open, as if to conspire with the thief in his punishment of the happy pair. Never one to ignore such good fortune, Peter at once effected a silent entry. He crept across the hall towards the stairs, in clear view of the embracing pair had they drawn apart. The stairs creaked, but how loud must they yelp to disturb a loving pair? He made it to the boudoir where, boldly switching on the light, the first thing to catch his eye was a massive padlock, its hasp secured to the top of a tallboy. It was the final clue, left by Sophia herself. No messy, protracted search was needed. This padlock said to him, loud and clear, here are my jewels.

He quickly covered the tallboy with sound-deadening blankets from the king-sized bed, ducked under them and, with consummate ease, bypassed the hasp and its absurd padlock by levering the top surface of the tallboy adrift. The gaping top drawer now revealed a huge black case. Peter took charge of it, and Madam lost her jewels.

An array of fur coats were left sleeping as Peter made his retreat, but not before he had slipped open a dresser and pocketed a pair of lady's black silk drawers. Back down the creaking stairs he went, covered by a new and vociferous Italian banter in the lounge. He'd had all the luck which daring demands – for the time being, anyway. A pal from Hoxton, waiting in the Jaguar, pulled away quietly as he slid into the passenger seat, sweat coursing down his brow in the summer evening. He caned the jewel case. It was crammed with boxes of all sizes, and he straightaway found a diamond suite, followed in quick order by an emerald suite, one in sapphire, one in ruby, a string of black pearls, a bunch of finger rings, earrings and bracelets. It was a pirate's ransom.

He was trembling. A frisson of pure fear swept through him. He'd cracked it, but what of the hoot, the consequences? He pushed a radio button. Appropriately for the occasion, the Haydn C-minor sonata filled the car. It made Peter feel like Zeus taking his throne on Mount Olympus.

Back in Pont Street, in a room used as a slaughter, they viewed the haul. It was not unlike the stock of a West End jeweller's. Then a cockney voice brought him down to earth.

'There'll be a right fucking scream about this. You're sure to be in the frame. Best get offside for a while.'

Peter's insatiable vanity longed to be in the frame. What was the point of being top man if it was his private secret?

The Hoxton stalwart's remark had been almost an understatement.

The theft was headlines in all the national papers, a tearful Sophia everywhere, as it transpired she had committed an even greater sin than relying on the padlocked tallboy. She was uninsured. The gems, she wept, represented her life's struggle, and she could not replace them.

Peter knew that she would recover and collect again, that this was but a temporary set-back in the life of a world-famous star, a strong, durable actress who would be more careful next time. Time was on her side.

Eventually she appeared on TV, looking dark, serious and very beautiful.

'The thief will have no luck,' she said. 'I am a gypsy. I have cursed him.'

Peter was watching uncomfortably. A private promise from the actress to the thief. It got to him.

Long summer days were passed around Roehampton swimming pool where knowing glances and nudges followed him, nods and winks from the upper echelons of the Element who used to gather there. They made a nonsense of any denials: they knew, and he knew that they knew. It was only a matter of time before it got to the ear of the enemy.

He admitted nothing, but happily carried the aura of the man who had done it. He made other mistakes too.

Foolishly, a day or two after the theft, he allowed Uncle Ben in Highgate to buy only the diamond gems. Ben had conveniently, but falsely, asserted that the coloured stones were the most desirable.

'You should hold on to them,' he advised. 'Till the dust settles.'

Peter had acted stupidly because even a novice thief knows never to split a parcel, because receivers invariably feel they have missed the best of it and bid cowardly. This is exactly what happened when he sold the residue: he got slaughtered. Thank you, Ben.

Compounding his stupidity, Peter bought a midnight-blue 150S Jaguar, at a time when one of the Yard's most astute officers was on his tail. Chief Inspector Norman Hoggins's pipe-smoking, along with his unfashionable moustache, made him a rarity on the élitist Flying Squad. It didn't prevent him becoming a Commander in later years.

Most pipe smokers seem to be honest, reliable types, and Norman was of this ilk. And now his team, which included Charlie Palmer, became his shadow. They didn't conceal their presence and the game became dangerous, not to mention nerve-racking. Friends' homes were turned over and Peter, for everyone's sake, was forced to go to ground. He consulted a friendly solicitor, Ellis Lincoln, who kindly, shrewdly and competently parleyed with the élitist police officers. Ellis advised Peter to present himself at Finchley police station to confront the pragmatic Norman and be interviewed. It was an anti-climax. The only question he had to answer, since he had removed himself from his house in Belgrave Mews North, was 'what is your current address?' A more zealous and less scrupulous officer than Hoggins – as certain as he of Peter's guilt – would have fitted him up. This wasn't Norman's style.

Peter was released, and the cat-and-mouse game continued. Peter's nerves were sorely tested. He fled to the South of France for the late summer, with Billy Hill arranging a room at the Martinez Hotel – quite a chummy gesture, as Billy had reason to suspect Peter's associate Taters of trying to blow the safe at the 21 Room Casino, in which Bill had an interest with Harry Meadows of Churchill's Club.

Peter booked the Jaguar on the Dover ferry and he and his Hoxton pal motored down. At that time the Exchange Control Act was in force and it was as well that Peter had observed it to the last permitted pound. Waiting his turn to board the ferry, he caught sight of three men in spotless white overalls embossed with the word *Jaguar* on the breast pockets. His curiosity was quickly satisfied when a well-turned-out, distinguished man approached the car.

'I am senior customs controller here, sir. I wonder if you'd mind pulling into that bay in front of you.'

He moved the car into the bay, which was fitted with an inspection pit. The Jaguar Squad then closed in.

'We'd like to give your car the once-over, if you don't mind.'

Peter complied with resignation. It would probably be a long wait, but he asked anyway.

'Will I be on this sailing?'

'Afraid not, Mr Craig Gulston. It'll take a little time to clear you. But all things being equal, you should be first on the next. They sail every two hours.'

Mr Craig Gulston? If the controller knew his name, it was a police ready-eye. Patience was the order of the day.

The Jaguar men's skill in dismantling the car had to be seen to be believed as they literally unscrewed it down to small pieces. Hoggins was hoping that Loren's jewels were on the move, unaware that they were long sold. The abortive search ended and the atmosphere became almost cordial.

'Mr Craig Gulston, we have our duty to do,' said the controller. 'I dare say you know the source of our instructions. However, one thing I can promise you, you won't be delayed on your return.'

He laughed and waved Peter away.

'Trying to encourage me to smuggle?' Peter asked, having the last quip.

He lost Sophia's jewels at the gaming tables that late summer, while his suntan took so well that all and sundry started calling him 'Monsieur Bronzage'. But meanwhile he couldn't relax, he couldn't fuck, for the shadow of the gypsy curse darkened his mind. Sophia had her pound of flesh.

The tenacious Hoggins was to have his too. With him an enquiry was never closed – not one of this magnitude.

23

Go to Jail Again

LATE in the summer of 1960, he returned from Cannes the skint victim of the gypsy's curse. Wrongly hoping that his absence had somewhat relegated him on the police's list of priorities, he was now forced back by his gaming excesses to work. We know he was a target thief; now it was time to pick a new target.

Helena Rubinstein's arrival had the customary mention in the glossies. Her cosmetics empire prospered in the market-place and she had a penthouse in Kensington Gore – half the top storey of the Victorian block had been sliced away to make a large roof patio leading through a sliding door to the master bedroom. The roof was readily accessible by courtesy of a fire escape, which, to be reached, required only scaling an outer door in Rutland Gardens. The thief had previously cased the roof, only to be thwarted by the first of many electronic eyes he was to encounter in his subsequent career. The concealed beam threw an electronic ray diagonally across the patio, some eight feet from the bedroom window. Madam, having got her jewels the hard way, was not about to surrender them to any common-or-garden prowler.

A parapet running round the roof had a ledge some three feet below. Peter figured that, moving crouchwise, he could circumvent the 'ray' and reach the bedroom window. Foolishly. Creeping along the parapet, he heard the fatal 'clink' as the alarm activated. Seconds passed before he was aware of the alarm bell shrilling at ground-floor level. It was on top.

He took off down the fire escape, four stairs at a time, vaulting the gate in time to conceal himself in the basement area of a private house before the enemy appeared with two odd lots and dogs. The Chelsea police always had a fast response-time and, unlike in Mayfair, with its dodgy alarm bells, one couldn't take liberties there.

He was not to learn his lesson. A week later in Marylebone, having a crack at a modest flat put up by a chauffeur pal, feeling uneasy as he could find no rear exit, his fears were compounded by his pal thundering on the front door.

'Get offside. The law are here!'

Out on the stairwell the pair were marooned as hostile voices rose from below. His companion's dexterity in opening a landing window adjacent to a sewage pipe gave them another chance but, descending the pipe, Peter's luck ran out at second-floor level. The pipe gave way.

Peter was hurled backwards into space. Foolishly, he put out his arm, hoping to break the fall; all he achieved was a broken thumb, a disjointed elbow, and a stunning blow as his head bounced off the concrete of the yard area behind the flats. He was pulled to his feet by his pal and they each took off in a different direction, every man for himself.

Peter hobbled to the southernmost end of the block where, confronted by a wall he couldn't climb, he was forced to double back through the block and out into the street. He walked straight into a burly and youthful police skipper, who marked him down as an easy target, put off his guard by the thief's dishevelment and patent injuries.

'Looks like you're nicked, Chummy,' he chuckled confidently.

Peter's resolve did not desert him. As soon as the words were uttered, he grasped the sergeant's tunic with his good right hand, all in one movement, and caught the bridge of his nose with a head-butt. The astonished skipper dropped like a sack of potatoes and Peter stepped over the prostrate (but not unduly damaged) figure. Luck now returned. The street was deserted except for the Q car and he legged it to Marylebone Road, where he hailed a taxi.

'Take me to Hounslow,' he croaked, ashen-faced and in agony. The adrenalin that had anaesthetised him had evaporated and the pain was sweeping in.

'It'll cost you, guv,' said the wily cabbie. He knew something was amiss. 'You OK?'

Peter nodded and the cabbie headed south.

Pain and despair were gutting him by the time they arrived. But it was Dr Tony's day off.

'I think I'd better drop you at a hospital, guv,' chirped the cabbie. Peter said OK, the pain overriding any further pretence. When he was dropped, the cabbie copped his four fivers with the words, 'Be lucky, pal.' He knew he'd been party to a minor drama.

It was one of the thief's most rewarding memories, benefiting from the skill of an orthopaedic surgeon at Hounslow General. Watched by a gaggle of eager students, the man pulled his exposed thumb-bone back into place and then delivered a none-too-kind rabbit punch to knock his forearm back into its socket. The surgeon too was pleased with his success, though he made light of it with his students, one of whom stitched Peter's wounds. They felt that Peter should be kept in overnight, but he discharged himself against advice and tubed it back to his friend Chelsea Ted's place in West Kensington. Belgrave Mews North would be off limits for the time being. After all, the felled skipper had had a good look at him.

Ted's wife Vera put him to bed in a back room. He languished there for ten days, the angel Vera ministering to his pain. Poor Vera. The following year, cancer was to ensure a premature trip for her on the celestial omnibus. They get impatient in heaven.

He recovered slowly, the fall having done more damage than was superficially seen. A blot on the horizon was that he was required to appear at Marlborough Street to answer a careless driving charge, a matter in the pipeline for some time. First, he returned to Belgrave Mews North where all seemed well: no one had been enquiring after him.

He went to Marlborough Street. Leaving, he was accosted by an old friend.

'Hello, Peter, remember me?'

Peter certainly did. It was the tenacious Norman Hoggins.

'You're needed for an ID parade at Paddington. A young skipper was bashed by someone leaving a break-in at Marylebone. He answered your description.'

There was a confidence in Hoggins's voice which frightened the thief. It looked like time up again. Ellis Lincoln, present for Peter at the parade, advised him to say nothing.

'It's police witnesses on the parade. I think you'll probably be picked out, though I must say Hoggins seems as straight as they come.'

He *was* picked out by Sergeant Cumberlidge (assistant commissioner in later years -- Peter's head-butt did not impede his career) but Ellis Lincoln's presence saved the thief from a belting in the cells, normally a mandatory feature expected by those who bash coppers. However, Hoggins's interest in the Norwegian Barn trespass guaranteed no bail and the notes went to the magistrate. He was remanded to the Old Bailey and was on his way down for twelve months, so he thought.

Judge Bernard Gillis presided, while the thief was represented by a non-tryer, Billy Rees Davies, QC and MP for the Isle of Thanet. Davies was a one-armed hero of the desert campaign, whose constant rudeness to the trial judge -- a Jew -- was to make the normally optimistic Peter fear the worst. But why should Rees Davies try for him? Peter was guilty. And, with a chief inspector from the Flying Squad appearing in a relatively trivial matter, Judge Gillis got the message. He did what was required of him. Peter copped a three-year term.

He wilted. He was demoralised. Trying to attribute it to his brief's rudeness, he knew in his heart that he was discounting the Loren sadness and the gypsy curse. Given that, the term was not unduly harsh, though strictly the offence before the court did not warrant it.

Wandsworth, changeless, depressing, swallowed him up for the next two years. For the first he sewed mailbags, then moved to outside works. He was finally rehabilitated on a G, H & K Wing scheme – an outside working party at Send Detention Centre in Surrey.

The G, H & K Wing scheme was a speciality of HMP Wandsworth, a rehabilitation programme for recidivists serving two-to-four-year sentences. Entry to the scheme was at the governor's discretion, after you had done a year in the main prison. It was the brainchild of Principal Officer Jenkins and included courses, classes, debates (on occasion with the Oxford and Cambridge Unions) and other activities of an improving nature – but the main perk was that you could be considered for six months on a hostel, working out and earning real (as opposed to prison) wages. Like any other radical or liberal idea to improve the convict's lot, it was abused and derided by the Prison Officers' Association.

Peter, naturally, applied for the hostel parole. At the board, he was asked a single question by Governor George Gale, MC.

'Is it true, Gulston, that you have communicated with a man called Billy Hill?'

There was no hostel for Scotty and his life, insidiously, continued to slip by. On his final release he was thirty-two. Already four and a half years of his life had been spent behind bars and he had little or nothing to show for it. Worse, he was doomed to follow the same self-destructive path, a prisoner to his passion and with no serious desire to escape. Reflecting thirty years later, the kindest thought he can muster is that his ruling passion was a drive beyond his control or ken. Perhaps he had a subconscious desire to punish himself, as a Freudian shrink would probably argue. Perhaps genetics had laid this in his path. Who knows?

An unpalatable comparison is with those sad, sick sex offenders – he'd seen so many of them – who go through life touching up little boys and girls, and then pay for these urges which they cannot comprehend in ostracism and castigation. How quick we are to use the adjective evil about our fellow humans who are less well in control of their latent passions than we are.

In the same way, the obscene passion of larceny hung round Peter's neck like a stone. In his more lucid moments, he might have struggled with it, but he could find no key to release its weight. He was trapped in vanity, loneliness, and Walter Mittyism.

Where does a passion start? Where does it end? Do we have any control over it? 'You have got to be careful what you want when you're young. You're sure to get it,' said Dorothy Parker.

The thief's great passion was first in evidence when he was a teenager. Peter Craig Gulston was a product of Belfast, but Ulster's Protestant morality had failed to strangle him, for he escaped into his own Walter Mitty existence. Looking back fifty years later, after a recent two-day visit to an old friend in Ireland, he believed he'd escaped the worse of two evils: bigotry. That is surely the most depressing dungeon.

His family origins were as yeoman farmers at Castle Cat, in the north-east of the unhappy province. As an only child (though he had an unrevealed stepsister), he had a loving childhood. No deprivation factor played a part in his degeneracy.

As far as recollection allows, he was always light-fingered – a euphemism with which the better-bred seek to dilute their progeny's blatant dishonesty. He didn't grasp the concept. To him, everything was mitigated by adventure and risk, the dry mouth, the sensuous arousal. Flirting with disgrace? What the hell is disgrace? He was a guest at the banquet that had been attended by Oscar Wilde; he was feasting with panthers. Peter had always felt a kinship with that other Irishman. Disgrace and ostracism had been a subconscious lure for them both, and both were to pay the price. Notoriety was preferable to obscurity and they courted it assiduously. Although Oscar was not an Aquarian, Peter was – and this is a profoundly Aquarian trait. If one's fate is truly in the stars.

Despite a Belfast public-school education, he was throughout his teens the wrong'un of police parlance. Earliest memories of stealing are associated with the need for money to gamble – pitch and toss and three-card brag, played in a garage in Ashley Gardens, where a small shop traded. Pens at school and florins from his father's untenanted trousers were early transgressions. It was shameful, and yet all part of the apprenticeship in the art of larceny. Stealing can be a profession. You serve your indentures and then, undetected, you gradually become more ambitious.

He was to burgle his first house at perhaps sixteen or seventeen.

This large, semi-detached Victorian property, also in Ashley Gardens, was the home in which Hessie McClurkin lived and (in the mid-1940s) died. If gossip was to be believed, she died in disgrace, with an affinity for American servicemen isolating her from her Presbyterian relations. The unforgiving Ulster factor again.

Hessie died alone; the house was shut up, locked and left unattended, a sepulchre. The 'lone couch of everlasting sleep'. It was something of a coincidence that Hessie's and Peter's morality should converge in the house in Ashley Gardens, almost as if fate put it there to accommodate their passions. Perhaps the die was cast there. Perhaps if Ashley Gardens had not existed, his life would have taken a different course. All this is speculation.

Hessie's garden became a play area to Peter. Surprisingly, the neighbours on either side of the decaying house did nothing to deter trespassers. Perhaps they were Presbyterian and feared guilt by association. Eventually, then, curiosity got the better of the boy as he peered into the antimacassared gloom. He found he wanted to see inside.

An extraordinary, narrow side door, rebated at an acute angle, would get the odd boot to loosen it as he passed. Eventually it gave, and a gap appeared. Peter approached and shouldered it aside.

Pungent, stale air assailed his nostrils as he entered a time-warp of dust and cobweb. The room, a lounge, had a table laid for a meal — it could have been a scene straight from Dickens's *Great Expectations*, the feast eternally laid for Miss Havisham's wedding, which would never take place. Only the rats were missing.

Everywhere valuables caught his greedy, excited eye. A couple of bottles of Scotch – at a premium in 1947 – stood unopened on a cabinet. He annexed them, along with a handbag containing a quantity of cash. When he left the room, closing the door behind him, he found sunshine penetrating into the blinded house. He decided to explore.

Hessie's bedroom drawers revealed masses of silken underwear and stockings. Handling them was erotic in the extreme, almost like molesting Hessie herself. The teenage thief was too young to understand the complexities of these sexual stimuli, later to become part and parcel of his calling. But the memory of that sensuous moment, that first sexual trespass, never left him. He pocketed a pair of the disgraced, deceased Hessie's knickers.

Over the next few months, he removed all portable valuables from the sepulchre. Hessie, he told himself, would have understood.

Life in Belfast's smug, middle-class, Protestant enclave revolved around church, school and sport. He took part in all these, but now he had discovered a new, sensuous (and lucrative) game: burglary. It became, like masturbation which he had also discovered, a thing he could not lay down. Creeping about at night casing prospective targets made ping-pong at the Youth Guild very small beer. All conscience was suppressed in passion. Isn't it always?

Further characters were drawn onto the stage, to enable him to act out his Mitty fantasies. A fish-and-chip shop opened locally and the owner, an ex-serviceman, recognised Peter as a live-wire who spent liberally in his shop.

'If you come across anything, mate, I'll buy it,' he told Peter one day. Peter had found his first fence.

The greedy squaddie – no different from most of humanity, disguise it as they will – became privy to Peter's sorties and began to order specific goods, as do the professional receivers of today: radios, gold and silver articles, damask tablecloths, bed linen, booze and tobacco. These were premium goods in post-war Ulster's austere age. Peter, in turn, was introduced to dog racing at Dunmore Park and he found he couldn't steal quickly enough to sate his appetite for indulgence. It was a miracle he went undetected for so long. Meanwhile the *Belfast Telegraph* aired the police's concern that a sophisticated burglar was operating in the Antrim Road. That was probably Peter. Privately, he felt an important person.

Do you ask, surely his mother or father must have suspected something? Dad was in his sixties, perhaps too old to see it, too uninterested in a son already a disappointment academically. But reflecting now, Mother probably did, but she didn't want to exhume the truth. Her eventual emigration to America in 1952, to join her daughter Peggy, leaving Peter to his fate, convinces him she did know.

The theft of a gun, a .45 Colt, from a home in Benmadigan Park, led to his downfall. The political implications of a gun were prodigious even then, and the squaddie wouldn't buy either it or the ammunition he'd got too.

'Get rid of it, Peter. It's trouble.'

He couldn't bring himself to. Squiring a young lady to the Troxy cinema, he carried it with him, tucked into his belted trousers. Rising to leave at the end of the film, it slipped out and clattered down a couple of aisle steps before he could retrieve it. Betty saw. Later, in a shed behind her home, kissing goodnight, his hand found her suspendered thigh. She was trembling, but not with passion. She was terrified in her anxiety to bid him goodnight.

His next act of macho folly was to produce the gun in a local milk bar. What was the point of having a gun if you couldn't flash it? But word got back, and he was quietly detained on a Saturday night on his way to the old boys' hop in the school gymnasium, Ken Smiley and His Jazzmen in attendance. Though not carrying the gun, he gave it up meekly when confronted by his father and the police officers.

Detained over the weekend in Chichester Barracks, he got through this hiatus in his thieving career, tearfully sticking to the tale that he'd bought the gun off a man in a betting office. The gun was not, in fact, traced back to Benmadigan Park and so, at Belfast City Commissions, he was bound over to keep the peace for three years. No one suggested at any time that he was a burglar. Better if they had.

The incident ended his education at Belfast Royal Academy and there was no more rugger or ping-pong for him. He hadn't properly grasped the fact, but he'd isolated himself from his people for ever. Like generations of remittance men before him, he went to England to find work.

Eventually, he ended up working for Balfour Beatty in a gang digging the Woodhead Tunnel. They were camped up on the isolated moor above Sheffield, in the bitterly cold winter of 1948/49. He was the youngest man on the job, and camp life was full of hazards, but he learned to take care of himself and even to enjoy manual work. In exhaustion and the lack of opportunity, his passion for larceny cooled that winter.

Peter's criminal education, however, did not entirely cease. They used explosives to blast the tunnel, and he listened and learned all he could. He was not escaping his destiny after all.

After a year in exile, he returned to Belfast. He was not the prodigal son, but they were not unhappy to see him. All was for the moment forgiven.

Frederick Arnott Gulston, the author's father, had worked for the grain millers White, Tompkins & Courage for thirty years. Eventually he became their chief commercial traveller with his own car. It must have been partly the father's track record which persuaded the builder's merchant that stood opposite White, Tompkins & Courage to offer Peter a job. There had been a large number of applicants, but John McNeill & Co. were a progressive firm with a number of offshoots, and it was decided to give the successful traveller's heir a chance to win back his spurs.

The mundane office routine not only bored him; it frightened him. He was not up to the discipline that record-keeping demanded. He stayed there on borrowed time, and meanwhile the stone still hung round his neck.

A friend purloined a watch from a hotel in Portrush. Peter had a sight of it, and when Chummy was apprehended, he implicated Peter. A twenty-pound fine resulted at Portrush Petty Sessions. This and the publicity in the *Belfast Telegraph* put an end to his job and probably broke his father's heart when Frederick Gulston came upon it without warning in the paper.

Peter went back to the Woodhead Tunnel until the summer of 1950, when he returned again to Belfast. A chance meeting with a drop-out medical student and former president of the students' union resulted in the two of them making concrete breeze-blocks in a disused quarry in Glengormley, and Peter playing in an artisan rugby club. He was settling down to provincial life in the third division. 'The man who had the gun is light-fingered,' whispered the righteous, but never to his face.

It is probable that the hurt he caused his family by the Portrush conviction seared his conscience to a degree and, realising that his passion would only damage those who cared for him, he buried it. Leastways he did so for the next two years – helped by an exceptional man whose path crossed his, and whose surname he was later to take as an alias.

Peter's income was growing sporadic. Roy Thompson, the failed medic turned breeze-block producer, was having it hard on account of his penchant for horseracing. He couldn't make the breeze-blocks fast enough for the bookies, and perforce was about to dispatch Peter to new pastures. Then a pale blue drophead Austin Atlantic drove into the quarry. The driver had a florid face capped by a shock of untidy blond hair. He was tieless, yet had on an expensive suit. His boots were covered in cow shit. This was Crawford Scott, and he had that thing called presence.

Scott was a cattle dealer, some said a cattle *smuggler*, whom Roy had worked for in his summer vacations as driver-cum-book-keeper. Crawford, then about twenty-six, had paid little attention to scholarly matters, and he still needed a Man Friday to bridge the gaps in his education. Roy proposed Peter.

'Can he drive?' Crawford enquired in his soft Antrim burr. Peter was a learner, with little practice, but Roy laughed, 'He shunts about here. He manages the dumper. You'll have him driving in no time.'

A rapport flowered instantly and Peter had a new employer.

Crawford Scott could fill a book of anecdotes. He was a mentor to

Peter second only to George Chatham, but the influence was of a different substance. To Crawford, essentially a workaholic before that word was invented, stealing from others would have been anathema. However, no more guileful dealer could be found trading anywhere.

With Crawford in 1951, Peter got a taste for the good life, dining at the old Grand Central Hotel, learning to drive, and then swanning around the city in the first Mark 5 Jaguar ever seen in Belfast. On the other side of the coin he was little more than a minion, a gofer, doing anything from jumping cattle over the border to brushing them down in the Dublin Mart on bitter winter mornings. Cuffs around the ear, tirades over his shortcomings, were all part of his essential education at Crawford Scott's hands.

His boss's 'Do you follow me? Do you follow me?' still ring in his ears forty years on. He always had to confirm that he understood what he'd been told, and it was a lesson no schoolmaster had ever taught him so well. However, well driven and dined though he may have been, he was poorly paid and, carrying a book of Crawford's pre-signed cheques to pay traders, he was from time to time forced to divert the occasional cheque. Crawford probably knew he did it.

In time, of course, Crawford became a millionaire. Among other things he owned a large cannery and had racing interests, and was a fine man and a good father to his children (and, of course, in a way, to Peter). He died in 1992, but his son Homer carries on in racing as a trainer at the Curragh. The thief has never met the like of Crawford Scott since.

Fred Gulston died of a heart attack in 1952. It was in the early hours of the morning, in the bathroom, in his son's arms. Sadly, it must be said, the comforter's earlier conduct may well have contributed – one of many sins still to be discounted. Now Daisy, his bright, sharp-tongued mother, emigrated and Peter was left to his own devices and a thousand undeserved pounds of his father's money. Morally, he was not entitled to a penny of it, but Dad had left no will and, at just twenty-one, Peter had qualified under Northern Irish law to take the lion's share of his father's estate, splitting it two-for-one with his mother. He blew what his father had taken a lifetime to accumulate in three short months: another, as yet, undiscounted sin.

Dad's death and Mother's desertion released his degeneracy. His inheritance gone, he cashed one too many of Crawford's open cheques and became finally expendable to the cattle dealer. It was back to larceny by necessity.

He carried out a spate of break-ins. It was a protracted spree, ended by Peter's first taste of betrayal at the hands of a Shankill Road 'hardman' weightlifter whom Peter regarded as his friend. The Belfast City Commission had no option but to send him down for six months. The uncles and aunts, most of them Plymouth Brethren, were mortified. They mourned not for him but for 'the disgrace he's brought on us'. Peter was left to deal with his own conscience.

The governor of the Crumlin Road jail at that time was Lance Thompson, who had risen from the ranks and whose son 'Musso' was a good athlete and friend of Peter's. The connection did Peter no favours.

'Well, Mr Gulston, you've arrived here at last. We've been expecting you for some time, haven't we, Mr Holmes?'

The servile chief officer nodded, but Governor Thompson had not finished. He had heard about an incident when a lout bully had been shot in a billiard hall around the time Peter had the Colt .45. Gossip had it that 'the young student did it' – he hadn't, but when you give a dog a bad name anything is credible.

'You shot that poor soul in the billiard hall. Only your connections have kept you out of prison. Well, here you are now and I'm going to tell you, you'll be in and out of prison for the rest of your life.'

The prediction, though accurate, did little to warm Peter to the martinet. Thompson was another fire-and-brimstone merchant with a hotline to the deity. He clearly relished giving Peter a hard trip – perhaps intending it to be for his own good. But Nonconformists in power positions, and hung up on punishment, find equity beyond them.

Colonel White, chairman of the prison commissioners, had been a friend of his father's. Peter, condemned to the wood-yard, met the colonel by chance. It was a bitter cold day.

'It's not too bad here, Peter,' the colonel proffered.

The kindly man meant well. It's never too bad to the onlooker, as life was to teach Peter. However, after the meeting, the colonel asked an unwilling and ungracious Thompson to elevate Peter briefly to a storeman's job.

Such is the pettiness of prison life, Thompson's staff, anxious to please the martinet, contrived a theft of officer's kit from stores, thus confirming Peter's unworthiness, and he lost the job. The wood-yard, however, was in many ways best. Sidling up to Joe Coleman, an ancient safe-blower, possibly the only one in the Crumlin, he tentatively enquired, 'Joe, will you tell me how you blow a safe?'

The safe-blower looked at the skinny, round-shouldered youth with his burning blue eyes.

'Every man to his own game,' he jested kindly, in his soft, gentle voice. Yet he recognised a fellow live-wire anxious to learn, and later he explained the basics of his trade. It was all part of the thief's apprenticeship. Larceny is not sectarian.

At Christmas 1953, Christianity disgraced itself in the thief's eyes. A five-day home-leave system over the festive season had recently been devised for suitably trustworthy inmates considered to be of low risk and certain to return. The prerequisite was to have a home to go to, but the Plymouth Brethren were having none of it. They closed ranks.

'Let him stay where he is. He's hurt us enough.'

But someone prevailed on Thompson to allow Peter to stay at a hotel for the five days.

'Your connections are getting you out for Christmas,' the irate man blustered. 'I'm against it. Hotel indeed! You'll not be back . . .'

It was one his few wrong predictions, for Peter did return. After the best five days of his young life.

A very pretty girl from Cookstown, Colleen, had stayed by him and they found a room in a downmarket hotel on the corner of naughty Amelia Street and opposite the Great Northern Railway. For four days and nights they didn't surface. They screwed passionately, drank cheap red wine, and lived on bacon and eggs. It provided memories that made returning to the Crumlin for the rest of his sentence bearable.

'You'll be back,' was Lance's new prediction on his release. Since two-thirds of first offenders re-offend it was a good 2–1 on bet. Nor was it to be their last meeting. Twenty years later he was gliding around in his Rolls-Royce with a former fellow sufferer, Lord David Hamill, on board. Suddenly Hamill bellowed, 'Stop! There's a man you'd like to meet.'

Startled, Peter halted the purring beast and David jumped out at the kerbside. He was heartily pumping a stooped and elderly man's hand.

'And do you remember this man, Mr Thompson?'

He turned the disorientated ex-governor towards Peter as he alighted from the Rolls.

'Peter Gulston, one of your old boys.'

Thompson needed no reminding. He smiled benignly as he took in the gleaming car.

'Peter Gulston. Didn't I always know you'd do well? What a fine big man you are!'

One remembers what one wants to. The old martinet was no threat and Peter shook his hand gently.

'Good to see you, Mr Thompson. It's twenty years since you looked after me.'

'You know he's a big gangster in London now,' David bellowed. He always bellowed.

'I've read plenty about him,' Thompson acknowledged. 'I'm sure he's no such thing.'

Thompson was right, for now Peter was enjoying his five-year sabbatical in the London construction industry. Fearful of prison, tipper lorries were currently breaking his heart. He said, 'I've seen the light. I'm in construction now.'

After a final 'God bless the pair of you!' they were off, the minor triumph having cheered the both of them up.

'He was a wicked old bastard.'

Peter laughed. 'Difficult not to be in those circumstances . . .'

On his release in 1954, the Plymouth Brethren were anxious to get Peter offside. They prevailed on a friend, John Campbell, a former neighbour in Lansdowne Park, who most graciously offered him a job in his factory in Liverpool, a sack and hessian business. Campbell was probably what a Christian should be, with a lovely tenor voice. Having taken charge of the late William Noble's factories in Dundalk, Belfast, and Liverpool, he wanted to be a good friend to the family of the deceased.

Peter took Colleen to England. Alas, the passion was still active and the theft of a car brought an end to his Liverpool chance. Colleen, disenchanted, took off for London and he foolishly chased her. But he found himself alone in an attic room in Norland Square, driving a tipper lorry for A. T. Balch of Vera Road, Fulham. He later moved on to Chown, a local Paddington builder, driving their tipper lorries. He did not steal, his passion defeated by physical exhaustion, until fate cruelly intervened again.

Chown was a progressive company in the early fifties and Peter had a future with them until one Thursday night thieves stole an empty safe from their offices. All the employees were subject to a CRO by investigating police, and Peter's record came to light. The managing director, who went on to become a millionaire, was short and sour.

'We're unable to employ someone we cannot trust. I'm aware you had nothing to do with our break-in, but you've been using the tipper for private work in the evenings, contrary to our instructions to garage in our yard at Queen's Park nightly.'

And so it went on. Some prat copper from Paddington CID had got him the bullet spitefully, vengefully. An arsehole. Or was it that bloody stone again? Yes, he'd used the tipper in the evenings. Most of the basements of elegant houses in Bayswater Road had had Blitz rubble shovelled into them, and in the early fifties it was still there. So Peter would clear a basement for twenty-five quid over a week of evenings, which was tough going: filling baskets in basements, humping them up the steps, and hoisting them onto the tipper. He'd been doing one such job for a Peter Pieters, who owned the Grantchester Club in Craven Terrace. He was moving the club's rubble when the proprietor of a smaller club next door, idling on his doorstep, hailed him.

'My, you're a strong one. I could use you as a cellar man a couple of nights a week.'

This was 'Tiny' Evans, a six-foot-four Mancunian. His offer was tempting, but at the time Peter's evenings were fully committed clearing Goering's litter. But later, sacked by Chown, he called back and was employed as cellarman-cum-doorman. It was a dangerous job in postwar London, with American servicemen coming into conflict with market-working cockneys in the area. Thieves also used it.

Tommy, a local trench-coated second-generation Irishman and a big spender, was friendly.

'Hello, Pat,' he said. 'Ever go screwing?'

Peter knew the cockney vernacular.

'Yes, I did a bit back home. They locked me up for six months too.'

He was anxious to establish his credentials and he did.

'I've got a bit of work in Archery Close next to the old graveyard in Bayswater Road. Fancy making one?'

Smashing their way through a roof door, Peter proved competent and Tommy passed him on to Taffy Raymond, just home from Dartmoor.

'This Irish kid's a bit useful,' he told Taff. 'A bit mouthy, but plenty of bottle.'

Peter was on his way.

24

The Thief Impaled

B Y early 1983 Roger had still not surfaced. Then a couple of valuable paintings went missing in Mayfair and the job had Taters's hallmark. That, combined with his absence, made Peter sure that Taters was in funds. You never saw him when he was holding – only the tables or the bookies did.

Then Clyde was on the trumpet to the club.

'I've seen something I fancy in Mayfair. I'm there now. Fancy coming over to meet me?'

Peter said he'd be there.

'Great. See you outside the Silver Vaults in half an hour.'

Clyde was taking Mayfair seriously now, after his successful debut. If he had the Silver Vaults in mind, *very* seriously. This was a well-guarded target.

He was standing on the corner of Brook Street in his bomber jacket, the ciggy drooling from his mouth. He looked suspicious, but the tracksuited Peter probably did too. Wasting no time, Clyde took control. He'd been doing his homework.

'I been up and had a shufty. I fancy a booth on the top floor, from the rear.'

Peter nodded in agreement. For a number of reasons he'd never considered the Vaults, regarding them as a no-no. He would certainly never back them. But he decided to do so now, and found himself in Horse Shoe Yard where single-storeyed premises abutted the rear of the Vaults.

'I fancy if we find a triple-extension ladder we can get to this roof,' said Clyde, indicating the empty single-storey warehouse. 'Once we're on its roof we use the triple-extension up to that fourth-floor window. It's not protected.'

Clyde was right. A triple would reach the seemingly vulnerable window of the Silver Vaults. Fate, kindly again, led them to a triple-extension ladder unattended in Avery Row. It was lying on the stage of a high scaffolding. Clyde shinned up.

'May as well have it now. Might not get another chance.'

Peter liked the boy's aggressive logic and concurred. Walking the heavy ladder up to Brook Street, Peter tried to assume an unconcerned look for passers-by. He'd been moving ladders in Mayfair for thirty years, ever since that first sortie to the Curzon Street furrier with Taters, when he'd learned that the public pay little attention to any business not connected with themselves.

An empty building in Brook Street housed the ladder in its basement. This was only a stone's throw from Horse Shoe Yard, and an unlikely place for the losers to go looking for it. Clyde, cigarette *in situ*, took it all in his stride.

'Piece of cake. The sooner we pop it the better.'

He'd got the flavour.

They returned to Horse Shoe Yard a night later. A light drizzle was falling and it was dead as a kipper, with the exception of a private drinking club in its extreme corner. Peter drew Clyde's attention to the bogie.

'Let's get it up as quickly as possible. There's a drinker there. Not a lot of activity, but you can't be certain.'

The heavy ladder took some handling before it could be stood upright against the empty warehouse offices. Sod's law operated. No sooner was the ladder up than the club door pinged and a punter left. He must have been pissed, for he didn't even glance at the furtive pair or their ladder. They ran up and, on the flat roof, drew the ladder up behind them. They were in a vulnerable triangle of light and at the mercy of a host of windows. They rested in the shadows, observing the windows for any possible sighters.

'It's OK,' Clyde hissed. 'Let's get this bastard up.'

Ever tried to get a triple-extension ladder up to as acute an angle as possible? It's difficult, time-consuming and noisy, but Peter's experience stood them in good stead, for Taters had tutored him well in the early days. Clyde was willing enough, but he was both a physical lightweight and clumsy when required to hoist in unison with Peter. At last, though, it was up, directly under the lintel of the unprotected window. They took another break to assess the spectator quantum. All was well.

Years of manual work, penal and otherwise, had toughened Peter, but hoisting the ladder had taken its toll. He panted and the sweat of effort trickled down his armpits and scrotum.

'I'll go up and open the burnt,' said Clyde. 'If the bell should ring I'll be livelier than you.'

Clyde was prepared to take charge, just as Peter had been with

Taters when first working with him in the sixties. Roger needed a bit of pushing, but Clyde was a live goer who'd see little fraught in the V & A. Time to swap horses?

Caning a sash window at ground level needs a little skill. Working at the top of a fifty-foot extension, it requires both nerve and balance. But Clyde made light of it, and the window was raised. Silence. Almost certainly it was not alarmed. Peter joined Clyde, lugging a dozen mail sacks under his free arm, and they went through. They were in one of the booths that traded from this floor of the Silver Vaults.

Peter, as usual, was in a lather of nervous sweat. He donned his glasses to examine the hallmarks on the glinting silver pieces that were lined up before him, but the lenses steamed up and his pencil torch was dim. With Clyde getting at him to hurry, they filled ten sacks, which they lugged down to the flat roof and into the empty premises. Oddly this had no ground-floor exit, so Clyde slid down a drainpipe into the Yard, collected the station wagon, and signalled Peter to throw the sacks down to him. They left the time-wasting ladder *in situ* against the second-floor Vaults window.

From where he was, Peter had a view through to Bond Street, and was considering exiting there when the arrival of a Q car with two coppers changed the game-plan. He returned to the flat roof and hissed down.

'Clyde, I think it's on top. The law are pratted up in Bond Street. Piss off. I'll meet you in Hanover Square.'

Peter prowled about the roof. It was now drizzling heavily and he was looking for an alternative to the descent by the now-slippery drainpipe. He toyed with the idea of going over the top of the pitch roof that separates Horse Shoe Yard from Lancashire Court, but that looked an even trickier option. He must descend the drainpipe.

Fifteen stone going down a moist drainpipe in soaked leather gloves and slippery crêpe-soled boots is a recipe for disaster. With little purchase, he slid out of control down towards a ring of malevolent (and forgotten) iron spikes which cuddled the drainpipe. He came to a shuddering stop in searing pain. A spike had penetrated his right foot, six inches of it impaling him. He lost his balance and swung down, spiking himself again through the back of his thigh.

A lifetime of desperate situations had given him reserves. He used his right hand to ease his impaled buttock off the spike. But he couldn't position himself at enough of an angle to raise his stuck foot. There was blood everywhere. He thought, 'If I don't get my act together I'm going to die here.'

With a savage twist of his free hand he wrenched his foot and ankle free, hearing the bone shatter as he let go of the pipe and collapsed the last three feet to the ground. He landed on his back and blacked out.

He woke. The pain was indescribable, but through it he was still aware of the impending police presence. He must get up, must . . . must.

Struggling to his feet, he noticed his suede boot squelching as it filled with his claret. He dragged himself to Brook Street, almost fainting. But to faint was a luxury he couldn't afford. He forced himself on, and was rewarded by the sudden arrival of Clyde, on the prowl, drawing the station wagon up beside him. The agony receded. He knew the law were not going to have him.

Then a chilling thought struck: the blood on the spike! Finding a duster in the car, he implored Clyde, 'I landed on the spikes at the foot of the pipe. The law are on to us. Before we go, give them a wipe. Please . . .'

Clyde didn't fancy it one bit, but he did Peter's bidding. Courage is the hallmark of the trustworthy conspirator. Afterwards they drove to Hendon and Diana's, where Peter's warm Dettolled bath turned crimson as the disinfectant bit him and he yelped with pain.

'Peter,' Diana begged him, 'you must go to hospital. You're bleeding to death.'

She drove him to Edgware General where, admitted to Casualty, he was sewn up and fed painkillers. He passed out and they kept him in overnight. The crucifixion was over, at least for the time being.

In the morning an alert registrar examined the stitches.

'What bloody idiot stitched these wounds. They're infected. Christ!' He eyed the sallow Peter, suddenly curious. 'How did you do this?'

'I fell from a ladder onto a wooden spike ringing a tree in my garden. Yesterday evening.'

The gimlet-eyed registrar looked unconvinced.

'In the garden? Well, I'm going to have to give you the appropriate antibiotics. And I think your ankle's broken, almost certainly a Potts fracture. How did you manage that?'

'I wrenched my foot to get it off the spike.'

The truth came more confidently. The registrar looked impressed.

'Very stalwart of you – and I expect very painful. We'll X-ray your ankle when the swelling goes down. Do you know why it's called a Potts fracture, Mr Gulston?'

Peter felt bloody and, frankly, couldn't care less.

'Potts was a surgeon out riding in Rotten Row. His nag threw him, but when he fell one ankle was still twisted in the stirrup. He instantly diagnosed a fracture, since when that particular type of break has been known in the trade as a Potts.'

Peter's lie about being in the garden caused him to be given ineffective antibiotics and it was two weeks before the infection disappeared. (The moral here: never tell a doctor a lie, never tell a gendarme the truth.) However, he was otherwise lucky in his treatment. The rota orthopaedic surgeon was a Mr Trickey, famed mender of footballers' knees. He'd fallen into good hands.

Trickey was even more worldly-wise than the sceptical registrar. Conducting a group of students past the prostrate Peter, he observed, 'Interesting injury here. Potts fracture, self-administered. Normally found in burglars who have fallen off the roof.'

The eminent man's urbane smile, as he jested, revealed nothing. Another clairvoyant, or can you not fool top men?

On discharge, Peter, very sorry for himself, opted for a small back room in Wandsworth belonging to an obliging Irish pal. Hobbling about on crutches, he was very poorly and disconsolate, and the injury would leave him with a permanent limp and an ugly red scar on his crooked right foot. At the time, it was doubtful if he would ever walk properly again, much less play tennis and, even now, writing about it, his foot twitches and shudders and he must flex it sharply to make it stop.

One consolation was the silver – until he contacted his accessory. The news Clyde brought him plunged Peter into new despair.

'It's *not* silver, Peter. It's fucking Sheffield plate, isn't it?'

Of course, he should have realised. However high and inaccessible the window, it was unprotected and therefore unlikely to give access to a valuable target. Some people call it 'easy money'. Peter thought not.

The raid was a cock-up from start to finish, entirely his fault too. Clyde had behaved impeccably. He supposed the truth was roofs at fifty are a bit like kisses. They come expensive.

Three months of purgatory followed as he did his penance in the Wandsworth garret. Only his Irish landlord's wife administered to him from time to time, but in truth he wanted to be in purdah. The relationship with Diana dimmed to obscurity and he took refuge in porn and music to serve out his time.

He rang the club from time to time to get messages. Nothing from Roger. His son Craig never rang. He was sad, self-pitying, on the verge of despair. The pathos of Dante's words swarmed over him. 'I did not die, but nothing of life remained.'

The only person who was glad to see him limping around the club again was Lena McGee, the Sligo belle and caterer. The beef burger was on again and his months of self-catering in Wandsworth made it more than attractive. He got himself a pint of lager from the bar to wash it down. Lena came over with her pad. Thirty years in London had not diluted her soft Sligo drawl. He felt at home.

'God, I never thought I'd see the day when Peter Scott drank beer, wounded or not. And how did you do that?'

Very little went on at Paddington that Ma McGee missed. It was tell the truth with bad intent time.

'I fell off a roof. Impaled myself.'

'Do you know, I believe you. The beef's lovely today.'

'Yes, I'll have the *boeuf bourgignon*. And have a drink, Lena. A Remy? A small one'll do no damage.'

'Ah well, only a small one then. There are enough drinkers in our family.'

Harry, Lena's husband, was polite and tame when sober and unbid-dable in his cups.

'Michael's been reading a book by a copper,' Lena told him. 'Could you be the man he says robbed film stars? Did you rob film stars, and do the other things he says?'

Her eyes were sparkling mischievously. He asked, 'What exactly does the book say I did?'

Peter was smiling. He knew the probable answer.

'Oh God, it's too embarrassing to pass my lips. He says one fellow who robbed them of their trinkets would take a pair of drawers. And wore them too.'

'Lena, I gave up wearing ladies' drawers years ago.'

Still, he felt his cheeks redden. Truth, even after thirty years, would find its mark.

'Well, whoever the society crasher was, he wore women's knickers. And knowing you, I wouldn't put it past you.'

She gave him one of her 'don't you dare deny it' looks.

As noted already, the thing probably started with Hessie McClurkin and her silken knickers. A dozen years later, he'd amassed a pres-tigious collection, which he displayed on a set of antlers in the hall in Belgrave Mews North, fluttering in the draught like battle honours every time the door was opened.

One of the proudest trophies was a black semi-transparent pantie girdle. It was all he had to show for his pursuit of Elizabeth Taylor's gaudy gems.

He'd been introduced briefly to Taylor in the Star Tavern by the ebullient Paddy Kennedy. It was probably the year the violet-eyed beauty moved on to marry Mike Todd, abandoning her father-figure, second husband Michael Wilding. Even in her halcyon days, those hips amply needed the then-fashionable pantie girdle, as Peter noted, his eye spotting the tell-tale bulge of the seam-line even before he'd registered the ten-carat solitaire ring.

'Do you really steal jewels?' she enquired, coquettishly covering the vulgar bauble with her other, unadorned hand.

'Bloody right he does,' Paddy guffawed. 'Fucking everybody's.'

'Well, I guess I'm going to be the exception,' predicted the beauty.

Mike Wilding had fallen by the wayside when Peter launched the first of several determined assaults to prove her wrong. Taylor had decamped with Eddie Fisher, the permanently adolescent hubby of her 'close friend' Debbie Reynolds. Eddie sang.

The impetuous young things headed secretly, and in a blaze of publicity, for England. Their arrival time at Heathrow was printed in the dailies and Peter was there to greet them, tailing their ivory Bentley Continental until he discovered the love-nest, in Englefield Green, Berkshire.

The rain was bucketing down on the Saturday evening as Peter and his sidekick, the 'Swan', drove from London to the 'secret' address. With a ladder already found and concealed on the night he'd tailed them, Peter was sure that conditions were perfect. All he needed was a bit of luck.

The driveway started with a sharp bend and could not be seen from the house. This was inviting. A minor hazard was high barbed wire, recently erected on the perimeter wall for the loving couple's sake.

'Odd,' he told his accomplice, the rain dimming his voice. 'All this barbed wire and the front gate's open. Listen, I'll slip round the back and take the ladder. If it looks sweet I'll go for it. You go up the drive and watch the front of the house. Any activity, mark my card.'

The Swan was an inexperienced raider. He nodded.

The house was well lit but the presumed master bedroom, which faced the Green, glowed only dimly, encouraging Peter to hoist the lightweight aluminium ladder to one of its windows. Clambering up, he found the ladder sinking into a sodden flowerbed but, undeterred, he easily reached the sill. He was elated to find the window slightly open.

Carefully he eased it up, the sound being muffled on the inside by the heavy, drawn drapes. He drew them aside, gaining sight of the empty bedroom. Climbing another two rungs, he was able to lean through the window, the dresser being an arm's stretch away. The only discernible item on it was a ruffle of black silk.

He was about to make entry when a series of torch flashes bounced off the wall beside him. Turning, he thought he could see The Swan outside the grounds, waving his arms in alarm. He snatched the black silk, closed and latched the window, and slid down the ladder fireman fashion. It took a second or two to unplug it from the flowerbed, but take it he must. A missing pair of drawers was one thing, but a ladder at a bedroom window was proof of somebody's intent.

He retracted the ladder, slunk round the perimeter and out through the gates. He dumped the ladder in the copse opposite. Then The Swan was at his side, breathless yet chuckling to himself.

'You won't believe this. I was sidling up to the front of the house when what d'you think I see? Only a police car with a pair of coppers watching me. They were pratted up under a garage lean-to. I headed for the front door but they were out before I made it. "Can I help you, sir?" "Press," I says. "I'm trying to get an interview with Miss Taylor." "What paper you with, then, sir?" "*Jewish Chronicle*," says I. "Sorry, sir, Miss Taylor's not giving interviews. Afraid you'll have to leave." So I walked back down the drive and glimmed you. Don't fret, they're sweet. They got back into the car. Good job I'm a yid.'

The Swan found it vastly amusing, Peter less so.

'Let's get offside. We'll come another night. Fucking unlucky. I'd the burnt open, about to go in, when you glimmed me. *Fucking* unlucky.'

Peter didn't mention the black pantie girdle in his bin. He was foolish to take it and knew he was. But with no visible signs of entry, they'd probably be, at worst, one of those domestic mysteries . . .

Peter came back a week later, alone. The ladder was gone and a police car was parked at the gates. Maybe it had been her favourite pantie girdle but, whatever, it was too hot a number. There would, he reasoned, be other chances.

Nearly ten years elapsed before he got a second chance, when Stan the chauffeur appeared with some news.

'Liz Taylor's taken a house called Foxwarren. She's coming to

London next month. Interested? I used to drive for the woman who owns it, a Mrs Fisher.'

But more of that later . . .

Sitting with Lena, Peter saw again the antler horns at the foot of the stairs, decked with all his victims' knickers, the black pantie girdle in pride of place. It took an earl's daughter, visiting him, to point out how vulgar and infantile the display was. They were banished the same day, for ever.

Lena grounded him again, the brandy making her bold.

'Well, *did* you take the stars' drawers?'

'Took Liz Taylor's pantie girdle once. Couldn't wear it, though. Too tight.'

'Get away with you. I never know when you're spoofing. Here, isn't that the girl you were chatting up last year?'

Lena indicated the bar. Chelsea was there with a gaggle of young men. She wore a black pencil skirt and a white sweater, bra-less. Her auburn mane was swept up Scarlett O'Hara style.

Limping, even lumbering, across to greet her, he felt very ancient. Stupid to be arrogant enough to desire her. She saw him.

'Where have you been? Fallen down a mine?' she asked gaily, playing to her gallery.

'Twisted my ankle on court. But still up to giving you a hit.'

The exchange amused the company. They looked to Peter like the law. He was swerving to the changing room when she trilled out, 'Can we have that hit tomorrow, then?'

Peter looked back and nodded.

'See you here at two.'

He went back to Sutherland. Sitting on his bed, Mahler's Eighth lent an obscure pleasure to his sadness. Then, removing his sock, the truth was confronted – the 'mended' ankle was swollen. It glowed purple and crimson. The memory of that night made him shudder then, as he flexed his foot, the horror receded. Chelsea's long legs took the stage and his eyelids drooped.

A prompt Chelsea turned up, pouting.

'It's bloody raining, and I did so want a hit. I've been on a promise for months.'

So Peter took her to Harrow Road Indoor Tennis Centre, impressing Chelsea with the thoughtfulness of the gesture. She played com-

petently, enjoying herself. He managed all right, with his ankle well
bound up.

Afterwards, in the swanky bar at Harrow Road, the pair relaxed.
On her second Teacher's, Chelsea confessed, 'I'm reading law at
Birkbeck. Too poor to afford a tennis coach.' Her green eyes glinted
with mischievous humour. 'Too pretty to have to, either. My dad tells
me you pass yourself off as a coach. Why does he refer to you as a
bit of a mystery man?'

'Probably because I talk a lot of bollocks. From time to time, when
I have a few quid, I'm Jack the Lad. But I'm a bit of a hybrid amongst
the still-life at Paddington. I used to be a scallywag.'

He tailed off, hoping he'd said enough to encourage and not enough
to repel. A delicate equation.

'Scallywag? That sounds intriguing. Have you retired from scally-
wagging, then? I'm pretty respectable myself. You get that way at
twenty-nine.'

Peter digested the unsolicited testimony. He could be in with a
chance. Sitting with legs akimbo on the barstool, her taut sweat-
soaked knickers drew his eye beneath the tennis skirt. Catching his
look, she assumed a more modest pose.

He dropped her back at her flat in Maida Vale, where she kissed
his cheek lightly.

'I'll try to come to Paddington tomorrow lunchtime.'

But she made no show at lunchtime and a disappointed Peter took
refuge in cognac before taking an afternoon kip in the TV room. In
the evening, Ferdie arrived by chance just as Peter was venturing out
in the icy air for a hit under floodlights. The temperature had dropped
to several degrees of frost.

'You're going to take me out tonight,' Ferdie boomed. 'It's about
time you did.'

He was done up like an advert for macho sartorial elegance, in a
superbly cut Prince of Wales check. He looked at Peter's racquet.

'You must be fucking mad, going out to play in this weather.'

He was right, it was a form of madness, but also a therapy for life's
larger madness. Once you're afflicted by the bug, excessive heat, rain,
frost, even snow are all met with the same disregard.

'I'll be an hour,' said Peter. 'Will you wait? I'll feed you if you do.'

'Suppose I must. I'll be in the bar.'

Back from his ordeal, Peter showered before rejoining Ferdie.

'Who's the bird over there?' Macho Man growled, and inclined his
head. Peter followed Ferdie's nod and to his surprise saw that the bird

was Chelsea. Seeing him, she advanced, more seductive than ever in her *femme fatale* ensemble of pencil skirt and white crossover sweater. And she was on her own.

'Hello, Peter. Couldn't make it at lunchtime. Sorry.'

'Chelsea, this is a pal of mine, Ferdie.'

But turning to introduce them, Peter found Ferdie had disappeared.

'I think I've scared your friend off.'

'Probably just gone to water the flowers.'

'More likely to comb his hair.'

'Hey, I've an idea. I'm taking Ferdie out for a meal. Care to join us?'

Chelsea's eyes narrowed. 'I'm not sure I like the look of your dandy friend. I'll think about it.'

A sheepish, groomed Ferdie returned. He made a good impression, referring to his BA from a minor university. Not a word about his brothels. Meanwhile, Chelsea's obvious intellect impressed the vice king and he was courteous and attentive. It was agreed they would dine together.

They ate in an upmarket Chinese joint on the corner of Maida Vale and Sutherland Avenue. Ferdie and Chelsea were enjoying each other's repartee. Paying the hefty bill made Peter wince. He'd have to be out and about again soon.

As they left, Ferdie suggested they go on to a Soho club, but Peter made his excuses.

'I've been playing tennis since three o'clock. I'm bushed. Why don't you two go on, make a night of it? An old man needs his sleep . . .'

His voice tailed away. It was a cop-out, but Chelsea didn't demur. He wasn't sure whether he expected her to, though her earlier distrust of Ferdie was no longer in evidence. Peter left them, mildly sad. He'd played a little game and lost. So how bad?

All hell broke loose as he came into the club the next day. Chelsea's dad, ashen and shaking with anger, curtly beckoned him to the bar.

'Peter! Fellow you left Chelsea with last night. What's his name? Where can I find him?'

'He's called Ferdie. He's got club interests in Soho but he's domiciled in Florida. I meet him here, we have the odd hit. Is there a problem?'

'There is for him, when I find him.'

Just as Peter was beginning to feel cornered, Chelsea arrived. She looked lovely but wan, fragile even. A silk scarf was hoisted around her neck.

'Hi, Pop. Yes, I'm OK now. Peter, can I have a word?'

She led him to a table in the empty dining room. Tears were moistening her sea-green eyes.

'Just who *is* your friend Ferdie? Why did you leave me with that maniac?'

There was now a vagrant tear on her cheek. Peter suddenly remembered the episode of the dinner with Rachel, Ferdie in drag . . .

'You appeared . . . compatible,' he stammered. 'I felt like a gooseberry so I left you to it.'

Guilt spread like a rash as he saw the welling tears.

'It was *you* I wanted to be with, not that beast. Wait till Dad gets hold of him. Dad's got connections, *police* connections. So have I, if I need them.'

Peter turned a shade paler under his tan. Police? What the fuck had Ferdie got up to? Chelsea had stopped crying now and she went on, speaking fiercely, 'I went back to his place for a drink. I know that was stupid of me, but I assumed I was in control. My job teaches me to be. Then he was prancing around in a pair of tights with his big knob bouncing around. He was threatening to sodomise me. He's got a massive knob, your Ferdie. He said he'd been in cabaret with it, stripping. We were pretty pissed. It was even funny, until he got me round the throat and started strangling me.'

In an almost confidential movement, she lifted the neck scarf. A dull red weal showed on her neck. Peter was horrified. Tears were flowing again as she said, 'There was no sex, actually. I mean not with me. He jerked himself off.'

'Christ almighty! If I'd known . . .' Guilt clogged Peter's throat.

'Well, you should have. It's your fault. You must have known he was a weirdo. And it was you I wanted to be with . . .'

He felt it *was* his fault. He stretched across and held her hands in his, then lifted one of them and stroked the flushed neck with the back of it.

'I was already unhappy,' she went on. 'I'd just split up with my chap. And then you left me with that rat.'

Peter felt angry and bloody. He was trembling.

'Right! I'm off to have a word with him. Wait here till I return.'

'OK. But say nothing in front of Dad. He wants him arrested, but I can't afford to let that happen. And do take care.'

She had perked up again. It made the thief even more vengeful. He roared up Wellington Road, jumping the lights at Swiss Cottage in his rage, and pulled up at the Hampstead flat, tyres screaming. He had no plan, only rage. He felt for the tyre lever under the seat.

When he pressed the bell the intercom came to life instantly. A woman's nervous voice asked who it was.

'It's Peter Scott. I've come to see Ferdie.'

After a little hesitation the door buzzed and, pushing it open, he took the stairs two at a time. A slim, anxious, attractive woman, aware for sure of the drama, stood in the flat door. Peter had met her before – she was a neighbour, in love with Ferdie.

'Ferdie's not here,' she said. 'He went to Florida this morning. He flew, naturally,' she added as an afterthought, as if to assist her credibility. Peter pushed past her without excusing himself.

'I've come to see the parrot. Is the parrot here? Pretty Polly! Pretty, pretty Polly . . .'

'No, it went back to the shop this morning. Ferdie'll be away for a long time. He may not return.'

Peter glared at her and began a cursory search of the flat. The wardrobes were empty. Satisfied, he turned to the neighbour again.

'If he phones you, tell him I've been. And if he comes back, tell him to expect the police.'

He forced his face into a patently false smile.

'It's probably for the best that he's not here. Goodbye and thanks.'

Then he walked back down the stairs. Back at the club, the bar was closed and Chelsea and her dad gone. It *was* his fault. Thank God Ferdie'd had it away on his toes. What Peter might have done to him did not bear thinking about.

He'd miss the parrot, though.

It was his lifelong *modus operandi* – toss the thing you most want to the wolves. The self-deprivation was inexplicable, unless that was really his buzz . . . He didn't know.

Lounging back beside the club's steamed-up verandah window, his inner lament was interrupted by someone tapping. Wiping away the condensation, he saw the bespectacled, grinning face of Roger. He was beckoning Peter out.

'Hello, stranger.'

Shivering in the biting cold air, Peter grasped Roger's limp hand.

'Where've you been? It's been months. But you look well.'

Roger still wore his enigmatic Buddha smile. He was suited and booted as never seen before – by Peter, at least.

'You're limping. Tennis taking its toll?'

'No. You want to come in?'

'No thanks, let's go back to your attic and get you into a suit. I'm going to take you to Mayfair for a gargle.'

Mayfair for a drink? Had Roger gone off his canister?

Driving down Park Lane, Peter told him of the fiasco at the Silver Vaults. He also mentioned that he'd visited Zilli's and mentioned the key to the offices in Bruton Place which accessed the roofs. Roger listened attentively.

'The key's interesting. There are a couple more possibilities on that roof area. I've been to India myself. Always wanted to go. The Mystic East's my scene. First Calcutta, then Cooch Behar, bloody amazing. The extremes – wealth, poverty . . .'

'Where in Cooch Behar? I was once friendly with Bia, the Maharajah, and his wife Gina. But sadly I blotted my copybook just before he died. He was a good head, though.'

Roger scowled.

'Do you ever stop dropping names? I expect you'll know the club we're going to. It's in Shepherd Market, the Maisonette. I enlisted recently.'

'Hang on, that's Ruby Lloyd's place. I've been *persona non grata* there for the last ten years, since Ruby got it into her head in the mid-seventies that I tied her up and nicked her tom. She slipped Wally Virgo up to go me. He was CID governor in London then. Wally knew I was a straight-goer at the time and, better still, he knew I never, even when at it, attended to friends, *or* the friends of friends. But Ruby wouldn't have it and after that I was admitted only with bad grace. Then one day it surfaced when I was there with Diana and I blew my top and behaved badly.'

'Worry not,' said Roger. 'There's been a change of management. Ruby's either ill or dead. I want to see a bird there. And talking of birds, did you get on the firm with Chelsea?'

But Peter's mind was elsewhere by now. The distant past had raised its head again . . .

That evening he drank too much brandy and, going to bed, he hoped to dream of Chelsea. Inconveniently, only a vexed Ruby Lloyd surfaced in his unconscious, flitting across the ceiling strapped to a chair and squawking like a parrot, 'I know it was you. I know!'

Then an ogre-like face approached the harridan in medical garb, brandishing extractors to force the gold from her strident mouth. Wally Virgo's bald head hovered above the captive in the chair, pointing a 'your country needs you' finger at the felon. Suddenly

Peter himself was in the chair, a dentist's chair. Virgo leaned over him, drill humming in his hand.

'Make a clean breast of it, if only for your Queen,' he was saying . . .

Peter woke with a start, clammy with fear. Only his mouth was dry. Bollocks to brandy. He got up, filled a glass with ice-cold water from the tap, and sat sipping it on the edge of his bed.

Wally Virgo? It was the memory of Ruby Lloyd which had brought him onto the stage of his dream. And Virgo had indeed pointed the finger, thirty years past. At four o'clock in the afternoon, in broad daylight, Helen, Dowager Duchess of Northumberland, had been deprived of her gems from a momentarily unattended limo in Eaton Square. Her chauffeur had gone to the door of the mansion block to squire the Duchess out. It was a simple strike, but within the hour an additional hazard had surfaced for the felon, whoever he was. He couldn't have known it, but the Duchess had just been off to tea with the Queen Mum. The story goes that the gracious highland lady had immediately rung the Factory demanding action. Well, that was Wally's story the following day, after he'd sauntered into Paddy Kennedy's.

'Peter, can I have a word?' the sonorous Wally intoned. He drew the thief to one side. 'The jewellery's got to be put back. The Queen Mother's furious.'

This water was getting deep. Peter looked surprised.

'Quite rightly. But why me, Wally?'

'We have an excellent description of the man and it fits you to perfection.'

Peter realised that this, for once, was a step beyond a fishing expedition. Care was of the essence. He remained shtum.

'So can you tell me where you were at four o'clock yesterday afternoon?'

'Four o'clock? Bad luck, Wally. I was having drinks with a maharajah in Durham Place, Chelsea. Gilly Bengough was with me.'

Gilly's was a handy name to drop in the circumstances. She was the sister to Piers Bengough, janitor to the Royal Enclosure at Ascot. But Wally was more interested in the Indian.

'What maharajah?'

'Of Cooch Behar.'

Wally frowned. 'Well, he won't remember. He's always pissed.'

'The young lady from Moyses Stevens, the flower arrangers, she wasn't. I chatted her up. Gilly was sober too.'

The frown turned to a scowl.

'What time did you get to Durham Place?'

'Three-thirty.'

'What time did you leave?'

'Some time after five.'

It wasn't the worst of alibis for a scallywag to have. Wally was pissed off.

'I propose to check what you've told me. For your sake, I hope you're telling the truth.'

Disgruntled, Wally took his leave to carry out his checks. The result was an end to Peter's drinks in Durham Place for, two days later, a petulant Maharajah, sitting alone in Paddy's, beckoned him over to his table.

'Peter, I enjoy your friendship,' he said in his beautifully modulated tones. 'However, when the seamy side of your life manifests itself in my home in the shape of two uppity policemen to whom you have given my name as an alibi, it's time to draw stumps, I think.'

The cricket analogy told all. Bia didn't look at Peter as he spoke. It's fatal in cricket to take your eye off the ball, but Bia was prepared to chance it.

'Even worse, they questioned my recollection when I confirmed your whereabouts. And, most extraordinary of all, they suggested I might have been in my cups at the time . . .'

Peter breathed out. Things had gone from bad to worse – but they could have been worse still.

'Bia, I'm sorry. I was forced to account for my whereabouts at the time I was your guest. I didn't have any option.'

Bia now looked him straight in the eye, as if playing a Bedser in-swinger.

'I realise that. But a suspicion lurks that you contrived this. You have used me, to say nothing of the mortified girl from Moyses Stevens, to carry out a particularly unpleasant theft.'

The Maharajah was getting out of his pram. Peter retaliated.

'Bia, there are no pleasant thefts.'

'But good God, man, the Queen Mother's involved. Is nothing sacred to you?'

Peter raised his eyebrows. Clearly the British Raj had not disappeared entirely.

'Afraid I can't afford to enjoy the morality you can. I'm sad you see me in this light, but actually I'm not sorry to expose you to my moral deficiencies. It'll allow you to cut me dead.'

Bia left then, irritably. He'd taken his eye off the ball and his off-stump had gone. Never again did he speak to or acknowledge the thief. He was a very charming man who'd accidentally fallen into bad company. He was safer in the pavilion.

Bia's final nemesis came playing polo, not cricket. He fell from his pony, which contributed to his early demise a few years later. Gillian Bengough married one of her own ilk and often laughed about the incident in later years. Commander Wallace Virgo was sent to prison in connection with porn corruption matters, though his conviction was later overturned by the Court of Appeal. The Duchess of Northumberland never got her gems back, while the Queen Mother had another glass of port and forgot all about it. The thief, whoever he was, was never caught.

The moral of this tale, again: lie down with dogs and expect to catch fleas.

25

Golgotha's Men

Lust rather than guilt drove the thief to seek Chelsea at the tennis club. After the night out in Shepherd Market, Roger had found female company; Peter was left with his nightmares – imprisonment, pursuit, the burden of his sins. All excesses have a price.

In Chelsea's absence he was hitting on Court Ten with Paula, an ash-blonde Irish exile, when Dr Fell himself materialised, his glasses glinting like sabres in the sun. Peter strolled across. Roger didn't waste words.

'A good night, was it?'

Before Peter could reply he briefly stated his business.

'See you at one o'clock at the back door, OK?'

He didn't wait for a reply. Watching the lank figure striding away, Peter's emotions clustered around an inexplicable anxiety.

'Peter, who in God's name was that? What an odd-looking man.'

Paula, like Lena McGee, missed little. Peter believed female Celts are in their nature witches, aware of vibes that should not be ignored.

'Is he a crook or what?' she asked.

Peter smiled, feeling oddly reassured that his own intuitions were shared.

'He's a porcelain restorer, nationally famous. He's been repairing a piece of bisque I dropped.'

A sceptical scowl in Paula's eyes told him she didn't believe him. She'd have done better to concentrate on her backhand.

'I'd say he was better at smashing things than repairing them.'

She'd seen what Irene had earlier suggested. Could they all be wrong?

'Look,' said Peter, 'if you took your racquet back sooner and got your feet comfortable, the backhand would be less of a mystery to you. Then you'd be in better twist and you wouldn't malign one of nature's great aesthetes.'

She practised the swing.

'Great aesthete my arse. He's sneaky-looking. Mind you don't trust him.'

On the dot of one, Roger swept up to the back door and revved the Triumph. As soon as Peter was inside they were off to Richoux's. Peter opened the bidding.

'How did you make out with the bird last night?'

Roger ignored him, throwing the Triumph around corners in his usual reckless, unnecessary fashion. At the first stretch of straight road, he came back with his own leering question.

'Who was the blonde you were playing with earlier? You *do* find them, I must say. Seen anything of Chelsea?'

Peter in turn ignored the sally and reported instead on the abortive attempt on the V & A in the snow. Roger seemed sincerely gutted by the news.

'Fucked it up, have you? I suppose the old prat was with you. I *told* you I wasn't ready for it. Why didn't you dwell the box?'

'It's not fucked up. We made a successful withdrawal. The old prat did what was expected of him. He's a colossus, he always performs well, age hasn't changed that. But we were unlucky. The gaff's got a bock on it.'

Roger glared at him. Later, settling into a comfortable restaurant seat, Roger returned to the V & A. He was still angry.

'How could you take a seventy-year-old up on the roof of the V & A?'

'I didn't. He took me.'

'OK, forget about that for the moment. What's on the cards now? I'm nearly skint. That trip to India did the damage.' Roger winked, knowingly. 'Goa has expensive temptations.'

'Expensive temptations are everywhere, Roger. The art is to ignore those that are not of the essence.'

Peter was tucking into a Richoux Special as he steered the conversation back to business.

'There's a couple of moves on the books. I fancy a silversmith's in St James's called How's. I found it over Christmas. I would've been better off giving that a shot than fucking up on those Silver Vaults in Bond Street. I could have died there on the spikes. Had to fracture my own bloody ankle to release myself.'

Involuntarily, he reached down to comfort his still-tender ankle.

'Yes, I heard,' said Roger. 'Shall we stroll over to St James's and have a look? I need the exercise.'

Ten minutes later, with the Triumph on a Mount Street meter, they were sauntering down Ryder Street. Something was bothering Roger.

'I wish you wouldn't wear that tatty tracksuit. People keep taking it out of us.'

Experience had taught Peter that his dress didn't matter. Only really outrageous behaviour or stupidity attracted unwelcome attention. The passing public were thinking about mortgages, school fees, the parking meter; not sniffing out possible felons on the street.

'You'll have to learn to live with my idiosyncrasies. I've had to.'

They turned into Pickering Place, that quaint fragment of Olde London in which How's held its business. Reviewing the display like any window shopper, Roger was clearly taken with the target.

'Has it been tried?'

'This is St James's. *Everywhere*'s been tried.'

Roger moved a little way down the street, squinting covertly up at the roofline.

'Where's the out?'

'Come with me.'

Well aware of Peter's obsession with bolt-holes and escape routes, Roger had known there would be an out. He allowed himself to be led back up St James's, right into King Street and right again. Here was Crown Passage, another Dickensian backwater where, midway, scaffolding jutted out above a hoarding.

'It's not complicated, Roger. We go over the hoarding through this renovation. The scaffolding lets us across the passage and we're then on a roof directly behind How's. It's twin-pitched, Georgian or earlier. There's probably a skylight and below that a trap-door, alarmed. So we're on red alert from the second we tamper with it.'

Peter's hands moistened as he visualised the scene.

'I've already confirmed that the showroom is on the first floor and it's grilled from the stairwell. It's a case of cutting the paddy and we're in. From the stairwell, we can observe the courtyard below and watch the law arriving to answer the alarm.'

Roger nodded attentively.

'What can the police do?' Peter went on. 'Report the premises secure and call up the keyholder. They'd have to see or hear us to surround the block. My guess is they won't even leave a sentry. We can load up and scarper before they get access.'

'What if they sniff us out when they arrive?'

'We scarper. They'd have to be bright to work out where we disappear to. I rate this a freebie.'

Roger considered. He saw the entire coup. No need for seconds.

'I like it. Very much. What do you think we can claw?'

'If we clear the showroom they'll hoot for a million. This is important Scottish silver – my man on the Continent will swallow it up. So
we could end up sharing maybe eighty, a hundred long ones.'

Peter stole a sidelong glance at Roger. He still hadn't mentioned the
role he'd envisaged for Chatham.

'There is one thing, Roger. You know my old sidekick Taters? He's
out again. He was with me when I found this. He marked my card.'

The lie was absolutely necessary if the old hussar was to be cut in
on this. It had to look as if Peter owed Chatham one.

'Taters will be the sentry, minding our backs in Crown Passage. So
we'll probably have twenty-five long ones apiece. Not the worst
night's work.'

Expecting protest, he faced the glinting lenses. But Roger did not
appear upset, just practical.

'Well, it's pointless nicking it if we can't make it come up to its
proper ecret.'

Roger was right. Peter would contact Didier first. As they retreated
back to their chariot, a shop in Ryder Street caught Roger's eye. He
stopped, beckoning Peter to his side.

'Pity you haven't got someone who'll buy dolly mixtures. Look at
these.'

He was at Pawsey & Payne's window, opposite the old Eccentric
Club. It showed a fine display of equine canvasses – Herrings (Senior
and Junior), Fearnleys, possibly a Stubbs on the back easel. Only a
few years ago he'd stood in front of that same window with a short-
arsed dealer from the west of Ireland, who fancied the stock, as Peter
told Roger.

'I asked my dealer pal what he'd bid and either he underestimated
my guile or he was just running off at the mouth. So he said twenty
thousand for any dozen of what was on display. The same night, still
in a state of shock at the size of the offer, I nicked sixteen or seventeen
of them. Bashed the door, did a hurry-up, a bunch of sighters from
the Eccentric Club calling out for me to put the pictures back. Oh to
be young and valiant again!'

'And did he pay?'

'Yes. Twenty-five grand, by cheque. After that he parted with
another one hundred and fifty grand, always by cheque, over a
fifteen-month period.'

It had been the beginning of a beautiful friendship. Like a shopper drunk on credit, the dealer picked out targets, mostly in Mayfair but with a few excursions into St James's. For more than a year, Peter filled him up with valuables: Keith Banham's enamel French striking clocks from the corner of Grafton Street, paintings from Richard Green in Dover Street, William Temple's Regency furniture from Haunch of Venison Yard, furs from Bruton Street. Peter had gone to war and ended up, inevitably, with the eight-year stretch.

Roger wanted to know about the dealer.

'People like that are never around when I get gear. What happened to him?'

'Disappeared.'

'Where?'

'Presumably to knock out the stock he'd bought from me.'

'Can he not be resurrected? He'd be useful for this lot.'

'My man on the Continent's just as reliable, and no chance of any kites. Why shouldn't he have his chance? After all, we're in the Common Market now.'

They got back to the Triumph in time to forestall a taut-skirted slattern as she began to scribble a ticket on her pad. Peter felt an urge to boot her up her ample arse. He resisted. As he opened his door the 'excess' flag popped up on the meter.

'Bad luck, love,' he murmured as they mounted the chariot.

As they roared away, Peter began to consider where society would be without offenders against the law. There was a whole chain of employment and revenue which depended on them. Traffic wardens, clampers, motoring fines. Security consultants, alarm contractors, glaziers, locksmiths, police, forensic scientists, lawyers, judges, clerks, probation officers, screws, prison visitors, welfare comforters, hostels . . . Without malefactors, many of the righteous would have little enough to do, little enough to live on, and little enough to make them *feel* righteous. Sinners are a much-maligned, very necessary commodity.

Small wonder the expedient Pontius Pilate found those two felons to liven up the show at Golgotha. Sinners were required, if only to be told, 'You shall be with me in Paradise . . .'

Paradise. Faith's ultimate reward.

Roger, swinging the Triumph into Berkeley Square, interrupted the daydream.

'You're very quiet. Spotted another victim of yours?'

They were thundering up Brook Street, past the site of Peter's recent Golgotha in Horse Shoe Yard.

'No. I was thinking about the Crucifixion. Well, more about the two thieves who the myth says were nailed up alongside. The wrong one got to Paradise, you know.'

Roger, concentrating on his driving, said nothing. Peter's foot twitched as he caught the briefest glimpse of the spikes that had impaled him. He rambled on, 'But where is Paradise? Hell, I suspect, is where we live. The repentant thief shouldn't qualify for Paradise, too easy an out. Faith is the necessary bollocks to keep the demands of human nature at bay.'

Now they were stuck in traffic. Roger, bored by the lack of progress, suddenly took to the theme with interest.

'OK. Why did the wrong one get to heaven?'

'Think about it. Suppose it's you and me up there with the Nazarene. We've never heard of him, never met him until now. We've been up on the cross for hours. There we are: weak, thirsty, dying in pain, and the only thing to distract us is the Romans taking the piss out of Chummy between us. Maybe we've even caught sight of the caption, "King of the Jews". We're Jews too. Could it be our king? If so, he's a bit naive. He wasn't expecting the lynching, never even been to one before. Word is, he doesn't really know why he's here. *We* know why we're up here. We've anticipated the possibility all our lives, because we're thieves. We know fuck-all's going to get us down again.

'Next thing, Chummy asks for water, they give him vinegar. He rambles on about forgiving them, because they don't know what they're about. Crap. They know exactly. So now there's blood running down his face from the crown of thorns some Roman wit's locked on his head. We see that. We feel a bit sad for him. Special treatment, you see? And it's very odd having this amateur up here with us. One of us is listening. Seems his father's abandoned him or whatever. Then we see that tart from the bazaar, lurking down there in the gloom. She's crying. But she'd cry for no one. Chummy wasn't a punter of hers, surely? Now the squaddies are rowing over his cape. And why's it getting so fucking dark? Maybe the Nazarene *has* got a bit of muscle in the next world after all.

'So Muggins tries it on. "Any chance of getting us down out of here, mate?" Chummy don't seem to hear, maybe he's gone on. Cunning bollocks, the second thief's on a different tack. He's sure nothing's going to get them out of this wrought, so he backs a long-shot. A show of faith. "Leave him out. We're here by right. We'd a good run. Him they swapped for that scumbag pickpocket Barabbas.

That was a crooked heat. But you know what the fucking Romans are like when the Pharisees gee them up. Line of least resistance . . ."

'In spite of his bitterness, he nearly laughs but naturally it hurts too much. Knowing the game's up, he takes the piss. "Hey," he says, "remember me when you come into your kingdom." He can hardly keep a straight face, but he has to say it, just in case. Then comes the line that stops the show. Chummy raises his nut and finds his tongue. He talks to the second thief. "Today you will be with me in Paradise." Then he drops his head, the curtain falls, and the end's a guess-up.'

Roger, driving again now, was interested.

'So . . . ?'

'The point is, the poor bollocks who first explored the idea of Chummy's power – very likely in some dim sort of faith, you know – got a knock-back. The other one, the guy who only added a few quips on the end, got a ticket. That fair?'

Roger slowed the car. His smile had gone. Something Peter had said had got to him. But he came out of it after a few seconds, mocking again.

'Who knows, Peter? Perhaps even you've got enough plus points to make it through the gates.'

He dropped his passenger by the rear door of the Sanatorium. Before walking away, Peter leaned through the open door, speaking quietly.

'The best time to pop it will be Saturday night, when the law's poncing around the West End. Meet me here at seven. I'll have Taters with me.'

'Anything I should bring?'

'A cane. I'll have the bolt-cutters and half a dozen sacks. We can use the Triumph, you handle it very well.'

Roger nodded. His lenses glinted one last time.

'See you at seven, then.'

He roared away.

On the dot of seven, Roger found the ageing conspirators at their point of loiter in Delaware Road. Peter made the introductions.

'Roger – my old pal George Chatham.'

'How do?' Taters mumbled, climbing with difficulty into the back of the car. He looked like the most unpromising of accomplices you could imagine, and Roger said nothing. He was sulking as he drove off – with exaggerated care, out of mock deference to Taters's age. A long time later he broke the ice.

'Bit old for this game, aren't you, George?'

Taters summoned his dignity.

'Got to do your best when you're skint, son. Young or old.'

Roger sniggered.

'Feels like I've enlisted in Dad's Army.'

'Don't fret, Rog,' said Peter. 'He's as sound as a bell. Got more experience – and scalps – than the two of us put together.'

But Roger had made his point. He picked up speed and soon they were nosing into Duke Street.

'Park in King Street, opposite Crown Passage,' said Peter, assuming command. It was action time.

But there was no space. They shunted further east and, twenty yards on, found a slot.

'You're not going to pop the silversmith's in Crown Passage?' It was Taters from the back, a plaintive whine. '*I* did it, a year or so back.'

'George,' said Peter, patiently, 'we're using the building site there to cross Pickering Place. It backs onto How's, the silversmiths. Remember? We found it together.'

Backing into the parking space, Roger sounded unimpressed.

'Don't tell me you done that too, George?'

Meekly, Taters picked up the fanny which Peter had floated on his behalf.

'No, but I did show it to Peter last autumn.'

Roger killed the engine and Peter went through the game-plan.

'George, Roger and I are going over the hoarding into the site. Once we're in, I want you to aim the tools over. Keep your eyes on the pub. We'll have to cross their roof and they're the only likely sighters. OK, we're off now. Mind us over.'

Leaving the car, Roger handed the toolbag to George.

'We won't need the big Stilsons. I've brought an eighteen-inch pair of bolt-cutters.'

He smiled without humour.

'Easier for you to lug over, George.'

He and Peter went over the hoarding sweetly and the equipment followed: bag of tools, sacks.

'George,' Peter hissed through the hoarding. 'Dwell in King Street. If they arrive, that'll be the most likely place. We may be a little time.'

There was a ladder inside the renovation, simplifying the initial ascent. To cross the scaffolding to the pub roof was more demanding. They were on view. But there was only the thin figure of Taters looking up from the ill-lit passage. Then they were tiptoeing across the two rooftops, before arriving at a skylight set into the twin-pitched Georgian slates of How's. The point of entry.

'Roger, I'm going to raise the felted skylight. It may be belled. More likely, the trap-door below will be. Once I put the cane to it, we'll be on offer.'

The skylight offered no resistance as, gingerly, Peter raised it. His cautious torchbeam revealed an attic into which they dropped, moving towards the predicted trap-door. Peter located the point of least resistance with the end of his heavy steel cane.

'Ready? Here we go.'

The cane prised the two-centuries-old timber. The frame crackled, resisting the shock of trespass, but then the cane found purchase and the trap-door surrendered. The alarm bell wailed dimly below them, amplified in the hollow well of the courtyard. Its real purpose was not to alert the law but to unnerve the thief.

Peter ignored it. He attacked the task in hand, swarming down the ladder which had been provided from below, as if thoughtfully. As if for his benefit.

Now he was on the third-floor stairwell and adrenalin was coursing through him with its old, familiar, sensuous excitement.

Roger joined him and they slipped down the rickety stairs, finding the expected grille between them and the treasure-house. Roger sliced the paddy with the bolt-cutters, but a second lock, set in the grille itself, still defied them. Roger applied the cane. There was a loud crack. They were in.

Net curtains covered the windows overlooking the courtyard. Peter stationed himself behind them, waiting for the enemy's entrance.

'Shtum, Rog! The law are here.'

Roger had been pulling the sacks into the room when Peter glimpsed the peaked cap of the skipper of an area car. They froze, hearts pounding, mouths dry, their eyes riveted on the set below as the uniform sniffed around. Peter prayed he knew the drill. Check the premises for signs of entry, find none. Think of looking round the back, then realise there was nowhere to look, because this courtyard backed onto the gable-end of a more modern building on The Mall. Then radio in asking for the keyholder.

Dozens of faulty alarms are activated in the West End nightly, and it's impossible to leave a police presence at every one. High-value premises get preference, however, and this could have been one of them. That – plus the fact that he couldn't inspect the rear – might encourage the law to dwell.

But in the lamplight of the yard the young skipper's face showed no sign of suspicion. He simply raised his radio and alerted Control. Over and out. He stepped back, took off his cap, and scanned the façade. Then, as if satisfied, he replaced his cap and disappeared out of sight, back to St James's.

'I think we've cracked it,' Peter whispered. 'Quick as you can, load up.'

The glittering silver was arrayed in cabinets around the wall. Methodically, they began filling their sacks, with Peter keeping a weather-eye on the scene below. They would be back, but when?

They filled four sacks, then moved the weighty silver to the roof via the ladder. The booty clanked ominously. Once up, they took a blow on the roof while Roger gave a confident grin and the thumbs-up sign. Then a creak alerted them to another presence. It was Taters, panting as he hauled himself onto the roof.

'It's on top!' he gasped. 'The law have cars at both ends of the passage.'

The young skipper had been too wide for them. Peter put his finger to his lips and crept towards the parapet which overlooked the court-yard. He peered over. The skipper was there again, looking up, but, if he saw Peter, he gave no sign. Only the squawk of his radio broke the silence. Peter retreated.

'Back to the building site. I fancy they know we're here.'

Roger went to lift a sack.

'We'll take one with us,' he said.

'No, leave it,' hissed Peter. 'The silver will rattle.'

They left empty-handed, having now only their liberty to preserve. Their tenuous luck held, for they regained and crossed Crown Passage not a moment too soon. Growling dogs were now dragging their handlers towards the hoarding which the thieves had traversed only seconds earlier.

'They're on the pub roof,' a harsh voice bellowed behind them. 'We have them!'

It was a delusion. They were on the roofs to the east of Crown Passage. A minute or so later the would-be thieves grounded in Angel Court, some hundred yards further on, and right opposite Roger's parked car.

Heading for Goldhawk Road, no one talked. They were exhausted, depressed at losing the prize, elated at the close shave, each aware that the old hussar's courage and guile had saved them. If this was Dad's Army, Roger really had better enlist.

'Can you drop me at Netherwood Road?' asked Taters.

There was a Greek spieler in Netherwood Road. He was going to play it up. But this time he didn't have to act the mendicant, or mention his need to collect laundry. Peter thrust a fifty-pound note into his gnarled hand, holding it for a second to say thanks.

When Roger dropped Peter at the tennis club a few minutes later, he was contrite about Taters.

'He's a game old boy. I feel a bit of a prat myself.'

And you're entitled to, Peter thought. But he didn't say it. They had lived and might fight another day.

How of Edinburgh are long gone from Pickering Place. They are housed now in secure first-floor premises in Albemarle Street. Peter believes that to have lost their stock in 1983 might easily have been to the old firm's best advantage for, in the interim, silver prices have collapsed and How's would have done better collecting the insurance and going into some other trade.

26

Impressionist Days

ANOTHER Christmas was not far off, and the failure at How's still rankled. Then a minor miracle put him in funds. A pal from the north turned up with the keys to a warehouse too good to turn down and, with the help of Steve, a penniless club member whom Peter persuaded to provide transport, about a hundred video recorders were spirited away.

Steve, who had also once helped Peter pillage a museum, was recently called to his early death from a vile cancer.

'I only ever did two dishonest things, Peter,' he told the tearful thief, 'and they were both for you.'

'Never you mind, Steve,' he'd said. 'Put them down to me when you get up there. I've so much to answer for and the extra won't matter.'

'I'll leave the back door open for you,' Steve grinned. Ever a lovely man. It must have made a change for the angels to be sent a diamond, with so many righteous shits battering on the door.

In the wake of the videos, Taters was back at the club for another helping of Lena McGee's fare.

'Just come from court,' he said, sprightly as ever, piling into a plate of stew. 'Got probation for the Bourne & Hollingsworth turn-out. I suppose you'll be having a pop at it now?'

Taters's indiscreet visit should have alerted Bourne's but they missed its significance. The store was still waiting to close down, like a great stranded whale awaiting the tide. So Taters was right, it was on the cards.

Suddenly, slyly, Taters pushed the boat out.

'You got any money?'

'Why, is it sub time again, or the bloody laundry? No. That sly look tells me you've got something to sell.'

Taters gave an insipid grin. 'I've got a painting. I've had it for a while. It's pawned with a bookie for two grand, but it's worth a lot more. You got anyone for it?'

'Who's the artist?'

'Matisse. The gallery wanted a quarter of a million. I hooked it out of their showroom in Mayfair.'

Pride came into his voice. 'It was on an easel. I used my wire hook. Remember we did the same at Wildenstein's, getting the Renoir?'

Peter didn't instantly recall that. But he'd read of the Matisse theft all right. The *Daily Telegraph* had announced that it was the work of a sophisticated gang of art thieves, stealing to order. The reality was, Taters had found a solo move. Not the first of his to be put down to gangs and plots.

'What's on your mind, then?' asked Peter, his greed stirring.

'Redeem it for two grand, give me another two for myself now and a further two later. If you have someone. It's cheap at six grand.'

Suddenly Peter remembered the Renoir. Taters had slaughtered it to an arsehole from Brighton for a mere five thousand. Given the intervening inflation, he was asking even less for the Matisse.

'I'll make a phone call. Can't use the one here, I think it's tapped. I'll be ten minutes.'

In his villa at Waterloo, Didier picked up the phone after the first ring.

'Pierre! *Ça va? Vous êtes très content?* You have something for me?'

'A Matisse. You probably know about it. I can lay my hands on it but what should I pay?'

'Yes, I know the Matisse. Not so simple to move, but I have a contact in Arles. Myself, I would like to give maybe five, six thousand sterling. I know it's small money, but it is not easy with a famous canvas. Would that buy it?'

'Not quite. Seven and a half thousand and we could take charge.'

'OK. Midday on the day after tomorrow, usual place. I come personally, you understand?'

'I understand.'

Peter returned to the club, having negotiated a fifteen-hundred-pound earner. He found Lena McGee delivering Taters's second helping of apple crumble. In a whisper she confided to Peter, 'George looks like a sparrow, though he's a fine old head. And his appetite – well, he eats like a lion, so he does.'

Peter sat down. 'George, when can we pick up the parcel?'

'Now, if you have the readies. Your friend can move it? I'll have to have my two grand before you can take it, but the other two can wait a couple of weeks. OK?'

Forty-eight hours later each of the three principals in this little farce was *très content*. The only unhappy one was a bit player, the bookie. He thought he'd nicked a Matisse for two grand. Yet even he could afford to smile, as Taters was sure to do the two thousand with him. And the Matisse? It went back to the place of its inception, somewhere in Provence.

A few days later Peter contacted Clyde.

'You can have a look at Bourne & Hollingsworth again. It's back on the probable list. Taters's problem there's resolved itself. Do you know Richoux's in South Audley Street? I'll meet you there tomorrow at two.'

Clyde appeared shortly after two, casual as ever, fag still dangling.

'You like it here, don't you?'

He ordered a banana split and lounged inelegantly on the moon-shaped bench seats.

'Had a shufty, then?' asked Peter

Sure he had, and he was enthusiastic. 'You were right, they're closing down, they're having a closing-down sale. There's loads of pussy. The two upper floors are empty, so I thought we might do a break-out.'

'No, we can't dwell up. Taters did that and was either seen or security got on to him some way. So it's our old friend the ladder again. Up to the first floor canopy and on from there.'

'Hang about,' said Clyde. 'I pratted up last night. An old boy locks up and goes off to a mews house in Eastcastle Street. I'm sure there's no security there at night. Fancy meeting me tonight and watching it?'

Clyde's excitement was infectious and Peter's resolve strengthened. You need a bit of a push at fifty.

It wasn't always that way. In the sixties he'd needed no pushing in the Fur Wars. He'd appeared hell-bent on self-destruction – falling in love and finding so many Judas Iscariots as the thirty-pieces-of-silver mob queued to collect their prizes. He now recalled the words of a retired copper from around that time who had buttonholed him at Sandown races.

'So many people with their arms around your shoulder were putting it on you. We felt sorry for you on the Squad. It came in your favour in an odd sort of way.'

This was Bill Baldock, a one-time Chief Inspector on the Sweeney. A chum with him was less sympathetic. Terry O'Connell, an Anglo-Celt, formerly a Commander at the Yard, sniped at Peter unkindly.

'You always talked too much. I was too bloody straight. I could have nicked you a number of times, and your wife Jackie. You were a flash Harry.'

Flash Harry? Maybe. Peter smiled. There was still the flash Harry in his make-up, and now he was off crusading again with Clyde, like Cervantes' Knight Errant, tilting at windmills, not on the sands of Granada, but in busy Oxford Street. What he had in common with Quixote was a priceless obsession, a master passion.

Peter arrived early for a final chilly, dank recce. He quickly calculated that they would need up to fifty mail bags to shift the anticipated haul. The GPO's habit of leaving them scattered around made them fairly simple to secure and, prowling around Hanover Square and environs in the gloom, he totted forty sacks unseen, which he stowed in the BMW's boot. Some of the most precious years of his life had been spent hunched over the needle doing eight to an inch. It was a very special purgatory. The idea of them filled with mink gave the thief a pleasing sense of revenge.

The ladder proved more difficult. One he had his eye on had been paddied up since he last sighted it, but he finally found one slumbering unprotected in a basement in Eastcastle Street. He must have cut a quaint figure tottering along in the twilight with the thirty-foot aluminium extension ladder, rating the odd glance, but none from officialdom. He smiled to himself, recalling Taters in Mayfair in the thirties. Under similar circumstances, he'd fannied a suspicious young copper with, 'I'm eloping, Officer.'

And he'd been believed. Such was the innocence of half a century ago.

Reaching Wells Street, a voice from a doorway startled him.

'You eloping, mate?' It was Clyde. 'Don't know how you avoid a pull. You look sussy.'

Clyde still had a little to learn about the public's threshold of interest.

Peter padlocked the ladder to a lamppost. He, at least, knew of the existence of thieves.

'Has the minder left yet?' he asked. Clyde shook his head as they took up their vigil near the store's side entrance. Suddenly the threshing of bolts alerted them.

'That's him now,' Clyde whispered as an elderly man tested the locked door with a vigorous shunt of his arm. They followed him and, as Clyde predicted, he went straight to a house in the Eastcastle Street mews.

'He lives there,' said Clyde triumphantly. 'I bet no one's in the store overnight. They rely on an alarm system at ground-floor level, but there's no system on the first-floor windows.'

He was probably right. A final jaunt around the perimeter of the once-great London landmark revealed no lights. In cockney parlance, Clyde summed it up succinctly.

'The joint's as dead as a kipper.'

Their last task was to make sure they could neutralise the street light adjacent to the entry point. From his pocket Peter produced a key and fitted it to the inspection box at the foot of the lamp. The key turned. Everything was falling into place. Only a sonic in the fur department itself could thwart them now.

'There's a lot of pussy up there. We'll need wheels. I can ask a pal in Hendon.'

Clyde was certainly on the ball, but vans from unknown pals in Hendon were unattractive to Peter.

'It's not a problem. A mate of mine at the club will lend me his van.'

The pal was Steve, who was skint and would welcome the five-hundred-pound fee Peter would pay him.

D-Day found Peter, who never stinted on preparation, in the fur department shortly after opening time. There was not a sonic in sight; the window in the ladies' changing room was unprotected, and he located a store-room under the stairs next to the fur department. Sneaking a preview, he saw it was stuffed full of fur garments. A scan of the store-room's door jamb revealed no alarm system. If there was an electronic Judas here, he couldn't detect it.

'Can I help you, sir?' A blue-rinse matron in a severely tailored suit pounced.

'Perhaps,' smiled Peter. 'My wife seems to have disappeared. I thought I might find her somewhere round here.'

'Well, you won't find her in there. That's a store-room.'

Her suspicion evaporated under the warmth of the thief's charm. Satisfied he was neither a punter nor a sneak thief, the elegant floor-walker went her way; the thief likewise, knowing now that the fur department was at his mercy.

Steve, yet again suborned, was nervous about parting with his van.

'Be careful with it. I can do with a monkey, but what if something goes wrong?'

'If you haven't heard from me by eleven o'clock tonight, report it stolen.'

It was early evening and Peter wanted to be certain of a parking spot directly under the assault canopy. Steve's old Volkswagen van chugged into Wells Street, farting as it went. The van was decrepit but it would just pass muster. It was taxed and clean, and would keep at least a casual constabulary at bay.

He found a space and, with time to spare, rewarded himself with a large Hine in a pub on the corner of Eastcastle Street. He realised he was close to the scene of the old hussar's greatest triumphs of thirty years past: the first Great Mail Bag Robbery was enacted here and Taters was still irked at the way Billy Hill had claimed the laurels for it. Never mind that. Peter took the coincidence as an omen. Once a good battlefield, always a good battlefield.

Clyde arrived, and together they observed Bourne's locking-up ritual.

'Taters is somewhere about,' Peter told the young blade. 'He's our outside man. Mind us from the street.'

The late decision to include Taters found no fault with Clyde and now, from the shadows opposite, Taters shuffled into view and greeted them with a question.

'Everything OK?'

The street was deserted and Peter, using his key, turned the street lamp out. The canopy and entry point beside it were now in almost total darkness. The ladder lay innocently on the pavement beside the store wall.

'Now,' hissed Peter, galvanising Clyde into action by hoisting the ladder. Peter belted up with the sacks and tools. Clyde scampered up behind, drawing the ladder after him. Then, crouching on top of the canopy, their eyes scanned the garishly lit Oxford Street for possible sighters. Windows opposite were not to be ignored and Taters, lingering watchfully in the shadows, indicated with a thumbs-up that all had gone well.

The broad, deep ledge above the canopy had a rebated leaded window let into it. A flick of Peter's gloved knuckle broke the pane but the glass, retaliating, sliced through the glove and now a trickle of blood was draining into the leather turtle. The handle inside resisted pressure, and now Clyde took charge, using the jemmy to force it up. At last it relented, the window opened, and Peter clambered into the room. He hesitated, embracing the silence, listening for any alarm. Nothing. He ushered Clyde in before closing the window.

'What do we do if the law comes?' whispered Clyde.

Hugging his torn paw, Peter played dad.

'Very little we can do, son. They'll surround the block and we'll be nicked.' He chuckled. 'But it's more likely we're about to have a nice touch, so let's get cracking.'

The initial anxiety was already passing, and an adrenalised calm took over. They moved up the immobile escalator towards the fur department. A great sales banner was stretched across the ceiling above them: EVERYTHING MUST GO! Peter pointed to it.

'Look,' he whispered. 'We're expected.'

Among the furs, the first hazard was neutralising the battery-operated buzzers, fixed on each row of garments to thwart hoisters. That done, they methodically packed the most expensive furs on display into sacks. They then turned their attention to the store-room, whose door offered little resistance to the cane.

They worked in silence. Only their heavy breathing and the odour of sweat was discernible to ear and nose. An hour had passed from the moment they'd begun the assault before Peter allowed himself the luxury of a look-down into the street. He caught sight of his ancient doppelganger, patrolling up and down to signal all was well. Clyde took time out to light a fag. They had filled forty sacks, and the remnants left were only the rags – very poor-quality foxes, which are uncertain sellers even at the best of times. Retreat was next on the agenda.

Dragging the sacks, two at a time, down the escalator to the first-floor exit window was a pilgrimage of eighty yards. Ten trips and both men were bushed, panting, latent fear burning precious energy. But now the haul was assembled beside the window.

Peering out, the thief waved to Taters to alert him of their exit. Only the dull roar of traffic in Oxford Street was audible as Clyde passed the sacks out to Peter on the canopy. They were now at the point of highest risk. Clyde lowered the ladder on Taters's signal and shinned down, opening the side loading door of the van.

'Right!' he hissed. 'Let's go.'

Peter, with a maniacal energy that belied his years, flung the sacks down to Clyde who, in an unbroken movement, aimed them into the van.

'Fuck it!' he said suddenly in a stifled voice.

A family group was sauntering down the darkened street. Clyde busied himself with the van while Peter crouched stock still on the canopy. Then the strollers had passed, without a glance. The transfer complete, Peter scrambled down unobserved, lowered the ladder, and was laying it in the gutter just as Taters joined them. Time to go.

'Well done, lads,' Peter praised as they crossed Oxford Street and were cruising sedately down Regent Street towards the sanctuary of Peter's garret in Wandsworth. The old van, puffing and farting, did its duty while Peter and Clyde, each wrung out emotionally and physically, sweated in silence.

They dropped Taters off first.

'We'll pull out twenty-five garments for you, OK?' Peter told him.

Taters's face told them he was not pleased. He seized on the imagined slight.

'Can't you let me have a few quid now?'

No mention of laundry. Peter bunged him two hundred pounds.

'Be in touch tomorrow,' he said, driving away. The play money had to some extent appeased Taters, but Peter could see that the old gladiator felt he was being treated shabbily. However, Taters's feelings were not paramount at this time.

'You didn't mention you were pulling in Taters,' Clyde said. 'Why not?' His grin told Peter it was only a lightweight enquiry.

'You might have rucked if I had. I thought it best to present a *fait accompli*. He played his part. There's plenty for us all. Sorry. I dare say I should have told you.'

They parked outside the backwater house and stored the booty in the small back bedroom, with much the same alacrity as they had removed it from B & H. If there were any sighters around, minding your own business was a basic ground-rule in those back streets.

The bedroom was filled to the ceiling with sacks, leaving them about sixteen square feet in which to examine the haul. A preliminary count adduced they'd clawed a hundred and seventy-five furs, mainly mink coats. Clyde acted perplexed, scratching his head.

'I thought we had more than this. I'm choked.'

He'd just been in a half-million-pound heist. How choked can you be over that? If you're a Lloyd's underwriter, maybe.

'Well, we'll get a lot more next time.'

Peter's sarcasm was wasted. Clyde looked up eagerly.

'Great! When?'

They chose garments in turn, Peter picking for Taters.

'Clyde, before you shoot off, let me have a full-length coat. I'll put one from mine with it. My pal with the van must be covered.'

'Two coats?' Clyde wailed. 'A grand for the loan of an old banger?'

Peter gave him a bland look.

'Don't whine. It did its job. More important, it came from a sound source with no chance of post mortems. Money can't buy that.'

With an impatient tug, Clyde drew a black mink from one of his sacks.

'Right,' he said, 'I'm off now. I'll get a black cab. I'll be back around

seven this morning and pick mine up. Sweet? They'll fit into my
BMW.'

After Clyde had left, Peter settled down alone on the mink moun-
tain. Sleep was impossible, with adrenalin still pumping. He made
some rough calculations. Eighty garments, worst way a monkey
apiece, more if punted individually. Forty thousand, then. He'd bell
Diana. He could have a draw and cover Steve for the loan of the van.

'Hello, darling, I'm having a little party over the water,' he coded.
'Like to come? Bring a few quid with you. You'll have to pay your
round.'

Diana was pissed off being belled at 2 a.m. Yet shrewd enough to
know it must be in her favour.

'Can't it wait till morning?'

'Could, I suppose. But maybe all the booze'll be drunk.'

Diana caught the thread. And she smelt an earner.

'I'll see you in forty minutes.'

Relaxing at last, he dozed off among the furs, to be woken by the
doorbell twittering. Diana.

'Hello, lover. I hope it's worth my while. I loathe south London.
What've you got?'

If she had been sleepy, the sight of the fur brought her rudely
awake.

'Jesus,' she wheezed. 'You done Harrods again?'

Peter said nothing. He just indicated the sacks that contained his
share of the loot. She began to open them one by one to peek inside.

'Why can't I look in those other sacks?'

Peter explained that they were Clyde's. Always sensible, even at
such an obscene hour, she was placated. She knew Clyde would probably be letting her see them himself, soon.

Then Peter gave her chapter and verse.

'OK. Here's the bottom line. I want seven hundred apiece for the
full-length coats. Most of them are on a four-grand mark-up, some
even more. The jackets must make three hundred a lump. The fox,
wolf and raccoon we negotiate on. But at those prices, you'll have
plenty of room to move.'

Diana grimaced.

'Behave yourself, you cunt. We won't fall out over a few quid.
This lot'll take some time to move. How many garments are there,
anyhow?'

'Eighty are mine.'

'Eighty! You could open your own salon. Where'd they come from?'

'Bourne & Hollingsworth.'

'Well, like I said, your corner alone will take some moving. And remember, I'll probably have Clyde's on my plate too. Also, I'm going to Spain tomorrow for a couple of weeks. Will five grand keep you sweet? It's all I have at home.' She paused and screwed up her nose, scheming. 'I'll arrange another two for you on Monday. Meanwhile, *do* stay out of Rousseau's.'

She bent over and, working quickly, selected eight black Glamma minks.

'These will cover me for the readies. OK?'

Peter chortled, as he might joking with a naughty child.

'OK,' he said, lighting her cigarette. He knew she was into the gentleman bit.

'Right, well I can't have all this at my place when I'm away. Make a list of what I'm taking, prices too. Keep a copy for yourself. Then sack all this lot up and we'll meet in the morning. How about the car park of the tennis club? What time does it open?'

Peter grinned. The faithful would not approve of their car park being sodomised.

'Nine a.m. I'll be there with the van at nine-fifteen latest. Your Granada will take them comfortably. You can leave the eight you've just picked out too. You don't want to cross London at this hour with them on board.'

Diana nodded. It made sense.

'What if the Squad pay you an early morning call?'

Peter found a wan smile.

'I'll get ten years and you'll do five long ones. But fret not. They won't be missed till the morning. We left it sweet.'

Reassured, Diana smiled back.

'See you at nine-fifteen, then. Don't leave me hanging about. I've got a plane to catch.'

A peck on the lips and she was gone. He knew she wouldn't sleep. She'd scheme all night as a lot of pub landladies flitted through her computer brain.

Meanwhile, he had plenty to do. He sacked and twined the furs as the blood adrenalin began to fall. As he finished, he felt tired and bloody old. Fifty-three? Too old for West End commando strikes. Yet he was also pleased in his arrogance. He could still perform.

He dozed off, until the buzzer jolted him awake at seven. It wasn't the Squad, but Clyde.

*   *   *

The huge boot of Clyde's BMW took most of his share, but a couple of sacks had to ride in the back floor area. The odd early-morning sighter passed, barely noticing them. Then Clyde was away with a flourish while Peter, dog tired, humped Taters's whack into the van. He was in Fulham within ten minutes, where Taters awaited him with a pal.

'Hope I haven't copped for all the rubbish,' he wailed.

Peter growled. 'You got pick for pick, same as us. There was no rubbish, it was all quality gear. Now, if there *had* been any, I'd have been tempted to drop it on your plate.'

Without further dispute, Taters took off, while Peter, heading for Maida Vale, had time for a café breakfast before his next stop at the club car park.

When he arrived at nine, the car park was deserted. Diana and a friend arrived minutes later, drawing alongside the van. She had her boy Rupert with her too. The Granada boot swallowed up the fur.

'Got a list for me?' she rasped. The late night and the dawn meeting had done her larynx no favours. Peter nodded.

'Yes, and I've got a duplicate. It includes a rough price guide.'

'Darling, Rupert will meet you in the café on the bridge at Baron's Court. Monday, midday. He'll give you two thousand. Meantime, take care, try to be sensible. Give Rousseau's a miss. You're not getting any younger, you know.'

Diana meant well, but it grated. He already knew he was a prat. He growled.

'Enjoy Marbella. Give the plastic gangsters a kiss from me. See you Monday, Rupert.'

The Ford Granada pulled away at modest revs, while Peter withdrew into the clubhouse. Truth is often a poisonous snake and he felt stung. The call of the tables and the flesh still rendered him vulnerable, yet the piper would have his shilling. Peter would relax. The touch would cushion the next six months, while his shrewd Diana made the stock fetch the right ecret.

When Steve appeared, he found Peter asleep in the bar with a brandy in his hand. He shook the thief gently.

'Everything go well?'

He was chirpy, hopeful, and anxious all at once.

'So-so,' Peter yawned. He reached into his wallet and passed an astonished Steve his monkey. 'Just so-so.'

Then he ambled off to cab it back to Wandsworth.

27

Chelsea and Memory Lane

PERPLEXINGLY, not a word of the theft appeared in the press. Had larceny in the eighties reached such proportions that a six-hundred-thousand-pound heist was not worthy of a mention?

Diana, as predicted, took several months to sell the parcel, but Peter ended up with the estimated forty thousand for his corner. It allowed him to ignore Roger and his phone calls, and the lingering ghost of the Jewel House.

Taters? He'd done his furs the same week, for a pittance, and the layers got every penny of it almost as quickly. Clyde bought a timeshare in Spain and a surfeit of Lebanese Black, and spent the summer amongst the successful gangsters of the Costa del Sol. Diana had a good earner, keeping a couple of coats for herself. Steve paid the rent and surprised the landlord. Finally an insurance broker in the City drove the governor in Marylebone mad with his migraine. One way or another, the Bourne & Hollingsworth turn-out spread a little happiness . . .

A young and ambitious DI was bashing his governor's ear, holding out a detailed print-out of the theft and its investigation.

'Same blood group again at the pussy theft. The computer comes up with an old face – Peter Gulston. Know him?'

The commander, a worldly man near retirement, chortled.

'Know him? Chased him half my life. Scotty's my age. He's probably hoisting at Harrods now.'

The senior officer paused reflectively. He was no lover of computer science, but he ought to cover his back.

'Let's not rule him out until we see what the collator has. The insurers are never off the trumpet. Have a word with West End Central too.'

The minus points were mounting. The thief was on borrowed time – but then so are all sinners.

He found Chelsea again, ensconced at the club bar. Seemingly she'd forgiven Peter's sacrificing her to Ferdie's peculiar lusts, and they played a little tennis before sinking the odd bottle of wine at the bistro in Lauderdale Road.

'My mum's from Kerry,' was her opening shot. The Celtic connection warmed him to her and, well in funds, he fished for a tryst. But he was not on.

'Peter, I'm still seeing my ex. I'm not ready to get re-involved, however lightly, not at this moment in time.' She paused, sipping her drink. 'I know you're not responsible for what happened with the caveman, so let's be friends, play it by ear. Is that all right?'

He knew the small monologue, fetching and sincere, came from the heart.

'Pals it is, then,' he said, giving her a boozy peck. But her next remark startled him.

'One of my father's guests the other day knew you. He's a retired commander from the Yard. And guess what? He said you were a jewel thief and you once stole Sophia Loren's gems. He thought your name was Gulston.'

'Oh, Chelsea, that's all old hat,' said Peter. 'I deny nothing, so you can believe what you like. I can't imagine your dad will approve of me, anyway.'

Chelsea pouted her lips, then smiled, charmingly and enigmatically.

'Look, I'm thirty years old. Reading law and supporting myself. Dad's got every confidence in me and says you're an amusing rogue. I suspect he's right at that.'

The twinkle in her green, distant Kerry eyes told him ground-rules had perhaps been arrived at. He slipped an arm around her waist and held it tightly enough to indicate that lust was not too far away. Scoundrels, even ageing ones, sometimes have lethal charm. Fascinating in small doses, it may kill in full measure, without the charmer even knowing it.

Chelsea's virtue was hoist on the petard of her curiosity. The 'pitfall and gin' may have helped, as did his temporary spending power and the many small subtleties that the hardened fornicator carries around with him. So the charade advanced.

One night he picked her up from her college. It was a bitterly cold evening and the image of her tripping across the pavement in a translucent silk blouse and pencil skirt compounded his lust. She shivered beside the car and he draped his overcoat over her shoulders as he ushered her into the warmth of the BMW.

'You look very chic tonight.'

'Thank you, kind sir,' Chelsea simpered. She was mocking him yet pleased. 'I do like old-fashioned good manners – men who open car doors for women and light their cigarettes. You're making a good impression, Mr Scott.'

The dark Kerry-green eye looked him over. He was wearing a double-breasted grey hopsack suit which concealed his bulk.

'You look smart. Rather like a High Court judge.'

God forbid. Or were his middle-class Irish antecedents creeping up on him suited and booted?

'I thought I'd show you off tonight, take you to Sheila's for a drink. It's a little jerry in Lanark Place. That's why I'm spronced up. To complement you.'

'I know Sheila. My chap used to take me there. She's super for her age.'

It was a faint disappointment. He'd hoped to break new ground for Chelsea tonight.

'Yes, Sheila's wonderful. I used to threaten her with marriage, writing notes under the pseudonym Dr Mad. She said I made her laugh.'

'Did she ever take you seriously?'

'Not bloody likely. She's much too wise. One husband, one long-time paramour. She's not a believer in third time lucky.'

Chelsea giggled. 'You are Dr Mad, but nice mad. Not like your macho transvestite chum. He's certifiable. Ever hear from him?'

'No, but I'd hardly go on about it if I did. I still feel guilty, you know.'

Chelsea leaned across and planted an affectionate, firm kiss.

'Don't. I'm a big girl, I can look after myself. I shouldn't have gone to the flat legless, it only encouraged him.'

'Most young women would fancy screwing Ferdie,' Peter offered in mitigation.

Chelsea yelped. 'I told you – I didn't screw him!'

I wonder, Peter mused, but only to himself . . .

Sheila's was crowded, meaning there were some twenty customers in the ill-lit, claustrophobic bar. Peter, none too politely, elbowed his way forward. Sheila sat bunched in a corner with a gaggle of syco-phants, as if the Gunpowder Plot was on again. Several malicious eyes did a quick appraisal of Chelsea. A bitching voice was just discernible above the banter.

'I don't know where that old cunt finds them. Is he well hung or what?'

The speaker knew only too well he wasn't, particularly. Still, better to be cunted off than ignored . . . A Teacher's and a brandy were put before them, the barmaid mouthing, 'That's with Sheila.'

'Cheers, Sheila.'

No one could accuse Mrs Kelly of being parsimonious, and for a few moments Peter and Chelsea paid court to the cabal, and then Peter called a round. The barmaid showed her worth.

'Sheila *and* her company?'

Peter gave the bitch a curt nod as he drew Chelsea aside to talk to her alone. The round was costly. Sheila's team never stopped scoring goals with the customers' inferiority complexes and supporting vanities.

Later Sheila joined them on one of her occasional walkabouts, to greet the faithful. Not unlike Ma'am at one of her garden parties. Chelsea and she indulged in those mysterious platitudes that women seem to have at their fingertips. Then Chelsea excused herself.

'Just go and powder my nose.'

Sheila pounced.

'She used to come in here with a copper. A right big-headed bastard, one of the governors in B Division. Lost no time in telling me she didn't fancy him.'

Peter smiled. Sheila's directness, at least, was appealing.

'Yes, I know. They're having a sabbatical from each other.'

'Sabbatical or not, you be careful what you tell her. You do go on a bit at times.'

It was true – almost like he didn't care. He gave Sheila a kiss and she was off to mingle some more. The thief had a regard for Sheila's intuitions. Perhaps he *was* tempting fate, fooling around with the enemy's lady.

But fuck it, that was half the buzz.

Chelsea's knees, gleaming in Lycra, swung onto the barstool, aimlessly lethal, mesmerising. She caught him looking.

'What are you thinking?'

She knew bloody well and immediately laughed. 'Yes, I *am* wearing stockings.'

She'd read his fornicating thoughts and he was embarrassed. A voice from across the bar rescued him. It was a local bookie.

'Hey, Peter. Hilly died last week. There's a small piece in the linen tonight.'

Peter acknowledged the news.

'Yes, I saw it in the nationals. Headline was "KING OF THE UNDER-WORLD DIES".'

'Did you know him?' Chelsea asked. 'Was he really king of the underworld?'

Peter considered the question. Billy had probably been the most pragmatic of villains; should have been a banker really. If he'd waved his pen as effectively as he arced a razor, there was no telling where he mightn't have gone.

'I knew him well for twenty-five years. He probably saved my life once, a long time ago. I knew he was ill, had been for some time. Must drop Gypsy, Bill's old woman, a line. Still lives in Moscow Road.'

'Saved your life? Tell me about it. Please.'

'Well, it's worth telling . . .'

He'd hardly be likely to forget it.

'Maria Callas was rumoured to have rented a house in Farm Street, opposite the Catholic church. I was poncing over the roofs after her bits and pieces. I got up there through a long-time empty in the same row, a derelict house it was. I must have been heard, because a resident started to hoot. In my haste to scarper, I took a chance on a drainpipe on the derelict. It started to come away and to save myself I punched through a sash window, sliced my wrist savagely. Then I fell through a glass conservatory roof below.'

'Were you badly hurt?'

'Didn't think so at the time. I knew I'd cut my wrist, but I got back to the Jaguar in Hill Street all right. A pal of mine, Bristow, was driving. Sitting in the passenger seat, I thought at first I'd pissed myself. But I hadn't. I was sitting in a screed of blood from a gash in my arse. I couldn't stop the wrist pumping, couldn't go to hospital — remember, I was top of the pops in the early sixties as far as the filth were concerned. So Bristow drove me straight to a nurse chum's home in Ladbroke Grove.'

'Are you making this up?' asked Chelsea.

'Making it up? You don't fanny about falls. Anyway, the nurse tried a tourniquet but it was no good, said I must go to hospital. Can't do that. So I bell Billy in Moscow Road, wake him up, thinking he might have a tame doctor. He has, in Hounslow. Or rather a pal, Percy Horne, who in turn has this doctor pal. So off we go, Bill still in his dressing gown and slippers. Sod's law. At Hounslow we find Doctor Tony's at some function near London Airport.'

Peter felt a bead of sweat running down his forehead as he told the tale.

'All the time I'm pumping claret so Percy has another chemist pal and we find him. He takes one look at me and whispers to Percy, "Take him to hospital. He's bleeding to death!"'

'Remember the old fifties movie, *Odd Man Out*? James Mason shot on an IRA bank raid in Belfast? He spends most of the film running around bleeding to death. Well, I didn't relish the starring role for myself. I was shit scared.'

'What happened then?' Chelsea was enthralled.

'So we discover Dr Tony's at a dress dance at the Oriel Hotel. We go there. It has a glass-fronted crescent entrance and from the car I can see Percy joining the revellers. He's found Dr Tony who's all negative hand signals. It looks like a no-no until suddenly Hilly springs out of the car, bounces into the hotel in his dressing gown and jamas. A very startled Dr Tony suddenly has a fistful of fingers tapping on his chest. I can see it all happening. And then, of course, Dr Tony *would* help, after all.'

Twenty-five years later, Peter still recalled vividly the scene at the quack's surgery, Hilly in his night gear swearing these were not gangland frolics while a none-too-sober dinner-jacketed Dr Tony prepared to sew him up.

'This is going to hurt,' Dr Tony barked. 'I'm pissed and you've lost a lot of blood. Drink as much of this water as you can, now!'

Peter, delighted at his deliverance, quaffed the water, gritted his teeth, and lived to tell Chelsea the tale.

'All he'd take by way of thanks was a bottle of Scotch, which I gave him when he took out the stitches later.'

Chelsea's eyes were as big as emerald saucers.

'Well, you were fortunate they were all good friends that night.'

She was right about that. Bill, Percy, Dr Tony had all combined to save the thief. Then she went on, spoiling it.

'But isn't it a bit over the top, the "saving your life" bit?'

'Well,' he laughed, 'that's how I tell it.'

He gripped her Lycra knee, his fingers following its contour round to the flesh at the back of her thigh. The trespass went unchallenged and it made him bold.

'Fancy a nightcap at Sutherland?'

Chelsea swerved.

'Didn't you go to Billy Hill's funeral?'

'No. Gypsy had it private. Didn't want the press vultures.'

They left the jerry. Driving into Clifton Road, he was uncertain about his next move. Chelsea solved the problem.

'OK. Let's have a look at your place, then. I bet it's quite chic. I can't imagine you living only with a bed, it's too bloody obvious.'

She giggled. Peter had alerted all and sundry as to the sparseness of his gaff.

'I just moved in . . . No time to furnish it yet. So it's booze on the bed, take it or leave it.'

Chelsea viewed the place stoically. She was more fortunate than most, for he'd changed the sheets that morning and the central heating for once was working. Nielsen's Second on Radio 3 helped relax her as she perched on the bed with a tumbler of Scotch, her skirt rucked back to expose an acre of Lycra which drew the thief's gaze. The scene had an impersonal, remote quality, not unlike Tracy waiting for a punter's reward, all in the dull glow of an orange bedside lamp, the green eyes resigned to the déjà vu of it all.

So they kissed in a dispassionate way, that being part of the script. Then Chelsea shed her skirt, whore-like in the orange glow, and her inordinately long legs in their sheeny cladding aroused his (these days) reluctant manhood. The purple knob, the silky legs, the orange glow . . . They fucked.

'Nielsen has a good effect on you,' said Chelsea. And, in the autumn of his libido, it had indeed been one of his better performances. A shade too clinical perhaps, but maybe that was the way Chelsea liked it, to keep affection at bay. Yet her lovely body more than compensated for her curious remoteness. She was smoking a cigarette now.

'You're the seventh man I've slept with. Am I a slut?'

Peter considered the rather sad unsolicited confession.

'Slut? You potty? You're a healthy modern young woman who's been very gracious to an old roué.'

Kissing her tenderly on the forehead, he felt suddenly guilt-ridden. He knew that 'the vine has tender grapes'.

'Then I'm not a whore?'

Words were inadequate to the situation. He cuddled her instead. She was a fragile waif playing at sophistication but not sure of her lines and deserted by self-esteem. The sexual revolution had done little for her.

Suddenly Hilly was dragged back for an encore.

'So you never answered my question. *Was* he king of the underworld?'

'King? There were more princes than kings. Bill spent most of his youth behind bars. He waited a long time for the throne, not unlike Wales. But he got there at forty-odd, having given the dungeons a miss for some time. Hill controlled Soho but not before he'd served as a trench soldier himself – which is more than you can say for most gangsters now.'

'You despise gangsters?'

'Despise them? That's too strong. I don't rate them. They have nothing to offer the thief and are best given a wide berth. Most are ponces and few have got any arsehole – real arsehole. I suppose they've got their own debased brand of bottle, intimidating others.'

'Did they intimidate you?'

She was challenging his ego, trying to get the measure of him.

'A few tried,' he admitted. 'I swerved with a mixture of Irish charm and contrived madness. I was never unaware of how dangerous they were, but it was a render-unto-Caesar scenario if I really found myself adjacent. The Twins flexed their muscles once or twice with me. My style didn't suit, which I guessed, so I kept mostly out of range. Everything's politics really, even in the so-called underworld. You're on your toes an entire lifetime.'

'Are you still of them, then?'

Her green eyes glinted.

'Probably . . .'

He hugged her, feeling a sudden affection which had previously been absent. His hand found a conical tit and began to stimulate it. An encore looked on.

28

A Reading in Aldgate

THROUGHOUT the thief's years at Paddington Tennis Club the atmosphere was one of male chauvinists, largely past their sell-by date, accepting a neutered fate without stoicism. Of the women, only those harpies most determined to hone their skills at the least sporting of sports stayed any length of time.

But with the spring sun, and the advent of Wimbledon, a trickle of new members was seduced into taking their playing tests. Few of them lasted but, during this hopeful season, the resident eunuchs would be in rut, constantly praying for some naive damsel to deliver them from their agony. They squirmed in their threadbare chairs whenever – briefly – the odd pretty girl did appear in the bar. More often than not, she would cast an eye over the still-life before her and be on her way.

On one such day, Major Keith St Clair Pringle tannoyed Peter into his office.

'Peter, like you to meet a new member.'

A pert, pretty, auburn-haired girl rose to greet the thief, so often the Major's 'courtesy hitter' and one of his few pals at the Sanatorium. Keith flashed him one of those 'we're on thin ice' looks.

'This is Fiona Kennedy. I've taken the liberty of promising that you'll give her a hit tomorrow morning.'

Peter knew how thin the ice could be. Shaking hands, he smiled and lied.

'Delighted to, Fiona. Peter Scott. I'd love to hit with you.'

Next day, forty-five minutes of frenetic tennis established that, though untainted by coaching, Fiona possessed an excellent eye and a lot of determination, scampering round the court and hacking everything back. Tea with Beauty afterwards was the reward.

She was a TV presenter. She sang too, and was engaged to a very bright TV documentary producer from a Gorbals background who had recently moved to London. Singing and tennis were her current priorities and Peter didn't try to disillusion her by explaining that it took five years minimum to get to grips with the cruel art of the latter. He didn't know about singing.

'What do I owe for the hit?'

Fiona paid her way. Most Scots do but, in her case, financial distress was clearly far distant. Peter blurted out, 'No charge. It's a pleasure to hit with a trier.'

'And what do you do apart from playing tennis?'

Pigeon-holing. The middle classes cannot resist it. He considered, maybe for a fraction too long. *To tell the truth with bad intent beats all the lies you can invent.*

'I wheel and deal. My needs are few. The club's more or less my life since I got hooked on the drug.'

Fiona was puzzled, and a little alarmed.

'Drug? What drug?'

'Tennis. It's an opiate for those whom life has passed by.'

Fiona scarcely concealed her disappointment. His perennial suntan and general demeanour gave him the look of a successful man. She wasn't to know that the illusion was generated out of criminal arrogance. Kindly Fiona found a platitude.

'I'm sure you could do anything you wished. Can we hit again?'

He nodded benignly, reasoning that nothing is for nothing with the unfair sex. 'Tomorrow, perhaps?'

The tannoy called him to the phone and he left her.

'Hello, squire. Richoux's at four o'clock, OK?'

Roger. Replacing the receiver, Peter felt the irrational shiver down his spine. Dr Fell was back.

Roger was on the half-moon couch.

'Hello, old man. Been on the courts? Saw Cicely at Bognor. She sends her regards.'

Plummy-voiced, Roger was fannying for any earwiggers. Peter was more direct.

'I thought you were dead.'

The heavy, exaggerated drone of conversation which filled the place allowed them anonymity, though they parleyed in *sotto* tones.

'Well, I'm not. Now, the V & A. I fancy having a pop at it.'

'Really?' Roger had surprised Peter yet again.

'Yes, but there's someone I want you to meet first, someone I have considerable faith in. She's a clairvoyant.'

He held up his hand. Peter's evident astonishment put him on the defensive.

'Don't laugh. Emma will prove you wrong. I have absolute confidence in her. OK?'

Peter scanned the limpid eyes behind their thick lenses. Was he serious? The sallow, bony face told him he was – very deadly serious. He decided to play along.

'I'm not laughing, Roger. I'm superstitious myself. Are we not both Aquarians? And me, I like the myth of Christ. You've got to have a myth in our game.'

Roger seemed reassured.

'Well, Emma's predictions, advice – whatever you want to label it – have astounded me in the past. I consult her on most things. With something like the V & A . . . well, it's a must. She's saved my bacon a couple of times.'

Peter nodded sagely.

'Is a seance expensive?'

'It's a *reading*, not a seance. There's no specific charge. Emma leaves it to you. I normally give her a hundred quid.'

'OK. Let's see if I've got this right. You want *us* to consult Emma before we tackle the V & A?'

'Correct. In fact, I make it a condition of my participation.'

Alice in Wonderland, thought Peter. But harmless, surely . . .

They tubed it to Aldgate. As they rattled along side by side, Peter watched their images reflected in the carriage windows opposite. Two fucking lunatics. Seances and prayers for permission to trespass, if you please!

They found a black cab and sat in silence as it wove through a maze of council estates, before pulling up at a prim and tidy terraced house. Roger gave the door a hearty bang.

'Emma, it's Roger,' he bellowed. 'I've brought a friend.'

The door opened on its security chain. Even those in touch with the psychic world must take precautions here on earth.

'Oh, Jesus, it's you. Dad, make a cup of tea for the lads.'

'Hello, Emma. Peter's from your country.'

She gave Peter a searching look. His forename would pass muster, Catholic or Protestant. It was a favourite with the Celts. Emma herself was a Juno, while Dad could have passed for Joxer in O'Casey's play. Who, Peter wondered, would play the Captain? In a Dartmoor production years ago it had been himself, for he'd been well equipped then, a peacock down to his claws. Peter nodded politely at Emma's greeting and Dad's tea. She'd become, on reflection, a little too anglicised for Juno, though she'd not lost all the trappings of her west of Ireland traveller origins. You'd sight a flock of her type on any fair day over there. She had dark, mean eyes which darted about like those of a horse trader weighing up a pony.

'I'd feel better if he'd take off those dark glasses,' she said. 'Give us a look at the eyes.'

Roger had dictated dark glasses for the cab ride. Peter now took them off, confirming her fears. He looked the perfect image of the absentee landlords who'd persecuted her ancestors. His distinct Ulster intonation evoked further hostility in Emma's beady eye. But she wasted no time getting down to business.

'So it's a reading you're after. Not sure I feel up to it today. I'll do my best, though.'

She rubbed her hands together, as if seeking inspiration. A faint perfume of whisky permeated the air around her.

Roger beamed, delighted.

'Do Peter first. May I sit in?'

So Dad was banished and Emma fished a dog-eared pack of Tarot cards from the sideboard.

'I can't say I'm on form today. I've had an odd day. I'll try.'

Emma ripped the pack open, bade Peter cut, and laid four cards down cross-fashion. Every one told a tale. She pondered their significance.

'You must shun a fair-haired girl. She's a bad omen. God, I've rarely seen so much money in the cards. You're going to be very lucky . . .'

Peter was bored, cynical towards the mundane, predictable predictions. Roger sensed it.

'Emma,' he interjected. 'Peter and I are going on a bit of work. Can you say if it's safe or not?'

Emma picked up the thread at once.

'I see a tall building. It's brightly lit. White, I think. You must not go there, you are not welcome.'

Peter's trespasses were never welcome. However, the information delighted Roger.

'But are we going to be lucky together?' he almost shouted. Was Emma deaf?

'Very lucky. Yes, you can do what you want, but avoid the tall well-lit building. Is it a church? God, I see it so clearly.'

'Tell us more about the white building, Emma.'

Emma reshuffled the cards and Peter cut once more. A further two cards were turned.

'It's very bright inside. Do not go there.'

Her voice had taken on a strident, emphatic ring, and Roger fell silent. Then they proceeded to Roger's reading. It was of a domestic nature though he, too, must avoid bright lights. He seemed satisfied again. When it was over, Emma stuffed Peter's two twenty-pound notes along with Roger's fifty into her ample bosom. As they left, two brightly lit tower blocks illuminated the dusk. Were they white, though? Difficult to tell. Roger strode briskly.

'We'll have to leg it back to Aldgate. We won't find a cab here. What did you think of Emma?'

Peter was sorely tempted to speak bluntly. The phrase 'an unmitigated load of bollocks' sprang to mind. But, aware of the value of the bollocks to his co-conspirator, he observed simply, 'Strange how she hit on the tall white brightly lit building.'

It was as far as the thief was prepared to go.

'Yes. Wasn't it just?'

Roger's voice was awed, with a reverence suggesting he'd just been on the road to Damascus. Seen the burning bush.

They arrived at Aldgate tube.

'Two to South Kensington,' said Roger at the ticket office.

Peter didn't have to consult Emma to know what he had in mind. They came out at South Ken and crossed Cromwell Road where the V & A confronted them, rearing up like a great Sphinx, a flood of light giving its façade a distinctively whitish hue . . .

Neither spoke, but they both knew. The target had fallen victim to the gypsy curse. Peter was oddly both amused and relieved. They wouldn't find their luck at the V & A, at all events. They repaired to a wine bar off Abbey Road, where Roger relaxed as far as he could (not very far) and asked what alternatives were available.

'After all, she said we'd be lucky.'

Peter, too, was in his way a magician. He pulled another target out of the hat.

'You remember I obliged Zilli's last year? I think it'll stand another visit. I have access to the roof from offices in Bruton Place. I have a key to the premises, actually.'

Yes, Emma would be accurate about one thing. They were going to be lucky.

A week later the French leather connection was obliged once more, this time to a modest hoot of a quarter of a million. The windows in the well had remained vulnerable; it seemed nothing had been learned from the previous visit by Peter and Clyde.

Two days later Chief Superintendent Stephenson called a meeting at West End Central with his troops.

'Most of you probably know about Zilli's in Bond Street being obliged again. Someone's taking the piss and I'd like some movement on the enquiry. We do have a small lead. Chummy may have been seen in Bruton Place: fortyish, suntanned (funny in winter) and tracksuited. Anyone we might know?'

An old hand who'd never got higher than sergeant took a fag from his lips.

'Governor, I've seen an old face prowling about in a tracksuit. Ruddy complexion too. Peter Gulston. He tuned us up in the sixties in Mayfair.'

Stephenson perked up.

'Now that's a coincidence. The Commander brought his name up over a break-in in St James's recently. Calls himself Scott now. Yes, he did tune us up in the sixties. I spent a few nights on canvas stools waiting for him. Tom, see if the collator's got anything, will you? Anyone know where we can find him?'

Respectfully, a fresh young aide raised his paw.

'Sir, I play a bit of tennis at Paddington Club. He hangs about there. Flashes the cash too, at the bar.'

'Well, that's it, then. Let's have a look at Master Peter, shall we?'

The Super felt better already and, from that moment, time began to run out for the thief. Go to any well too often and you'll surely fall in. Peter *was* taking the piss. He was doing it purposefully. And why not? It was the one, the only game he was good at.

There was another copper taking an interest too, who belled his ex.

'Chelsea, I hear you're seeing that flash prat Peter Scott. True? Apart from being old enough to be your dad, he's a villain. The word's about it's on him, Chelsea. So if you're serious about coming into the job, drop him out. OK? Drop him out.'

Mayfair Gems and a Greek Tragedy

In 1993 Peter attended a memorial service in Farm Street for one whom he had once obliged – Margaret, Duchess of Argyll. One or two surviving victims of his passion had rolled up to pay their respects (or shed their crocodile tears). Among the mourners he recognised the Duchess of Rutland.

Afterwards the thief sat beneath the plane trees in St George's Gardens, as Father Beattie's words to the reluctant turn-out a few minutes earlier struck home again: 'We shall all need someone's prayers some day.' And then the memories of four decades flooded back. Swarming with impish delight among the leaves of the plane trees, the ghosts of his well-deserving Mayfair prey swarmed in the air.

There was Mrs Arpad Plesch in 1959 at her home where the ghastly Hilton Hotel now stands, and that most talented of actresses, Maggie Leighton, then married to Laurence Harvey, who was deprived of her gems in 1960 in Bruton Place. He attacked Sylvia Ashley's property adjacent to Lord Lambton's home in South Audley Street; he pillaged Bert Taylor's wife's gems from a penthouse in Park Street, among them a diamond and ruby brooch of the Taylor Woodrow emblem, which showed men pulling on a rope. Then there was Lady Pleydell Bouverie, visited via the roof in Grosvenor Square, and Lady Zia Wernher, whose home had stood scaffolding-clad on the other side of the square. In 1964 there were attempts in Stratton Street on Anne Bancroft and sorties on the roof of the Dorchester to the Messel Suite, unsuccessfully to attack Liz Taylor's treasures. He recalled finding the Duchess of Bedford's tom in a concealed security drawer under a vanity case in her town house in St Anselm's Place, and in the same mews he recalled a visit to the old showman Jack Hilton and the Aussie wife he married in later life. He remembered Viscountess Jacqueline de Ribes being chloroformed in Claridge's (of all places) and deprived of jewellery that she'd borrowed from a Parisian jeweller.

There were a couple of escapades in Green Street. He chased Linda Christian's bits and pieces when she stayed at Charlie Clore's home in Park Street. And twenty yards away, on the corner of Green Street, stood an old hospice from where the thief launched possibly his last attempt to play Raffles in the eighties. It was a crack at Mrs Frank Sinatra, who was also Groucho Marx's widow, a collector of gems and on most thieves' books. On this occasion the Sinatras were guests of Cubby Broccoli, producer of the Bond films, at his Green Street home. The gable-end of the house abutted the flat roof of the annexe to the then-empty hospice, and this was the launching pad for Peter's attack. Entry to the gardens at the rear was from Woods Mews, where twenty years earlier an American woman had lost fifty thousand pounds' worth of gems. Now a thirty-foot extension ladder was hoisted over the wall beside a phone box and the plot was set in motion – not without risk, for he humped the ladder across the enclosed garden under the eyes of a hundred possible sighters.

He pitched the ladder from the roof of the nuns' annexe to the gable-end balcony on Cubby's home and ascended. Suddenly he was vulnerable to a new bunch of sighters in Green Street – the press. Even in the autumn of his warbling, Sinatra still attracted the *paparazzi* and this sub-species of human life was camped out in the porch of the house opposite. One of them wasn't sleeping.

'Hey! What do you think you're doing?' It was an animated, none-too-friendly bellow from the street. 'You the press? You'll fuck it all up for the rest of us.'

Thank God he'd taken Peter for one of his own more daring brothers. A discreet enquiry to the law and the thief would have been nicked. Instead he made an orderly retreat, abandoning the ladder on the annexe roof. The Sinatras had had a close shave. And it was as near to a James Bond operation as Cubby was likely to come up against in real life.

Back in the early sixties, a random prowl around accompanying a young man who was later to be jailed for his part in the Great Train Robbery had led them to Woods Mews. Peter shinned up a three-storey pipe to an open bathroom window carelessly left ajar. The house was seemingly deserted. A pouch of fine gems put him in funds and he bought his first E-type Jaguar. Forays in Belgravia with the same party deprived, amongst others, Rixi Marcus, the international bridge player, at her Lowndes Lodge, Cadogan Place home. Rixi lost her jewels. The wife of a military man and steward of the Jockey Club, Colonel Hornung, living in the same block, also lost her bits and pieces.

There were, rarely, victims who caused genuine regrets. One was

Odette Hallows, GC, a brave and gracious lady. If the thief had known the occupant of the house in Aldford Street where he trespassed, he would have passed, always a great respecter of courage and suffering.

Mayfair had always been his particular oyster. His second love was country-house work, for which the ladder was indispensable.

In the late fifties, tired of relying on chance to provide a suitable ladder near the attack site, he had several aluminium expandable ladders specially made to his requirements by a pal in Shepherd's Bush. Folded, they fitted into his car boot; expanded, they would scale an eighteen-foot wall.

He took one such ladder with him to Charlbury, the Tudor dower house of Blenheim Palace, which was home to the Marquis of Bland-ford and his recently acquired consort, Christina Onassis.

Sonny Blandford had brought his attractive, sad Greek wife to be immured at Charlbury. Her whole life was, in retrospect, a long Greek tragedy. After a youth played out in the malicious world of the great ship-owning families, she was dumped by the toad-like Onassis in favour of Maria Callas. Maybe it was out of pique that she then opted for the blue blood of M'lord Anglais. It was an example of how the swinging sixties licensed the world's jet-set to play musical beds as never before. The coarse Greek tycoon Onassis was of course a prime exponent, and it was not long before he sent the diva to a melancholy early grave after he'd traded her in for the widow of the Irish-American stud Jack Kennedy. Swing they deserved to do, most on the scaffold. They were a gutless and selfish crew.

It should have been a simple robbery. The initial recce revealed that ladders on the estate were at a premium, all housed and padlocked, so the thief imported one of his own customised ladders and chose a compost heap in which to secrete it.

A couple of entries to the house showed the sleeping arrangements (separate bedrooms) but failed to locate the Greek's gems. They were probably in a safe in the gun-room, which the thief did not attempt to enter, knowing that country-house gun-rooms were invariably belled. So he decided on a more daring procedure. He would catch Christina coming back from a formal function, when she would be certain to be tommed up and, relying on the likelihood that they would not be properly put away until the morning, he would enter the house and thieve the baubles while she slept.

On the last of several nights spent impatiently waiting for Christina and Sonny to return from a function, he was at the rear of the house, lurking in the garage and stable area. He was dressed for the role, in a dark polo-neck sweater, cheese-cutter grey strides, and cheap throwaway brothel creepers with crêpe soles. The latter would be disposed of after the job. Forensically, a burglar's shoes are the most likely item of his wardrobe to give him away.

Suddenly the limo purred up on him. It swung into the yard and immediately he was caught in its headlights. He ducked down behind a wall. They must have seen him!

Apparently not. The motor died under a lean-to garage and now the sound of a fierce verbal exchange told the thief that his presence was far from the couple's minds.

The aristocracy have a long history of marrying wealthy wives, getting bored, finding fault and discarding them. They make the Maltese look very second-rate!

Car doors slammed, but the invective continued. The thief heard a gasp and everything went still. Then a tall man strode alone towards the house and silence returned, except for a gentle sob in the night air.

The thief, perplexed, had ambivalent feelings about what he thought he'd witnessed. He walked across the yard and entered the lean-to to confirm it. She was slumped across the bonnet of the car, sobbing quietly. Her couture dress and fabulous jewellery evoked no greed in the thief. She actually looked no more than a small child in distress. He bent down and helped her up.

Christina gave him a startled glance but immediately, astonishingly, composed herself.

'You must be the man who left his ladder in our compost heap,' she said.

The comment baffled him for a moment or two, and then the inference became clear. The police knew that the attack was imminent. Was she warning him in return for his kind gesture? Was it a way of scoring off a heavy-handed spouse? For a moment the two of them, the Greek millionairess and the thief, clung together in a tight embrace. The moonlight played around them as if they were trysting lovers.

There are no fairy-tale endings, neither for the highwayman nor for the pretty marchioness. She was never to be robbed at Charlbury but did escape from there, returning to Greece to marry Stavros Niarchos, but this union was also short-lived, curtailed by her premature death, the gods in need of an angel.

Sonny, as Duke of Marlborough, was to have his own cross to bear, in a son and heir called Jamie, who has shaped up well in degeneracy, pimping for dope, spraying dud kites about, knocking taxi drivers, behaviour that finally landed him in the slammer.

There are two or three faces, now breathing that rarefied air on the sixth floor of the Yard, who in the sixties formed a special Fur Squad and loitered on roofs in wait for Peter the pussy bandit. In 1964, the thief had been apprehended leaving premises in Beauchamp Place. As he lay banged up, bloody and battered, in the cells at Chelsea nick, Superintendent Maurice Walters made a savagely pertinent remark to him.

'You broke their hearts in Mayfair,' Maurice told him grimly. 'You're not going to break mine.'

These were suicide years in the thief's life. Finishing his lagging in 1962, with little capital and few (if any) friends, his options had been limited. His private passion swiftly and easily prevailed. They were years in which he stole a couple of million pounds' worth of fur and a fortune in jewels, had an affair with a transvestite, fell in love with a fashion model, married, and was betrayed first by a friend and then by his own arrogance. Destination Purgatory in Dartmoor. So whose heart was broken?

Between 1963 and 1964 not a furrier in Mayfair or Knightsbridge was exempt from the thief's attentions. Nor were Marylebone and Kensington neglected. But with the Fur Squad in existence, it looked like only a matter of time before they nailed him. The Great Fur Robbery at Mitzman's in Bruton Street, however, gave coppers and the trade a respite. Peter bought a second E-type Jaguar, this one a V8 hard-top, and took himself off for a second time to Cannes.

Arriving at the Martinez, he found Billy Hill sitting in the foyer.

'Hello, Peter. I want you to do me a favour. I'm here with Meadows and Botibol – leave them out, will you?'

Bill's appearance was no coincidence, for he rarely left anything to chance. The warning about Billy's two erstwhile partners in the 21 Room Casino stemmed from a fracas in Harry Meadows's Churchill Club in Bond Street earlier that year, where Peter was infatuated with the warbler-cum-hostess Jackie Whitehead. A punch-up at the club had resulted in Harry's son Andrew getting a clump, which to get sweetened, leaving the law on the touchline, cost the thief a monkey. Bill had arranged this accommodation, but Harry still smarted, growling 'that guy's an animal' whenever the thief's name came up. In addition, Taters was under suspicion for trying to steal the safe from the 21 Room offices.

Bill, here in Cannes, was calling a truce. But it was an uneasy one, not destined to survive.

The thief, in truth, had few friends. Not only does the calling attract Judases but in the Element Peter's arrogant middle-class Ulster attitudes endeared him to very few. Even Taters and he were partners only out of expediency. They were not pals.

But Peter had one friend in Cannes that year, a man who for twenty years supported him and stood for his madness. This was David Ruben Gliksten, the eldest son of Stanley Gliksten, who built a timber empire and owned Charlton Athletic Football Club. When Stanley died in the mid-fifties he left a fortune to his sons David and Mike. But what warmed David to the thief was the Celtic connection, for Stanley had married out of his faith, finding a wife from County Cork. David's Irish connection dwarfed his Semitic ancestry and he lived all his life as a surrogate Irishman.

David was a little past forty when the Reaper called. He drank himself to death in Kinsale in 1979 – well, it was not only wine but also melancholia which killed him. 'Happier may he find his nights than ever he found his days . . .'

But in happier times, David was staying with his first wife Jean in the Martinez. Peter and the Glikstens casinoed, imbibed, swam together. More foolishly, David had a phone to hand on the *plage*, to play the horses back in the UK, and Peter himself soon got involved. Quickly he went two grand behind. He got out of it by pressurising his credit with David. None too subtly, David tested Peter's loyalty.

'Peter, I've been gambling at the 21 Room. There are rumours that the chemmy's not straight. Have you heard anything?'

Peter suddenly found himself in the 'middle'.

'I don't get in there,' he said. 'I'm *persona non grata* with the management.'

Alarm bells were ringing in Peter's conscience. He felt loyalty to Hilly for staunching the claret after the Callas turn-out, and also to David because he was a pal wanting a straight answer. Peter had to be cautious. He knew that suspicion was rife in the early world of legalised gambling in London, and thought it would be best if David stayed away from the 21 Room.

'Look, David, we're both babes in the wood, really. Amateur gamblers. If I were you I'd give the London casinos a miss.'

'That's difficult at the moment. I owe thirty thousand to the 21 Room. Of course, I could settle, but if I was sure I'd been cornered in a crooked game, that would be a different kettle of fish.'

'You want my advice? Pay and give those tables a miss.'

Peter thought he'd found a compromise that would preserve his own welfare. He didn't much like being in the middle, for biblical advice is profound – a man cannot serve two masters – and part of the secret of life is to avoid Hobson's choices.

A few days later, David was dining with a man who (unbeknownst to him) was one of Hilly's pals. He repeated the conversation with Peter verbatim and, not unnaturally, the man gave chapter and verse to his friend. A heavy banging on Peter's hotel-room door brought home the dangers of getting middled. Hilly stood there – once again in his dressing gown.

'You told Gliksten not to come to the club,' he snarled, his brown eyes glinting with menace. 'There are more ways of being a copper than going down to the nick, you know.'

Perhaps Bill knew some.

Unable to deny what he'd said, and angry with himself for his loose mouth and David's naivety in repeating the conversation, Peter had no choice but to take the tongue-lashing. Bill, of course, relented in time – he could afford to, if only because Peter had lost much face by being put so grossly on the defensive.

The 'holiday' went from bad to worse when the only sexual conquest of the month cried foul. This was Delphine, a well-bred, basically serious American who, on this day, was squiffy with an excess of 'Mistral', the local wine, at lunch. Then, in the back of a motor boat off Levant, she succumbed to the thief's pressing flesh.

A further savage homily was in store for him after his friendly seduction. Coming down to the *plage* the following day, the impressionable East Coast socialite seemed to want to put the relationship in perspective.

'What's my position now?' she queried.

'You're my girl,' Peter appeased, gallantly. He wanted to please her, but instead the comment made her furious.

'Well, I'm *not* your girl. I suppose you think it's clever getting me drunk and doing what you did?'

Apportioning blame away from herself, perhaps to excuse any small pleasure she may have felt, Delphine was beside herself.

'No one will be your girl. Not me, for sure. You're shop-soiled.'

She turned away. *Shop-soiled?* Monsieur Bronzage blushed beneath

George Chatham aged 16, captain of London Schoolboys football team, 1929 – 30.

The Duke of Wellington's swords were stolen from the V & A by George Chatham in 1948. They have never been recovered. A conservative estimate of their value today would be £5 million.

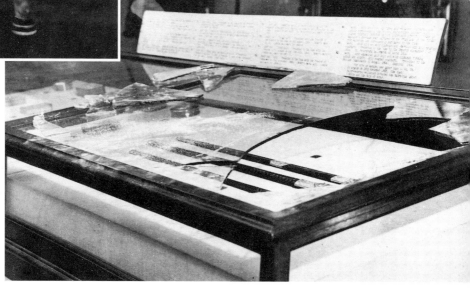

Peter in Mayfair: 'George, I found a way in.'

George 'Taters' Chatham and Peter in the Park, 1992.

'It all was to go, so was Peter – to jail for four years': the Antique Porcelain Company of New York's showroom in Bond Street, Mayfair, 1983.

'A friendly roof in Bond Street', scene of much pillage by the thieves.

The gentleman thief at the Paddington Lawn Tennis Club, c. 1982.

Wedding number 4: Elaine was aged 24, Peter was thirty years older (1984).

Milenka, a socialite from Prague, with Peter, New Year's Eve 1990.

Peter and a friend in Regent's Park, 1989.

Anyone for tennis? Peter and Ralph Halpern in Regent's Park, 1993.

Peter and a friend in Regent's Park, 1989.

Anyone for tennis? Peter and Ralph Halpern in Regent's Park, 1993.

Wedding number 4: Elaine was aged 24, Peter was thirty years older (1984).

Milenka, a socialite from Prague, with Peter, New Year's Eve 1990.

'Peter Scott will play tennis and encourage', according to his card.

Gary Engleman's young lady Alison. As a young pro, Gary looked like going all the way on the tennis circuit.

Margot and Roz keeping bad company, Regent's Park 1993.

A hug from a friendly pupil –
a tennis coach's perk.

his tan. Thirty years later the sear of her words lingers. Perhaps she had summed up his whole life, then and now.

It had been a bloody holiday. Back in London, and under observation, Peter knew that the Fur Squad were bracing themselves in Mayfair and Chelsea for a renewed assault, and had been doing their homework. A certain Stuart Pulver, formerly of Pulver et Cie in Davies Street, was possibly a receiver; Sammy Ullah's butcher's shop in Camden a possible stow; and a pensioner in Biscay Road, Fulham was being watched. Neighbours reported late-night activity there, with sacks going in and out.

The pensioner was Jim Pointing, an old sidekick of Taters who as far back as the early 1930s had got a four for an attempt on Lampard's the jewellers in Notting Hill Gate. His home was where the pair housed their gelignite and propane kit: it looked as if they were already now on borrowed time.

In fact the use of explosives to blow safes was already out of date by the mid-sixties, manufacturers having countered the safe-blower with the modern technology of anti-blow bars. Even the portable oxy-propane kit had decided limitations, though a certain modest door would make a profitable exception.

30

Third Thoughts Pay Dividends

I N September 1964, Peter was watching a television programme about a north-east town experiencing the worst of unemployment. The Labour Exchange vault would be cash-laden . . .

Suddenly the telephone rang. It was Taters.

'You watching television?'

'Yes,' said Peter.

'And are you thinking what I'm thinking?'

Great minds on the same wavelength. The trip north became a formality.

An inspection of the vault door gave him an idea of the difficulty. The propane bottle coupled to a small oxygen cylinder gave around twenty-five minutes' cutting time. But it would not all be needed. The ancient Cox and Coles door's locking bar could be exposed in twelve.

In all the vault took fifteen minutes to open, but it was to prove a disappointment. There was not a coin in sight. All the vault housed was a table-tennis table, folded in half. Driving back depressed and perplexed, Peter pondered on the disaster. They'd done their home-work – pay-out was later that morning. Could the money be delivered by a security service on the day? Had to be. It was the only expla-nation.

Stopping at Scotch Corner, an obscure and uninvestigated possibil-ity struck him. He thought about it all the way to Grantham, where he turned round and headed back up the A1. His hunch would have to be tested. Back in the vault he found that the folded ping-pong table was supported around the underside perimeter by a six-by-two timber – an unusual feature. Folded over, it created a box a foot deep. Peter opened it up and found that some bright spark had devised the idea of stretching a wire on hooks under the rim, and from it had hung the money bags out of sight.

The journey back to Biscay Road was a pleasant one.

The Labour Exchange success inspired Peter to oblige a more pres-tigious one in Victoria. He went on a recce the night the dosh was there, one week before the planned attack. A public toilet at first-floor level overlooked the target, which stood conveniently next to a doss-house. Relieving himself there, Peter saw that he had company – very likely a cop on obs. Later, watching from another vantage point, Peter became interested in an empty office block opposite the target. There was a persistent glow of cigarettes behind one of its windows. A police presence. The enemy were smartening up, and Peter again appreciated the wisdom of his policy – never skimp on your planning. This time it had preserved his liberty.

The penultimate safe he blew with Taters was in a Gas Board prem-ises in Essex. Once it was tilted onto its back, Taters gave it a small shot and the door flew open. Their reward in today's money was about seven thousand apiece. But the last time they played safe-blowers together they tackled an old John Tann in a Fulham Road furniture store, and it jammed. After that embarrassing débâcle, they slung the Polar Ammul gear, delighting old Jim Pointing. Fifteen years later, Jim was to tell Bert Wickstead of the Serious Crimes Squad, 'I never wanted it here. Peter asked me to keep it for him.'

He wept in Mancini's pub, recounting his treachery. Poor, sad old Jim. Never got into the witness box. He passed away quietly six months before the crucifixion.

Unattached, living on his nerves, Peter's persistent relaxation was whore-hunting. He was comforted by those understanding madonnas, plentifully found in corners of the metropolis as far apart as Cable Street in the east and Kensington Church Street in the west. Providing affection for the unloved and the unlovable, they are assured of a paradise as certain as the one who dallied in the dusk at Calvary.

Golgotha's megastar done the righteous mob like a kipper that day by the well in Samaria. The Pharisees – and there are more of you than you think – presented the tart to him for his (hopefully flawed) judgement. They were already raising stones to crush her, champing for the off, but the ever-gentle Nazarene idling in the sand knew a thing or two. He fronted the zealots.

'He who is without sin cast the first stone.'

There were no punters. Cowardly eyes to the floor, they were bested again as they slunk sheepishly away.

'Go and sin no more, woman.'

The Nazarene didn't believe for a moment she wouldn't offend again. What he did, which the godly find so difficult, was to *forgive* her. Little wonder the Magdalene wept at Calvary.

So, Kensington Church Street was a cruising area for the Magdalenes of the sixties. With the local burghers still to get their act together, a tart could always be found there, and Peter spent many a twilight lingering at the corner of Bedford Gardens in his car, watching in the driving mirror for the relief of a passing madonna – slingback shoes, silk-clad legs, tripping past and promising ecstasy.

Then one summer's night in 1963 his degeneracy was put to the blade. She came tottering past, her legs so divine in silk that business became a must. He honked the horn of the Rolls and she shimmied up, all belted leather coat and bouffant hair swept up.

'Hello, darling,' she trilled as she slid into the passenger seat. 'So the chauffeur's got the car tonight?'

Peter was casually dressed. He probably did appear incongruent with the Rolls. Nonetheless her words made him bite.

'Yes, and the chauffeur's wearing a thousand-pound watch, too.'

A painted claw pounced on his wrist and cast a pawnbroker's eye over his kettle.

'So he is,' she amended with marginally more respect.

'Have you got a place?' said Peter, lust cramping his breath. 'If not, we can go to mine.'

An anxious look appeared in her pretty eyes.

'Have you read about the brothel in Lancaster Mews this week in the press?'

Of course he'd read it. A transvestite bordello had been raided there by the enemy. The penny dropped.

'Out, you bitch, out before I chin you!' he thundered.

But she knew more about lust than he did. Before he could stop her, a hand was creeping courageously along his inner thigh in defiance of his outrage. The skirt was hitched up, the superb limbs were exposed shimmering to his attention. Her voice, an octave lower now, simpered.

'So you don't think I can get you at it?'

Peter, helpless, found his hand wandering up the silken ladder to her bulging gusset. He was a million, and she was Shirley, the tit and stocking making up for the (inconvenient?) thick knob swinging flaccidly till he penetrated her sweet arse. Nature took centre-stage and 'she', too, stiffened and without further aid spunked. It was the most perverse of thrills. It must have been, for he spent a thousand quid with her over the next couple of months.

Twelve years later came a sequel to this episode. He was kerb-crawling in Gloucester Road and caught sight of an elegant, plumpish woman searching for a cab. He slowed to admire her. It was Shirley. What odds that? She got him in one and at once joined him in the BMW.

'Darling.' The voice was even deeper now. She planted a kiss. 'You look wonderful. Still hunting whores?'

'Maybe. You still at it?'

'Don't be silly, darling. I've had the operation. I warble in Germany. I'm Anna now.'

She hesitated. 'But I do recall you were a super fuck – only I'm not sure you'll fancy me now that I'm straight.'

But Peter had to find that out for himself. And she was right. He'd been mad for Shirley but Anna left him cold. Now what do you make of that?

31

Love, Marriage and Dartmoor

FALLING in love is demanding enough for the innocent. It's torture for the sinner. As the Celtic ditty cautions, *I'd rather be in jail myself than fall in love again*. Love invariably arrives at the sinner's most vulnerable time, more often than not a pleasant rash that outstays its welcome for one or other of the conspirators concerned. For love *is* a conspiracy, a private game in its nature, fuelled by the desires and needs of the players who find themselves expecting more from it than love can ever provide. In essence the thief has found love to be a greed for reciprocated affection, and that its players are rarely worthy of what they desire. Loving is the most selfish of virtues.

Cupid's arrow was poised one Sunday morning in 1963 in Ruby Lloyd's Maisonette Club in Mayfair. It was the most common, and least durable, of reasons – physical attraction.

Catwalk model Jackie Bowyer was having man trouble. She had extracted herself from a tiresome middle-aged admirer who she now found was issuing threats against her. The troublesome swain was an acquaintance of Peter's, on the fringe of the Element but not so close that he would need respectfully to ignore her cry for help.

They chatted together at the club, surrounded by disapproval, a sea of scowls. Peter was calculating how a cuddle might reward a Sir Galahad who stood up for her, and they left the club together, tipping Miss Bowyer from the hot fat of the frying pan into the flames themselves, for passion and lust were about to take centre-stage. How unfortunate that she should have met the thief when she was so vulnerable. If she had been on a winning turn he wouldn't have rated a second glance from her. But such is the fell clutch of circumstance.

Yet, spreading his cloak, even a thief possesses stature. Soon they were inseparable. Poor Jackie, giving her heart to the thief, became swamped in the first rush of excitement which his degeneracy stimulated and so, very selfishly, he fucked up the life of a very vivacious, trusting young woman for seven years. First, he alienated her from her family and circle of friends and lured her into his reprehensible way of life.

Socialising with Peter in the austere upper sanctum of Paddy Kennedy's pub, Wally Virgo, then the governor at Gerald Road, became a devotee of Jackie's charm and beauty. He also observed the comings and goings – the Twins, Billy Hill, and one or two heavy faces from south London among others – and if he was still smarting about the Duchess of Northumberland affair, he didn't show it.

'You're keeping bad company, Peter,' he cautioned. 'When it suits, your new pals will shop you.'

But sound advice is wasted on youth. One of the south London firm became privy to a recce that Peter was making in South Wales, a wages office at Six Bells Colliery, Abertillery. Peter thought he might be able to tunnel into it and take charge of a quarter-of-a-million-plus payroll which would be housed there overnight. He'd discussed arrangements with Chummy, whose credentials were impeccable in the Element. Chummy agreed to travel down with the thief, but cried off at the last moment. Peter, hotted up, seeking a break from the Fur Wars, shot down to Wales alone in his E-type Jaguar.

In the still of a pitch-black night he parked, looking amid the dour slate of the Rhondda like an intruder from another planet. He opened the bonnet and loosened a couple of leads, and then legged it up the hill to the colliery itself. On the way he passed a rebated phone box, but missed the copper skulking inside. At the top of the hill he could see the ghoulish coal mine, a shantytown of outhouses and sheds, visible in the glow of a solitary sodium light on a fifty-foot pole. Then, as his eye accustomed itself to the gloom, he saw a dimly lit, red-blinded window: the wages office! A closer inspection was a must.

Peter figured that, if challenged, he was at worst a trespasser whose car had broken down. He prowled adjacent to the target window. He peered in. A Monmouthshire constable's helmet badge glinted in the inner gloom. Treachery was revealed.

His retreat in controlled, nonchalant haste was probably foolish. A more leisurely departure might not have provoked the response. Anyway, he'd gone about twenty yards when the colliery was flooded by the glare of a host of sodium lights: This Is Your Life, Peter Gulston. Two rugby-playing coppers, sprinting from cover, laid firm hands on him.

'What brings you here, then, boyo?' a young giant bellowed.

'My car's broken down. I'm looking for a phone.'

'And do you have a name?' the giant hollered, giving his arm a twist to aid his memory.

'Gulston, Peter Gulston, and my car's packed up. It's in the pub car park at the foot of the hill.'

Anxiety and the policeman's painful embrace gave his answers a desperate ring. 'That'll do for now, boyo. Car packed up, eh? We'll see.'

Arrested, and charged initially with trespass, he received a visit in his cell the following morning from a Sergeant Harry Glover, the local sleuth. A sinister complexion was about to be cast on the trespass.

'Peter, we've found a substance under the passenger seat of your car. We think it's gelly. Can you say anything about it?'

Peter had plenty to say. Fearing the worst, he lost his urbane cool and screamed 'Plant!'

'We don't do that up here, you know. We're not the Met.'

Glover's words did little to console the thief as he was remanded in custody at a special hearing later that morning. He was permitted a phone call and asked Jackie in London to alert David Gliksten of his plight. David had been at school, Marlborough, with a Cardiff chum whose family had a legal practice there and he instructed them. The same day, Alan Roberts Thomas, a former Crown Prosecutor for the city, arrived at Abertillery police station and agreed to act for Peter. He was a charming, astute adviser, and they would eventually become friends.

At their conference, Roberts Thomas went to the heart of the matter. 'We have a problem with this substance. Can you think how it may have got into your car?'

Peter had no idea, no recall of any substance at all. It was foolish and he should have.

The 'gelignite' find inevitably entailed a remand in custody, and reception staff were confused and envious as they counted the two thousand pounds which the thief had in his kick when arrested at the colliery. To them it represented two, perhaps three years' wages.

'Never seen so much money, boyo,' growled Piggy Wall, counting it for the third time and still not getting it right. 'Always have this kind of cash to hand, have you? Haven't stolen it, have we, Mr Gulston?'

It was a rhetorical question. The grumbling Wall was none too pleased at having to thumb through all this paper and record it on the prisoner's property sheet.

'Why didn't the police hold on to it? Bastards didn't want the responsibility, that's what.'

Piggy had hit the nail on the head. He knew that if there'd been the slightest question that the cash was stolen, the law would indeed have held the money. Finally arriving at a consistent figure, Piggy sighed in mock relief.

'Nowhere to keep it at the nick, lad. Am I right?'

Banged up, Peter paced the freezing cell, mentally tracing back the events of the night before. The law had not been there by accident. Had he been lollied? His mind went back to Chummy from south London and his late withdrawal. But he was sound as a bell; it was nothing to do with him! Maybe he'd been downright unlucky and stumbled into a police surveillance exercise. But that wouldn't account for the 'gelignite' find, though it was difficult to believe that coppers in the sticks were getting up to the Yard's tricks. Harry Glover had seemed as puzzled as Peter at the find. Nothing made sense as he drifted off into a shivering sleep.

A day later, the distraught Jackie turned up to visit. The chic model girl, on the first of what would be many pilgrimages to the visiting rooms of jails, handled the bleak surroundings stoically. She even uttered the most flawed (and most necessary) of clichés: 'I'll wait for you, darling.'

The mandate of emotion bested logic here. It would have been better if she'd called it a day there and then. But, alas, the obscure, pleasurable agony of passion took five years to abate. Cupid had fired a cruel arrow. It delivered her into the underworld of Peter's master passion and tainted her with its selfish attitudes. Fifteen years later she was to call in the tab.

It was by means of a privileged late-night visit, a week later, that Alan Roberts Thomas relieved Peter's Mafeking. He was breathless, genuinely elated.

'Peter, great news. The so-called gelignite is nothing more than a sweetmeat. It's a slab of marzipan! Not surprising, of course, that they thought it was Polar Ammul. It was a green slab, almond-flavoured, and sweating under your passenger seat. How did that get in your car?'

Peter had totally forgotten about the marzipan. He'd bought six bars of it earlier that year in Moretonhampstead, going to visit a pal in Dartmoor, and now he remembered how, in the visiting room, Mickey had devoured the other five, while rejecting the sixth on the grounds of its unattractive green colour.

'Can't eat that one, mate. Got a bilious look about it. Looks a bit like Polar Ammul.'

On the way back to London he'd slung the sweetmeat on the seat beside him. It must have been shunted off as he threw the phallic

Jaguar round bends, only to linger there awaiting discovery by Harry Glover's mob.

The result of the forensic test meant that Peter was bailed at his next appearance in the sum of a hundred pounds, having been charged only with conspiracy to trespass.

The committal was held in a shanty-like schoolhouse at Abertillery. The embarrassment of their mistake over the 'gelignite' spurred on the Monmouthshire Constabulary in their attempts to justify their (quite accurate) belief that a major London villain had come to plunder in their beloved Wales. Such things must be discouraged, but how?

They knew a thing or two about expediency in the Principality. So they added to Peter's holding charge of trespass a new charge, conspiracy, in company with Albert James Healey and persons unknown, to break and enter the wages office of the Six Bells Colliery and steal two hundred and forty thousand pounds. Albert James Healey? Who was Healey?

Billy Rhys Roberts was briefed. Arriving in his ancient Rolls-Royce, he murmured, 'They're pulling out all the stops for you. I think it's going to be messy.'

The prosecution paraded their witnesses and exhibits – gloves, torch and marzipan – and Peter was bailed and committed for trial. Bailed again and back in London that evening, Peter took a phone call from an agitated Welshman.

'Peter? Harry Glover here. We have a bit of a problem at our end. The exhibits in your case have disappeared. When we adjourned for lunch they were there.'

Peter couldn't believe what he was hearing. What was this? Another crooked move by the police to rescind his bail? Harry went on.

'Well, after lunch the clerk of the court thought we had them, and when we were leaving we thought we had them, but in fact they were nowhere to be found.'

'Harry, I hope you're not suggesting that I took them.'

'No, no, boyo. But you know that Mr Kutner who was with you?'

He did indeed. Among the group of Peter's pals who had travelled with him for the committal was the inveterate West End gambler Brian 'the Swan' Kutner.

'What about him?'

'We checked him out, see? The Jaguar he was driving wasn't taxed.

And he was last to leave the courtroom. Could you ask him to give me a ring?'

Suddenly Peter grinned to himself. He remembered Swan's joking remark, 'Best place for all that fucking gelly is down the toilet.'

Could the Swan have flushed them away? Peter belled him and got a laconic, 'Really? Don't know anything about it, Peter.'

Confess? Not the Swan.

Peter's bail was not rescinded. But this was a mixed blessing, for bail is a fickle prostitute at the best of times, in essence a form of double jeopardy. It represents a chance to go back to work and recover your losses, at the grave risk of putting you in substantially more rasher. It almost demands that prats fall for the 'up for none' syndrome, and Peter was no exception in finding it attractive.

One kind of retribution arrived swiftly. About an hour after being married to Jackie at Kensington Register Office, he was using (or trying to use) a public phone where he picked a fight with the wrong man. Insisting on access to the box, he'd initially knocked down the apparently gangling youth who, getting back to his feet, gave the liberty-taker a good belting, leaving him unconscious and hospitalised. The man was a German elephant trainer with the circus at Olympia, and had once boxed Carl Mildenburger, the German light-heavyweight champion. Summary justice indeed.

The honeymoon in Las Palmas was marred not only by his pair of black eyes, but by the happy couple falling in with unfortunate company – Charlie Mitchell and his wife Pat. Mitchell, five years later, was to offer to QE the Kray twins and in 1988 would be kicked to death outside a Marbella nightclub.

The ebullient Charlie had a small Starting Price office in Lots Road, Chelsea, and, on their return from the sun, Peter had two thousand pounds' credit with them ready for the racing at Cheltenham. Meanwhile he burgled a furrier called Francis in Beauchamp Place, Knightsbridge, on the Chelsea manor of Chief Superintendent Maurice Walters. He entered an empty on the north-east corner of Ovington Square, which allowed access through its rear to the roofs of Ovington Mews, running alongside the backs of the western side of Beauchamp Place.

Following this strike, he went to the Gold Cup on the Thursday with about three grand in readies. He proceeded, like the prat he was, to oppose the greatest steeplechaser of all time, Arkle. As the big race approached, his cash had shrunk to two thousand pounds. Mill House opened at 5−4, with Arkle a 2−1 chance. On the rails, Peter asked two and a half thousand to two on Mill House to win and was laid it. This was a crime in itself, certainly for an Irishman. Peter had had his card well marked as to Arkle's ability. Had he become so Anglo-Saxonised that he could see nothing beating Mill House?

Soon the big English horse was drifting out to 11−8 while Arkle's price had ominously shortened, and was now 7−4. Peter found a telephone and called the SP office bookmaker in Lots Road, giving him a minor heart attack by pressurising his credit to have a further two grand at S.P. on Mill House. His total bet on Bill Gollings's horse would be equivalent to at least forty thousand today, a breathtaking wager whose size occasionally comes back to haunt him in the park, as he hits tennis balls to prats for a tenner an hour.

Jackie, wearing a new custom-designed wild-mink coat (made by Stuart Pulver in Davies Street) had a five-pound forecast on Arkle to beat Mill House and Peter was alerted to his destiny by Jackie's elated screams as they were coming to the second-last.

'My horse is catching up!'

He was, too. Lowering his bins, the thief watched sourly as Arkle skipped over the last and drew easily away from the totally devastated Mill House. With that race went all Peter's money and Mill House's panache for ever: a sad day all round.

He did not have the money to settle at Lots Road, but the earlier visit to Francis the Furrier was fresh in his mind. He had found a divine entry point, impossible, he thought, for the enemy to work out. So he decided on a matinée. The weekend found him dragging a dozen bulging sacks out of Francis's and back along the roofs of Beauchamp Place. The original entry point had still not been properly secured, laughable as it seems.

Peter paid his due, but moaned about it to an unsympathetic Charlie Mitchell, who philosophised, 'You go screwing either to pay or play. What difference?'

How astute the lout was.

Meanwhile Maurice Walters called a council of war at Chelsea police station.

'Some smart Alec's taking the piss out of us. The furrier in Beauchamp Place was done again.'

He passed around a photo of Peter.

'We think we know who it is and believe me he'll be back. We propose to be there. So have a good look at Chummy.'

Morrie was right. A week later Peter was creeping along the same track to another furriers in the row, Fabian Furs. The troops were in place and no sooner had Peter dropped into the basement area to find an entry than whispering voices on the roof alerted him to the enemy. He was trapped in a basement. Only with his strength doubled by fear was he able to rip out one of the bars protecting the window and get into the premises. Once there, he found himself locked in and spent vital seconds smashing through a secured door to the first-floor shoe shop.

By now the law were in the basement area and in hot pursuit. The door to his escape into Beauchamp Place from the shoe shop was a deadlock, giving no quick exit. In desperate circumstances, desperate tactics are required. He threw himself backwards at the plate glass window, only to bounce off and back into the arms of a hostile, baton-wielding enemy. They bashed him unmercifully. Head, ribs and kidneys suffered, claret was everywhere, and he was pissing blood for weeks afterwards. The whole scene took place in semi-darkness, the young officers probably scared themselves and taking no chances.

With Peter safely housed at Chelsea police station, a delighted Maurice Walters agreed that he could have a doctor, who immediately insisted that Peter be hospitalised.

'Mr Gulston's not going to hospital if I have my way,' said Maurice. 'He'll leg it.'

The first quack faded into thin air and a second opinion was sought. This second doctor stitched Peter's head up and gave his back a cursory examination.

'He's fit for court in the morning,' was the verdict.

Maurice had half of Scotland Yard there that night to gaze upon the prize through the judas hole in his cell door. The following morning a major operation was planned and Peter was being held incommunicado. Back at the flat at Edith Road, all Jackie knew was that 'one of our aircraft is missing'. She fretted until morning, when Morrie and his troops booted down the front door.

In their search, their eyes fell on the wild-mink coat that Stu Pulver had crafted, and it became a suspect item. Stu, when they asked, had no purchase tax number.

So now Jackie, too, was in the frame. From that fateful Sunday morning six months earlier in Ruby Lloyd's, via the flat above a Wimpy Bar in Parade Street, to marriage and the pleasant flat in Edith Road, she now found herself in the dock of Number Two court at the Old Bailey with Peter, Stuart Pulver, and Sammy Ullah, an employee of Pulver's. It was entirely Peter's fault.

Others spun that Monday morning by the Fur Squad were Charlie at Rannoch Road, Fulham, Jim Pointing in Biscay Road, Taters, Fred in north London, and Pulver's wife in Bayswater. And then came the big break. A butcher's shop cold store in Camden was found to conceal a clutch of mink coats from the previous year's carnage. Pulver, for God knows what reason, had kept a selection of furs from a number of break-ins, all identifiable. The Yard had cracked it.

That old friend Conspiracy was now on the agenda again. It is often a flawed weapon in the armoury of law enforcement agencies. In effect, in seeking to make it stick, the prosecution do not have to prove anything, merely to paint a picture and allow the jury to use their own common sense as to what that picture represents. Hence, presentation is crucial: *telling the truth with bad intent beats all the lies they can invent.*

The business at Cardiff was still unfinished. Who should turn up to lead for the Crown but the thief's old adversary from Windsor Sessions, Kenneth Jones, QC. The trial judge at the assizes, Mr Justice Danny Brabin, was, they said, fair, but an upper-spectrum man, well aware of local needs.

They were pulling out all the stops. Chatting in friendly fashion to Rhys Roberts, as barristers are wont to do in the Alice in Wonderland theatre of justice, Kenneth Jones observed, 'Your friend Gulston certainly believes in going equipped. Eight years ago in Windsor he was arrested with a thousand pounds in his pocket. Inflation drove him to have two thousand with him at the colliery. Do you think it might be carried to influence police officers?'

The old pleader Rhys, who unlike Jones was not destined or wanting high office, smiled benignly and nodded.

'I think Peter had been to the races. There is no suggestion that he attempted to corrupt.'

But the glint in Kenneth's gimlet eye did little to reassure.

'Yes, and that day at Windsor he'd been to Ascot. Odd that, don't you think? Very odd.'

Lords of Appeal find the use of the time-honoured weapon of sarcasm hard to resist in their written judgements. Kenneth Jones, heading for high office, did not neglect it in spoken comment. In the meantime he made a perfect Pilate for a crucifixion.

Rhys Roberts lost heart once he learned of Peter's capture in London. Knowing he'd get scant sympathy for a bail abuser, he trod gently; Kenneth Jones had all the ammunition. In the end, the soppy jury at Cardiff, having glimpsed the 'wide boy' from London and his elegant wife, over-enthused. They found him guilty of both conspiracy and theft, and he got three years. Not unnaturally, this allowed for the possibility of appeal. The very personable solicitor Ellis Lincoln, of Lincoln and Lincoln, was acting for him in London, while his barrister brother handled the appeal against the dual convictions handed out in Cardiff. Their Lordships agreed to a man that it was wrong in substance that both matters had been put to the jury. However, this did not leave Peter in the clear.

'But Mr Ashe Lincoln, what was your client doing at the colliery wages office at two in the morning? You might well think we would apply the Proviso in this matter.'

Ashe Lincoln got the message. The Proviso is the Appeal Court's final bastion against administrative errors that might otherwise allow the guilty to go free. It goes something like this: 'Notwithstanding the points raised, the court sees a general picture of guilt in this case . . .'

The swingeing sentence for what, by any stretch of the imagination, was only a trespass stood. But fate, not always cruel, was to allow this to work in Peter's favour when he came to trial at the Old Bailey over the Fabian Furs job, for Judge Bernard Gillis, presiding, had a long memory. He had given the thief his three-year lagging back in '61 for the break-in attempt at Marylebone and for giving Sergeant Cumberlidge a crack on the nose as he was legging it. That had been a top-of-the-range sentence.

Roger Frisby led for the Crown. On Peter's behalf, a young barrister was briefed by Ellis Lincoln, while Jackie was defended by Jean Southwell, also destined for high office.

In Peter's earshot, Stu Pulver's barrister warned his client against giving evidence for Jackie in respect of the origin of her mink coat.

'Mr Pulver, as matters stand you are probably facing a sentence of twelve to eighteen months. If you give evidence on the Gulstons' behalf I cannot give you the same assurance. Please think carefully.'

But Stu didn't need to think. He knew Jackie's mink coat was not part of her husband's carnage, and that it was only an issue because he lacked a purchase tax registration number. Gallantly, he played the game.

'I must go into the box. Jackie is totally blameless.'

'Be it on your head, Mr Pulver.'

On his head it was. Jackie was acquitted and Stu's staunchness earned him a three-year lagging for receiving stolen goods. Thirty years later the thief still feels indebted to him.

However, the conspiracy charge failed. Sammy Ullah was acquitted and the Crown was left with a guilty verdict on Peter in respect of being on enclosed premises – which carried a maximum two-year penalty. But that was not quite the way Roger Frisby saw it for the prosecution. Addressing Judge Gillis on the merits of tough sentencing, he got out of his pram.

'M'lud, the Crown maintain that all these matters are connected. I propose to draw your attention to a section on being on enclosed premises that carries a maximum of ten years.'

The thief was horrified, until he saw that Gillis was unimpressed. Frisby pressed on, 'Then if I could draw your Lordship's attention to Gulston's bank account over the last year. Over one hundred thousand pounds have passed through it, most, if not all, cheques made to "pay cash". Where was the origin of these monies?'

But Gillis, bearing in mind that Peter was already doing a savage lagging from Wales, spiked the Crown's guns. Flicking idly through the damning bank stubs, did he find something likeable in the sinner?

'I wonder, Mr Frisby, how many people in this court have written three cheques to Oxfam in the last eighteen months, as I see the defendant has done?' Then, turning to the prisoner, he continued, 'Gulston, you have been found guilty of being on enclosed premises. This is a matter for the maximum sentence which the law permits me to pass: you will go to prison for two years, to run consecutively with the three years you are already serving, making five years in all. Take him down.'

Could it have been circumstance which allowed such a lenient sentence? The jury was still out considering their verdict on his wife Jackie . . . Brabin had topped him up in Wales . . . and, most likely of all, Gillis remembered the top-of-the-range lagging he'd handed out to Peter three years before.

Half an hour later, down in the cells, Ellis Lincoln arrived to announce Jackie's acquittal.

'She should never have been charged, old man. Maybe they thought you'd hold up your hands. Not the worst of results, a bottle and an acquittal.'

Ellis Lincoln was both kindly and wise, as most Jewish pleaders are. Perhaps they know a thing or two about suffering. Ellis's abrupt departure from the legal system, struck off in his prime, was greatly regretted by all those who required a solicitor to put up a genuine fight on their behalf. It's neither wise nor fashionable among the privileged arseholes at the bar to make any real effort for the criminal ilk. Real pleaders are few and far between – the Lord Chancellor's office sees to that.

Jackie was on the front page of the nationals the following day giving her pleader, Jean Southwell, a big hug. Her modelling career, after an initial hiccup, continued unabated. Maurice Walters retired a happy man to a job in security and poor Stu Pulver lost his wife – a lovely Spanish diving champion – who scarpered taking everything he had. He never really recovered.

Mayfair was to enjoy a four-year respite, for now Peter was heading for Dartmoor via Wandsworth. They were to be years of traumatic disturbance right in the middle of the swinging sixties. But – like General Douglas MacArthur – he would return.

32

A Lucky Escape

In November 1983 Chief Superintendent Stephenson was already hotted up over Peter's second assault on Zilli's, so it was an act of total madness when the thief confirmed Stephenson's worst fears. Herman Furs in Conduit Street was accessible from a flat roof off a fire escape in Burlington Place. The premises were about a hundred and fifty yards from West End Central nick.

A scaffolding of five storeys lay adjacent to the roofs in Regent Street, offering an escape route in an emergency. Observing his usual *modus operandi*, a mock run was devised, purposely activating the alarm system in order to get a measure of the police response. Curiously, this never arrived. The felon then returned for real. Lowering his ladder into the workroom, he took an inordinate time to force the cupboard open and fill two sacks with stock. It was almost as if he had a death wish – if so, the wish was nearly granted.

Turning into Burlington Place where his BMW was parked, he ran straight into the arms of a young constable answering the alarm. Quickly, the thief threw the sacks to the surprised copper and got a head start back up the scaffolding. Looking down, he caught sight of the enemy swarming up behind him, their torches glaring as they shouted.

'Give yourself up. You're surrounded.'

They had clearly expected the break-in and were out in strength. The pre-rehearsed emergency plan took Peter to the roofs, where he'd left a stairwell window open in an office block in Conduit Street. As he skirted over the Regent Street roofs, the enemy were still at his heels, but reaching Conduit Street he got through the bolt hatch and secured it behind him. He sat there on the stairwell for a full five minutes, bushed by his exertions, sure he was trapped, his heart pounding. A glance through a window overlooking Conduit Street confirmed his suspicion.

Finding a second wind, he explored the basement. It led to an internal well, visible but not accessible from the roof, which backed onto Regent Street. Crashing a rear window to get into the well, he heard a cry from the roof.

'He's down there,' a cozzer on the roof shouted. 'I think I can see him. Give up, you fool, you're trapped.'

From the well he accessed a Regent Street travel agent's. He made up his mind to crash out of the door into the late shopping crowds. But as he peered out, nerving himself to do it, fate played him a scurvy trick. A child, sitting on Daddy's shoulders, gave an excited scream.

'There's a man in there, Dad.'

The brat was swiftly joined by the cavalry. He was truly trapped.

Luck came to his aid – or maybe fate relented. Doubling back up the stairwell and finding a small section of fire escape that ran from the third to the fifth floor, he saw that a window into an office was ajar. Stepping gingerly across, he prised it open with his fingers and hauled himself through. It was a solicitor's office, and the roof mob had missed his entry to it.

But they had got access to the building, and now he listened as they tramped up and down the stairwell in which he had previously lain hidden. They tried the solicitor's door but clearly had no keys. They went away to try other doors while Peter baked. After a couple of hours the police presence had dwindled to a solitary copper posted in Regent Street. The thief returned to the stairwell via the fire escape. He decided to take a chance.

Opening the office block's door, he found Conduit Street deserted, so he walked briskly back to his car. He reached Burlington Place in time to see it being grab-lifted into a police removal lorry. He spent a restless night after going back to his lair in Wandsworth. Sutherland Avenue must be given a wide berth while a plausible tale was devised. He phoned the police in the morning and reported his car missing but, to his surprise, the traffic section's pound knew nothing about it. He then belled his brief, Raymond Davis, and asked could he phone around and locate the car. Raymond could.

'Peter, your car's at West End Central. You can collect it any time.'

Raymond had spoken in a carefully non-committal voice. Peter's silence prompted him to ask, 'Are you all right?'

'Yes, yes, I think so. I dare say you'll hear from me if I'm not.'

Let sleeping dogs lie. Peter gave West End Central a miss for the day. A nocturnal visit to Sutherland Avenue revealed that he'd had visitors: the door had been forced, the law had been there. He was a wanted man . . .

A day later he took the bull by the horns, ringing West End Central. He spoke to a CID sergeant and, yes, he could collect his car tomorrow. Euphoria swept over him. Things were not as bad as he feared.

When he called, a hard-faced tec took him to an interview room.

'Well now, Mr Scott. Or would you prefer Gulston?'

Peter remained shtum.

'What was your car doing parked in Burlington Place?'

As Peter trotted out his fanny, the sergeant's steely gaze did not waver.

'Why have you taken so long to collect it?'

'I thought it was odd the car was here and not in the car pound.'

'Well, I'll tell you right now, I don't believe you. There was a break-in at Burlington Place on the night in question. A suspect was chased and you answer to the description of the man. I propose to put you on an ID parade, *if* you agree. Do you understand?'

'Who'll be attending the parade?' Peter queried, stomach in boots.

'A young uniformed officer chased the suspect. We propose to assemble the parade now. Do you agree to appear?'

'Yes.'

'Would you like a solicitor present?'

Peter shook his head and the tec went on.

'We're collecting volunteers now. It may take half an hour. You'll be put in the detention room until we're ready.'

Forty minutes later, a dapper fledgling Inspector in uniform put his head round the door.

'We're ready for you now, Mr Gulston. You may choose any place you like in the line. It will be scrupulously fair.'

As he'd expected, no one assembled looked remotely like him. He chose to slot himself in at second from the right. Seconds later, a flushed young uniformed officer rushed in. Peter had to smile as the youth whizzed past him at breakneck speed, barely giving him a glance and ignoring the Inspector's advice that he should take his time.

'If there's anybody there you recognise, just tap him on the shoulder.'

Peter had his fingers crossed and, as if to answer his wordless entreaty, Chummy tapped a member of the public, the second man from the left. The face of the 'victim' broke into a broad grin. He was a pin-striped business type, surprised at being positively identified in such haste. Catching Peter's eye, he held up two fingers. Peter didn't cotton on at first, but then – could it be . . . ? He was second from the left, or second from the *right*, depending on which side you were looking at the parade from.

It was a bitter pill for Chief Superintendent Stephenson to instruct his sergeant to release Peter. In full view of a uniformed posse in the charge room, the embarrassed tec then had to return a pair of bolt-cutters, which he'd found in the boot of Peter's car. Finally, collecting the BMW from the small basement garage, the thief proffered a hand.

'No hard feelings?'

Chummy knew better than to let his feelings show. He gave a terse, 'None.'

But, as Peter was aware, nothing was over. The game had only just kicked off.

33

St Peter Calls

CHRISTMAS is a bloody time even for a well-balanced family. For the solitary sinner it was purgatory. No cards, no presents, not a word from his son Craig. Loyal to his mum. The thief took refuge in self-pity, but in his heart he knew he was reaping what he had sown.

A surgeon pal, a brother Aquarian, had offered a tentative invitation to his home in Dedham, Essex. But his charming and bright wife found the thief tiresome, tolerable only in small doses, and the thief, different, even outrageous by their house rules, was in two minds about accepting. He knew he would be required to do his cabaret act, play the amusing Celtic conversationalist to a gaggle of unimaginative Anglos, and he wasn't sure if he wanted to pay his entrance fee.

Early on Christmas Eve, he was playing a few quid up in Rousseau's, still undecided about the invitation. It was the callow side of Peter's nature always to look a gift horse in the mouth, even on Christmas Eve. Doing a rare double at rummy, a loser offered him a lady's gold Longines watch for a hundred sovs. So now equipped with a splendid gift, he decided to travel.

He arrived at the spacious fifteenth-century cottage at ten. His appearance – dishevelled, unshaven, wearing a grotty tracksuit – was an impertinence in itself. The housekeeper briefed him that the house party were dining out, at the nearby Talbooth Restaurant. Perhaps he'd join them? All Peter wanted was a bath and a kip but such prosaic self-indulgence was not permitted. On their return from dinner, the gaggle insisted he shave and change to attend midnight Communion. Yet for all his wickedness, he was unable to emulate that peculiar religious hypocrisy that the bourgeoisie develop at festive times.

On Christmas morning, determined to escape, he bulldozed the male players to the pub for a pre-lunch drink. Disapproving wives were ignored – his second rick. The men returned punctually, but a hostile air prevailed. The ritual of gift exchange was going badly. She gave him a bar of toilet soap. He gave her the watch. It was regarded as over-the-top.

Yet in his cups he felt so jolly that at lunch his hostess's brittle patience gave way. Laying a mini-portion of fare before him, she snapped, 'You won't need much, you're full up with booze.'

'Bollocks to this,' said Peter.

So he left the table and bowed out. In five minutes he had packed and departed, with none prevailing on him to stay.

Driving back down the A12 to London, he was both ashamed and pleased. There was intermittent traffic and he relaxed as he drove, possibly too much. He felt detached, almost trance-like.

Then it happened. The BMW switched to auto-drive, shuddered, and threw itself against the central reservation. Try as he might, it would not respond to his steering. Just as abruptly, the car tore away to the left, shot across to the hard shoulder, and stopped on the incline on the embankment that supported several bridges crossing overhead.

Bewildered, he thought for a moment he might be dead. The damage was substantial, and the atmosphere strange. There was no traffic on the A12 at all. The silence made him feel he was caught in a time warp. Either that or the gin and tonics were having a delayed effect.

Reality took over again. He knew he'd fail a breathalyser, so he gathered his wits and made off up the embankment to distance himself from the vehicle. What the hell had happened? Was he pissed? The odd detached feeling lingered, or reappeared. He felt as if he were programmed.

There was a village three-quarters of a mile away, the sign said.

Off he trudged to find a phone box, the evening now beginning to draw in. He almost felt at peace with himself, pleased in an irrational way at how the debauch of Christmas had gone.

The village was a church, a pub, a shop, and a clutch of upmarket houses. The brightly lit phone box advertised life, and there was life indeed, for it was occupied by a youngish woman with two children. Waiting ten yards from the box, he could see the woman's face. She was crying, the tears flowing freely down her cheeks. Peter was chilly, but loath to hurry the sad woman, so he walked towards the church, finding it open. The warmth inside allowed him to doze off in a rear pew.

He was awakened by a none-too-friendly voice.

'You can't sleep here. I'm locking the church.'

Peter gave the agitated vicar his blandest smile.

'Sorry. I've been waiting for the phone box. My car broke down. I'm afraid the box has been occupied by a lady for some time.'

The beady-eyed cleric viewed him suspiciously. Suddenly he barked, 'You've been drinking.'

Not only a Christian, but an observant one! Before allowing Peter to reprimand him for his impertinence, he continued, 'The woman in the phone box has domestic problems.'

The unsolicited testimony put Peter in control. In his best theatrical voice, he bellowed, 'And shouldn't you be there to comfort her? Doing something useful on your master's birthday?'

The vicar, startled, began to back-pedal.

'You can't help that one. She's unbalanced.'

'You could try, anyway,' Peter snapped, tired of the charade. 'If you're unhappy with me, phone the police. I'll be at the phone box. I can't escape till I've located help.'

Leaving the godly man in his temple, he found the woman still telephoning. He took up a position where she could see him through the glass. She was still tearful, gesticulating in despair as she talked, until at last she vacated the box. She had only one child in tow now. She apologised wanly for the delay. Peter bent and spoke to the child.

'And what did Santa bring you today?'

The attractive little face was bereft of self-pity as the girl mumbled, 'Nothing this year. We're not having presents this Christmas.'

Instinctively his hand went into his pocket.

'Well, we can't have that,' he said, his voice dropping an octave. He thrust a ten-pound note into the child's hand. 'You buy yourself something with this. Santa often comes late, you know.'

'Mummy,' she said, 'can I take it, please?'

The forlorn woman put up token resistance, then thanked Peter in a quizzical way before setting off with the child. She went a pace or two and then turned back.

'Who are you? I've not seen you round here before.'

'My car's broken down. I'm ringing a friend to pick me up.'

'Perhaps you'd like to wait at our place till he turns up.'

Unbalanced or not, she was more gracious than the prat cleric. Peter rang John, then a loyal friend. He agreed to drive up from Southampton to collect him. It would probably take a couple of hours.

So the unlikely trio – the thief, the brittle lady, and the happy child prattling away – set off down a winding road.

Feeding her pony was paramount with the child. She told Peter that she hoped her sister had already done it. At the end of the lane a cottage came into view, with a paddock and stable annexed.

'There's not much by way of food in the house, I'm afraid,' the woman said. 'I'm in a sticky patch.'

Without warning, her explanation turned into a gush of confidences.

'I'm a schoolteacher who wants to educate my children at home, but my husband's left me for a young woman and refuses to support us as long as I insist on keeping the girls from school.'

Peter thought suddenly that it was the fucking vicar who was unbalanced.

The cottage, though smart, smelled dank, and he organised a fire. He felt ill at ease, compelled to help. At last, bidding them farewell, he thrust a hundred pounds into the reluctant woman's hand.

'Brighten the holiday up,' he said, and was off down the lane to meet John.

As he trudged along he pondered the extraordinary events of the last twenty-four hours. He'd been propelled from the tables of plenty, denied sanctuary by the Christless vicar, only to find a distressed family in need of his help. On a day normally of joy. Was it a coincidence? Did it have the hand of the Master about it?

John provoked a long silence when observing, 'I suppose you know the church you sheltered in was St Peter's?'

Chief Superintendent Stephenson returned from the holiday to a meeting with officers from the Regional Crime Squad. A collator clued him up.

'We've been keeping tabs on Scott over the holiday. He was in the Ipswich area, where exactly we couldn't pinpoint. The next sighting is more pertinent. He abandoned his BMW, damaged, near Brentwood. We think he'd been plundering in the area and was possibly taking a stoppo. The local lot are chasing it up. Oddly, he hasn't recovered his vehicle.'

'Ipswich . . . I'm more concerned with what the bugger is up to in Mayfair. We had to let him and his thirty-six-inch Stilsons go recently. We thought we had positive ID but he wasn't picked out.' There was despair in Stephenson's voice.

A Commander present spoke up.

'He's a bit long in the tooth to be responsible for all your current problems, Dave. This last break-in at the furrier's – hardly the action of a target crim.'

'He gambles, sir. Needs must. Does his money and finds a soft target to tide him over. You recall his old sidekick, Taters Chatham? Blew a safe one week for thousands and out house-breaking the next. More important, the current gossip is that he believes he's on a crusade and the Deity is helping him.'

'God help us if that's the case.' The Commander allowed himself a smile. 'Chatham . . . God, he gave us many a headache. He's in his seventies now. Bit of shoplifting at worst.'

'Selective shoplifting, if rumour is to be credited. We've had a Renoir and a Matisse go walkies over the last year.'

'Well, let's hear from the Essex mob. Meanwhile I think it's best if we target Master Peter for a couple of weeks. Might find out what he's up to.'

The Commander had the last word.

At the club, Helen told him that a Betty from Green Street had rung. Could he phone her? He dialled the Mayfair number and Betty's aggressive New York twang answered.

'You want a hit indoors? I got a court at Harrow Road at three.'

Why not? She was a good sport and hostess.

'OK, I'll pick you up at two-thirty.'

Turning into Green Street, snowless now, the yellow peril were about and he couldn't park. He took a right into Dunraven Street, ending up in Woods Mews where he found a meter. Lucky battlefield of '63, he thought.

Admitted to the comfortable art-infested flat – Betty not only collected but painted professionally – he gazed down on the gardens behind. He was amused to see the solid Staveley attached to the rear of a house opposite. He'd once relieved a careless American tourist of fifty thousand pounds in gems from that house. What would they come to now? He smiled wryly to himself. All passé. He couldn't climb pipes today, or ever again. It made him feel quite sad, with the ladder as his last ally.

On court, Betty Zondheimer made up in enthusiasm what she lacked in skill. She was also the most valuable of friends to the thief, albeit entirely unwittingly. She was a widow who, apart from her modest tennis and ghastly chicken dinners, had a hidden asset – a lock-up cellar which she did not use. Peter, without mentioning it to Betty, who remained unaware of his deviousness, found numerous uses for the place, once he'd fitted a mortice to give him access with his own key. Here a multiplicity of swag was stored for long periods, giving the thief a private vault just where he wanted it – a slaughter in the very heart of Mayfair! One drawback was the presence of an old acquaintance in the same building: Bobby Butlin had the penthouse above Betty. It would have been, to say the least, awkward if the thief had met 'the camper's friend' in the basement area of 71 Green Street, for Peter's special skills were not unknown to Bobby.

However, Peter used the slaughter on numerous occasions in '84. Chief Superintendent Stephenson was to discover it a shade too late to assist his diligent enquiries.

Roger was anxious to work again. The rubbish from Zilli's had made small monies.

'What about giving the roof in Bond Street another visit?' was his opening gambit when they met. 'Still got the key to Bruton Place?'

Peter still had the key. Better, he had two possible targets. But he was no longer the aficionado of Dr Death. He fobbed the oddball off.

'Too warm up there now. The penny will have dropped at West End Central. But I have an order for a few dolly mixtures in St James's. I'll know more about it next week.'

'Uh-huh.'

'By the way, you were right about Chelsea. She's almost law. Reading it at Birkbeck College with a view to joining the filth at privilege level. She's gone back to her boyfriend. I got the sack.'

Roger was visibly shaken.

'Did she know you were at it?'

'She saw me as Dad's Army, yesterday's man.'

Roger, clearly piqued, felt he might be getting the bum's rush. He rapped out a curt 'I'll be seeing you, then.'

And he was off. It didn't matter. Peter had the lively young Clyde in mind for his next excursion to Mayfair. He felt at ease with Clyde.

34

Dartmoor Years

CLYDE was beaming.

'I was in Sheila's with Di last night. Met a guy you were in Dartmoor with. Brian?'

'Brian Turner, probably. But he's never been a fan of mine.'

'Yes, Turner, that was him. Got a handshake like a vice. He didn't give you a bad blowdown.' Clyde chuckled. 'Said you were mad, though.'

'In Dartmoor,' said Peter seriously, 'if you weren't mad when you arrived, you sure as hell were when you left.'

In the early sixties D Wing in Wandsworth housed those serving five years or more. A security boffin had built a workshop on two levels at the end of the wing and at right-angles to it, so that you went directly from your box to labour. HT (Hard Tack) 1 and HT2 were security shops where Category A and special-watch prisoners had to work. A careless joshing conversation Peter had with Officer Chitty in the workshop about copping for staff and smashing through the windows adjacent to the wall came home to roost. The following day the thief was on the ghost train with another prisoner, Alf Alpress. Alf went to Parkhurst, Peter to Dartmoor.

Danny Malone was the governor. He was a tough, fair Anglo-Celt who had performed with courage for the Army during the emergency in Cyprus. He was a man's man, no crooked heats. But you fucked him about at your peril.

Peter was back sewing mailbags under the awful 'Arab' in Mailbags 1 and he wanted out of there. So he went on Governor's Application, for a change of labour.

'4711 Peter Craig Gulston, sir. Application for a change of labour.'

Malone viewed him not unkindly.

'What did you have in mind, exactly?'

'I'd like to work in the quarry, sir. I find the mailbag shop . . .' He hesitated, looking for the right word. 'Tedious. Soul-destroying to a man in the prime of life. I'd like some kind of physical work, sir.'

'Well, Gulston, I don't think I can let you outside the walls just yet. You have an appalling record . . .'

He ran his eye over the file in front of him.

' "Friendly with several of the Train Robbers and Billy Hill." Is he the old gangster? I remember from our records that we had him with us. Well, whoever wrote this report certainly had it in for you. Fortunately I run my own ship here. So, no quarry just yet, but I see Works are forming a small squad to concrete an area inside the prison. That will be hard work. You up for it?'

Peter certainly was. Open air was what he craved.

Geordie Waugh was a small bantam cock of a screw from the north-east. Opening Peter's cell door the following morning for labour, he joked, 'I hope you know something about laying concrete, Gulston. Because I don't.'

Four other cons and Geordie made up the squad, none of them very anxious to graft. Peter broke their hearts and the steward's estimates by concreting every rock base inside the walls. He sometimes even bribed the team to work. One young prisoner on the squad, Paddy Henery, was both powerful and a bully. Geordie Waugh was so intimidated by Henery that he would not take the party out until he'd confirmed Henery had taken his Librium – it being then fashionable to allow prisoners access to anti-depressants. (That ended but today they turn a blind eye to illegal drug-users. Anything to keep a happy ship.)

Henery, aware of Geordie's apprehension, led him a dog's life. Initially the young man respected Peter, for they were both Irish, but with a bully nothing lasts and one morning he challenged a working method Peter had suggested to Geordie Waugh.

'You work if you like, you cunt.'

It was a declaration of war. Peter swallowed hard. He knew that, sooner or later, he would have to take Henery on.

Henery bet on horses, with tobacco the currency. Peter accepted bets on behalf of a pal who ran a book on D Wing. One afternoon Henery slipped into the officers' mess and learned of the results before anybody else. He then called a bet with Peter which the thief, knowing what Henery was about, pretended to accept. It was a foolish thing to do. The young bully would want paying. Peter had no intention of being after-timed by a cunt, dangerous or otherwise.

In A Wing you were paid with your working party, when your officer got a chance on the prescribed afternoon to bring you in. The four of them from the concreting detail queued with Geordie Waugh in the almost-deserted A Wing.

'Don't forget my two ounces,' Henery reminded Peter in a voice full of menace. Peter tried to make light of it.

'Behave yourself, Paddy. You know you didn't pay on, nor did I accept it. I knew you'd got the result.'

'If you don't pay me, I'm going to give you a belting in the recess.'

Geordie Waugh watched and listened with interest. He wasn't going to interfere. Henery was going to have his come-uppance, he was sure. He had such confidence in Gulston. The thief, although he had little appetite for taking on the brick-shit-house-built bully, was not going to be mugged off after being after-timed.

The wages were handed out and Peter received another gruff request from Henery for the snout.

'Fuck off, Paddy. Think I'm some kind of a cunt?'

In fact, Henery did. He beckoned Peter towards the recess and Peter stepped into the darkened area. He was thirty-six, the bully twenty-three. He would see if a little guile would help, and Henery gave him all the help he needed. Mouthing obscenities, he stupidly started to take off his battledress jacket. Peter pounced when the sleeves were at elbow level and booted Henery up the balls. He dropped like a stone, crawling in under the jaw-box for protection. Frightened, angry, remembering old scores, Peter booted Henery until his hobnail-booted foot ached. Geordie Waugh simply watched impassively.

Peter was exhausted and he turned it up. A bloodied Henery crawled out, groaning cheerfully, apparently unconcerned.

'If you hadn't have got in first I'd have done you.'

He gave a bleeding smile. Suddenly Geordie Waugh exclaimed, 'You've had that coming a long time, Henery.'

Peter, wiser in victory, knew full well the truth of Henery's words. It might very well have been oh so different. Later, in D Wing, Henery showed his utter madness. Standing in a recess queue he deliberately drenched a south London gangster in boiling water. There was no comeback.

The steward, or Danny Malone, got tired of funding Peter's concreting campaign. And now, at last, he got his transfer to the quarry. He arrived there on a cold, dank morning in '65. Few were working. The men stood huddled in twos and threes, resisting the cold.

He teamed up with a handsome young armed robber from north London. His name was Mickey West. Peter tried to persuade Mickey of the virtues of killing time with work, but he was not easily convinced.

In one corner, near the mouth of the quarry, was an ancient crusher shed to which stone was barrowed from the perimeter face. At one time, bogie tracks were in evidence around the face, but these were now defunct. A couple of old bogies lay idly to one side, overgrown with weed. Peter thought, why not relay the track and restore the bogies, then draw the broken stone from source, then manhandle the bogie to the crusher ramp? He put his brainwave to Abe, the elderly quarry master. Abe, Devon-bred and born, had seen lots of wide-boys and was suspicious. But seeing Peter's obvious enthusiasm he agreed.

'If you can lay the track, lad, we'll get the bogies fixed.'

And so a track was laid, Peter so absorbed in it that he found time flying. The only possible way to do your bird was to bash it to death. But one or two of the Jocks carped.

'Working for hostel already?'

'But of course,' Peter confessed instantly. Six months in a prison hostel in the metropolis was the ultimate prize when you finished a long one, working outside and enjoying the odd weekend at home. Only about one in four copped it and Peter certainly wanted to be among the chosen.

Even in prison, there is a 'best' to be found, though it varies greatly with the individual. In the thief's case it meant interminable exercise, studying French and economics, and the profound solace of classical music. He even penned sonnets to Jackie. Strangely, looking back over a quarter of a century, they do not now seem unhappy days. He was in love. Jackie wrote and visited regularly, but he was hearing about her even more often.

What Peter found more disturbing was the fact that never a week went by without her appearing in the press, the senior member of a group of a dozen models who were trail-blazing British fashions worldwide. Alas, in her forced sabbatical from the flesh, she damaged herself in some insidious way as she 'waited' for her man. Daily, inexorably, they grew further apart – she vibrant and alive, he in a criminal time warp.

They were traumatic years for the prison service. The swingeing sentences passed on the Train Robbers (which had doubled to thirty years the previous top tariff for their crime) had a knock-on effect throughout the prison population. This, along with the horrifically stupid preventive detention legislation of '48, has brought about today's crisis. Prisons are not only packed to the point of desperation, they contain a growing hard core of long-term offenders, as well as hordes of social inadequates, who shouldn't be there at all – other than to appease society's cop-out from responsibility for their kind.

Prison staff are not by their nature, or inclination, pleasant people. Most resent their being in the job at all. Nowhere more so than in the arsehole of nowhere, Dartmoor. Sub-standard accommodation and anti-social hours were among the hardships endured by staff, and were so well known that an officer who had done his five-year stint on the Moor became entitled to choose his next station where, if he wished, he could remain for the rest of his service. The professional prisoner knew only two breeds of staff: those you could use and those you couldn't. The former were to be cosseted assiduously, the latter to be given a wide berth, a distinction as valid today as it has ever been. This is a fact that anyone foolish enough to contemplate a life of crime will be able to confirm for himself.

Percy Batt was Peter's landing officer on B Wing. He was a regimental sort of guy, but not the worst of the breed, and they gradually found an accommodation. While modest privileges were an acceptable currency between them, neither ever pushed the boat out too far. Another far more fateful acquaintanceship was about to be struck.

Having won his spurs grafting in the quarry for eighteen months, Peter qualified to go on an outside working party. The Duchy of Cornwall was demolishing a number of cottages scattered around the domain, five to seven miles distant from the prison. He and a couple of others, along with a works officer, all equipped with packed lunches, would set out daily. At the same hour of the morning, three other working parties gathered in the assembly point and one of them, the farm party, included a stooping, bespectacled, prematurely grey con who approached Peter on the first day, as they were all waiting to leave. This was Stan 'the Chauffeur' Addersman.

'Hello, Peter,' was Stan's opener. He used a sycophantic tone. 'You may not know me, but I've put up one or two bits of work you've gone on.'

Having established his credentials, Stan prattled on about having lots of solid work still to be attended to. At first Peter was wary of him, but in the end he got to like him. It was the beginning of a more fateful friendship than he could know.

Another of the outside parties, the leat party, was detailed to work on an old mill-race out on the Moor. And included in the leat party was Frank Mitchell. The press eventually dubbed him with a misnomer that stuck, the 'Mad Axe-man', but Peter was acquainted with the real Mitchell, his small perk being to be spared the embarrassment of the unfriendly hugs which Frank inflicted on staff and inmates alike.

Mitchell had been in prison for fifteen years, surviving on a promise from Danny Malone that he'd be released before Malone retired. With his maverick attitudes, Frank was a headache to the staff, but Malone got the best out of him. He even trusted Frank to hump a great axe about with him on working parties. The children in the village loved Frank: after all, he was really only one of them. He was also an overgrown, over-muscled fitness fanatic. But for all that Frank (and others of his ilk) did much to make the lot of other prisoners better. They bucked the system and often won through, while at the same time being prepared to pay the price in the block or with loss of remission if they lost. When they did win some degree of licence for themselves, this would spin off for others. A lot of cons even today owe their privileges to men like Frank Mitchell.

Malone was retiring soon, and Frank was still waiting for his date. Then he decided to wait no longer. The day his east London visitors spirited him away by limo from the leat party was an unfortunate day from the thief's point of view. Jackie had arrived on visit the day before in a caravanette and, on the actual day of Mitchell's escape, Peter got permission from the party officer to be absent on the pretext of locating a Christmas tree in a nearby plantation. In reality he'd arranged to meet Jackie in her caravanette and, a little further along the road, they had thirty minutes of ecstasy on a mattress in the back, curtains drawn, Peter rutting and panting in his hobnailed working boots. It was farcical, but needs must.

By the time of evening roll-call, when Mitchell was missed, Jackie was still inside the perimeter, around which the law quickly set up roadblocks. Though not detained, her presence was noted, which led to armed police surrounding Edith Road one evening a week later and searching her home. Meanwhile, in the prison, the hunt for Mitchell meant that all working parties were stood down indefinitely, so that on A Wing television was the only diversion for a day or two. A final irony of the Mitchell evacuation was when the news showed police with dogs searching a cottage that Peter and his pals had been demolishing. Peter watched, knowing that Jackie, late on the evening of the escape, had been due to leave him his Christmas parcel in a dustbin at the cottage: tobacco, fowl, confection, pud, the lot, all concealed by a layer of firewood. Suddenly, on screen, the bin came into view. A huge Alsatian dog on hind legs sniffed it and Peter knew it was on him. He was right. Later that day he was called to the Centre. He stood in the corridor outside the governor's office. Suddenly the door swung open and there, laid out on the floor, were the captured Christmas goodies.

'Looks like Santa's called,' Peter observed to the assembled worthies. The new governor, on his first adjudication, smiled.

'Yes, but who's he come for? Someone will have to accept responsibility, or the whole working party may have to be abandoned.'

The thief gave it the only shot he had in his locker.

'I believe some misguided person may have left it for me.'

The governor rose from his seat and selected from the heap of Fortnum's fare a can of bicarbonate of soda. He showed it to Peter, whose indigestion was legendary at the M.O. Room.

'Some misguided person who knew you pretty well.'

Back to the bloody quarry and with an extra week to serve, he struggled on, until his 'home leave' was due. He had actually got Hostel, but after he had a screaming row with Jackie in the visiting room, the new governor had told Peter in the crispest tones, 'I am not prepared to confirm your hostel release. Frankly I'm surprised you got it in the first place.'

Now Jackie and Peter had passed the point of no return. Hostility emerged, and the loss of Hostel was the straw that broke the lady's back. The compensation probably did little to help. Peter was granted home leave three months before his discharge – five days in London. They turned into a nightmare.

Jackie, still trying to keep the marriage alive, picked him up by cab from the prison gate. They caught the rattler at Tavistock, travelling in an empty carriage before picking up the Devonian express at Plymouth. Crassly, with nothing but sheer animal drive to excuse him, the thief forced himself mid-journey on a lady not quite ready, satisfying himself but repelling her. It was the first of many mistakes he was to make during that furlough.

A drinks party was arranged at Edith Road for that evening, a roomful of Jackie's friends from the fashion world assembling. There were none of Peter's ilk except a lone David Gliksten, sitting boozily in the hall, unhappy in the company of swingers. At one point he was promising Peter five thousand pounds on his release, suggesting he buy a tipper lorry and start a legit business. But David monopolised Peter most of the evening, causing the first of many rucks with Jackie.

'You paid no attention to me all evening,' the lady bleated when all her guests had gone. Peter, who'd worked his butt off to keep the swingers' glasses topped up, began to realise just how far they had grown apart. The savage quarry culture cannot accommodate drawing-rooms in Kensington. Yet, loving the lady and unable to please her, he became impotent and angry. He slept on a loveless couch.

It went from bad to worse. Nothing he did found favour with Ma'am. Finally he snapped.

'Bitch! Bitch! BITCH!'

And he did what he now thinks the lady – unconsciously – wanted him to do, to absolve her guilt. He slapped her.

Back at Dartmoor, he got a letter from Brazil, where Jackie and the Associated Fashion Designers girls were trail-blazing again. 'Dear Peter . . .'

Working by then on a forestry party, he cut and felled trees furiously from morning to night. Only work eased the pain. He hardly spoke to anybody. Taters, who'd arrived at Dartmoor the year before, smarting from a six-stretch for a jeweller's in Leicester, observed Peter's behaviour and told another Fulham pal, George Newberry.

'I think Jackie's given him the elbow.'

Taters knew the hazards and he himself was always on the knife-edge of a similar fate, being currently (and fearfully) in love with a certain Amy Buckingham.

Peter was discharged in October 1967. There was no one waiting for him at the gate. Travelling to London on the Devonian, he and two fellow dischargees drank and scoffed to the tune of seventy-two pounds, a bill eventually paid by Peter. Arriving at Waterloo, Bill Smaller and Smithy were pissed, the thief stone-cold sober. He was about to face his own Waterloo.

Jackie was there on the platform with a hairdresser chum, Mary, who greeted Peter and hugged him, while a sullen Jackie hung back.

'Peter, Jackie's not too well,' said Mary. 'She needs a little time to think things out, so she's going to stay in the country for a few days.'

A bellow from Bill Smaller distracted him. Peter turned to wave goodbye, then turned back to see the two girls legging it out of the station. He caught a last glimpse of them leaping into a taxi.

Only the cats greeted him at Edith Road. Dear old Tigre, who knew how wounded he was, rested on his chest purring as he stretched out on the bed. He was distraught, confused. Yet fate had another brutal card to play. Casually looking through the wardrobe, astounded at the volume of clothes she'd accumulated, his eye caught a letter poking out of one of the coat pockets. It was addressed to a Jennifer Statler in New York and written in Jackie's handwriting. In her haste to decamp, she must have forgotten to post it. Peter opened the letter, which gave chapter and verse. Jackie had a new beau, a model-boy from the Brazil trip. Never had she been so in love. But it was the callous observation 'Peter will be devastated', penned so coldly to her Yankee chum, which forced tears from his eyes, tears that Dartmoor could never have caused him to shed.

When his tears were staunched, anger took their place, and he flipped his lid. He started a bonfire in the back garden with all Jackie's possessions, including, wickedly, stupidly, her trunk (which he had had made in La Verne, a Dorset prison, the year before and covered with the unlucky royal purple cloth), full of a lifetime's photographs, as well as the sonnets he'd written in Dartmoor and the portrait he'd had painted of her in oils. That autumn evening in 1967 a little of him died as he roasted his most profound emotions at the stake of bitter malice. He stopped loving that night and he would, indeed, never love again. It was as if the swirling flames gutted his soul. *'Twas only a slight flirtation, a pity the fellow died.* But if there is any extravagance from which the career criminal must distance himself, it is love and marriage. They will extract a far greater penalty than any court can when time is called.

David Gliksten held his hand, plying him with Bloody Marys. He'd let Peter have the five thousand as promised, but in their respective miseries tippers were forgotten. In due course Jackie's young man, fearful of Peter, returned to his Kraut wife. Jackie, pragmatic as ever, decided to come back home. It was small consolation for Peter; the marriage was now terminally flawed. Jackie knew in her heart that the man she loved had only been deflected under threat from her thief husband. And she had other reasons for hating Peter. He'd hospitalised her when she flung a glass of wine in his face, catching her with a reflexive back-hander. She arrived at St George's with a swollen cheek and eye. A doctor exclaimed, horrified, 'You must have hit her with a hammer to have inflicted such damage. Her cheekbone has collapsed.'

Peter cringed in shame. 'Sorry, no hammer,' he said. 'Just a back-hander in rage.'

Subsequent examination led to a milder prognosis. Jackie had a chipped cheekbone. Peter felt even more bloody – he was a brute to have struck her, and he knew it. Out of hospital, she elected to come back to him at Edith Road, but the carping continued in the run-up to Christmas.

'I'd rather you went thieving than got pissed with Gliksten every day.' She had a point. Her dalliance had given him an excuse for rescinding the promises of reformation, although he may not have needed one – the trenches of pillage were always beckoning, his destiny inescapable.

It was time to regain his self-respect. Jackie was desperate to have a baby, even with a brute for a potential father, and it seemed the only possible salvation for the marriage. In the misery of his guilt-ridden, vodka-soaked mirage, Peter struggled to find the bottle to perform criminally again.

Stanley Addersman was the catalyst. Currently the chauffeur was still languishing in Dartmoor but, before Peter himself had departed, Stan promoted a bit of work: Mrs Raphael's emeralds. The iffy bit of the plot was the mandate that he must strike over Christmas.

'The gear will only be there then,' Stan asserted.

The target was a Dutch barn-type house on the western perimeter of the J. Paul Getty estate, Sutton Place near Guildford. Peter recced the house but, try as he might, he couldn't face a Christmas assault. However, a week later, the continued domestic battle drove him down to Sutton Place on New Year's Eve. He found a house party in progress.

The thief skirted the cattle-pitted field and approached the balcony of the barn, which was ablaze with festive spirit. He quickly found a ladder, knowing there was no point in hanging around. Either Stanley was reliable or he was a wally. He propped the ladder up against the first-floor balcony, scaled it, and drew it up behind him. Then he erected it again under one of the bedroom windows. All was going well.

An unlatched sill simplified entry. He was in an oblong master bedroom. He went to the door, opened it cautiously, and heard the festivities below. Then he closed and locked the door from the inside before ransacking the more obvious possible concealments. There was not a bloody smell of the prize. He searched the en suite bathroom. Nothing. Back in the bedroom, he was about to give the linen cupboard a spin when he heard someone turn the door handle. As he continued his search with increased urgency, a timid knock was followed by a man's voice.

'Is there anyone in there?'

Peter tossed the bed linen to the floor and a pouch dropped out. He pocketed it and made for the window, with the door now being hammered by Chummy, who was bellowing in rhythm with his blows.

'Open this bloody door!'

He was moving back down the ladder to the balcony when he heard an excited scream.

'He's out on the balcony!'

Then, as he lowered the ladder to the ground, he heard an outside door opening. He slid down and took off just as the entire house party spilled out.

'Stop thief! Stop thief!' they yelled. But he was already gone across the field.

He headed for the coast. It was too dangerous to risk the London road and he had a pal with a caravan at Pevensey Bay. He stayed there for the night. When he inspected the take, he found a specimen eight-carat emerald and a six-carat to go with it. He'd had a touch, all right. The profits allowed the thief and his wife to have a month in Las Palmas mending bridges, trying to develop respect, trying to have a child. Stan the chauffeur came home a month later. He'd seen news of the burglary in the papers, but was surprised nevertheless to draw his whack.

'I'll make you a rich man if you'll listen to me,' he told Peter. He was delighted to find a thief who paid on *and* showed respect. Stanley was very strong on respect. One was even required to respect his fantasies, such were the complex sensitivities of the owl-like finger-man. Stanley was probably the most enigmatic male ever to have come into the thief's orbit.

The couple returned from Las Palmas reconciled for the moment and in good fettle. Soon Stanley suggested another prestigious victim, Dr Hugo Simpson, supremo of the emporium in Piccadilly that bears his name. Dr Simpson practised in Harley Street and Stanley from time to time shunted him about. One of his tasks was to call at the consulting room to pick up and deliver parcels, occasions on which the enigmatic ferret missed little. No sooner did any of his masters turn their backs than Stan had a shufty.

'There's a big safe on a plinth, right in the middle of an annexe just off the consulting room. They keep the family jewels there – I know, I collect them sometimes, take them to a house in Sussex.'

It sounded like a possible touch. Peter called in a pal to effect a key entry from the street and then the surgery.

The Harley Street house had multiple consulting rooms, unoccupied at night and weekends. On the other hand the basement was a liver for the caretakers. Peter and his pal found that there was indeed a big Chubb safe, totally impregnable to the convenient mini-propane kit of the amateur safe-breaker. It was for an expert to decide whether oxy-acetylene or arc cutting was required.

The job was a fuck-up from the start. They attacked the safe on a Saturday with oxy-acetylene, but first ran out of oxygen and then flooded the surgery, cooling the bubbling, burning safe with water. Miraculously the trespass went undetected overnight and they had a second bite at the cherry on the Sunday night. But the safe defied all the inept safe-breakers' best shots. They left a fortune behind.

Peter blamed himself. He'd let control slide into the hands of a lightweight team. They were game enough, but lacked finesse. Stanley was hopping mad – but not for long. He'd located the whereabouts of an even bigger celebrity target: film star Natalie Wood.

The petite actress was cohabiting with an English film director in Pimlico. It appeared on the face of it an uncomplicated strike, though the full recce would require a nocturnal vigil. When he told Jackie not to expect him in that night, she was sceptical.

'I don't believe you're out working. You're seeing someone.'

To convince his wife he took her on the recce. It was bitterly cold as they lingered cuddling in a doorway opposite the address, waiting for the upper house to be unoccupied and the road deserted. Peter planned to hoist a ladder up to the balcony window and confirm the whereabouts of the au pair, who actually lived in the basement. It was a cold wait and went unrewarded. By 10 p.m. they retreated frozen, the mission unaccomplished. He invited Jackie to accompany him the following night, but she said she was satisfied he was not trysting. She would stay indoors.

Things fell into place, as they will for the tenacious. The actress and her lover went out and the au pair settled down to the telly. The road clear, he moved the ladder swiftly and effected entry through an uncatched sash window. Tenacity found its reward. Natalie's jewellery, lying on the dressing table, funded the long vigil.

Natalie Wood died almost twenty years later. Other victims of the thief were already close to their deaths when he trespassed. The beautiful, neurotic Vivien Leigh was deprived of some of her gems. They were in a handbag in a mill-house near Uckfield a few months before she quit this life. Calling some local Chelsea police to an unsuccessful break-in, Katie Kendall was foolish enough to confide to them that she hid her gems behind a bath panel. Sadly, the coppers gossiped, unwittingly marking Peter's card. It was not long before the angels beckoned her, too. At Montagu Mews, Marylebone, home of Dawn Addams, alias Princess Mattrissimo, Peter left a footprint in the bath.

A lady Inspector announced that it was a vital clue and would lead her to the culprit. She failed and the emerald-set brooch of a boy on a dolphin was never to return to the Prince's Italian family.

This bit of work had a sequel. Peter was lunching with Billy Hill in Paddy Kennedy's when Dawn arrived with Vasco Lazlo, an artist whose wife Lila's gems Peter had once stolen. A note arrived from Dawn to Bill, written on her lunch menu, which promised she would do a striptease if he could recover her gems. But Peter (by this time older and wiser) did not confide to Hilly that he had her gear and Dawn never danced. It is possible Hill had a freebie anyway. Dawn had a penchant for old men.

When the elderly assessor who'd stuck up the work drew his whack, he told Peter, 'I went round to comfort her over her loss and was stunned when she lifted her skirt up and asked me if I liked her legs. You see me. I'm fat. Even ugly. Can you imagine? I'd not screwed for years, but I did that day!'

Judy Garland was renting Sir Carol Reed's house in the King's Road when Peter encountered her ascending the stairs, alone in the house in the early evening. She was somewhere over the rainbow, spaced out of her mind. The thief escorted the sad warbler to a couch. She was pathetic, bewildered at the reception she'd had at the hands of a hostile Palladium audience. She thought Peter was staff and he simply played the part, lying her down on the sofa and fixing her a drink. He took nothing that night, feeling more like bunging her a few quid. Then, before letting himself out, he murmured over her, 'The Wizard's leaving empty-handed. Your money's not valid in Oz, Madam Judy.'

35

'May the Baby Have Long Legs'

JACKIE got pregnant in the autumn of 1968. The Gulstons rejoiced. In due course Mr Wynn Williams delivered a boy child at Queen Charlotte's. Mum and Dad were delighted with Craig Patrick.

At the turn of the century, when a mother-to-be was having a final drink in her East End local, the toast was often 'May the baby have long legs' – a boy was destined to be a thief, and if a woman was blessed with a boy these words were intended to enhance his ability to scarper from the law.

Babies being expensive, it was mandatory that Peter went to graft. A large cache of cigars purloined in St James's bought the pram.

Stanley's extraordinary knowledge of the whereabouts of the transient wealthy was invaluable to the thief in the late sixties. He was privy to the comings and goings of people who inherited the mechanics of ostentation with their lifeblood. In 1969 *Mame* was in town, and Stanley had been shunting Mame herself, Ginger Rogers, about. The ageing hoofer's parsimony was legendary – she'd mugged the cast off with boiled sweets at Christmas when they'd been expecting a few quid. Nor had she ever greased Stanley's palm – a fatal error, for he promptly revealed the whereabouts of her loot to Peter. According to Stan, Ginger kept her tom in Harrods' Depository. He, or one of his pals, would collect it on nights when she was socialising. It was on one such night, getting to Ginger's penthouse roof from a block of flats adjacent, that Peter found the upper-floor bedroom window ajar, but grilled with diamond-crossed wire mesh. He would have to return with cutters.

The thief and his pal Bristow approached the target a second time, and were alarmed by a plain-clothes presence, identified only just in time. They decided to stay clear and take refuge in the Rutland Arms. Back on the roof an hour later, with the copper gone, Peter started snipping the grille. The section he cut whined and pinged as it yielded. Someone inside heard the noise – possibly Ginger's maid or companion, a woman anyway – and came into view, creeping up the stairs.

The thieves desisted, knowing they could live to fight another night, since it would take a minute examination to detect the section of grille he had snipped. They went back to the pub, had a quick drink, and went their separate ways. But Bristow was to get no further than his car. A CID team sprang out and challenged him.

'You've been observed trying car door-handles, chum,' a Taffy cop growled. 'And looking in basements. What's your game?'

In fact, Bristow was legally (and conveniently) employed to repossess motor cars whose owners had fallen behind on their payments. For that purpose he had a clutch of tools and a Gladstone bag full of keys. Finding them, the mob howled in delight.

'Looks like you're going equipped too,' said the copper.

Bristow was quickly nicked, hauled off to – where else? – Gerald Road, and charged with being a suspect person. At midnight, Peter too was arrested, under protest, at Edith Road. He was also taken to Gerald Road.

It was a minor charge. They expected to be acquitted, but they were remanded in custody and eventually banged up for six months.

With Peter free in the summer of 1970, Jackie put her cards on the table, unsteady as it was.

'I cannot tolerate any more police tramping over my home. Craig deserves better. I think, if you love us, you will let us go. I really would like a divorce.'

Jackie had rehearsed her speech, but she omitted the most pertinent reason. That she had found a Sir Galahad, a certain Trevor Bailey.

'Well, I don't think you're telling me everything. I think you've met someone. I'd be obliged if you told me straight.'

'How can I tell you anything? If I have met someone, you'll only go round and bash him. That's all you know, frightening and bashing people.'

Peter pondered. What a bloody awful CV. Anyway, bashing-time was over. It was letting-go time, love's cruel ultimate mandate, and he let Jackie and Craig go – to a stranger. It was a crucifixion of sorts, but it gave tears that no nails, however savage, could produce. And he had only his own arrogance and passion for thieving to blame.

The petition Jackie presented read like a horror story, never mind that she was technically the guilty or adulterous party. No unpleasantness, however small, was omitted, and no slight was ignored. How the hell do women retain such trivial memories? Or was it always a gathering of ammunition, anticipating the conflict from day one?

He found out soon enough who Sir Galahad was, and he had alarming connections. Trevor Bailey's father was a one-time Commissioner of Police in the Bahamas and before that governor of the Yard's murder squad. Within a year Bailey was to have liquidity problems, Jackie foolishly having left her share of the now-valuable family property at Edith Road to Peter. She had made it a willing forfeit for her defection, about which she now began to have second thoughts. She even pushed the boat out, offering to return to the thief, but there was no room in his heart for a reconciliation. He was hunting now for something new, and all the time waging a ruthless war with society in his sorrow. Stanley was finding him victims weekly. It was a lucrative time.

But the flat was a tomb. The only living things were Cindy the Labrador and Tigre, the oddest of tabby cats, which Jackie had left behind. Tigre knew how sad the master was and compensated by perching on his chest, purring and looking into his eyes as he lay mournfully on his bed. How much more caring are our pets than our lovers, he thought.

Despair and loneliness can unhinge decency. Peter prowled about at night walking the dog, seeking out carelessly curtained windows in basements in order to pry on ladies disrobing. Earl's Court was his favourite pitch, with its plethora of bed-sits and transient exhibitionists. Well, that is what the peeping tom liked to think they were as he masturbated to his private fantasies. He must have been a sorry sight as he skirmished in the dusk and darkness, night after night, to the point of exhaustion.

In these circumstances it was hardly likely that he would renounce the one consistent passion of his life. Victims over the years 1970 to 1971 were drawn from the most deserving in society – the most deserving of being deprived, that is. The prats actually believed that their wealth was an accumulation of their honesty and skill, with avarice and selfishness never in evidence. The list comprised a sizeable chunk of *Who's Who:* Viscount Blakenham, the sad Chairman of the Conservative Party who committed suicide, in Holland Park; Mrs Marnie Heinz of 57 varieties, at Binfield, after he'd failed her at Hay's Mews; Cubby Broccoli in the charade with the paparazzi at Green Street; the Guinness family at Upper Phillimore Gardens, where he missed the safe and had to content himself with a haul of silverware – a change in luck for them since their nubile daughter had recently slipped from the marital clutches of royalty; Shirley MacLaine, actress, at Winkfield; an Arab prince in Warburton Street, Mayfair; the Earl Lloyd George in the sticks in Wiltshire. All fleshpots, deserving of a visit.

The previous spring, languishing in Wandsworth for a couple of months prior to a transfer to Eastchurch, he got friendly with a well-set-up young man who worked in the library there, an amateur house-breaker named George Bethnal Alexander, who claimed to have held a commission in the army and to have served with the SAS. Now he was anxious to learn the ropes of larceny.

When Alexander was aimed out of the prison library, gossip had it he was a sneak. Others warned Peter, 'Be careful. Alexander's a wrong 'un. He grassed the whole library up.'

But Peter ignored the gossip, choosing to give the greater credibility to Alexander himself. Foolish thief. He had admitted a second Judas to the Garden of Gethsemane.

Alexander looked like a soldier, and was built like a lion. But he had the heart of a mouse; he was a jelly-baby when the cell door shut. Not his fault, but Peter's, for giving him a high handicap rating on appearance alone. The words of Bobby Melrose, the old Scottish safe-breaker, echo the truest of all truths. 'If you attach more integrity to a man than he deserves and then he lets you down, the fault is yours, not his.'

Bob the Dog was right. When he came out in 1970, Alexander looked the thief up. He was of good appearance and anxious to learn, and Peter was tempted to use him. A decade later he was to pay the forfeit for his faith in the soldier – the chocolate soldier, alas.

George was housed in a rented pad at Burghclere with a common-law wife, a light-fingered hotel receptionist, Laurie, who always wore long-out-of-fashion mini-skirts. Madam, feeling that Peter was using, not educating, George, found the thief not to her liking.

Alexander was not with Peter when he burgled Shirley MacLaine at Winkfield, near Ascot. He was eventually to tell the jury an imaginative version of the events of that night. But in the main, Alexander crept out on his own. He did well too, plundering with no mean skill and bringing the loot to Peter in London to dispose of. It was Peter's commission which irked him.

'You get me poor prices. You take too much.'

The apprentice burglar wanted a freebie with Peter's contacts and the skills he had learned over a lifetime; he didn't want to pay for his education. Laurie thought he would do much better finding his own buyer. The idea was to end in disaster.

Alexander had stolen a collection of antique watches from a collector in the Banbury area, which he brought to Peter. Their usual meeting place was the Swan Tavern on the Bayswater Road. On this occasion it was bloody luck that Stanley Addersman should appear. Although it was the first time they had met, somehow the pair colluded that day, unbeknownst to Peter. Inspectors Eist and Birch found property in Stanley's garage in Smallbrook Mews which almost certainly came from Alexander. Birch had long been obsessed with capturing Peter; Eist had recently moved to St John's Wood from east London. It was to be a further misfortune for Peter that he would be one of the investigating officers on the Lloyds safety deposit break-in in Baker Street in 1971.

How the pair of coppers got on to Stan was then and now a mystery. What they did manage to wring out of him with attractive options was the demise of George Alexander.

'We don't want you, Stan,' Eist told him. 'Tell us what you know about that flash prat Scott. You owe him nothing.'

Eist's needs went unanswered. Stan still cared for Peter, perhaps in fear, hardly in respect, for like most of his ilk in the lower divisions of crime he respected little other than his own liberty. Peter's time was not up, but Alexander's was. Stanley offered him up without a second thought.

'I won't say anything about Peter, he's packed it in, but I do know where an active friend of his who's cracking away lives.'

It was a good trade.

'What's his name and where is he living?'

'I know him as George. He's living in a rented house at Burghclere.'

'Where in Burghclere?' Eist smelt blood.

'Can't say, only been there at night. It's up a lane.'

Stan kept it vague, but it was enough for the pair of experienced officers to be able to locate the property after calling on local estate agents.

Peter had warned Alexander, 'Never have anything crooked in the house.' George knew better. Eist and Birch found the most damning of clues, a leather gun case bearing Earl Lloyd George's name, though the Purdeys were absent. A Rover car in the drive turned out to be a ringer. It was time up for George Alexander.

'Looks like you're nicked, chum, but there could be an out. What do you know about Peter Gulston? You might know him as Scott.

Looks like he's dropped you in it. It's him we want. Use your nut. Let's do it the sweet way, George.'

It was an offer Alexander could not refuse.

George failed to keep a meet in London. Peter rang Burghclere. A hostile, suspicious Laurie answered the phone.

'I thought you might know where he is. The police have nicked him.' She railed on in unfriendly fashion, 'You're the only person who knows we're here.'

She said nothing of Stanley having been a visitor and at the time Peter was unaware of his visit. It perplexed and mystified him – clearly Laurie was pointing the finger at him.

Alexander was eventually bailed, Peter getting him surety, but by then a pal in Maida Vale had alerted him to what was happening – a terse 'Peter, a prat called Alexander has put it on you, mind your back.'

Unaware of this, Alexander fronted Peter. 'How did the police find Burghclere?'

Non-committally, Peter murmured, 'George, I think it best you drop me out for a bit. In the meantime I'd give the game a miss.'

'Still can't understand how the police found me and Laurie.'

'Keep your nut down, George. I'll be in touch.'

The thief found it difficult to control his anger, but haunting him like a spectre were old Bobby Melrose's words about misplaced integrity. After all, he had been warned about Alexander's duplicity. The library mob in Wandsworth had it in one – he was a sneaky, grassing prat. And Peter had to find him!

An event prior to Alexander's arrest convinced the thief it was time to kick the ball into touch – an attack mounted on the ancient pantry-vault at the home of Patricia Hastings Bass over the Prix de l'Arc de Triomphe weekend of 1971. While she and Mrs Paul Mellon watched the great Mill Reef capture the crown, back at home a burglar was winning his spurs, removing the door frame and gaining entry to the pantry strongroom. His prize included a twelve-carat diamond and the most magnificent of emerald brooches with a surround of sixteen matched one-and-a-quarter-carat blue-white diamonds. Georgian silver was spirited away in two cricket bags.

Alexander saw a report on the theft in the local rag and challenged Peter.

'Did you do that?'

Like a prize prat Peter denied it a shade too coyly. George was having none of that. His face was pained as he asked, 'So why didn't you take me?'

The hit was grossly undervalued by the loser, a rarity in the larceny business. The lovely Patricia thought she had lost about twenty-five thousand's worth of property. The large diamond alone sold for more than that. But the great horsewoman was more concerned about the loss of a couple of racing trophies, the Royal Hunt Cup being one.

At the races at Sandown, Peter was buttonholed by an ex-copper working for security.

'Mrs Hastings Bass would love to get her cups back. Fellow who could organise it might get the odd good tip.'

'Patricia wants her cups back? What about her tom?'

'She's not concerned,' was the terse reply.

This casual exchange gave Chummy the idea that Peter was privy to the theft. It was to earn him a strong pull journeying by car to Ascot races. A Flying Squad team headed by Charlie Palmer stopped him on the motorway and gave him a spin.

'Where are you off to, then?' Charlie queried.

'Ascot races.'

Nothing found, they parted amicably.

Drinking in the bar under the members' stand, Peter was with a couple of swells when they were joined by the handsome Hazel Lyons, another of his deserving victims.

'I've just seen . . .' She dropped the name of a major-domo in race security. 'The Flying Squad are here. They're after a famous jewel thief.' The company evaporated. Alone, Peter was joined by the ex-copper he'd met at Sandown. Flustered and nervous, the man blurted out, 'Bertie's hopping mad.' He was referring to Ascot's senior steward, His Grace the Duke of Norfolk. 'The Flying Squad vaulted the turn-stiles, flashed their briefs, but would say nothing to the local mob about what was up. Some ass has told Bertie they are on to a cat burglar suspected of robbing Princess Margaret and Patricia Hastings Bass. All hell has erupted. You'd best leave. Bertie wants the man off the course.'

Peter was amused by the ex-copper's embarrassment and decided to leave, but not before he had quaffed a bottle of Tattinger Blanc et Blanc.

Patricia's cups turned up in due course in a station locker. HRH was to the thief's knowledge never burgled, though in fact she had a near-shave at her cottage hideaway near Margot Reading's home in Sussex. But that's another story.

36

A Roof Too Far

Wɪᴛʜɪɴ a few days of Peter's recce at the Antique Porcelain Company in March 1984, Didier was on the trumpet, confirming that he had made contact in Milan and that the porcelain could be discounted. Peter gave the encouraging news to Clyde, who was lukewarm.

'Well, that's that, then. We'll pop it. Now you tell me how we have it away without damaging it.'

'Not easy, son. But this is what I have in mind. Two, possibly three, tall, oblong cardboard boxes pre-packed with sponge and a sack of sawdust to pour over the china once we've filled them. We may damage a little because we must perform at speed. From the moment we crash in we've five minutes to load up and scarper.'

'What can we claw in five minutes, packing it so carefully?' Clyde asked, remaining sceptical. But Peter knew you could remove a fortune in five minutes if you'd planned properly. He had in fact already researched the stock. A dealer pal had spent an hour in the showroom fannying the well-bred girl assistant, getting her guts.

'This is some of the finest antique porcelain in the world,' she'd gushed as she led him round, occasionally putting a price on an item. 'We deal in the main with museums who want to supplement their collections. It's a very specialised market.'

She had naively assumed she was talking to an aesthete, but the thief's pal had more of an ear for the price tags. A J. J. Candler pair of Meissen jays could leave Bond Street for two hundred thousand dollars.

'Dollars?' queried Peter.

'Yes, the culture-hungry yank's the most likely punter.'

Chummy went on to brief Peter in detail as to preference items. It was an hour well spent. Then Peter prepared the packing – three stout cartons that had once housed storage heaters. He stapled and glued rope grips to the boxes. Then he cut two wedges from the end of a piece of two-by-one timber, to slow the enemy's entry through the double glass doors of the first-floor showroom. He threw the remains of the two-by-one slat into his waste disposal. This was also the result of a lifetime's training.

They parked the station wagon on the corner of Bruton Place directly outside the door, which stood between the two entrances of a now-defunct nightclub. This middle door led into the offices and the roof. Apart from the Guinea restaurant, a one-time haunt of Peter's, the mews was as dead as a kipper.

With little fuss they used the key and found themselves adjacent to the sash window with the bell frame. The catch was still open. Sliding the sash up, Clyde had a quick shufty with the torch-beam.

'OK,' he panted. 'Ready?'

Getting the nod, he pushed straight through the bell bars and at once the familiar drone commenced. Now it was a question of police or security response-time. Peter passed two cartons in to the lively Clyde. They had no difficulty sighting the treasures, for the showroom was lit up at the front to make the first-floor display visible from Bond Street. They worked swiftly and in silence, raping the showcases and displays. Five minutes later they had removed most of the items without a single breakage.

'Time up!' Peter commanded when Clyde showed signs of wishing to dwell. Obediently the young man slipped out to the flat roof and the thief gingerly slid out the two, now very heavy, boxes. He then returned to the double doors and tapped a wedge under each before scarpering.

From the roof they humped the two cartons into the empty office, negotiating the narrow stairs down to the mews. They looked out. The mews was empty so, with Clyde taking up sentry duty at the one-way entry from Bruton Street, Peter loaded the booty into the station wagon. Seconds later, they had slipped confidently away. Mission accomplished.

They had a short shunt. Betty Zondheimer's vault in Green Street was the destination. Betty would have had a heart attack if she'd known. Clyde was none too happy.

'Are you sure about this slaughter? What if somebody gets busy and finds it?'

Peter was sure, all right. You'd have more chance of being canonised a saint than have a copper stumble on the loot here. He poured a liberal topping of sawdust into the boxes, sealed them with tape, and they were off. Clyde was still uneasy.

'When do we get our hands on some readies?' he bullied.

'Clyde, behave yourself. I explained this. It will take a little time to place the gear, probably a month, maybe two. If you're skint I can let you have a draw.'

'I'm not skint. Look, I'll leave it to you. Drop me at Maida Vale tube.'

Fag in hand, he disappeared down the Underground, leaving Peter with some hard thinking to do. He was certain that West End Central would fancy him for this one. He'd be gutted if they didn't, come to that. And he suspected that he and Clyde had done some serious damage in terms of the hoot.

Peter was right. The following evening a placard announced: 'MILLION-PLUS THEFT IN BOND STREET'. The heat was on.

An event in Bedfordshire allowed Dave Stephenson to put his plans in motion. The Duke of Bedford's home at Woburn Abbey was burgled and antique silver valued (by His Grace) at five million pounds was stolen. The computer put Peter up as a likely candidate, so the head of the Bedfordshire CID, Chief Superintendent Pickett, decided to give him a spin. Courtesy, however, required him to contact Peter's local division and alert them first. Harrow Road told Pickett that this was the second enquiry they'd had in as many days. West End Central were also sniffing around the occupant of the address on Sutherland Avenue. Pickett immediately belled Stephenson.

'Pickett here from Dunstable. I'm told we have a common interest in one Peter Craig Gulston, alias Peter Scott. CRO 19720/54. We'd like to give him a spin, but I gather you have your eye on Chummy yourself.'

'You fancy he had your silver? I wouldn't think so myself. He's been taking the piss out of us in Mayfair for the last year. Still, I'd rule nothing out as far as Master Peter's concerned.'

'Well, it looks very like his handiwork, so we certainly want to spin him if it doesn't queer your pitch.'

Pickett was pressing but respectful. Stephenson saw a move.

'I think we can work something out,' he said.

Didier knew all about the strike when Peter rang him two days later. He had seen the size of the hoot and didn't want to rush things.

'Pierre, I have read about your good fortune. For my part I think it better if we have a – what do you say? – a breathing space. Let things settle. Ring me say in a month, OK?'

Peter understood and agreed. Meanwhile the tennis club became his bake and, playing one night under floodlights on Court One, he noticed a face lurking on the clubhouse verandah, braving the chilly night. Peter was certain it was the law, having a blimp at him.

Two nights later he left the club around 8.30. Back at Sutherland five minutes later, he was taking refuge in the Mozart Requiem on BBC Radio 3. Just as he was about to grill a chop for dinner, there was a light tap on his door.

Whoever it was had circumvented the street door, for his bell had not rung. As he went to answer, he had a gut feeling that it was a spin, and a look through his judas hole confirmed it. A posse of young men stood on the stairs and landing. As he opened the light-framed door he was pushed backwards by a zealous young stalwart who was bellowing, TV-fashion, 'Police. We have a warrant to search these premises.'

His anticipation of resistance amused the thief, though he understood why. For many years his Criminal Records Office file had boasted a heavy red-underlined health warning on the front of the folder: 'APPROACH WITH CAUTION. THIS MAN WILL RESIST ARREST'. Chatham's file had an identical inscription. However, the sergeant was quickly satisfied that on this occasion the suspect was tame. He told Peter, 'There's been a break-in at Woburn Abbey, the Duke of Bedford's home. A large quantity of valuable silver was stolen and you answer to the description of a man seen in the area.'

He thrust the warrant under Peter's nose. Glancing at it, the thief saw that the document was fully effective.

By now there were eight or nine men in the bedroom/lounge. This was an unnecessarily large turn-out, since the flat was bereft of anything other than a radio, a bed and, in an unused bedroom, some belongings of a former tenant, Peter McGee. Slowly, Peter began to realise that all was not what it seemed. A clearly senior officer in his own age group was in attendance, champing on his pipe and saying little. The sarge from the sticks was spearheading the search, but when Peter also recognised the face who'd been skulking on the tennis club verandah a couple of nights earlier, it suddenly began to look like a joint operation.

'Enjoy the tennis?' he joshed.

Chummy ducked his nut, ignoring the quip. He didn't want Sir to know he might have been sussed on obs. When an elegant-suited prat came out of the kitchen holding a wooden slat from his hot-press, the pipe-smoker nodded, becoming more animated. He was now tapping the uncarpeted floor with his toe. The boss-man, Peter decided. Suddenly a bombshell dropped.

'Where did you get these?'

One of the mob held aloft a green cloth which he unwrapped to reveal a dozen large spoons. Peter grabbed one. Confirming that they were indeed silver, his arsehole fell out.

'Have you cunts come to fit me up? Where did the spoons come from?'

The tantrum resulted in his being swiftly restrained and handcuffed.

'We found those in the empty bedroom.'

'That stuff's not mine.'

'Whose is it, then?'

Calmer now, Peter tried to make sense of the charade.

'It belongs to the former tenant. I look after the flat for him. His name's Peter McGee.'

The pipe spoke.

'Where is this Peter McGee now?'

'He's in Madrid. He's a linguist, teaches there.'

The skipper now took the initiative back.

'You're under arrest. We propose to take you to Dunstable and hold you for further enquiries.'

It must have been midnight before they got there. The station sergeant read him his rights and asked, 'You know why you're being detained?'

Peter nodded and was ushered to a cell. He had been there only minutes when a dapper man opened the door and introduced himself as the head of the enquiry, Chief Superintendent Pickett. He was bland and to the point.

'You know why you're here. However, you can help yourself. I want to recover the Duke of Bedford's silver. You either had it or you know who had it. Do I make myself clear?'

Peter nodded. He knew it was going to be the Mad Hatter's tea party again. Bollocks unlimited.

'The old man,' Pickett said, referring to His Grace, 'has gone on local radio and said he'll give a hundred thousand for the return of the silver. No questions asked.'

Peter was not the culprit at Woburn, but his conscience reminded him that he had indeed once deprived the Duchess at St Anselm's Mews and later that night sat rubbing shoulders with the sybaritic Duke at Winston's nightspot in Clifford Street, Mayfair. Pickett held up his hands.

'I know, I know. It's irregular. But the old boy's done it and we can live with it.'

The feudal system had not apparently died out in Bedfordshire, at least as far as the constabulary were concerned. But Pickett's respect-fulness had a pragmatic thrust.

'I can stand over this deal. Better, I can advance twenty thousand up front if I receive proof the silver is, well, in certain hands.'

Peter saw the drift and went in with, 'What kind of proof do you have in mind?'

'Let's put it this way. If I had a Polaroid photo of the silver alongside a packet of cigarettes of a brand of my choice, then I would know I was dealing with a man who might well wish to return it.'

Pickett was confident of his facts, even gave the impression of being someone who could be trusted. But one thing was for certain: he was a capable, dangerous cop. Events were to justify the judgement.

'What about those silver spoons that were supposedly located at my home?'

Peter got to the heart of the squeeze – for a ball-squeeze it was. Pickett airily waved a non-committal hand.

'They're a minor inconvenience. Do you think you can help?'

'I can try – I do get to know things – if I'm satisfied this is a bona fide offer.'

Peter was fannying, but he stumbled on.

'I can't say much more for now.'

Pickett seemed satisfied, at least that they understood each other. He rose to leave.

'We'll release you on police bail in the morning,' he said brusquely. The cell door slammed.

Peter slept little, wondering about Chummy back at Sutherland Avenue with the pipe. It was all too simple, too easy.

Pickett swung his door open early. 'We'll process you soon. But before you go I think the Met are coming to have a word.'

And Peter was certain what that was about.

The door swung open for a second time and in one smooth move-ment Superintendent Stephenson rushed in, slipping handcuffs on the thief.

'You're nicked, friend,' he chortled, barely able to conceal his elation.

'What's this for?' asked Peter, managing a grin. He was amused at being cuffed when already in the cells.

'You'll find out when we get to London.'

Alongside Stephenson was Chummy with the elegant suit, who had also been on the spin at Sutherland the night before. They travelled back to London in near-silence, though it appears the thief did say something, it being alleged at the committal proceedings that he'd volunteered, 'I'll probably get ten years for this.'

He couldn't recall the prediction, but if it had purchase, it could only have been made in relation to the Woburn silver. At all events, he was kept in the dark as to why he was being brought to London. Before their arrival at West End Central, he was treated to a tour of Mayfair, Stephenson laughing brutally, 'You've cracked a few here in your time.'

Peter nodded benignly. 'A few hundred, I expect.'

The tour took a serious turn in Bond Street, with Stephenson pointing out specific premises – Zilli's, Marie Claire, Wildenstein's, the Antique Porcelain Company.

'You done all these in the last year or two, didn't you?'

Peter smiled and said nothing.

At the cop shop a lady Detective Inspector was to conduct the inquisition. She was attractive, Helen Mirrenish, polite, incisive. But she was pissing into the wind. At termination, she really surprised him by announcing, 'You'll be released on police bail till a week today, when you'll be required to report back here at two-thirty. A decision will then be made as to whether to charge you.'

The nylon of her stockings crackled as she stood up. Stephenson then appeared briefly, playing a cameo role in the interrogation.

'Do yourself a favour and find that porcelain, OK?'

So now, as he trundled out of the nick, he had a double mandate: the silver from Woburn and the china from Bond Street. He would need the most astute of genies to keep everyone happy.

His first stop was the offices of Davis Hanson, solicitors, in West Kensington. Mr Raymond Davis, on being given the facts, was consoling.

'Peter, I don't think the wedge on its own is good enough. It was found in, to say the least, odd circumstances. No, I think you will find they'll have more – or rather, will *need* more – to charge you.'

Raymond had been a long-time confidant and friend to the hapless thief and was always cautious with his pronouncements. Peter felt reassured. He phoned Clyde's mum.

'Tell the boy I've been nicked. Best he stay away. I'll be in touch when things improve.'

He was sitting on a bench in Hanover Square gardens a week later, contemplating reporting back to the nick to answer his police bail. He had little cash in hand and a parcel of china which he could not discount. He'd been back to Green Street and gone through it, discounting a couple of gold boxes in the haul for movers. He'd then called John, a quartermaster pal, and had him remove the parcel to the safety of his home in the West Country. If he were going to be out of circulation, Clyde had to have access, and John was accessible.

With a heavy heart he rose from the bench and ambled down to report to the desk sergeant at West End Central. The sergeant went to the phone, belling the crime squad room.

'A Peter Gulston, reporting on bail. Any of your mob there?'

Whoever 'your mob' were – CID probably – they were out, or maybe not ready for him. The sergeant returned to Peter.

'Mr Gulston, can you report back in half an hour? No one seems to be about.'

The thief went back to the gardens, his spirits raised. It seemed there was scant interest in his appearance. As he returned to the nick, he was beginning to think that Raymond Davis had been correct after all: enough they did not have! He was met by the sheen-limbed lady Detective Inspector, who put him in the waiting room in the hall.

'Hang about there, Peter. You confused us with the name Gulston. We have you bailed as Scott. Won't keep you long.'

All very casual. Too casual.

After a while she returned with Stephenson.

'Hello, Peter. Didn't expect to see you. Come upstairs to my office.'

He followed Silken Limbs up the stairs. Even in his anxiety he found it possible to fantasise about rumping her. Fear and lust in tandem. They all three sat down in the office, her stockings glistening as she crossed her legs. She smiled. She knew the effect she was having. She ignored it and got to the business in hand.

'You know why you're here? A wooden wedge, one of two found at a break-in at the Antique Porcelain Company in Bond Street. It appears to have been cut from a slat of wood found by one of my officers on an observation brief at your home in Sutherland Avenue. He found it in your airing cupboard. Can you offer any explanation for that?'

Peter, mesmerised by the stretch of stockinged thigh, shook his head, but remained shtum. Putting down his pipe with deliberation, Stephenson interrupted his reverie.

'Peter, I've decided to charge you with the break-in. Do you wish to say anything?'

What was there to say? A bland silence reigned, until Stephenson broke it.

'We'd like to have another look at your flat and I propose to take you there now. You understand you're under arrest?'

They went to Sutherland in a bloody convoy of two cars and a police lorry equipped with tools. Dave Stephenson puffed at his pipe contentedly. When they got there it was a twenty-foot wooden ladder, sawn in half, which fascinated the Chief Super this time.

'We can't work out what it's doing in your flat. We're going to take it away with us. Where did you get it, by the way? And why is it sawn in two?'

Peter smiled co-operatively. 'It's a long story. A builder pal of mine left it here. He was working on the guttering.'

'Guttering, eh?'

But it was clear Stephenson saw more sinister connections. A couple of cops set to work with wrecking bars, tearing up the floorboards. Others stripped panelling. Half an hour later, with nothing found and the flat looking like a bomb had hit it, a disconsolate convoy trundled back to the nick, where Peter was housed in the cells.

'Phone my brief, please?'

The duty sergeant, as law required him to do, took refuge in an old chestnut.

'I'll have to clear it with the officer in charge of the enquiry.'

Although the law decrees that the accused has a statutory right to a phone call, the small print gives a get-out clause. Should the officer in charge see this as interfering with justice, he can forbid it. The bottom line, in spite of all the waffle, is: if the law doesn't want you to have a phone call, you don't get one. It has no virtue at all for society. It's a banana-republic ploy and it has led to a spate of acquittals in the Appeal Court. The sooner the small print is amended the better.

But Stephenson had no objection to the call, and Peter relayed his plight to Raymond Davis, who told him, 'I'll have a barrister at court on Monday morning.'

He did, but despite the circumstances of Peter's voluntary surrender to police bail, an application for his release at Marlborough Street was rejected out of hand by the magistrate. The police were objecting.

'There will be no bail in this case,' the bench ordained. 'Over a million pounds' worth of property is missing.'

He was remanded in custody for fourteen days to the Scrubs, where he found a number of old acquaintances languishing: Jimmy and Johnny Knight had a problem, and so did Tony White, who was accused of the bullion turn-out at London Airport, later to be acquitted. The thief was back home.

On his next appearance, having a natter in the cells at Marlborough, Stephenson gave Peter a pleasant shock.

'Can you get a couple of sureties if we don't object to bail today?'

He could try. A campaign of phone calls persuaded two of the gang at Paddington – Chris and Ken – to stand for five thousand. However, it was a struggle to persuade the martinet on the bench. Before you can make a second application for bail, there has to be a change of circumstances. And the fact that the law were now anxious to have Peter back on the street is not necessarily what the Act has in mind. However, finally getting the drift from Stephenson that they wanted him out and about, the bench announced that it would set bail at two sureties of fifty thousand, one being from the thief himself. Peter's brief had a hard struggle.

'Your honour, the accused is an elderly man. As I understand it, he is working as a tennis coach. He simply does not know persons of such stature as can support a fifty-thousand-pound bond. It says much for his standing that two members of his tennis club are prepared to stand in the sum of five thousand pounds, an enormous amount for them.'

Very reluctantly, the martinet agreed. He was probably puzzled as to what the change of circumstances meant. Stephenson was a straight-goer. He was letting the thief out and about so he could recover the porcelain.

A copper from Harrow Road had been fired into him – a policeman's policeman, lantern-jawed, handsome. He had a bit of advice.

'Stick that porcelain back and do yourself a favour. You could get lucky and not get committed.'

Peter knew he needed some plus points, but putting the parcel back was out of the question.

Shortly, and unwittingly, he was to get a host of minus points when the Bedford silver was recovered by workmen at a water-pumping station near Woburn Abbey. Neither the theft nor the recovery had anything to do with him, although others were convinced that he had 'arranged' the find, including Dave Stephenson, Bruce Laughland, QC, the eventual trial judge, and his own pleader, Stephen Batten, QC. More likely the astute Pickett had been a shade too cunning for someone who had bitten at his carrot, and the wily copper had recovered the silver.

And the silver spoons? They are still at Dunstable police station. In 1988, in response to an enquiry from Peter, Pickett wrote, choosing his words with care, 'Mr Scott can collect his property from Dunstable PS whenever he wishes.'

He never found the fare to Dunstable.

37

The Muck-Away Years

NINETEEN seventy-two was to be the year Peter absconded from his passion for larceny. It was the ever-enigmatic Stan the chauffeur who unwittingly allowed the thief to make his exit.

That summer Stanley pointed him towards a Nigerian entrepreneur and chief called Shonabarrie, who Stan suspected was smuggling money out of Nigeria. Stanley had been ferrying parcels from London Airport to the Chief's home in Kensington Court, and told Peter, 'He has a safe in one of the rear bedrooms.'

Peter had come to respect and value the most oblique of Stanley's titbits. Stanley had already baited the thief's vanity with stories of armed staff protecting the house of the Shah's sister in Sussex and a secret cellar under the dining-room table. Peter had made a successful and lucrative sortie there the previous autumn.

He was less lucky now in removing Chief Shonabarrie's safe, losing it down the lift shaft in Kensington after a comedy of errors. A chat with a copper acquaintance in Ruby Lloyd's a few days later eased him into retirement. The copper told Peter, apparently in all innocence, 'A little firm left a fortune behind in Kensington the other evening, lost a safe in a lift shaft. Talk in the office is there was over a million in gold, cash and gems – some Nigerian chief's pile. I bet they'd be gutted if they knew.'

You will never know how gutted, Peter mused, but he showed no twinge of interest. If he was being sussed out, he did not bite.

Nevertheless, it was a bitter pill to swallow. It was time to turn it in.

Between 1972 and 1977 Peter was a straight-goer. Turning it in was a personal commitment. Fear, a sufficiency of money, the subconscious desire to show Jackie and his son that he could do it the hard way, all contributed. But like most resolutions, it needed determination, a lack of fantasy, a desperation to escape from the passion of a lifetime. Finally it was the improbable challenge of honesty that gave Peter strength.

But knowing you're making an effort is not always enough for the hitherto compulsive sinner. Other eyes are more cynical. In the former thief's case, he had to convince the law, who publicise in parrot fashion their favourite platitude: a leopard never changes its spots. They would not admit the possibility that the spots might fade so much as to be indiscernible.

He had to be seen at toil. Not property-developing, not dealing in motors or second-hand furniture, but visible hard graft. Peter chose to go back to an old sweetheart, the tipper lorry. Even the most biased of coppers can't miss seeing a tipper and its driver at work. So he bought an AEC Marshall – registration number NLC977K – from Arlington Motors and puddled up to what was then the biggest muck-away job in north London. Into the hillside in Hendon, Hammerson Group were building the Brent Cross shopping centre, and Mike Farrell, a smart Mick from Longford town, had the job from McAlpine. He'd taken it on at a loss until he was indispensable. Then, with the job secured, he bargained for the right price.

The secret of any muck-away job is to have a muck-shoot, a tip, within viable running distance. The driver must do a minimum of five loads a day. An equally live wire from Edgware made the job a beano in this way. His name was Jeffrey Turland, and his skill was to persuade local worthies to provide him with land to tip on – land that just avoided regulation under the Town and Country Planning Act. Charming local landowners up and down the A1 and A5, the Farmer, as Jeffrey was known, secured several tips within a forty-minute round trip, enabling Peter to do ten loads a day, knocking up a monkey a week and more. All that summer of '72, the grey Marshall, with Peter Gulston Haulage painted on it, belted up and down to Hendon.

After six months behind the wheel, the redundant thief fancied he knew the game and began to expand. This was much to his solicitor's dismay, for Raymond Davis knew a thing or two about haulage since, prior to the advent of British Road Services, his dad Yiddle Davis had the largest haulage business in east London. So Raymond knew the hazards of vehicles and, finding Peter hell-bent on getting expansion capital by mortgaging Edith Road to Lloyds Bank, whose manager, John Hobern, counselled caution.

'Peter, you can have an excellent income from letting the flats at Edith Road. You're flourishing with your vehicle as an owner-driver. But I warn you, if you do expand, you'll never find drivers to duplicate your work-rate.'

Of course, the fledgling contractor, hell-bent on tycoonery, paid scant heed. By the following year he had four tippers and was learning at first hand the nature of the beast. Peter had chosen an industry in which one's past is not of the essence, for the tipper-haulier is at the arsehole end of the construction business. The memory of all Peter's past skeletons was eroded by effort, and by the climate of corruption in which the construction industry thrives. A lot of media coverage is given to police corruption, and there is of course some. But in construction, more bribes change hands daily than in criminal circles in a year. Peter had made an expedient choice of field in which to exercise his new-found morality.

Yet the scene was so petty in comparison to his previous activities. Never in his five years grafting did he find the petty fiddling attractive. He refused to play the game and suffered to retain his dignity.

There were five self-contained flats at Edith Road; the contractor lived in the garden basement. During the early seventies, he built two bedroom extensions at garden level, eventually triumphing after the usual cavorts with Hammersmith Council over planning permission. One of the bedrooms was to provide a room for Craig to occupy on visits. The other was a guest bedroom with en suite shower. These improvements radically increased the value of the flat. Better still, they disguised from the prying eyes of the taxman his growing wealth.

One of the upstairs tenants died and, now in control of the third floor, he modernised it. Then the tenants on the top two floors moved away, and he set about self-containing their flats, which gave him three flats he could let to unsecured tenants at the going rents. Only Mrs Adler remained at ground-floor level, thwarting his new-morality greed. The contractor behaved disgracefully towards this widowed lady as he set about trying to get her out. If God should exist, Peter will one day find it far more difficult to justify this – not to mention his harassment of tenants in some stable-houses in Perrers Road which he bought in 1974 – than all his felonious persecution of the fleshpots. It is no defence that the evicted were better housed in the end. People are entitled to have their roots undisturbed, and many are content in run-down areas. Rehousing in better accommodation often spells loneliness. The man was correct – property is theft.

But becoming, to his eternal shame, a harassing landlord was not an imprisonable offence, and it seemed there was a broad swath of things decent people could get up to, safe from prosecution, merely having to square their activities with themselves. If there is any justice in the misfortunes that befell Peter later in life, it was due to this. In his dash to put criminality behind him, he became a greedy, ruthless prat. Dante's words were 'by different sins being sent to different depths'. Be assured, the righteous plumb those depths and society sanctions it.

And so life went on in the new greed. As a thief, his largesse had known no bounds. Now, in his reformation, he counted every penny. But all the time fate was marking up the minus points, waiting impatiently to return him to his old, more generous way of life. Meanwhile, the contractor was growing fat. Even his Savile Row suits could not conceal his bulk, and the once-slim Peter now scaled seventeen stone. And he was drinking too much – gallons of brandy. It was a prerequisite of the construction business to be a good drinking companion, up for a jar with the lads, able to do business while socially imbibing.

Meanwhile he met a new chum, Patricia Esdale, an attractive Scottish girl engaged at the time to Hugh Fraser, then the owner of Harrods. They met at the Maze races in Northern Ireland, where she'd come to buy a couple of horses for the show-ring. Peter was in the company of his old mentor Crawford Scott and his bookmaker pal Barney Eastwood. Barney (later the manager of boxer Barry McGuigan) and Crawford had horses in training with Mick O'Toole, and it was a crony of Mick's who was squiring Fraser's fiancée.

Introductions done, it was established that they were both staying at the Europa Hotel. And that they were attracted to each other. The horse dealer Frank Barry took a dim view, advising her, 'Best steer clear of that fellow. He's a London gangster.'

He was probably right to warn, but what his motives may have been is less certain. Perhaps he felt the 'gangster' might mark the lady's card as to his own horse-trading activities. He might have fancied her himself. Whatever the truth, Lindsay Esdale's ex was capable of looking after herself. She was merely stimulated by the warning.

They dined that night at the Europa. Later, groping one another in bed on too much wine, she put it to him directly.

'Are you a London gangster?'

She exhaled a plume of cigarette smoke.

'No. Sorry to disappoint you. I'm in haulage, but I was in the distant past on the fringes of the underworld.'

Pat clearly did not believe him yet, departing the next day for Stourbridge, she granted him a phone number.

'I hope you'll ring when you get back to London,' she lied.

But the phone number was a wrong one. It took four or five calls to an increasingly irate colonel in Gloucestershire before the penny dropped. He did not see her again for a year. By coincidence it was in the bar of the Europa Hotel, where she was sipping claret with her mother, and still procrastinating over the nuptials with Sir Hugh. Mum, a well-preserved thespian originally from Bangor, County Down, took a shine to the contractor, confiding to her daughter, 'He's very handsome and I think he likes you too. What is he complaining about . . . this wrong phone number?'

The attraction was confirmed when Peter had a winning turn at the races and decided to buy a dress for Pat from Bradleys in Wellington Place, Belfast. But Hughie was to get wind of the dalliance that year. As it developed back in the Cotswolds, with Peter and Pat frequently dining at the tables of the local gentry, Hughie took to ringing up the hosts to warn them who they were entertaining.

'Enjoying the gangster's company?' he would yelp. Fortunately the hosts were invariably too well bred to make an issue of it. And by now Pat had decided not to marry Hugh, had called off the engagement, and was seeing more of Peter.

The contractor, in retrospect fortunate to last five years, hoped that his legitimacy would distance him from the gendarmes. In reality, the minus points were still building up. Alexander, out of prison and after a job as a chauffeur, had the cheek to ask for a reference from the contractor – and got one. If Peter was hoping to let sleeping dogs lie, there was not a chance. One evening, on his return from work, he found Alexander waiting in the gloom of his Edith Road lounge. How he had gained entry was academic; in rage and fright he belted him. Alexander offered no resistance, content that he had baffled Peter. More minus points accruing.

That same year it was sauce for the goose time. He was burgled twice at Edith Road, being deprived of his modest collection of antiquery. Painful as the losses were at the time, cheques totalling nearly thirteen thousand pounds on his Vicula policy softened the blow, while rendering him uninsurable. It was his professional pride which was really dented. He assumed his lightly protected home was out of bounds for local herberts; hopefully he'd been burgled by strangers or, even better, by someone bearing him malice. He'd learned the hard way never to cling to wives or possessions!

He had half a dozen tipper lorries by 1973, but a moment of petty greed nearly undid his self-imposed exile from larceny. One of his drivers brought in an elegant chaise longue in brown velvet. It matched the colour scheme at Edith Road, so he bought it with a cheque for a hundred quid, ignoring the facile tale the driver spun him as to how he had acquired it.

'They were dumping the contents of a show-home in Camden Square, mostly rubbish. I copped the sofa for carting a couple of yards of rubbish off the site.'

Bound for Cork with Mike Farrell, he was asked to leave the plane as it was about to depart. The Flying Squad were in attendance. They had been to Edith Road earlier and conveniently found the front door unsecured – no Peter, but a diary entry recorded the flight to Cork. Back to Edith Road for a cursory spin, which revealed nothing, but their card had been marked as regards the chaise longue. One of the team growled, 'Got a receipt for this sofa?' He was gutted when Peter produced his cheque stub. Nevertheless he was taken to Hammersmith police station, and later given police bail. Peter felt sure that if he had bunged them a few quid the matter would have been forgotten. But why should he? He was a straight man now. Charged with handling, he and the driver appeared at the London Sessions where Judge Phelan was on the bench.

When the pair were found guilty, Phelan remanded them to Pentonville overnight and the next morning gave Peter a two-year suspended sentence and fined him a thousand quid.

Lord Scarman sat on the appeal. Peter gained a partial victory in that Scarman reduced the fine to one of two hundred and fifty pounds. More importantly, what he said that day was to influence another sitting of the Court of Appeal in 1980. 'Peter Gulston has a long criminal record, but this offence is of the most modest nature compared with his record. He is a man who has built up a business, he employs twenty men. Clearly he has pulled himself up by his bootstraps. He deserves consideration.'

Initially there appeared to be a bonus on the day in question, but as it concerned a female the contractor was aware that what started off looking like a bonus was likely to end up an unrewarding experience. As he sat in the well of Number One court, he got chatting to an attractive lady barrister sitting next to him among the gaggle of spectators.

'I'm here to watch my brother. He practises on the northern circuit. This is his first appearance at the Court of Appeal. Are you connected with the law?'

'No, I'm in demolition and haulage. I'm an appellant myself.'

'Really?' There was a hint of alarm in the pretty green eyes.

'Low-key stuff, connected with my lorries,' he fannied.

Brother did well – his plea was allowed. Portia was ecstatic.

'Gosh, didn't he do well. I must take him out to lunch.'

Peter smiled and, on impulse, thrust his business card into her hand.

'If you fancy a drink some time, you can ring me.'

'"Peter Gulston",' she read. '"M/D Gulston Campbell Ass. Ltd."
Bless you, Peter, I may just do that. My name's Clovis, by the way.'

He felt sure she would phone. She did.

He picked her up in Fulham and they noshed at the Guinea in
Bruton Place. Clovis practised at the criminal bar. Peter revealed none
of his special knowledge of that field; he was discreet for once. As
they left the Guinea, Clovis caught sight of the brightly lit hostess club
at the turn in the mews.

'What's there?' she enquired.

'It's a hostess club – booze and birds.'

'A strip club? I've never been to a strip club.'

'Well, we'll change all that. I know an upmarket one in Kingly
Street. I use it to entertain business clients.'

The basement in Kingly Street was an exclusive hostess club featur-
ing an all-night cabaret. The girls were all lookers. Sammi, a Eurasian,
was the star turn. In the past she had boogied with Peter. Of all things,
they had a common interest in poetry.

Clovis and he sat quaffing in the champagne oasis into the early
hours. Sammi joined them. Learning that Clovis was a barrister surprised and delighted her – like the thief she was an awful snob. They
gelled. The boss-man lingered behind the half-moon couch, puffing
at one of his interminable cigars. The club began to empty as the girls
bitched about the vices of the male. Sammi relaxed, her legs akimbo.
She was knickerless, and her immodest posture gave Clovis a view of
her shaven cunt. When she left them briefly to powder her nose, a
breathless Clovis nudged Peter.

'She's lovely. And she's wearing no knickers. I can't keep my eyes
off her. Christ, I must be pissed.' She panted as she spoke.

Sammi returned. Boss-man, watching the charade, read the tell-tale
signs and beckoned Peter over.

'I think they're up for it, Peter,' he murmured out of the side of his
mouth. Chummy knew a thing or two.

Sammi was kissing Clovis aggressively, while Clovis had her hand
on Sammi's gleaming thigh. They slid to the floor, Sammi contriving
to present her smooth crotch to Clovis's lusting mouth.

Boss-man was breathing heavily, eyes glued to the combatants. He seemed hypnotised, his cigar becoming ash-laden. Peter found the spectacle more bewildering than sexual, his feelings tainted with guilt. Eventually the girls called a truce and clung to one another with genuine affection. They had established their contempt for the male.

As they drove back to Fulham, Clovis was silent. On arrival he opened the passenger door.

'When shall I see you again?'

Clovis pounced with wanton tongue.

'See me again? You filthy bastard, you're a bloody degenerate taking me to that brothel. You should be locked up.' She tripped to the door briskly, turned, and spat out a curt 'Piss off' before disappearing into the bijou house.

Peter was speechless. Driving back to Edith Road, he consoled himself with the thought that he was the victim of ever-obscure female logic. Taking refuge behind their time-honoured accusations of 'It's all your fault' absolved them of their latent passions. Clovis would do well at the bar.

His old pal David Gliksten had lured him to Kinsale where he repented in large brandies at Doris's harbour bar. Dave had wife trouble which Peter stupidly got involved in, trying to get Mary Rose to return to her husband. He made an ass of himself. But Kinsale took infidelities in its stride and Peter forgave himself yet again. He was spending most of his leisure time in Ireland. Crawford Scott, his old mentor, had departed Ulster to live in Tipperary. His eldest boy was an amateur jockey who hoped to become a trainer. Crawford had a number of horses in training; it was a measure of his affection for the thief that he named one Peter Gulston. It was never raced and was later sold to the Swiss equestrian team.

When he visited Paul Doyle, a Curragh trainer who tended many of Crawford's mounts, the subject of this horse came up. Doyle ventured, 'Peter Gulston was a better horse than Peter Scott, and as you may recall that horse won some grand races in England.'

Peter Scott was another of Crawford's horses, named after one of his sons. The thief was delighted to hear that Gulston was a better Peter than Scott. The Scott alias that had clung to him like a doppelganger during the latter half of his criminal life had small appeal.

38

The Unseen TV Star

Expediency and greed find strange bedfellows, and here was the contractor-thief on an away night with Stanley Addersman again. He ignored his former doubts. Greed delivers us into the hands of the Philistines.

Yet that night was peppered with clues. From the start Stanley drove in silence, and each time Peter glanced at him he contrived to keep his eyes on the road while a faint perspiration tinged his brow. This was not the Stanley the thief had known, and a mild discomfort permeated him.

Coming to a sharp right turn above Chalfont St Peter, Stanley finally broke the silence. He was nervous, stuttering.

'That's the house, on the left.'

Slowing, he indicated a modest property at the end of a drive.

'You might be lucky and find she's out now.'

This was a *faux pas* that put the thief even more on his guard. Stanley must have known that Peter wanted his victims in when he called. It made certain that their bits and pieces would be with them – in most cases upstairs while they gaped at that burglar's friend, the television.

They turned down a long winding road which passed the side of the house, searching for a parker. Finding a friendly gate, Peter told Stanley to stop.

'Park here. I'll go up through the fields and approach the house from the back. You stay put.'

He trudged off suspiciously through the cattle-pitted, pyloned field. Seconds later he heard a car pulling away. He did not look back. Stanley was turning. Perhaps.

Approaching the faintly lit house, he caught sight of an ornamental gypsy caravan, which lurked ominously in the gloom. He was compelled to inspect it. He crept up the steps and peered in, pointing a smothered torch-beam into the darkness. But it was empty. Perhaps he was looking for a cop-out. Perhaps his bottle had gone or, at the least, his criminal reflexes were rusty. He steeled himself, creeping reluctantly towards the house. A lamp in the front porch cast a light through one uncurtained ground-floor window, where the regenerated thief saw a shadow flit. He froze, then gently turned about and drifted away into the night. The inner voice was whispering he must piss off, and he obeyed it.

Trudging back down the soaked and muddy field, he was sure he'd escaped from a trap. Stanley was not where he should have been and Peter began tramping down the road. Suddenly the limo appeared, purring past him as he crouched down.

'Stan!' Peter yelled. The car stopped and Peter got in. 'No good. Didn't fancy it.'

Stanley kept silent. His eyes stayed on the road all the way back to Hammersmith. They parted without a word. Neither could trust himself to speak, which they both understood.

An extraordinary sequel to this night out took place many months later, when Peter was idly watching the box at Perrers Road. It was a fly-on-the-wall documentary series following the daily affairs of the Thames Valley police. This particular episode concerned a plot to rob Laura, the Duchess of Marlborough. Peter watched fascinated as the Reading burglar squad, acting on a 'tip-off', staked out Laura's home. As the drama unfolded, it became unintentionally comic. The main problems for the coppers seemed to be, first, how to address the Duchess and, second, how to keep her two doddery house guests, a puffy baronet historian and a 'semi-famous' painter, in the background. They were sent to bed but they wouldn't stay there. Then a copper whispered in the darkness, 'Someone in the garden, guv.'

'Oh, how exciting!' Laura trilled.

'He's having a look at the caravan,' another copper murmured. 'Now he's approaching the house. Not a word.'

The tension rose and was then deflated.

'Seem to have lost him, sir.'

'Where's he gone?'

'Don't know. Looks like he scarpered.'

So the vigil ended and lights were turned on. Relief (the Duchess's) and disappointment (the police's) developed into good-natured banter. But how had the law been so confident as to have a television crew, of all things, on hand? Peter, by the time he saw this programme, knew the answer to many things that had puzzled him in the past. It was *him* they'd been waiting for, courtesy of a tip-off from friend Stanley.

The bizarre experience gave him goose-pimples. West Country Peter had been right. But what other damage had been done? And what a crazy way to find out about it.

It was his fitter, Dave from Yorkshire, who told him the truth about his haulage business prospects.

'Peter, it's time you packed it in. All the lorries need remedial work and there are no jobs about. So if I were you, I'd sell the bastards.'

He knew in his heart it was time up, and he unloaded the six tippers that were free of HP to a sharp cookie in Staffordshire for two grand a lump. Three others were dispatched to a pal in Ireland, to graft on the then-thriving motorway programme. When in due course the boom fell on Peter's affairs, the trio were working around Crossmaglen on the border, the finance company showing little enthusiasm for repossessing them.

It was a bitter pill for Peter to swallow. The flats in Edith Road were mortgaged to the bank; his sole assets were the house and stables at Perrers Road, devoid of any charge other than a ten-thousand-pound mortgage. The carriage-house was partially developed and two of the stables were taking shape as living accommodation. He could use some money to get on with the development.

An old, once loyal, pal turned up at the site in Perrers Road. He's seen Peter some six months previously, trying to tempt him to rob a private residence above a butcher's shop in Marylebone. Peter had blanked him then. His reappearance with the same story now was much more compelling.

It was an odd tale – a lady friend of his pal's anxious to see a possible last will and testament of a former husband of hers which for some complicated reason was in the hands of the couple who owned the premises. It had the ring of truth about it, and Peter decided to give it a whirl.

A recce of the butcher's revealed difficulties. It was in a narrow street – no chance of fronting it. Directly behind the shop was a well-secured college, the front door on security locks. In short, it had natural protection. It was one screwer that would have to be done when the premises were empty, and they would have to be approached from the roof. Fortunately there was an empty in the terrace in which the shop and the maisonette above were located. It was to be Peter's point of entry.

He was surprised by the ease with which he shed the cloak of contractor and donned the thief's mantle again. It was as if he'd never been away! Early one evening, watching the occupants go out for the night in the company of his pal, he caned the door of the empty and made his way to the roof, leaving Chummy to mind his back in the street. Tripping over the roofs at seventeen stone was demanding. Locating the skylight of the premises, he made entry with one twist of the jemmy.

It was a modest home, even dowdy, but when he opened a cupboard in the main bedroom he saw a small safe. Leaning against it was a pile of fifty-pound banknotes. He binned the cash and, searching on, found a coin collection and a couple of fur coats. He made his way to the floor above. It was a wilderness of junk and tat, but as he searched he continued to find banknotes stuffed in old handbags and drawers. He scavenged for the best part of an hour before retreating to the roof, now humping the one-hundredweight box safe. It was an effort to creep back to the empty. At forty-five and seventeen stone he was ill equipped for the task; only greed gave him strength and kept a coronary at bay. Back at street level his pal was not in evidence. Peter, unable to loiter, humped the box into the boot of his BMW and drove to Perrers Road. Later he would learn that his minder pal was holed up in a pub with a Scotch to bolster his bit-part. Best place for his ilk!

He had secured fifteen thousand pounds in cash. God alone knew what must be in the safe. He felt like an old lion in the comfort of his den, his immediate cash-flow problem solved.

Chummy turned up later, drew a couple of grand, being fined for not being where he should have been, and seemed satisfied, but suggested that the as yet unopened safe be housed at his home in Maida Vale overnight.

'What do you think is in it?' he hissed, elated.

'Well, if they leave fifteen grand lying about, I fancy the safe must be chock-a-block with readies.'

How wrong can you be? Cutting the safe open at Chummy's Maida Vale basement the following day yielded only a few papers, with not a last will and testament in sight. Peter gave Chummy the furs and coin collection to relieve his disappointment and balance the equity. They decided on a drink to celebrate.

'Let's go to Ruby's.'

Enjoying his drink later at Ruby Lloyd's Maisonette Club in Shepherd Market, Mayfair, he was introduced to two attractive mature women. He knew one of them by sight; he had seen her at the races over the years. Her name was Fay Sidler. Within three weeks he was to marry the fragile, grey-sheened, cashmere-coated Fay. She was eight years older than he and had been married five times, latterly to the late Willie Sidler who owned leather factories in Africa.

Peter had been drinking recklessly and was sweating buckets in his smart, too-tight Prince of Wales suit as they shook hands. Fay was to recall later, 'There I was in Ruby Lloyd's, immaculate, and I'm introduced to a florid man sweating buckets in a Prince of Wales suit. Not an attractive sight, I might tell you.'

Attractive or not, relaxing under the ghastly canvas of a reclining nude they were both animated and tossed down gin and tonics with abandon. Ironically, it was on this same couch under the same reclining nude that Peter met and was to come to adore Jackie Bowyer.

Fay confessed to her previous five marriages and was not coy about her age. 'I'm fifty-four, but I do look after myself.'

They gelled, establishing locations and people they had in common, but it confounded Peter when she let slip, 'I think I had a blind date with you once in the South of France. You failed to show up. Sidney King told me you had to visit a sick friend, otherwise we would have met fifteen years ago.'

It came back to Peter in his gin-sodden haze – his sick friend had been a visit to Suzy Volterra's pad in Eden Rock.

'My God, you're that Fay! I was supposed to join you and Sidney and Wanda at the Festival of Flowers in Nice.'

'Wanda has done very well for herself. You may know she married Lord Boothby. She's very grand now. I dare say she wouldn't remember either of us.'

Fay was a little pissed when he lured her back to the stable-house at Perrers Road. He got his first, and possibly last, plus point by putting the lady in his bed and bedding down on a couch in the lounge. His self-control had its reward when he was invited down to Fay's delightful mill-house at Thatcham, Chamber House Mill, the following weekend. Aware by now of Peter's fragile libido, and knowing the stress middle age induced in studs, she was patient with him.

They went on holiday to Ireland together and, dining one night at Concurren Lodge, she rounded on him. 'You're a court jester, everybody's idiot. You're not a businessman, you're a silly fellow.'

She had a point, such a valid one surely only a fool would have married her a couple of weeks later. What was the attraction? Loneliness, probably, both needing that little bit of each other that barely justified dining together, let alone considering marriage. But marry they did, in indecent haste, and set about tearing one another apart.

Shortly before the event, a jaunt to Belfast in a Rolls-Royce brought the pair to Peter's elderly uncle's home in Somerton Park. Robert Topping had little desire to see his nephew, Rolls or no Rolls. They were barely seated before Bert launched into an embarrassing tirade as Fay perched gingerly on the edge of her seat, holding a cup of tea the housekeeper had rustled up.

'You know you killed your Aunt Maude sure as you shot her, in and out of prison,' he biled on. Fay was rescued by the housekeeper who invited her to inspect the garden. 'Your aunt died of shame, that's what you have to answer for.'

Maude was Peter's father's sister. Her chronic arthritis having prevented her having children, she worshipped Peter as the son she never had. Her strong adherence to the Plymouth Brethren community in Belfast made Peter's antics particularly embarrassing to her. He had loved his Aunt Maude and recalled her anguish. 'How will I ever live it down?' she had wailed when he went to prison in 1953. He often pondered on the Christian alacrity to bemoan 'poor us'; it was never 'poor Peter'.

Bert's bitterness was not to be assuaged. He'd lived his life in the time warp of Belfast bigotry and was brimming with an unforgiving biblical zeal that predated the Troubles.

'I suppose you bought that Rolls-Royce with the money you stole. Call yourself a contractor now? That's a laugh. You'll be back inside again.'

Peter smiled thinly at the prediction. He could be right.

'Robert, if crime has done anything for me, it's allowed me to escape from the tribal prejudices of Belfast. Believe me, listening to you, it's cheap at the price.'

The Gulstons saw themselves out.

They were married at Hammersmith Register Office in 1976.

Peter threw all his energies into the Perrers Road development, which by now had attracted a stop notice from Hammersmith Council. Storm clouds were gathering. His companies were in the hands of the Official Receiver, the banks were selling him up in Edith Road, Jackie and Trevor Bailey were in the Family Division seeking to deny him access to his son, and Stanley Addersman was in some difficulty which he was about to unload at Peter's expense.

39

First Glimpse of the 'Old Grey Fox'

STANLEY surfaced at Perrers Road. Peter was loading a skip as the badger slipped past him furtively into the carriage-house.

'Trouble,' he murmured in passing. 'We may have to help the police.'

For a moment Peter was tempted to confront him with certain television coverage, but thinking better of it he said simply, 'Really?'

It was ten years to the month since their paths had first crossed in Dartmoor. The brief but direct opening remark reminded Peter of his belief that he was being propelled towards a destiny over which he had little control. It was the use of the pronoun 'we' which alarmed him. It was generally a preamble to sharing another's cross. As Stan's shifty eye continued to spell trouble, he listened.

'A very senior policeman is investigating certain people. He needs our help. I can't say much about it now, I'm sworn to silence, but I think it would be to your advantage to meet two officers on the enquiry, hear what they've got to say.'

Peter's silence forced Stanley to continue.

'If you don't help I may be standing opposite you in court,' he said with a courage Peter had never known him possess, 'giving evidence against you.'

Whatever trouble Stanley had got himself into he was about to dump on Peter's doorstep.

'I'll think it over. When you're in a position to give me details, come and see me again.'

A dull ache in his stomach told him that crucifixion was beckoning yet again.

A disconsolate Stanley made sure he had the last word.

'I've done you plenty of favours, remember that.'

And one or two disfavours too, mused Peter. As the limo purred away, he lost interest in loading the skip.

Act Two of the impending tragedy took place early one morning a week or two later at Chamber House Mill. From a bedroom window

Peter caught sight of a stranger lingering in the orchard beyond the mill-leap. A frisson of fear ran down his spine by way of warning. The stranger was joined by another man. The mating swans were clucking. He slipped on his tracksuit and trainers silently so as not to disturb the sleeping Fay and crept out.

'Good morning,' he greeted the men. 'This is private property. The swans are mating. They're best avoided.'

One of the men raised his bull-like head, bluish eyes gleaming with unconcealed malice. Peter felt he knew him, but from where?

'Yes, Peter,' Blue Eyes said. 'I'm aware I'm on your property, and believe me when I tell you all this' – he indicated the house beyond – 'will disappear if you don't listen to Stanley.'

Stanley's 'friends' left by way of a gap in the hedge. Peter was sure now that they were coppers, but try as he might he could not put a name to the bull-headed man.

Fay greeted him on the patio in her slip, her shrill tone reverberating off the mill-pond.

'Who were they, darling?'

'Not sure, may have been coppers. One's Merlin – all this is going to disappear, or so he says.'

Fay's pretty eyes narrowed as she thrust a cigarette between her rouged lips.

'Police down here? Surely not. What would the neighbours think?'

'I believe I may know what it's about. One of my skeletons from the past may have surfaced.'

'You know we don't discuss your past. You're a contractor now and you'd better believe it.'

If Fay had a past she never mentioned it. Her current wealth came from being widowed, and she was both generous and parsimonious as circumstances suited. Having recently started to support the mortgage on Perrers Road, she constantly griped about *her* money and *her* house. Peter's self-respect was waning. Diving into the icy water of the leat, he realised that the marriage was fragile at the best of times. How would it survive if a crisis arose?

The crisis emerged a week later, an agitated Stanley reappearing at Perrers Road.

'You really must come and meet the coppers. They're insistent. They don't want to force you to come, but their boss may make them.'

'I may have met their boss. A couple of coppers turned up in my orchard a week back. One seemed familiar.'

Before he admitted that he could not put a name to the face, Stanley blurted out, 'Wickstead? Wickstead's been down to your place?'

Peter gave an involuntary shudder. Could it have been Wickstead?

'I don't know if it was him, but whoever it was invited me to listen to you. It seems my lifestyle will change if I don't help him.'

'Did they say what they wanted?' quizzed an alarmed Stan.

'Not in so many words. They did infer you would clue me up.'

The modest hyperbole peeled the plot. Stanley began an interesting and dangerously full monologue, the gist of it being that a Serious Crime Squad was interested in a couple of acquaintances of Peter's and a trio of bent coppers.

'The enquiry is at the stage of being proceeded with or dropped. I think progress largely depends on you. I've told them what I know and they want to confirm it. The Commander is a very fair man, but he could turn nasty.'

If it was a Wickstead enquiry, Peter was aware of just how dangerous they could be, despite his five-year sabbatical from crime. 'Wicksteria' had already left havoc in its wake – the Tibbs and Dunn families, Bernie Silver, Reggie Dudley, and Bob Maynard, all behind bars in back-dated prosecutions orchestrated by the 'Old Grey Fox', Commander Albert Wickstead. Most alleged foul play, without any sympathy from the courts – with the exception of Silver.

Yet sitting in the comfortable mill-house, the whole world of crime seemed distant. Peter felt oddly immune from the infestation. After all, notwithstanding the trip to the butcher's, he was straight now and had not been behind bars for ten years.

Eventually he saw two officers from the enquiry in a hotel at London Airport. They talked in riddles but did confirm that they were attached to the Serious Crime Squad at Loughton, Essex and that their governor was Commander Albert Wickstead.

Fay was worried. Peter kept her abreast of developments. In the end he agreed to see Wickstead in Loughton.

Pulling in, uninvited, to the police car park in his BMW, he glanced up. Two pensive, malevolent faces gazed down from a third-floor window. It was Wickstead and his deputy, Mike Taylor.

The Commander put to him certain matters regarding a raid some years earlier on a bank depository in Marylebone. He suggested that certain officers had profited from the event with the assistance of a chum of Peter's.

'You realise these people made a fortune out of the raid?'

Peter conceded that this was the gossip.

'Well, I want you to find out where the money's gone.'

'I can try, Commander,' Peter fannied.

'Peter, I have to say that, should you not be able to help, there are a number of skeletons rattling around in your own cupboard. I do have a second string to my bow. Understand me? If you don't assist you'll have to take your chances.'

Fay was scant comfort when told the turn of events.

'You must do as he asks. Did Eist have his hands in the till?'

Peter grimaced. 'Do you think he'd tell me if he did?'

The only good news over Christmas 1976 was that the stop notices were lifted on Perrers Road. The development could now be maximised. Separate beds were the order of the festive season that year. Peter decided to alert his pal by letter to the events at Loughton. He wrote it late one evening. Thinking better of it in the morning, he slung it in the bin.

Back working at Perrers Road in early 1977 he found a note in the lounge. It was from Fay.

'I'm sick of this horrible marriage. I want a divorce. Stay away from the mill-house . . .'

The severance was neither unexpected nor unwelcome. A petition was duly served on him by Fay's solicitors. It contained twenty-four allegations, ranging from sexual deviation to dishonesty and violence, some of such a vitriolic nature that the petition had to be defended. Defended divorces, Peter was to discover, were purgatory.

Now living alone at Perrers Road, he succumbed to a deep depression, his lack of funds contributing. He had left the Commander and his team roasting in Loughton, hoping he had called the bluff of a paper tiger. He had forgotten the oldest of rules: *never kid a kidder*. Meanwhile he was struggling with a ghastly divorce and in danger of losing both his liberty and Perrers Road. A couple of his pals, implicated in the enquiry, gave no encouragement. Hart and Moore yelped:

'It's your problem, Peter. Say what you fucking like to Wickstead. Get yourself out of it as best you can. It's your own people who are coming it on you. We barely know them.'

Paddle your own canoe was the message.

It was indeed on him. Summoned one morning to Loughton, he loaded his Old English sheepdog into the BMW. At the time it seemed a natural thing to do; he couldn't have foreseen that the dog would verbal him up.

He never got to the third floor at Loughton. Going through the swing doors on the ground floor, he was confronted by an ashen-faced Wickstead, sitting behind a desk in the foyer area. Mike Taylor was at his side, paperwork everywhere.

'Sit down, Mr Gulston. I propose to charge you with a number of matters going back some years. It'll take some time. Would you like a solicitor present?'

No point, thought Peter. Fannying time was up.

A long litany of his past sins was read out. Stanley had forgotten little. A number of items were nothing whatsoever to do with him, but did it really matter? Time to be shtum.

An hour later the Commander had finished – at least, it seemed like an hour, confronted by these old skeletons.

'We propose to search your home at Perrers Road. My officers will accompany you. Regarding bail, I think I'll need a couple of sureties of ten thousand pounds. Can you provide them?'

The search at Perrers Road was fruitless. However, it was alleged that, jesting with the sheepdog in the rear of the car, Peter blurted out, 'I've been a naughty boy, Elvis. Looks like I'll have to suffer.'

The swamp conspiracy charge of breaking and entering premises in the London area and the home counties was laid. He was bailed through the good offices of a fellow contractor, Frank Ward, and a local chemist in Chiswick. He was further required to report to Hammersmith police station twice daily.

Life was at a nadir, but on reflection he realised he probably deserved it. It was futile to continue feeling sorry for himself; better to think positively.

The borrowing of a dentist pal's car after attending for treatment in Wimpole Street landed him in custody. The day before, his own BMW had been repossessed by the finance company. He borrowed the dentist's, initially to park it for him, got hiked up with good company, forgot to report at midday, and when reporting that evening, still in the borrowed car, found to his consternation that it had been reported stolen.

Banged up overnight, he appeared the next day at West London. The beak would listen to nothing. He was remanded in custody to Brixton. There things went from bad to worse. Further contemporary charges emerged of demanding money by menaces in respect of a hard-stand car park he'd built in Acre Lane, Brixton, for a Mr Ali whom he had threatened when he refused to pay, or so it was alleged. Another charge was laid regarding his company returns, the allegation being that his former wife Jackie Bailey was unaware that she was the company secretary and it was not her signature on the annual returns.

The two months he spent banged up in Brixton in the summer of 1977 almost destroyed him, travelling to three different remand hearings a week in the claustrophobic meat wagon, applications for bail being blocked at every turn. His sympathetic elderly barrister paraphrased his lot after yet another failed application. 'I'm afraid, Mr Gulston, we're pissing into the wind. You'd probably be better off making an application yourself.'

A couple of weeks later Peter did just that. The lay bench at Epping listened, and a young DI was indifferent as to whether he got bail or not. It was set at two sureties of ten thousand and his own of forty thousand. The sureties were difficult to find the second time around, and he was to be eternally grateful to his accountant, Peter Davis, and a surgeon pal, Peter Horswill, who finally saw him right.

It was half-past nine at night when he was released from Brixton. Raymond Davis, his solicitor, met him with further depressing news.

'You can't go to Perrers Road. Fay has moved in, albeit against her solicitor's advice. It's a condition of your bail.'

The kindly Raymond pressed a fifty-pound note into his hand.

'Where will you stay?'

'The basement flat in Edith Road is empty. I'll have to go there.'

'Good. My clerk will pick up your personal effects from Perrers Road tomorrow, and for God's sake be sensible.'

Fortunately there was a mattress in the empty flat and he slept like a log.

As he squatted on an orange-box the following morning, the enormity of his position became clear. It would at this stage have been very simple, even pragmatic, to have fallen in with the Commander's wishes, but by then he had developed a deep-rooted antipathy to the man. The more problems he presented Peter with, the firmer his resolve became. He was forty-eight years of age, had been absent from crime for five years, and had not a single accomplice or friend left in the calling. Taters was in the slammer. Worse, he had few ideas, only anger fuelling a longing for revenge.

As God is wont to arrange for those in despair, a minor angel was about to enter his orbit. Calling at a girl chum's home in Maida Vale, he met a friend of hers, Barbara Smith. The pair hit it off, the lady responded to moving into the mattressed basement at Edith Road with well-bred panache, and things began to take a turn for the better.

40

An Ageing Idol Returns to the Stage

Meeting Barbara, and the return of a master thief from prison in the shape of Taters, launched the campaign of 1977/78. Barbara's ample bosom being there to cry on, and Taters's great skills and strengths at his side, breathed new life into Peter.

With larceny at the helm again, it was not inappropriate that Mayfair should be the selected stage. The Waverton Street home of a ruling Kuwaiti family had long been on Peter's list of those deserving a visit.

The assault was to be launched from the small private garden at the rear of the house which could be accessed through a wicket gate in Hill Street, where a wall concealed the arbour. A balconied third-floor bedroom window was to be the point of entry. Arriving at dusk, the pair 'borrowed' a double-extension ladder left carelessly unlocked in Farm Street.

'Let's take that small ladder with us too – the double may not reach,' Taters hissed in the gloom.

Striding round to the wall and gate in Hill Street, they made an odd couple. Peter humped Taters over the wall. He opened the wicket gate and the ladders disappeared from the possible view of a newspaper-engrossed porter in the block of flats opposite. For his part, Taters never saw danger. Tonight, in his lust for revenge on society, Peter too was unconcerned.

The gardens were overlooked on three sides by private residences. It was not unlike being on stage as the sodium lights from the street illuminated the pair in the twilight. They were hostages to a hundred possible 'sighters'. Peter had ceased to care.

Taters was right. The double would not reach the balcony, and they were committed to lashing the single ladder to the double-extension. Fear and greed gnawed at Peter's stomach. Normally his bowels were most vulnerable; tonight he was unable to stop himself retching and spewing. Taters understood. He said not a dicky-bird and kept his nut down, probably having a quiet chuckle at Peter's expense.

With the ladder hoisted *in situ*, Peter tripped up it with the panache of a window cleaner going about his lawful business. As it bowed and swayed, he retched yet again as he approached the lashed section, but he pressed on to the balcony. Beyond the curtains, the bedroom was lit up. An unlatched, unprotected window was a bonus; it was ajar at the base. Peter eased the sash up and sneaked a peep through the now-parted curtains. The room appeared deserted.

Raising the sash, he crept in, going straight to the bedroom door. Voices came from below, servants moving about. Gently, he shut the door and wedged it and began his search. The first thing that caught his eye was an ancient Cox and Coles safe on a pedestal table. He wrenched the handle but it wouldn't budge. Moving on to the dressing table, he rifled through the drawers, finding a bundle of notes and a fortune in gems strewn carelessly in one of them. As he searched feverishly for the key to the safe he was startled to see his sixty-seven-year-old accomplice appear at the window.

'You've been in here too long. Don't take liberties – there's a lot of movement below.'

'Old safe here,' Peter hissed. 'I'm trying to find the key. Fret not – we've had a night's work from the dresser.'

He tried a last savage, two-handed twist on the brass handle, crashing it from side to side. There was a crunch and the door swung open; the lock had not been effectively engaged. A dozen gem cases met his eye. Many were empty, but half a dozen had their contents *in situ*, including a magnificent diamond bracelet. They'd had a touch.

Back in the garden, about to recover the ladders, they were thwarted as a face appeared at a window. They slipped away through the wicket gate and legged it to the Ritz to inspect their haul in the toilet and regain their composure. A couple of bottles of Tattinger Blanc et Blanc at the bar were mandatory, Peter peeling off a couple of fifties from the boodle he'd taken from the Arab.

As they left to hail a taxi, the thief was sure he heard a nightingale warble in Berkeley Square.

'Hear that, George? It's a nightingale singing.'

'Nightingale? You feeling all right? There's no birds here . . . well, maybe a few in Curzon Street. Give me a few quid to be going on with, I've a lot of laundry to get out tomorrow.'

And so it was that the thief returned to his destiny in the autumn of 1977. He was to commit carnage in the region of three million sterling over the next fifteen months, before curtailing his larceny in the Christmas holiday the following year, two months before his cameo for Wicksteria. It was especially rewarding during this period to be reporting twice daily to the nick, anticipating that every time might be his last. Someone up there *did* like him, for apart from one minor hiccup, he went undetected.

Only the defended divorce called a halt to the faith-protected spree. It was neither cheap nor private, getting the full press treatment. Fay had found an unlikely ally in the thief's former wife, Jackie Bailey. It was a bloodletting, as Mr Justice Balcombe was to remark during the proceedings. Fay's team ran with the old chestnut that Peter was a criminal adventurer.

Mrs Barbara Calvert, QC did her best but, deprived of the asset of a client's good character, was pissing in the wind. Balcombe found for Fay and awarded her a decree nisi on the grounds of what Peter had admitted to in the witness box – cuffing Madam once, swearing, and having a penchant for porn. The other unsupported allegations were dismissed.

A financial settlement hearing was to follow, Balcombe cautioning against it. The parties' solicitors came to an agreement: Fay would pay her own costs (Peter was conditionally legally aided) and give the thief five thousand pounds in full settlement, an odd accommodation for a criminal adventurer.

In all civil matters in which Peter was to appear, and there were many, he found that he was disqualified from winning on account of his bad character, bad characters having no audience with justice. A further reversal occurred in the Family Division when a second appeal by the Baileys before Lord Justice Ormerod succeeded. Peter was to have no further access to his son, Ormerod indicating that while a man awaiting trial on eight different indictments might well be telling the truth, it was not in the child's interest for his father to have access until the matters were resolved. The learned lawyer pronounced, 'It's purely academic who a child's father is. It is those who look to a child's needs who are of the essence.'

At the time Peter viewed this observation with a jaundiced eye. A decade or so later, he has learned to appreciate the wisdom of the utterance. Ormerod assuaged his plea by asking for a report from the Official Solicitor. It was to have unexpected ramifications!

Deprived of his child and his nest-egg in Perrers Road, his comforts were the ever-loyal Barbara and the fifty thousand he'd amassed during his current war with society's fleshpots. He survived, in anger. Wicksteria took what seemed a turn for the better for him when Michael Hill, QC announced at the committal hearing, 'This is no longer a case of police corruption. The Crown now intends to proceed on counts of dishonesty against the persons in the dock.'

Wickstead was about to retire and the second string to his bow was about to be played in a low key. Without Wickstead and the corruption factor, the case became small beer. Even the ambitious Mike Taylor lost the glint in his eye. It was to be a very minor crucifixion.

A new player surfaced when an Irish acquaintance turned up at Edith Road. They had met briefly at the races in Ireland. He made Christmas 1977 memorable by announcing, 'I've a couple of hundred thousand pounds to lay out. I'm in the market – for canvas, silver, clocks, fur. I hear on the grapevine you're at it. Perhaps we can complement one another.'

They went walkabout in the high-rate areas that offer such goods. It was on the pavement in Ryder Street that a galaxy of sporting pictures caught their eye in Pawsey & Payne's showroom. At an agreed twenty thousand, Peter spirited sixteen of them away that same night.

From then on it was an unrelenting campaign. A buyer of such potential does not surface readily. When one does, it is only right to fill him up quickly before he finds another thief. It reached a point where the thief convinced himself irreverently, irrationally, that he had a mandate from the Deity, and that angels were watching over him.

A daring raid on a provincial museum, where he narrowly avoided capture, rewarded him with a collection of bejewelled boxes. Barbara was unaware that the superb hand-painted watch that hung around her neck once belonged to a Queen of France. Peter kept her in the dark about his activities, although no doubt she suspected.

The carnage continued, Taters and the thief smashing their way through the fragile grille at Keith Banham's treasure-house of superb clocks in his premises on the corner of Grafton Street and Albemarle Street. Pure fucking madness at their age, challenging response-times and grilles in Mayfair. The pair deprived the aesthete Keith of a collection of finest French and English striker carriage clocks, many with hand-painted porcelain panels and faces, having it away on their toes as the law arrived. The Irish connection discounted the haul.

On yet another sortie with Taters, the Stilsons made short work of the bars protecting the rear of Richard Green's pricey gallery in Dover Street. Sadly, Peter had already sold his share to the Leprechaun when Taters's as yet unsold portion had to be returned to Richard to appease the wrath of a diligent copper at West End Central by way of a compromise. Taters was none too happy. He screamed the place down, and is inclined to do so to this day should the memory surface.

So it was that Christmas 1977 found the thief in funds. Despite Barbara's arrival, few extras had been added to the desolate flat. A bed-base had been found for the mattress; a television glinted in the light of the open fire in the hearth Peter had once built; a phone and a low-slung table were additional luxuries.

Having already been rewarded with a mink, Barbara dreamed of Santa bringing a lynx to keep it company at Christmas. Hermès in Bond Street allowed the dream to become a reality. In their window, pouting on a dummy, hung a lynx priced for those who can afford that thoroughfare, at nine thousand-odd. Foolishly, it was left on show nightly; perhaps they felt safe being no more than three hundred yards from West End Central nick.

In more sedate times, Peter would have passed, but in his fever of gratitude and divine inspiration, he decided to nick it. A bitterly cold night found him lurking at the corner of Bruton Street and Bond Street with a short length of scaffolding pole lying hidden by the kerb. He was there for hours before the roads approaching the crossing were clear of traffic. An almighty stab with the scaffolding pole in the appropriate place and the semi-bandit glass shattered.

The lynx was secured to the dummy, which had to come too. As he retreated down Bruton Street in the shadows, clinging lover-like to the dummy, a passing motorist gave him a startled look. Peter responded with a festive wave before dodging into the gloom of Barlow Place where his BMW was concealed. He stripped the coat from the dummy, dispatching the latter to a chilly rubbish-bin grave. He returned home inordinately pleased with himself.

Barbara gave him the darling treatment on Christmas morning, but she must have suspected something. She wore it a couple of times and then decided to sell it on to a girl chum.

'Too dodgy to wear, darling. Had a few funny looks in San Lorenzo's.'

41

Golgotha Time

THE Leprechaun had big eyes.

'I've seen some furniture in Haunch of Venison Yard that I could find a home for.'

William Temple traded there, exhibiting a few superb pieces of the finest eighteenth-century English and French furniture. Peter recced the premises. It was a well-known venue, approachable from the fire escape that took you to Phillips the auctioneers' roof from the north cul-de-sac in Globe Yard. The following night he worked his way across Phillips' roof to drop down to a fire escape leading to a picture restorer's and William Temple's premises, which were protected by a conventional alarm system. It must once have been a private house. A rebated office perched on the third floor. The Crittal window offered scant resistance to the cane. Entering, he heard an almost inaudible bell tinkle somewhere below. The same good fortune attended him as he had enjoyed at Max Mitzman the furrier twenty years before. He heard a gramophone record intoning, 'Intruder on premises.' It was directly in front of him; he silenced it with one belt from the cane.

Only a dim, lifeless bell spluttered on the staircase. He silenced that too, then went back to the fire escape to look for signs of the enemy. No one was coming. Twenty minutes later he was in the ground-floor showroom jemmying the access door to the yard. An acquaintance had been persuaded to attend with his van for a monkey. He assisted the thief in loading some twenty priceless pieces undisturbed and departing without any angst.

It all seemed to be going like clockwork until, chugging up a hill in north London, the van's engine cut out and refused to restart. An area car with two friendly young coppers stopped.

'Can't leave it here overnight, mate. Have to shunt it round the corner.'

They did just that with the coppers' help. Around a quarter of a million pounds' worth of goods, including Chippendale mirrors and commodes, was left overnight in the unsecured van. It was intact the next morning.

The pal who produced the van was in retrospect unhappy with his five hundred quid. There was a little unpleasantness in a pub some months later.

'You had me over that night in Mayfair when I put my van on offer. You mugged me off.'

He was pissed. It looked like fisticuffs, but a show of anger from Peter gave him second thoughts.

'You weren't treated like a cunt. I done the screwer. Had it come on top, I'd have carried the can. You got what you agreed to and were happy to get it at the time.'

Looking back, perhaps Chummy had a point. Peter's tronc system was often a little one-sided, but 'outside men' tend to price themselves out of the larceny market. Both Peter and Taters had dozens of volunteers to play 'outside man' expecting an equal cut. Experience had allowed the thief to dispense with such prattle. You got what you were worth.

The Irish connection was filled up as 1978 drew to a close. A massive strike in the Quorn country had thrown up a quarter of a million pounds' worth of Georgian silver, but now it was time to shut up shop. St Albans was the venue for his forthcoming trial in January. He had stolen between two and three million pounds' worth of property in sixteen months, probably drawing a quarter of a mill for his whack. More importantly, he'd got his self-respect back; he could face Wicksteria stoically and probably accept the anticipated bang-up in the knowledge that he'd had some sort of revenge.

Even better, he had fifty thousand in a bank in the Republic. Barbara and he had purchased and sold the basement flat in Edith Road and cut up the twenty thousand profit. Things were looking up . . . or so it seemed. But circumstances flattered to deceive.

The Crown had a strong cast assembled to support their case. George Bethnal Alexander was the main prop for Stanley Addersman's tale. His common-law wife Laurie was on the team too, as were the Baileys. Fay had pitched in by retrieving from the dustbin the note he had written to a co-accused and dispatching it to the police. A lady publican was to recall how Peter had told her that he'd robbed Princess Margaret and alleged he'd taken her on a recce to Liz Taylor's pad in Belgravia. There were a dozen or so others, all with evidence to give. It looked tough.

The judge was a local man rejoicing in the name of Hickman, and in keeping with local needs he was a theatrical-looking arbitrator, sporting mutton-chop whiskers and being excessively polite, even jovial. Be warned, though. Give the mutton-chop brigade a miss. Even when they're portrayed on the stage, they invariably seem to adopt a high moral position, and ought to be viewed with a jaundiced eye. On the bench itself, they are lethal.

Michael Hill's dark mane glistened brightly, as did his piercing eyes. He once again gave the impression of being a most dangerous opponent. Co-defendant Guy Hart's solicitor, Anthony Leader, had briefed, at enormous expense, Montague Walters, who was rumoured to have turned down a call to the Queen's Bench and a knighthood. Like all his brothers at the top of the profession, the QC's enormous fees almost guaranteed a result. Mr Ronald Gray appeared for Ronnie Moore, also an ebullient defender, while Peter was defended by Kenneth Machin, QC, a Recorder with a quiet, conciliatory air and a limp. He also had a habit when addressing the court of rustling his gown across his shoulders in a manner that Lord Denning has advised barristers against. Machin knew it was a crucifixion.

This was the cast that assembled in the foyer at St Albans, eyeing one another for clues. Montague Walters peered at the thief, trying to assess what damage he might be going to do to his client. His whole case relied on Peter Gulston not going anywhere near the box. They had a stilted exchange of pleasantries, with Peter finding little to like about Walters. Chief Superintendent Mike Taylor greeted the thief.

'Didn't think we'd see you. What have you been up to?'

Peter went on the offensive. 'Usual thing, robbing people.'

Taylor smiled. He was destined for high office and knew better than to bandy words with the quick-witted thief. Then Machin appeared.

'Mr Gulston, I understand you feel there will be difficulties for your co-defendants if you go into the box. It is my considered judgement, at this stage, that you do not do so. A whole hornet's nest could be disturbed. However, we shall play it by ear. It is essential you understand that my duty is to you and not your fellow accused. You do seem uncommonly anxious to protect them.'

'Hart and I were once pals. He's not too quietly putting it about that I coppered him. I'm on the defensive really.'

'Coppered him? Good gracious, man, there's only one likely victim here, and it's you. However, you've put crime behind you now. You've been honestly employed for nearly ten years – yes, yes, I am aware of the sofa business, but Lord Scarman's judgement on your appeal may well stand us in good stead. You're a reformed character now.'

Peter found it difficult to look Machin in the eye. The sixteen-month campaign in Mayfair was too fresh in his mind. He mumbled, 'I suppose I am. But what good will that do with Wicksteria? Past sins linger long.'

'What do you call it? Wicksteria? How apt. Well, we shall see, shan't we?'

Machin smiled in his concerned way. He knew it would all be uphill. And the real task he was facing was damage limitation. In his heart he was uncertain whether or not his client deserved to be crucified, for experience had taught him about smoke and fire . . . after all, had he not sat as a Recorder?

Michael Hill laid out his wares for the jury, immediately getting into soft ground when he had to acknowledge a letter (in the possession of the defence) from the Home Office to George Alexander which promised to review his sentence favourably if he performed well for the Crown. Hickman thought the letter nothing more than unfortunate, though an Old Bailey judge and jury would surely have had stronger views. Alexander was then called. He loudly protested about his last year at Blundestone prison, where he was kept on 'Rule 43', the special protection category commonly reserved for sex offenders and convicts who have turned informer. Now in the witness box it almost looked like he was not going to come up to scratch. But the ever-competent Hill placated and coaxed the scumbag back on course.

Peter glanced at the shire burghers constituting the jury. It was obvious that they found little attractive about Alexander as he recited the litany of his crimes – real and mythical – dragging Peter along in his slipstream whenever possible. Most of the time Alexander's eyes were admiring the floor. Occasionally he would look up at Peter aggressively, contradicting what he'd told Michael Hill, that he liked the thief and found him amusing. But he was here to settle old scores, maintaining that Peter had coppered him years earlier at Burghclere.

By now, of course, Alexander knew that this was a load of twaddle. His other visitor to Burghclere all those years ago was now exposed as a long-time police informer. It was he who had fired Birch and Eist to Burghclere. And now the Judases were in tandem for the Crown, along with Laurie, who'd coincidentally put Alexander away for his current seven-year stretch. Extraordinary what depths the Crown would stoop to in order to pick up crumbs.

Alexander's allegations did not stop there. To heap insult on treachery, he told the court that Peter was a bungling thief.

'I had to send him home one night he was so incompetent. My training made him, by comparison, second-rate.'

Peter thought it a pity that Alexander's SAS training had not taught him to keep his trap shut in the nick. Perhaps SAS men do not expect to end up there!

Later in his evidence, a shabby prompt from Hill drew another imaginative tale from Alexander.

'And what occurred when you and Gulston robbed the home of Shirley MacLaine, the actress, in Berkshire?'

Peter had spied on her in a state of undress and masturbated, Alexander alleged. Chummy had not even been there! His lie was an extension of his sewer-trawling blend of fact and fiction.

Claims about other work he'd done were confusing. He pleaded guilty to robbing Patricia Hastings Bass. Questioned by Kenneth Machin as to what he'd taken and what he'd carried it away in, he said he couldn't remember. Odd that a thief who'd apparently bested a vault door and removed gems and Georgian silver – along with racing trophies – in a pair of cricket bags could have forgotten such compelling details. Under pressure, he took refuge in an obvious lie.

'My memory's poor,' he stammered. 'I've done so many.'

Machin, by now uncertain what to believe, soft-pedalled from there on, barely challenging Alexander's evidence. Later, when Peter questioned his approach, he said, 'Fear not, Mr Gulston, Alexander is a poor witness.'

But it was Laurie Alexander who was to star for the Crown. The self-confessed hotel thief cooked Peter's goose. She was convincing in her certainty that Peter had, on several occasions, visited Burghclere and gone out with Alexander to plunder. She was an impressive and, in the main, truthful witness. She should have been, having had plenty of experience by way of shopping her husband. They probably deserved one another.

Most other witness statements were read, including the Baileys', which continues to hurt Peter even to this day. Few of the original squad gave evidence, and the pace of the trial flagged as it stumbled on into February 1979. Jim Pointing was by then dead. Peter was glad that the good old boy did not have to go through the ordeal. He'd never been up for it in the first place.

One more unfortunate weary for breath
Rashly importunate, gone to his death.

From time to time in the early morning before sittings, Stanley Addersman had been seen talking to Peter in an ABC café. He was already regarded by the prosecution as a possibly hostile and certainly unreliable witness.

'I'll do no harm,' he hissed at Peter as they queued for a cuppa before the day's agony. Hart, trooping about with Peter in the hope of consolidating his loyalty, hissed back, 'What did you have to stick me up for in the first place, you cunt? What did I ever do to you?'

But Stanley instantly swerved; Hart was not at all to his liking. Peter tried assuagement.

'Too late now, Stan. The damage is done.'

But he was wrong.

'Mr Addersman, tell His Honour and the jury what you know Peter Gulston to be, and what kind of things you may have done for him.'

Michael Hill was quietly leading Stanley towards his perfidy.

'Peter?' said Stan. 'He's a haulage contractor. I sometimes drive him about. And his friends.'

Stanley was not sticking to his lines. Hill tried again, a little more aggressively.

'But you know him as other things, do you not?'

'No, he's a successful haulage contractor and I like him.'

Everyone crucifying Peter liked him! Was it mandatory to love the thing you kill? Didn't Judas kiss the Nazarene before copping the shekels? Hill, anyway, saw which way the wind was blowing. He could not get Stanley near the script. He tried harassing him as to what he said on oath at the committal at Epping. Shades of an allegation of perjury emerged, which partially got Stanley back on track, but then lost him again when coming to Patricia Hastings Bass's racing trophies, which he had previously alleged Peter had given to him. They had in fact been recovered from a luggage locker at Waterloo, after Peter advised the law as to their whereabouts eight or nine years earlier. Stanley himself had lodged them there on Peter's instructions.

'You recall handling the pair of racing cups – one the Royal Hunt Cup, I think.'

Stanley nodded, encouraging Hill to proceed, but gingerly.

'What did you do with them after Gulston gave them to you?'

'Did what he told me. Threw them in the Thames.'

Peter, dockbound, started to titter. It was pure comedy. Hill held up his hands in surrender.

'Stay where you are, Mr Addersman. My learned friend may have a few questions for you.'

Defence counsel had been warned as to Addersman's temperament by Peter, who told them, 'Don't challenge him. Stroke his ego and he'll follow you kindly.'

In fact, Machin found little to put to him, and neither did Montague Walters. But it was Michael Hill in re-examination who drove a nail into Peter's coffin by suggesting to Stanley that he was not Gulston's friend at all.

'Not Peter's friend?' asked Stanley. 'What about the night at Binfield when I picked him up in Liz Taylor's Rolls-Royce, when he was bleeding to death?'

Hickman swooped, mutton-chops bristling.

'Mr Hill, is this matter on the indictment? Ah, it is not. Still, best I think if the jury hears about it.'

Poor Stanley – he was in limbo. Binfield was not part of the script. He told how he'd picked the wounded thief up at a flora-concealed phone box at Bracknell, wrapping a fur rug round his bloody legs, and driving back to London through a roadblock. Listening to this, Peter dropped his head into his hands. He had ceased to care. The tale had the ring of truth to it – for God's sake it *was* the truth! – and Stanley warmed to it as he crucified Peter.

Binfield House was a low dwelling of two storeys, but spreading some seventy yards across. It had a river meandering past, a swimming pool, stables and, inside, a magnificent selection of Georgian sticks. Peter had the latter sacked up and was about to descend the ladder to *terra firma* when a police loudhailer trumpeted out in the silence of the night.

'Intruder! Give yourself up! You are surrounded.'

Abandoning the loot and the ladder, Peter rushed downstairs to the gracious hall. He ran pell-mell to the east end of the house, and slung a chair through a window there. Then he doubled back across the hall to the west wing where, foolishly, he dived through a pair of French windows. On screen Connery and Eastwood seem to achieve this kind of thing with a skill that confounded the thief. But the outcome for Peter was two badly sliced thighs and shins. In the heat of the battle, such trifles don't at first register, and Peter's ploy of drawing the enemy to the first sound of breaking glass seemed to have worked. No one was at their post at the west end as he made his way down to the edge of the river. He heard a shout.

'There he is! Down by the stream.'

Torches glistening lethally, the enemy pounded towards him. He started to run towards the bridge on a public road, but thought better of it. He waded instead into the dark icy water and breaststroked silently, hidden by trees and shrubs, to the other side. He emerged adjacent to a pub at the junction of three roads. The enemy were in attendance but the gods were smiling too. A row of houses running at right-angles to the tavern threw up an empty, where the thief took temporary refuge.

Ripping a soaking sweater asunder, he devised a couple of tourniquets to staunch the flow of blood. Outside, yapping dogs confirmed that the search party had got a sniff of him, the law having set up a command post on the pub forecourt. As the barking dogs drew closer, he decided on a daring plan. He would return through the grounds of the house towards Bracknell.

Crossing the Wokingham Road, he could see the enemy as he hit the copse at the house's rear. He circumvented the torch-beams that were glinting at various vantage points, and followed the course of the stream. He was whacked and bleeding profusely. He could not afford to be seen by anyone.

Such is the nature of the calling. Everyone is the enemy. Even a normally friendly dog will snap and snarl and long to devour you. What had ever attracted him to the work?

It took an hour to cover the couple of miles to Bracknell. Crossing a sports ground, he found refuge in the most unlikely of phone boxes, on an estate at the edge of town. It stood beside the gable-end of a house set back from the road, and was almost totally concealed by bushes. It was late by now, and unlikely to be used, making a natural refuge both to hide in and call for assistance. He telephoned Stanley, who arrived dutifully to retrieve his patron, wrapped him up, and drove him away, passing through a police checkpoint with panache as Peter pretended to slumber regally in the back of Liz Taylor's Rolls-Royce.

Stanley told the court the whole story verbatim. Hard to equate, really. The same Stan who had snatched him from the jaws of God knows what was today crucifying him. He felt sorry as Stan completed his tale, his owl-like eyes apologising from behind rimless glasses. He'd made his point, though. And Hickman had recovered some of the ground lost by the prosecution. No one in that court disbelieved the story, yet it was not at all what a haulage contractor should be up to.

As the prosecution case closed, little had been said to damage Guy Hart, just twice-removed hearsay. Montague Walters set about making a submission for immediate discharge. He told Judge Hickman that Gulston was not going into the witness box, and accordingly nothing more could be adduced against Hart. The submission spread over two days, arguing either that Hart should be tried alone (which would be most unlikely to get anywhere) or that there was no case to answer in law. Hickman deferred his decision until the next morning and then concurred: there was, he said, no case for Hart to answer and he should have his costs. He was then discharged, trembling like a puppy dog as he struggled past Peter in the dock. Montague had certainly earned his refreshers.

When Peter's remaining co-defendant, Ronald Moore, went into the witness box, he spoke with authority, making a good impression on the jury. After this, it only remained for Peter to address the court from the dock. He spoke with all the sincerity he could muster. Yes, he had been a burglar. Yes, he had encouraged Alexander and given him tips, so a little of what the prosecution said was correct. But the moot point was, he had weaned himself away from crime in 1972.

Soon Peter was telling the jury a load of bullshit, but he felt constrained not to get too virtuous. His consciousness of the recent campaign hampered his appeal to the twelve decent citizens who would sit in judgement on him. God knows they looked a decent enough lot – some even seemed to like him, nodding a greeting if they passed him in the streets of St Albans. His forty-minute noteless monologue impressed Michael Hill so much that the QC, ready to address the jury from his own notes, quite abruptly put them to one side and spoke extempore.

'Members of the jury, I dare say many of you have come to like Peter Gulston. His charm is infectious. But underneath the bluff exterior charm lies a very determined criminal and we are required to address ourselves to the facts.'

Gray made a strong speech for Ronald Moore, and then Hickman summed up in the prescribed fashion. He was clearly a past master at avoiding any future wrath from the Appeal Court. But, then again, he was only doing what he had been educated and trained to do. Maybe even programmed to do. Justice, as has been many times noted above, is a myth. Expediency rules.

Moore was acquitted. Then it was the thief's turn.

'Guilty,' said the foreman, avoiding Gulston's eye.

Once he had awarded costs to Moore, Peter was left alone to hear his fate from Hickman, just as the thief had known he would be ever since the day Stanley had appeared at Perrers Road while Peter was loading the skip. Now, finally, Wicksteria was about to overwhelm his life, but not quite yet. Two more events must first be acted out in Hickman's theatre – the hearings relating to the forgery charge and to demanding money with menaces. It took another six weeks of waiting.

The trial for the charge of demanding money with menaces was hampered by the complainant Ali having more convictions than the contractor-thief, and he gave his evidence so poorly that the Crown reluctantly declined to proceed. Hickman blew a fuse. He insisted that the prosecution continue, but the young barrister stuck to his guns.

'The quality of evidence, My Lord, does not come up to credit. You have seen Mr Ali. I cannot think he has impressed the jury.'

Maybe not the jury, but anything said to Gulston's detriment impressed Mutton-chops.

As to the 'forgery', Peter had pleaded to it, agreeing that his 'company secretary' had not signed the company returns for the year 1976, and that a girl in his office had done so in her absence. But there had been no loss to anyone, and no intent. However, Hickman was not to see it that way. Furthermore, Peter had failed to appreciate the implication of pleading guilty. The 'offence' fell within the range of the two-year suspended sentence that Judge Phelan had passed on Peter in 1975 for receiving the stolen sofa. This sentence could be activated for the least trifle. Peter may have missed this; Hickman did not.

He put off sentencing the malefactor until the next morning, when he suggested that the thief's decade of freedom had been achieved by criminal cunning and corrupting police officers. He didn't say a word about the seven years in haulage. Apart from the hints about police corruption, Hickman had no further need to refer to Wicksteria, and indeed not a member of the team had been present at call-over time. The judge showed little more interest in Peter's antecedents, related by a sergeant from the Met who'd appeared in the demanding-with-menaces case. He was keen to get down to the business of sentencing. Listening, Peter felt the icy tentacles of retribution creeping down from the bench.

Five years for conspiracy to burgle, three years for conspiracy to handle stolen property, and twelve months for the forgery (activating the old two years suspended). At first, standing there in shock, the thief thought all the sentences were consecutive, which seemed to add up to eleven years. It was not until some time later, in the cells below, that he was informed by his brief that he was in fact serving an eight. Machin had arrived red and angry.

'Mr Gulston, I am as senior a judge as the man who has sentenced you. May I say at once that, in my opinion, Judge Hickman has given you double the maximum. I am sure we'll have it reduced on appeal.'

This was small comfort, for such is the barrister's standard patter to clients who get topped up. In reality, the Court of Appeal rarely interfered with the sentences of men with Peter's kind of form – not unless something was radically wrong.

He knew there was nothing left for him. He'd landed again on the dreaded square marked Go to Jail.

Which is more than can be said about Alec Eist, the detective whose corruption in the Baker Street case had spawned Wicksteria, and whose tainted relationship with Guy Hart was at the root of Peter's problems, culminating in his being sent down.

Eist did eventually stand trial for a wholly different piece of corruption, but he was acquitted. Justice of another sort caught up with him soon after. He died of cancer.

42

Wandsworth '79

DECIDEDLY sombre, Peter trundled back in the van to Wandsworth. Even the screws felt compassion for the ageing felon. During the long trial he had sent the odd drink over to them at lunch-breaks and they'd had a sweepstake among themselves as to his sentence. The highest guess had been two years – and screws are normally near the mark.

As if to show the depth of their concern, they stopped briefly in St Albans to buy him a cigar.

'Better smoke it now. It may be the last one you'll see for some time, Scotty.'

Hickman's words floated threateningly above the gentle feather of cigar smoke, as it wafted around his head.

'You're a danger to society,' Mutton-chops had growled. He had to believe it – it might well have been true.

Wandsworth was strangely cheering, like a homecoming. There had been changes. In reception where, previously, you did an abrupt right on entry to sit on benches opposite the staff desk and counter, he was now confronted with a desk immediately on his right.

At the same time, it was as if he'd never been away. The dialogue was exactly the same, although the tone was different.

'Name? Sentence? Court?' a civil-enough voice enquired. A quarter of a century ago it would have barked.

'Peter Craig Gulston. Eight years. St Albans.'

A pipe-smoking PO appeared. They knew one another.

'Hello, Scotty. Back to your correct name?'

He'd been Peter Scott doing a lagging there in '61.

'Afraid so, Mr B.'

Peter smiled, tactfully paying respect to the old jailer.

'Didn't think we'd see you back in the system.'

Mr B. bantered on, Peter and he each enjoying their seniority. Peter quickly discovered that Wickstead's victims boarded first class here. He passed quickly through a bath and medical and at nine o'clock was led across the slumbering prison's hallowed, polished centre and into D Wing. It was the long-term security wing and Peter, as a Wickstead boy, was located on D2, ground level. The cell exuded comfort compared to anything he'd formerly known inside. Twenty years had brought much change to Wandsworth.

Mr B. appeared on the landing, still enjoying Memory Lane.

'Something odd, Scotty. A pal of yours has just vacated that cell – Bobby Maynard. Lost his appeal today, gone back to the Island. Wickstead did him too, did he not, Mr Gray?'

Another ghost from the past, Dolly Gray, appeared, shuffling out of the wing's caged office.

'Hello, Peter. Gave you a slap, didn't they? Yes, poor Bobby. We were all expecting him to get a result. We all thought he was innocent.'

Peter had been in Mailbags 1 in the early fifties, when this ruddy-faced, shy officer had first joined. With his soft West Country burr, he was a long-time diamond and a first-class officer.

'Dolly! Yes, we all knew he was innocent but, like me, he was keeping bad company and he suffered for it. He's left the kennel nice and tidy, anyway.'

'He's done better than that. Look under the mattress.'

Peter flipped back the mattress to reveal a flat bundle of soft porn.

Dolly banged him up with a cup of tea and, as the door slammed, he suddenly felt a great weight lift from his shoulders. All the strain of three years of Wicksteria had come to an end. He even felt born again, in a way. He slept soundly.

Slopping out was still the practice. Shooting down first thing to the recess jaw-box to unload turd and piss was flash-point in the morning. A couple of old faces hailed him from the other side of the landing – one of them was Bruce F., who fed him from the ramparts when he had been on chokey at La Verne. The piss-taking abounded.

'What are you doing here, Pop?'

'Couldn't make the break, eh?'

Prison Officer Paddy Ryan still ruled the roost at the Hard Tack shop (HT2), built directly at right-angles to the end of D Wing. He was not impressed with Peter.

'You back again? Always had a lot to say. Well, stay out of my way and I'll stay out of yours.'

His harsh west of Ireland brogue had a menacing tone. He'd done well for his brood – a barrister son and a solicitor daughter were the long-serving officer's family rewards. Even he had mellowed.

'Ever see the other master thief, Arthur White?'

Arthur had always bemused and used Paddy with his intellect and guile, and the screw associated the two thieves as fellow sybarites, birds of a feather. But Ryan's soft spot for Arthur did not extend to Peter.

So there he was, sewing mailbags at fifty, eight years on his plate and already deciding on a lightweight war with Paddy Ryan to keep monotony at bay. It took him six to eight months before he got himself and Tony White promoted to the stencilling table, escaping from the soulless sewing. Paddy Ryan made a great fuss assigning the pair to a non-sedentary task.

'See you behave yourselves.'

The one light shining in the infinite tunnel of prison was his appeal. He lived and slept it. Someone asked him casually what he would do if he was successful.

'I'm going to play tennis. Yes, that's it. I'll learn to play tennis.'

'Scotty? Going to play tennis? The only tennis he'll play will be padder tennis.'

Padder tennis is played on a tennis court at La Verne with large wooden bats. None of the audience had a modicum of faith in the Court of Criminal Appeal.

At the beginning of 1980, when Peter had served ten months, he wrote to Raymond Davis, reminding him of Machin's words at St Albans about having the sentence reduced on appeal. Unknown to Peter, a minor angel was waiting in the wings: David Walsh, the ageing junior to Machin at the trial. Walsh had held a post where his experience stood him in good stead – secretary to the Court of Appeal. Having one's case put before a sympathetic bench was of the essence and Walsh, conversant with such matters, knew the drill. To succeed, be assured, you have to know the drill.

The initial application was to be heard at the Royal Courts of Justice on 28 February. The thief rolled up to the Strand, handcuffed to one of two loutish officers from Wandsworth. Lord Justice Donaldson, Mr Justice Kilner-Brown, and Mr Justice Wood were listening for Regina. Machin, leading Walsh, appeared for Peter. A short, chilling conference took place in a shrouded recess, outside the courtroom.

'Mr Gulston, you may know, it is now policy to grant leave to appeal and hear the appeal immediately. If we are called, that means leave will have been granted and we will be heard. I am confident of a reduction. If we're not called in, you'll go back and continue your sentence.'

Even before the impact of the words sunk in, a voice bellowed, 'Peter Craig Gulston!'

They were on court. But could Machin serve an ace?

The prisoner stood at right-angles to their Lordships, no more than twenty feet away. A row of benign faces under the wigs gave the thief hope, for he knew that judges' faces have a story to tell, if only for the fact that – hard set as they are in the duty of dispensing misery – on the odd occasion when mercy is about to make an appearance you can sometimes read the rejoicing in their faces.

However, Machin's serve was put under pressure immediately, when Donaldson enquired, on hearing of the allegations of police corruption of such interest to Wickstead, 'Mr Machin, could Mr Gulston not help? Or *would* he not help?'

Up to this point, they were only knocking up, padding the ball about politely. But the lobbed question needed answering. Machin shrugged his gown, hesitated, then answered in measured terms.

'My Lord, it is my opinion he couldn't.'

The Receiver relaxed. The ball was back in play, to be gently stroked back and forth. Then Roy Kilner-Brown punched one down the line which was to leave Machin flat-footed.

'Mr Machin, who authorised this very senior officer to make an offer of blanket immunity, for any offence he, Gulston, might ever have committed?'

Machin shrugged, turning his palms to indicate in silence the weight of the shot. It was a veritable mystery. Donaldson served again quickly and with little warning.

'Well, why in heaven's name did he not accept the immunity? He was told he would not even have to go into the witness box, was he not?'

Machin, who was moving better now, returned the sneaky ball.

'My Lord, one can only hazard.'

Peter realised that the set was going his way. He thought, why indeed did he not? The cops were the enemy. Hart and Moore were coppering him off. Why indeed?

The thief cannot now remember if there was a retirement. If so, they soon came back and Donaldson read the judgement. Peter's sentence was reduced to three years, the same as had been given to George Alexander in 1972. The learned Justice ended with the following pious hope:

'Speaking for myself, and I am sure my fellow judges will agree, I can only hope that the very clear indication that he is intent on now taking up a new profession as an honest citizen will be continued upon his release.'

He was reunited with a breathless Machin in the shrouded recess. Now he was doing only a lagging, and had served more than half of it. A stranger from the After Care Service appeared, thrusting a parole application form into his hands. It was clear their Lordships were prepared to support an immediate release for Peter.

'Fill that in,' said the official. 'A Mrs Horrobin will process it at Wandsworth. It'll take a couple of weeks, but you'll be paroled.'

Events were moving too quickly for Kenneth Machin. Realising that Peter's release was imminent, and not certain in his own mind that the thief deserved it, he advised, 'Their Lordships have been most generous. It's likely you'll be free presently. Please make good use of their Lordships' largesse.'

Machin looked shocked at having such a total victory, not certain that he'd even meant to. Peter boomed out in cheeky, grateful affection, 'Bless you, Kenneth. Well done. Do yourself a favour. Get married. You're a very decent man.'

Startled by the impertinence, Machin mumbled his thanks. He did get married and he is now a very competent judge at the Bailey, if on occasion somewhat severe.

Shipped out of D Wing, he joined Dolly Gray as tea-boy in G, H, and K Wing, a separate block built originally to house women prisoners. Now it was home to receptions, section 43s (nonces, protection cases, and the like), and the Punishment Block. It rejoiced in a small tea-room which the more discerning officers used in preference to the one in the main prison.

Dolly Gray was often on nights. He had a collection of old Wandsworth memorabilia and allowed his new tea-boy a shufty at it. Included were a number of old reception rolls, and Peter found the one for 1932. This showed that George Chatham was admitted to serve three years' penal servitude, being only one of seven in the whole prison to be classed as 'convicts' – prisoners serving a lagging or over. Today, there are four or five hundred men in Wandsworth serving three years or more: such is the inflation rate of British justice. When you consider that British prisons today have some 3,500 lifers locked up – more than in the rest of the entire European Union put together – you will realise just how out of kilter this ill-defined British justice is. If our prison-building rate is anything to go by, we are either in severe decline, or obsessed with punishment. It is probably the latter. The sooner the public school is abolished the better.

Mrs Horrobin, a charming grey-rinsed Anglo-Indian matron, expedited his release on a sunny day in May. As he was processed out of Wandsworth, Dolly Gray asked, 'What are you going to do, Scotty?'

'Play tennis, Dolly. I promised myself I would if my appeal succeeded.'

'Well, make sure you don't play it on the roofs of Mayfair.'

Linda, the wife of a chum, was having six months in Aussie, and offered her flat in Palace Court, Moscow Road. The Parole Board agreed to the arrangement. Peter stayed there eight months.

As he strolled from Moscow Road to his first meeting with his parole officer at Seymour Place, he cut through Hyde Park. It was a fine summer's day and young women sunning themselves, showing glimpses of their underwear, reminded him that he was back in the game, free. But he was also bitter. At war with himself and society, he could only hope that the tennis court would dilute the desire for revenge. In his heart he was sad that the vice of revenge lingered. He felt almost a traitor, harbouring thoughts of larceny.

Barbara and her claustrophobia were long since gone. She had in fact once braved Wandsworth, to give him details of the sale of the flat at Edith Road, and of his share. Then she said, 'Darling, I'm off to the States. I may write, but my handwriting's bloody. Good luck on appeal. Always love you.'

His millstone lingered in the shape of Diana, whom he met, or rather saw, dropped over a large Bell's in Sheila Kelly's corner pitch when Jack took him for a jar. Diana showed out with a wave to Jack.

'Who's that?' fate lured Peter to ask.

'Diana. Used to be married to Tommy-boy. But she's too warm for you.'

Jack laid it on the line, but the damage was done. Peter had found a new playmate.

He invited her to accompany him on a reprehensibly boozy shunt to visit the Horswills in Salisbury. Arriving, they found them out. Diana, unimpressed by his driving, suggested, 'Why don't we have a drink? We could get a room at a hotel, kip for the night. You drove very aggressively. I was scared at times.'

They found a room in a hostelry and set about a couple of bottles of champagne. Peter, pissed and none too sure of his courting tackle, tried to swerve as Diana listened to his bitching about Wicksteria. She was a worldly woman and knew all the ploys. She comforted the nervous lover with a skill that allowed Bert and his minions to evaporate in a haze of maternal affection, coupled with a sympathetic conclusion.

'Well, you can't bitch for ever. You won your appeal, got a few quid to come out to. How much did you say you had?'

Peter hadn't said, but Diana had been barked at by her ex, from whom she'd had a good settlement.

'Watch that gentleman burglar. He's a Paddy. He'll knock your few quid out in short order.'

Peter cashed his modest shareholding in Lonrho at a small profit (he'd put his portion from the sale of the flat into Tiny Rowland's hands). He bought a BMW and a Head tennis racket, in preparation for the new game. An urgent visit to Scotland Yard to claim paperwork seized by Wicksteria brought Mike Taylor and an A/C Crime down from the sixth floor to greet him in genuine amazement. They treated the thief like a long-lost friend.

'Peter! Do you know, we didn't have a clue you were out. A couple of phone calls from people seeking protection alerted us.'

The smiling, promoted Taylor clutched a sealed plastic sack, with Peter's former life in it. He introduced Peter to his governor, who had often chased Peter in the past.

'You nearly ran me off the road once, remember?'

Peter remembered but he didn't much feel like swapping cosy reminiscences.

'Which people are looking for protection from me?' he joshed. 'Whoever they are, they've only their consciences to haunt them. I'm not into personal retribution.'

Jock, Taylor's colleague, gave a loud guffaw.

'Wicksteria, you call it? We have another name for it.'

The edge in his voice revealed that he had been no admirer of the retired Commander.

Mike Taylor pulled the mule back on course.

'Peter, be sensible. You've had a wonderful result. Don't do anything foolish to spoil it.'

Peter's blue-grey eyes glinted. They told Taylor that there was little chance of the advice being taken. And yet it was true – revenge on morally weak prats and their wives was not on his mind. His war would be with society and its fleshpots.

'Absolutely right, Michael. Back to commerce for me. I'll cause your Judases no aggro, even though they may garrotte themselves in the knowledge that I'm out and about. By the way, I understand congratulations are in order. Your promotion . . .'

Taylor preened and smiled coyly. Jock, the more worldly of the two coppers, watched sceptically as the thief left.

'That fellow will be causing us a lot more trouble. I've never seen him so bloody polite.'

And Jock of course was right. The five-year campaign of the eighties was about to grow leaves and blossom, as surely as Wicksteria itself had done.

Diana was exported to Ireland: to Kinsale for booze and cuddles; to Mallow, where Peter picked up his deposit with the Allied Irish Bank; and to Belfast, as the guests of Lord Hamill and family. She made a strong impression in all three venues. Her elegance, her ability to drink Teacher's like water, and her mannish repartee attracted all. Much to Diana's amusement, David Hamill, the ebullient Belfast businessman located in Broomehill Park, summed her up in his hearty, bellowing tones, 'Diana's great gas. She knows more moves than I do.' A decade later, he was to learn that his spouse, Roberta, knew a few moves too, annexing his considerable business interests and leaving him to paddle his own canoe.

But wine and romance needed heavy servicing. Peter's few thousand was shrinking to a level that pointed him again at Mayfair. He chose to revisit an old target. The unfortunate, uninsured Bill Gibb had been at these premises when he'd been there first, but now they were occupied by Marie Claire. And like Bill Gibb, they too had a fur department.

Taters had been called in purely as driver, on a tronc split of two for Peter, one for George. Shameful, really. It rubbed it in that Taters was more or less past it. He quite rightly bitched about being excluded from the entry, but Peter reasoned with him.

'No one could help me if the enemy rolled up. I'm only putting you in it as you're providing wheels.'

George accepted the argument with bad grace.

So the nervous thief went in alone from an office stairwell in Bloomfield Place, breaching the wall straight into the couturier's showroom. It was a dull Sunday afternoon and he knew that he could be trapped there without warning. He could access the roof but no cat burglar's escape route presented itself, with a two-storey gable-end rearing up on one side and an impossible wall topped by another roof on the other. If West End Central arrived, he was entombed.

But luck held. The sonic on the premises did not pick him up, the bell he silenced, and he was able to remove eighty garments which were to net him twenty-five thousand. And so the 'Five Years' War' commenced.

The silver shop at the corner of Curzon Street and Half Moon Street was his next, solo strike. Peter used the estate agent's next door to access the rear wall of the well-lit showroom, where all their Georgian silver was cabineted or on window display. A sensor on the stairwell had to be respectfully circumvented and the porter of the Hotel Washington opposite was a likely sighter, able to see in through the shop window. But Peter's luck continued and he cautiously removed the treasures from the window and cabinet, sacking them up in the estate agent's hall.

More luck was required to load them into a parked station wagon in Half Moon Street, but here it seemed to desert him. Two uniformed constables were rounding the corner of Curzon Street, some twenty-five yards distant. They started bearing steadily down on him.

It was one of those contingencies that cannot be discounted when working alone. He'd been dealt a cruel card and was on the point of legging it, not fancying his chances one bit with half a century on board. But fate has many convolutions. Suddenly a Jaguar hooker-mobile came trawling its way slowly down Half Moon Street. The driver, seeking custom, became the focus of the young coppers' attention and they jumped out in front of her, torches brandished, signalling her to stop. Madam obliged, the driver's door was wrenched open, and she was none too gently dragged out.

'Hello, Cynthia. You're nicked. We've been observing you for the last half-hour. You've been tomming again. And had a drink, have you?'

Cynthia, in a semi-cultured voice, replied, 'I'm on my way home. I've just had dinner with a peer of the realm. Have you pair of cunts got nothing better to do than fuck me about?'

She was a little closer to the bone than she knew. Peter took instant advantage of the miracle, hoisting the remaining sacks into the vehicle under cover of the struggle now taking place as patent high heels and suspendered legs kicked at the restraining officers. Madam's voice had shed all pretence of sophistication.

'Fucking prats! Fucking *fascist* prats!'

Peter slowly and respectfully edged past the ruck in the mouth of Curzon Street, winding his window down and dutifully enquiring, 'Need any help, officer?'

A curt wave indicated that they had things under control, and the thief purred away with fifty thousand pounds' worth of Georgian silver. W. S. Gilbert was right about a policeman's lot.

It was such repeated, gratuitous good fortune which made Peter entertain his fanciful ideas of God being with him. The longer he clung to the illusion, the longer the luck lasted. Vengeance is mine, saith the Lord. Wrong. In this instance, vengeance was the thief's. So, even in the sure knowledge that he was self-destructing, the blood-letting went on.

A couple of provincial museums were pillaged at the behest of a dealer from Brighton, a new face on the scene introduced to him by his Moscow Road landlady's husband, Bongo. Then twin visits to Sidney Massin, trading as the House of Worth in Wigmore Street, reinforced yet again the luck-in-faith syndrome. The first time he smashed the window, snatching half a dozen or so superb garments and escaping as the law arrived through the basement of the adjoining block of flats into Welbeck Street, where he found a way into Easley's Mews and comparative safety. On his second visit, one Sunday afternoon, he holed the hapless furrier through a breeze-block wall from a childrenswear shop. Again he decamped as the law arrived. The gods were still smiling on him. Could it last?

The fall onto the spikes in Horse Shoe Yard and the subsequent convalescence in his garret in Wandsworth have already been described. They ended the dalliance with Diana. A first portent that perhaps he had displeased his masters.

As he hobbled around the tennis courts in search of fitness, another viper became reactivated – Trigeminal neuralgia. He had first had it in '78 at the height of his eighteen-month campaign. He described it as like having 'a viper in your mouth' when consulting his good friend Fergal Nally, a fine surgeon. Fergal told him, 'It's usually associated with stress or depression. You have a particularly bad case of it. Puzzling.'

He struggled with it stoically at the Eastman Hospital. When the drug Tegrotal failed to diffuse the ghastly shock-pains of the condition, only cryo-surgery gave some relief from the pain. The thief was reluctant to accept that this might be a celestial warning. But he knew that the stress of larceny did little to help the condition.

Then Taters was on the phone.

'Fancy meeting me at the Brompton Oratory? The scaffolding's up on the Polish Church. Gives us a bit of a chance with . . . you know what.'

Here we are, back where we came in when we met the pair of thieves in 1980. But tarry . . .

The tale is not yet fully told.

43

Wedding Bells Again

In the spring of 1985 Peter was baking for his Old Bailey appearance over the Antique Porcelain business when a crop of fresh hopefuls drifted towards the morgue at Paddington. In the clubhouse, a West End smoothie clubowner, Tony Engleman, introduced an attractive brunette to Peter.

'This is Elaine, my receptionist in Bruton Place. She plays a little tennis and has just joined the club. Could you find time to give her a hit?'

Engleman rarely wasted words. The handsome swarthy Jew had a panache that mesmerised women, but Elaine was recovering from the hypnosis and moving on. Tony found a squat for her, and was now sorting out an old 'player'. He was certain Peter would bite.

'Hello, Elaine. Glad to meet you.'

The thief extended a paw and Madam's eyes told him he was of interest. She obviously knew what she was doing and where she was going.

The resident still-life closely monitored Elaine that spring. Peter had the odd hit with the 'receptionist' but she chose to get hold of one of Chris Mitias's gang to screw, a worldly man-about-town (or so he thought) with a Porsche. But, having conquered with such consummate ease, he was mystified as to why he so quickly got the bum's rush.

'That little girl's a weirdo. I have a date with her and she fails to show. When I find her and enquire why, she tells me to piss off.'

Certainly, Elaine was a strange one. Handbag always crammed with money, she was a free agent who treated relationships just as casually as any hooker treats a transient punter. It amused the thief to watch the lady operate, but others were less pleased with her. Alan Waller, the club captain, announced one day, 'A strange little girl. I think she's mad.'

Waller may have been pompous, but he had a point. Peter knew him well – they had started the tennis pilgrimage together in '80 and

Peter lured him to the tennis club the next year when he himself joined. The pair had drifted apart after that. In spite of his grotty bookshop, Waller had a certain conservatism that appealed to the seedy snob element at the club. Peter was a good client of his book 'clinic', but Waller was always likely to opt for his own ilk. They had drifted apart in mutual irreverence.

Yet he too was flawed. Like seventy per cent of Peter's acquaintances, like Clyde, Roger, Taters, not to mention J.C. himself, he was an Aquarian. This astrological factor plays an inexplicable role in this tale. Several months earlier at a club dance, Marjory Orr, a friend of Fiona's whose star-charts found their way into the *Sunday Times*, had warned Peter of the significance of his star-sign. At the time, the thief – thinking it a load of bollocks – was more intent on pawing her attractive bosoms. He qualified only for a smart cuff. Exit Marjory. Enter Elaine.

Strangely enough, in his entire CV there was not an Aquarian woman to be found. It's all in the stars.

It was a lean spring. A foray to a provincial museum had kept the ship afloat while Taters, smarting at being left out of the pillage at the Antique Porcelain Company, was doing his own thing. Then, one morning that spring, he shuffled into the club.

'Found a furrier's in Marylebone we can have a go at,' he wheezed. 'It's a block in Clipstone Street. Better still, we can approach it from an empty there.'

'Empty in the block, eh? Well, we'd better have a shufty.'

Bolsover House in Clipstone Street threw up an odd situation. The main door of the block appeared to be permanently left open; in fact it was not even possible to secure it from the inside. The furrier on the third floor would have to be walled, a noisy business at night and doubly dangerous when the enemy have direct access to you from the street.

The empty, however, was perfect, coming out at fifth-floor level and leaving a trip of some thirty yards over a dozen roofs, with limited obstacles. This was an important factor for the pair, whose combined age was one hundred and twenty-seven. Most men of seventy-three were walking gingerly on sticks. Many were already in the hereafter. Peter supposed there was not another one in the kingdom who would contemplate crashing through a wall, humping a hundredweight of sacks of mink skins and coats over a roof five storeys up, with the sole help of a fifty-four-year-old. But there was only one Taters. The two of them were the last of a dying breed of cat burglars. Surely, they deserved to succeed.

Succeed they did. Jamming the front door of the block (ineffectually as it turned out) with cardboard, they belted their way through a party wall from the stairwell. As the gap opened they were delighted. The make-or-break circuit started to howl from inside the premises, as the diminutive Taters struggled through the gap to silence it. But the external bell kept silent. They followed their usual drill: back up to the roof, give the enemy twenty minutes and, if they don't show, get to work. They didn't show.

Taters went back into the premises and flung garments and skins out for Peter to put into his old enemies, now more friendly – a bundle of mailbag sacks. They had filled ten before a dishevelled Taters, poking out his fine old head, croaked, 'There's another cupboard high up. I can't get it open. Do you fancy coming in for a try?'

Peter didn't fancy it one little bit.

'Leave it out. We've got plenty. And we can't leave the stairs unguarded.'

So they humped the sacks over the roofs to the empty in number 2 Bolsover Street. Peter became irritated with Taters's slow progress.

'Come on, George, we can't be up here all night. Get a move on.'

As soon as he uttered the words, driven by nervous fear, he rebuked himself. 'You cunt, how dare you say a word to the old man? Just because your arsehole is bottly.' He felt better, bollocking himself.

They made two trips to get the haul to the empty where, resting in the gloom, Peter caught sight of them in an abandoned mirror. Sweat was streaming down his face, while the old hussar was crouched like a moulting eagle. His beak was open and he was panting, but he was dry as a bone, his aged skin utterly devoid of moisture. They would never see the like of him again.

At the right moment, they came out into the street and loaded up a Ford van that Peter had borrowed. It went sweet as a nut.

This was to be Peter's last foray into the fur trade. Taters? I'm afraid not. He still had a few mountains to climb, but it was to be the final matinée the pair would play together. Thirty-five years of joint pillage had come to an end.

But the strike had further significance. It led directly to the thief's third marriage – or fourth, depending on who you listen to.

As the weather warmed, a minor task he set himself when he arrived each morning at the club was to water the clay show court. Maintenance staff were thin on the ground, and the surface of the old court, laid in 1927, was often as parched as a desert, swirling with grit and heavily potholed. It was a time-consuming job, but Peter found it relaxing. Besides, on bail and cold-shouldered by most, he was anxious to be getting some plus points.

When he finished he would languish under a parasol, feet up on the table with a brandy in his hand. One day, Elaine appeared looking the part and dressed to kill. Tennis was not on her agenda for the day.

'I'm going to a fur auction,' she yelped breathlessly. 'Going to get a blue fox jacket.'

She looked very young.

'Don't,' said Peter. 'You'll get little wear out of it. The sleeves and armpits will scuff in a couple of months.'

'I don't care. I've promised myself a fur.'

'Want a fur, do you?' It was the voice of Flash Harry speaking now. 'Well, be here this time tomorrow. I'll have a full-length black Glamma mink for you.'

Elaine shot him a quizzical look, but something told her that the sun-bronzed, paunched Peter had meant it.

'OK,' she said. 'I'll see how good your word is.'

She turned on her heel and vanished.

It was sunny the next day and Peter had just finished his self-appointed task. His feet were up, the brandy was by his side, when Elaine appeared on cue. She said nothing and Peter casually indicated that she should go to the lady's changing room. She got the gist and shot up the stairs. Seconds later a delighted whoop revealed that she had found her present. She came back into the sunshine, belting the dark-sheened fur around her waist. On her, it looked very fetching indeed.

'Is this really for me? What have I got to do?'

'It's a prezzy. You don't have to do anything. Well, plant a kiss on an old man's cheek, if you like.'

Elaine did so, with some relish.

'Anyway,' she said, 'you're not an old man. You don't look a day over forty.'

The kiss and the specious lie were hardly cheap at the price, but such is the surreptitious malice of middle-aged largesse. Peter was not entirely sure why he'd indulged in it, but he reaped the 'reward' in feigned surprise.

'That type of bullshit will get you almost anything. I'm in my fifties, you know, but maybe the tan sheds a few years.'

'Why do so many members here ignore you?'

'You've noticed, have you? I'm on bail for theft. It's all a misunderstanding, it'll be sorted out. Doesn't mean we can't be friends.'

It all began there. Fifty-four to twenty-five, that was the age difference, but they did become friends, pals, conspirators almost, pisstaking together at the expense of the still-life. But like many young people in the West End scene, Elaine liked a snort of coke. The thief had one or two friends who had access to it and, though he'd never been a user himself, he was aware of the buzz it might give to a fifty-year-old's sex fantasies.

Elaine took to playing tennis with Peter daily. Then her sports car needed a service and the thief was helpful. Elaine took to visiting the drab flat in Sutherland Avenue, even staying the odd night, always sleeping with her jeans on. She saw the potential of the place and liked it.

Then, of course, the inevitable happened. In wine and powder one night, Elaine announced, 'I'm going to fuck you tonight. In fact, I think I'll be your next wife.'

She went on to achieve both these aims, proving how determined emancipated young women are in their freedom. Peter was neither pleased nor displeased. It was the natural consequence of his criminal largesse. With the mink coat, he had bought himself a wife.

But kisses at fifty are expensive, and supporting his resurrected lust, he ran into a touch of the shorts only a couple of weeks before his wedding date at Marylebone Town Hall, where Chris Mitias had sportingly agreed to be his best man. In fact, he tried half-heartedly to swerve. On their way to make some initial enquiries about marriage at the town hall, Peter procrastinated, dawdling beside the window of a friend's car showroom. Elaine, sensing his reluctance, struck at him with a viper's tongue.

'Do you want to get fucking married or don't you?' she snarled. 'Well, I do, so hurry up.'

She was mini-skirted and looked about sixteen. When asked about a special marriage licence, the ageing spinster at the register office asked, po-faced, 'Both over twenty-five? If not, you may need a consent form.'

The thief blushed. Over twenty-five? He felt like one of Captain Mainwaring's mob in the Home Guard. But Elaine was up for it. Sweetly she produced a birth certificate that showed she had just turned twenty-five. Here we go again, the thief thought, still feeling very foolish.

His pal Arthur had fired him up with a bit of money – he even gave them a car for the honeymoon and, with another old pal, Brian Turner, paid for the reception at Sheila Kelly's pub in Lanark Place. It was, all in all, an undignified time for the thief. He knew he had to go to work again, but he decided to put it off till after the nuptials. The honeymoon, though, would have to hold fire.

Sheila put on a lovely spread. Champagne flowed, but all the time the thief's mind was dwelling on the bit of work he had to attend to. He was due to return to his old happy hunting ground at Ascot, where the mistress of an Italian industrialist lived. Still hoping that Emma of Aldgate's prediction that 'you'll be lucky together' had some currency, he called up Roger. He concealed his inherent dislike of the fellow, for if they were indeed a lucky pair his disaffection was a small price to pay.

'So you married Elaine? You're a lucky man,' Roger joshed. 'But it looks to me like it'll need some funding. So where are we picnicking now?'

The myopic lens glinted in challenge.

'Ascot,' said Peter simply. 'I'm going back to an old bit of work. A chum marked my card as to the mistress of a wop millionaire. She accumulates baubles. I've been down there, spadework's done, ladder's *in situ*. Chances are above average.'

As he found himself obliged to encourage the prat, he suddenly felt in need of the gypsy's good-luck premonition.

'Ascot?' said Roger. 'Warm old manor. And they know you. Were you not nicked there some years back?'

Roger's prodding irked him and suddenly he came off the defensive, barking, 'Yes, it's warm. Yes, they did know me. Windsor, I was nicked at. Apart from that, I've punched holes in practically every property from the Wheatsheaf in Virginia Water to Swinley Bottom – and that was when it was the sole preserve of gentlefolk. Now it's all pop stars, Arabs, fashion designers, and scummy motor traders. The inept aristocracy, unable to compete, retreated further west.'

The snob in Peter was blossoming now. He went on, 'Of course, the *nouveaux riches* are more fearful of trespassers. They expect them. The old money didn't cosset themselves with alarm devices, cameras, sensors. None of those were about when I used to hold the court.'

Roger impatiently cut short the monologue.

'What about this courtesan, then? Will she have availed herself of the wonders of modern science?'

Roger's dry pragmatism put the thief back on course.

'Yes, she's got protection. But I think we can circumvent it. Especially with the bit of luck your guru Emma predicted for us.'

Roger gave a sardonic smile. He clearly felt small regard for the old thief but at least he seemed to think that Peter had a sense of humour.

'When did you go down there?'

'Last week. Had Elaine with me. She fancied she was up for it herself, but the twilight and owls hooting took the buzz out of larceny for her. So I secreted a ladder before getting Bonnie back to base.'

Roger let out a genuine guffaw of admiration and amazement.

'You're fucking mad.'

'I fancy popping down there tonight. There's a good parker at a pub not far from the house. You up for it?'

Parking discreetly at the pub, they soon crossed the fence that protected the estate. The moon broke through as they crept by the laurels and rhododendrons before skirting a stream beside a fine house. Peter was not humming hymn tunes – another of his usual nervous habits when on a bit of work – but whisper-singing *sotto voce*.

I'll tip-toe
By your window
In the moonlight
By the willow tree . . .

He knew in his water that they were about to be lucky. Carelessly drawn curtains allowed the intruders to observe Madam, a beautiful woman reclining on a sofa and glued to the box. Staff, in their annexe, were paying homage to the same god. Everything was in favour of Satan and his advocates.

They pitched the ladder to a bedroom window. Entry was academic, for the burglar catches were not on. Even with the most sophisticated protection, you have to remember to use it. Yes, it looked more and more like Madam was about to be the victim of Emma's prophecy – to her a curse. With professional caution, Peter let the torch's faint beam survey the bedroom. Moving on tiptoe, he locked the door from the inside and switched on the light.

A quick search of drawers in the dresser and tallboy revealed nothing. He located a couple of minks in a cupboard, which assured expenses, and then another cupboard in a rebated alcove caught his eye. It was locked, but the silver-steel jemmy prised it open effortlessly. There in front of him was a Chubb safe, quite ancient and with no combination, just a single keyhole. Pausing, he listened to the house sleeping, then tried the handle. It was locked. Maybe Emma was to be thwarted after all.

Having a final shufty round the gracious room, he noticed Madam's handbag on the floor, partly concealed by the bed's drapes. Pray God, the safe's key would be inside it. Before he could reach the bag, a hiss from the window startled him. Roger's pale face appeared like a grotesque vision of the Madonna atop the ladder.

'You're taking a long time.'

Peter, wiping sweat from his forehead, signalled that all was well. He rummaged through the handbag. An elongated Chubb key fell out, and it fitted the safe, turning silently in the lock. He swung back the door. An enormous gem-pouch met his eye; it immediately changed ownership.

Peter checked the contents hurriedly. His chum had told true: Madam was undoubtedly gem-oriented.

Tripping back towards the car in the moonlight, Emma took on a new status in Peter's eyes.

'We've had a blinding touch, Roger. I fancy there's around half a million in tom here.'

As they belted back along the A30 to London, Roger checked out the pouch for himself. Suddenly, he whooped in spontaneous delight. Peter inwardly whooped too. He had the Elaine support money now. No more madness this year, no more hurry-ups. Just snorting and rutting. Roger interrupted his reverie.

'What will it come to our way?'

'Enough.'

The assessors announced to reward-seekers and bounty-hunters a forty-thousand-pound incentive. It would be a ten per cent tariff, meaning that Madam had lost four hundred grand in jewels. Which was perhaps not all that much to an Italian tycoon, bearing in mind the corrupt house rules in that country.

Didier flew to Heathrow and a trade was called in his room at the Post House. There was no undignified haggling and Peter acceded to the Belgian's first shout.

'Peter, a superb parcel. I'll pay eighty-five thousand for it. It will be in two payments, one today and another in two weeks.'

Peter and Elaine took off on honeymoon to the Lake District, slipping into an old-fashioned hotel at Windermere. Checking in, he had been jarred by the receptionist's enquiry. 'And a separate room for your daughter, sir?'

'The lady is my wife,' the thief growled.

'But of course, sir. How silly of me. Will a fine double room over-looking the lake be all right?'

Meanwhile Roger and his 'friend' went to Marbella while Emma took her brood to Southend and a very attractive lady DI at Ascot began a long, hot, unrewarding summer of investigations. It would bring her to bitch to her handsome sergeant, 'They deserved to be burgled. Burglar screws not in, alarm off, safe-key left lying about. And *I'm* supposed to find Chummy.'

The Regional Crime Squad lost no time in contacting Dave Stephenson at Savile Row.

'Looks like your boy's enjoying his bail. The computer and the local at Ascot think he's been calling in there. Why did he get bail, by the way?'

Stephenson had to tell his Commander, 'They seem to want to put everything down to Scotty.'

They certainly did. Was it not in the cards?

44

Victor, or Little by Little

TATERS was to be nicked in that summer of '85. It got quite a lot of press coverage, a man of seventy-four breaching a wall into a gown shop in Kensington High Street on a Sunday afternoon. It was only discovered when the owner returned to the premises unpredictably and found a hole in his wall. A chase then ensued across the rooftops.

In his halcyon days, George would have shown the police a clean pair of heels, but youth prevailed and a young copper caught up with him. The Super at Earl's Court nick was a prat who took himself seriously and – when Elaine turned up at Peter's prompting to do the honours – determined to prevent the septuagenarian having bail.

'Mrs Gulston? Mrs *Peter* Gulston? You have a cheek coming here to offer yourself for bail. We know your bloody husband only too well.'

The zealot strode to the window, from where he could actually see Peter lounging against a car bonnet just outside the nick. It clearly irked the good man to see the tanned sybarite propped up by the sporty BMW. After the interview, Elaine emerged close to tears.

'What a rude man. He has it in for you.'

So does half the Met, Peter mused. Not to mention the Regional.

Back at the club, they held a conference of war. Elaine thought she might ask her dad – but he was still too near Gulstonville to be acceptable. Catching sight of that most romantically inclined of liberals and supporter of lost causes, Larry Adler, Peter called to him.

'Larry, a word in your ear.'

Larry had Victor Lownes in tow, but Victor was out of earshot as the harmonica player, whose face had come to look like that instrument, came over.

'Larry, an elderly friend of mine needs a bailsman, probably around five hundred, which I'll stick in, of course. I think you may have seen him around here once or twice. George Chatham.'

'Sure I have. You said he was a legend. I'd be delighted to stand bail for a legend. What have I gotta do?'

'What's that you're gonna do, Larry?' It was Victor, approaching with a stern look on his face. 'I don't want you to stand bail for evil men. I mean it, Larry.'

'Victor, I've given my word. It's for an old man. I can't say no now. Please.'

But Victor's stance was a moral one.

'Larry, I don't want you to do it. If you value my friendship.'

'Victor, you can't tell me what to do. I've a mind of my own.'

The pair disappeared into the pavilion to change and were still bitching at one another as they went onto Court Five. Peter hailed Larry.

'Larry, forget all about it. It was good of you to want to help.'

Larry smiled and waved. He was grateful for the bolt-hole. Lownes was riled even more and the bitching reached the level of invective by the time they came off court.

'I'm leaving now, Larry. You know I'm right.'

Peter and his wife were embarrassed by the exchange. When Victor reappeared from the changing room, suited and booted, Peter approached him.

'I'm very sorry, Mr Lownes. I don't mean to make trouble between you and Larry.'

'So you should be sorry, getting Larry involved with an evil man,' Victor barked, totally unappeased. It was the reference to evil which crashed Peter into overdrive.

'Evil man? Who do you think you are, you horrible prat? You spent your life bending the rules at the Playboy Club. You're one to talk about evil men. If we were somewhere else I'd teach you a lesson in manners.'

Out of the corner of his eye, Peter saw Larry disappear into the pavilion. Victor bulged with outrage.

'I'm going to report you to the committee,' he shouted. 'I won't have you talking to me like that.'

Peter was on the point of booting him up the arse, but Victor saw it coming and sped off.

Larry came out again.

'Peter, Victor fell off his horse last year, you know. He's never been the same old Victor.'

'Forget the bail, Larry. It was a kindly thought.'

A bailee was found eventually and Taters was free to pillage again. Victor Lownes did not report the thief; perhaps his actions were tempered by memories of his foolish battle with arch-schemer and top bookmaker Cyril Stein, which he lost.

*   *   *

Waiting for the trial at the Old Bailey was like waiting for Godot. It put an additional strain on both the thief's nerves and his outgoings. Elaine refurbished the flat, while Peter put in motion the transfer of tenancy into her name. He spent a lot of his time at Rousseau's, playing cards with his betters. He probably lost around forty thousand sating his weakness. Elaine, on the other hand, was not an expensive choice of playmate. She was a gentle little thing who really regarded him as a surrogate dad. She was greatly amused when he went out to work, telling her friends, 'Peter's out playing Raffles again. I wish he wouldn't!'

In her way, Elaine was an adventurous, talented woman. She had an IQ in the 130s and spoke French and Italian fluently. She was also a fine horsewoman, and not a bad tennis player, having once won a club tournament in Rimini. She had lived and worked in Italy for several years, when she drove tourists in a hackney carriage around Sorrento. (She prevailed on Peter to bring the nag back from Italy, and stabled it near Epping, close to her parents' home.)

There was no malice in Elaine. She was simply a lovely girl, seeking temporary refuge. But she also had a tough streak, which surfaced when needed. She may have liked a snort of Charlie, but it was not her master. Loyalty was Elaine's strong suit.

A much more worrying problem arose, however, when Didier didn't produce the second and final instalment of forty thousand pounds, and the number at Waterloo became unobtainable. 'Mr Reliable' had gone to earth.

Roger was unsympathetic.

'It's down to you, mate. He's your man. I look to you for my twenty grand.'

The boy was right – it was his problem. How to solve it was another matter. A trip to Brussels wasted a monkey, as Didier had vanished without a trace, his elegant premises boarded up. All Peter could do was bake and pull up what he could for Roger, who was still bitching. The anticipated restful summer was not to blossom and it looked as if Peter would have to go to work yet again.

Meanwhile, Chief Superintendent Stephenson had another strike on his plate in Mayfair. Though he did not connect Peter with it, the boss-man at the Central Robbery Squad at Finchley did.

'Dave, the armed robbery at Bentley's,' he said. 'We think Scotty might have been involved. Odd as it may sound, the word on the ground is that an out-of-work actor was conned into performing there, we think with Scotty, and probably waving a water pistol. Unaware that the robbery was for real!'

Stephenson got the pipe out, as was his wont in moments of stress. He took his time lighting it.

'Scotty on an armed robbery? No, no, not his scene. An actor with a water pistol? Christ! What makes you fancy Peter?'

The governor at Finchley had hunted Peter in his days as an aide, and he had a healthy respect for his abilities.

'MO. Who have you ever heard of who wedges the door of the jeweller's, locking himself in and others out, and then has an idiot bellowing to staff, not disguised, "Back! This is a robbery!" while he waves a pipe or a water pistol. And meanwhile he and his – this is important – *elderly* friend clear out the window.'

The governor hesitated. This was clearly a bitter thought.

'The old boy's doing it so calmly our mob think he's staff.

'"Open the door," they yell at him, rapping the window, "there's a robbery taking place."

'"Yes, I know," bellows Chummy, "I'm the one who's doing it."

'I'm sure as hell it's Scotty. Then he scarpers over the roofs.'

Stephenson sat up, alert.

'Almost identical to what happened across the street at the Antique Porcelain Company. Worth giving him a tug. But it makes no sense. The Regional think it was him at Ascot the other night. Some biddy lost half a mill in gems. It can't all be down to Peter!'

'Anyway, there's no point giving him a spin. The gear's long gone. I suggest we target him again. Heavy surveillance.'

The governor from Finchley nodded.

'Right. But we'll have to get authorisation. The budget may not stretch to it. They expect us to catch live-wires on shoestrings.'

As this exchange was taking place, Peter was sunning himself in the once-fashionable Queens Hotel in Southsea, lying around the pool drinking chilled wine. Elaine was getting bored.

'Can't we go back to London? It's dead here.'

On their return, an anxious Diana sought him out.

'They're spinning everyone. I think they're looking for a parcel of tom. How's the child bride? Got to you, has she?'

She kissed him lightly on the cheek and left.

But it wasn't the Regional or Stephenson or the targeting that sealed his fate. As he was having tea with a pal from Brighton, a third party joined them.

'Trevor, this is the infamous Peter Scott,' the Brighton man said with barely concealed irony. 'Peter, this is Trevor Davis.'

A tall, gaunt youth held out a flaccid hand. It firmed as they shook. There was a friendly smile on the lad's face.

'You like a furrier's, Peter,' the Brighton man said. 'Trevor's got one that needs attending to.'

With the porcelain tucked around his bollocks and Didier on the missing list, he swallowed the bait in one terse question.

'Where?'

It turned out to be in Marylebone. Anxious to give Mayfair a miss, he decided to pop it. Well, the lad had a nice smile, he looked determined, and the introduction was from the soundest of sources. He was up for it.

'Where exactly, Trevor?'

45

As Any Ageing Cat Burglar Will Tell You

It is not the élitist CID crime squads which are the thief's immediate enemies. As any ageing cat burglar will tell you, it is the uniformed, the sharp young bobbies on the beat, wrongly nicknamed Wallies, who present the greatest threat.

Now, in the autumn of '85, a Chief Inspector of that ilk in Marylebone lectured his flock.

'Right. Settle down. A determined thief has been seen prowling the Great Portland Street area. He's currently on bail from West End Central and we think he's found a target on our patch. We haven't the resources to follow him around, but even if we had I doubt it would be rewarding. What he's after is a matter of speculation, but he has a long history of fur and jewel thefts. Furs are the most likely on our manor. So if and when an alarm goes off on a furrier's in the next few weeks I want a lively response – from you lads on the ground and from the area cars. If there's the slightest indication of an intruder on the premises, I want the block covered. Understand?'

The audience nodded.

'Good. Any questions?'

A young skipper spoke up.

'Is there a description of Chummy, sir?'

'Good point. He's Peter Craig Gulston, alias Peter Scott. Six foot one, suntanned, often tracksuited. Fifty-four years of age, but don't let that deceive you. He plays tennis, keeps fit. There's photos and a description available in the CID office. It would be a feather in our cap to nab Chummy, but a word of caution – he will resist arrest. OK?'

The meeting broke up and the uniformed boys were on red alert.

At this time money was a constant source of worry to the thief. With the porcelain in the main unsold, he was gambling erratically and supporting Elaine's extravagances. It was time for the accommodation with Trevor Davis to bear fruit. The target was the Marylebone furrier's.

Making an entry in Portland Street, a fire escape led Trevor and the thief to the roof of the newish building concealed by Portland Street, Great Titchfield Street, and Mortimer Street. They got entry to the stairwell of the furrier's block.

A seemingly vulnerable hardboard wall was investigated with bit and brace. Experience told Peter it must be protected, but his young companion's enthusiasm clouded his judgement. The hardboard resisted until an audible click startled Peter.

'I think we've activated the alarm system.'

His young friend was less certain, thinking the old boy was bottly. They moved away, following the corridor round to a flat roof where they saw a window, just accessible. Peter then made another inexplicable error of judgement. He agreed that Trevor could bash the window and climb into the showroom. In his water he knew the alarm had been set off.

Inside, he was partially reassured by the existence of a bolt-hole in neighbouring premises, a building on Mortimer Street. They might use it if the worst came to the worst.

'The furs are in a padlocked cupboard. I'll need the bolt-cutters.'

No sooner had Trevor spoken than Peter heard voices from somewhere near the foot of the fire escape. It was the enemy!

'The law are here,' he hissed. 'We'll have to scarper.'

Trevor left only reluctantly. Back on the roof, they crossed to a trap-door on the roof in Mortimer Street, going in and securing the hatch behind them. They settled down to wait and listen. They would probably have to bake there all night – if they were lucky.

But minutes later, heavy feet above told them PC Plod had worked out their probable escape route. Someone was trying to raise the trap-door.

'Could have gone this way,' they heard a voice bellow.

Normally, secured premises would have been discounted, but not tonight. The coppers went on struggling with the trap-door.

'They know we're here,' Peter whispered.

The brace of thieves, now very alarmed, investigated their new prison. It ended in a go-nowhere stairwell bottom. They went to the front door of the block, which led out into Mortimer Street. A peep through the letter-box confirmed a police presence on the other side and put the dampers on the idea of making a dash for freedom by that route. They were trapped.

'We're surrounded,' Peter said. 'And I think they know we're here. Best chance, and that's not much, is that we conceal ourselves in the well and hope they quit the roof, and then we can climb back up.'

Trevor nodded in agreement. The law were plotted on the roof. They'd be finding their keyholder before flushing the building out with dogs. The pair sat on the stairs, each in his private misery, Trevor laconically puffing on a fag. They were trapped like shit-house rats and could only await the inevitable.

The enemy were so sure they were there that they dispensed with the key and shouldered the door down, charging in like cavalry through a breached wall. They soon found the timid pair cowering in the well.

'Well, well, look what we have here,' a young skipper laughed. 'You're nicked, lads.'

Both were remanded to Wormwood Scrubs for two weeks. On their next appearance, Trevor got bail. Peter roasted. He was visited daily by a then-loyal Elaine bringing lots of goodies. It was a novel experience for her, traipsing through the visiting room, admired by all.

So it turned out that he was in custody when the time for the Old Bailey trial came round. They were in Court Twenty-two – a poorly ventilated shoebox. Peter, on legal aid, suffered one of the indignities that often attend the defendant with a poor defence in law – a last-minute change of counsel, only meeting his new pleader, Stephen Batten, on the morning the case started. The Judge, Bruce Laughland, was concerned about this turn in events.

'Mr Scott, would you care for an adjournment to discuss your defence with Mr Batten?'

Not really, thought Peter. Batten looked sharp enough, but being nicked bang to rights in the Marylebone furrier's had taken the heart not only out of Peter, but out of his advisers. Looking at it pragmatically, Peter knew his time was up.

'I don't think we can put you in the witness box. The business of the Woburn silver will be canvassed by the prosecution. It could be very damaging. As it stands there's little against you – the wedge on its own is hardly enough. As to the verbals – I refer to your extraordinary admission when you returned from Dunstable with Chief Superintendent Stephenson when you said, "I'll get ten years for this" – I propose to make a submission that it is not admissible. I think we may well have it out.'

Batten had a fine grasp for a barrister seconded at short notice.

'Do as you see fit,' Peter told him. 'I maintain my innocence.'

But the thief's words were parroted and had a hollow ring which did not escape Batten. He went into action skilfully, having the verbal admissions ruled inadmissible. A quartet of senior police officers trooped into the box, telling of the search and how they found the wooden slat in Sutherland Avenue. The jury grew inquisitive, sending a note up to the judge.

'Why,' they wanted to know, 'did the police go to Sutherland Avenue in the first place?'

While this sensible question was ventilated, the jury was sent out. Chief Superintendent Stephenson went into the box. He told of West End Central's watching brief as the Bedfordshire police searched for the Woburn silver and a portion of Batten's attempt to conceal the matter was breached. Certainly the judge now knew of it. But the jury did not, and so the damage was limited.

Stephenson then told how his alert officer had noticed the slat of wood with the missing triangular piece, and how he, Stephenson, had had it sent for forensic examination. And so the tale of West End Central's 'good fortune' unfolded. It would surely have been a very foolish thief who, having cut a wooden wedge from a slat in his bathroom cupboard, replaced the slat in the cupboard and then left the offending wedge behind after burgling premises in Bond Street of property worth more than a million pounds. It was hardly the action of a professional.

It's a matter for you, members of the jury.

Peter was called to the box in the absence of the jury to give evidence on oath. He could throw no light on the wooden wedge. But, given the opportunity, he was able to deliver the following monologue to the judge.

'What I find extraordinary, my Lord, is the actions of the Bedford police, who find twelve silver spoons at the same time as this piece of wood turns up. They are significant enough to have me taken in custody to Dunstable and held. I am never charged with the Woburn theft. Nor have I ever set eyes on the silver spoons again. What's become of them?'

Peter's thrust was clear. If he was fitted up with silver spoons which then vanished, it was very likely the wedge was contrived too. Judge Laughland swerved cleverly, enquiring of Stephen Batten, 'I think the Woburn silver was recovered. Is there a suggestion here that your client was instrumental in its return?'

'My Lord, those are not my instructions.'

Batten's denial had a hollow ring, almost as if he believed that Peter had assisted in the recovery of the silver.

Batten did not call Peter into the witness box. He advised the jury that the onus was on the Crown to prove their case.

'Scott can throw no light on how the slat of wood came to be found in Sutherland Avenue. He certainly denies all knowledge of it. His going into the witness box would be of no assistance to you in your deliberations. He can give no explanation for its presence.'

The prosecutor was more direct, addressing Laughland in terms of the defence amounting to one of 'plant'. He asked the jury to recall the four policemen's evidence, and the quality of it. He reminded them that two were senior officers, with the inference that they were beyond reproach. In the absence of any explanation from Mr Scott, it would be difficult to reject the officers' evidence.

Laughland summed up fairly, finally telling the jury to use their own common sense. Then he sent them out.

Two to three hours later, when they failed to return a verdict, they were recalled to be told that Judge Laughland was now in a position to accept a majority verdict of any ten jurors. They retired again for a further half-hour and came back with a ten-to-two verdict: guilty.

The judge ordered a retirement before passing sentence. The court emptied save for the barristers and an elderly man sitting unobserved at the back of the court, who now became privy to their speculations. It was John, his quartermaster from the West Country, playing *doppelgänger*. The prosecutor thought twelve years was the tariff. Batten took the view that this was too severe, canvassing a sentence in the eight-year range. Ten years seemed to be a compromise, as the two huddled barristers bartered in *sotto voce*, probably unaware of the elderly man dozing in the gloom at the back of the court. They eventually rose to join the judge in his chambers, only to be met at the door by his clerk, who announced, 'Judge Laughland is returning. He is not in need of any guidance.'

The judge began in an exploratory fashion.

'I am not clear as to what part you played in this theft, which the prosecution seek to describe as a commando operation. You are a man of a certain age – fifty-four I believe – with a long criminal record, and now you stand convicted of a theft in excess of one million pounds.'

Peter faced Laughland stoically, thinking time up, time to pay, as the judge's not unkindly voice continued.

'A theft of this magnitude would normally attract a sentence in double figures. However, I take into consideration your age and your health which Mr Batten, your able counsel, has referred to. As to the part you played . . .'

Laughland paused, almost as if he were struggling with himself. 'The least sentence I can pass in the circumstances is one of four years. You will go to prison for four years.'

Coming quickly downstairs to the cell, a beaming Stephen Batten perched on a chair, legs crossed, cheroot in hand, and greeted him.

'What do you think of that for a sentence?' he asked, obviously chuffed. 'I was pleased you thanked Judge Laughland. It's a very lenient sentence. You have reason to be grateful to him.'

He got up to shake Peter's hand.

'Make good use of it.'

Which, as Stephen Batten would be surprised to learn ten years later, Peter Gulston did.

46

Books and Roses

IT was almost six years since he had last left Wandsworth, the old Alma Mater in Trinity Road, to win his appeal and be paroled. His return was in his stars, unavoidable, even an appealing destiny. He'd left the place then with larceny and revenge in his heart, a luxury he could not rightfully justify and which made it certain he would return, as surely as night follows day.

There was no Rolls-Royce processing on this trip. He was no longer a Wickstead Special. He went through reception leisurely to be housed in the reception annexe of G, H, & K Wing, but not before an old chum in reception, Roger Metzner, had marked his card.

'Hello, Peter, you had a result. You'll be delighted to know an old pal of yours is here, George Alexander. He'll be on governor's* tomorrow when he hears you've arrived.'

A chief officer sitting on the reception board recognised him.

'Back to Scott again? Used to be Gulston. Well, think you could keep your nose clean in the library?'

Peter nodded. It was a good berth in any prison but, as there was generally little or no work in Wandsworth, it would be an oasis here.

'Make sure you don't let me down,' the chief barked with mock severity.

He caught a glimpse of Alexander on exercise the next morning. George ducked his nut and Peter showed no signs of annoyance. It paid a dividend. Alexander got himself transferred to the Scrubs the next day. Peter's arrival at the library was more traumatic. The screw confronted him, legs astride, arms resting by his waist.

'Well, well. If it isn't Scotty come back to us! It must be twenty-odd years since you were in the G, H, & K rehabilitation scheme. Mr Jenkins's clinic did you no good.'

This was one horrible cunt from Peter's aggressive past, now paunchier and no longer serving on the discipline staff. The screw was spinning out his time in the library till retirement.

---

* To be 'on governor's' is to apply for protection.

'Don't think I really want you here, Scotty. Can't see you lasting long, can you?'

Peter viewed the laconic prat with a malice that he did little to hide.

'No, I don't think I'll last long. You're still the same horrible cunt that you were a twenty stretch ago.'

Best exit quickly, Peter mused, hoping to depart with dignity. But the screw had mellowed.

'Yes, you're right, Scotty. I was always a horrible cunt. You remember that if you want to last in here.'

It had amused the screw to be reminded that he was a horrible cunt; he took it as a compliment, even preened at the direct language. The hater and the hated had known where they stood in those days. Peter was directed to the 'books back' cubbyhole at the bottom of the sparse library. This was the pisshole end of the job, and pay got better as you progressed to the 'front office'. At the back of the library, Peter's job was to take the books in, check the readers' cards, and examine the returns for any damage.

'Don't keep any books for anyone and report all damaged returns to me immediately. And no spitting, please.'

The screw could not resist a jibe that brought back Peter's cardinal sin of the early sixties – spitting at staff when they weren't looking. The screw had a long memory.

And so the war of wills began: Peter retaining any book he was asked to keep and ignoring all but the most obviously damaged returns, while the screw baited him relentlessly.

The majority of the library staff were amateur prisoners, surprised to be there. Most were in for substance offences, wallies to a man – a Wiltshire landowner, a Yorkshire businessman, a couple of Yiddish car dealers. Not an old-time lag, burglar, or con in sight. The screw's only toy was Scotty. Scotty do this, Scotty do that; can't you write, Scotty? Go back to the cubbyhole; you're not up to the front office.

For front office, the screw had chosen a con who Peter knew had an old conviction for rape. They kept a healthy silence as Chummy, now doing a stretch for dope, still peddled his wares from the safety of the library, assisted by the indolence of the screw and his sidekick Sir, a wee, bitter, two-faced Jock prat who bellowed much and noticed nothing. He was always driving the professional librarians – women seconded from the local council library service – mad with his snide remarks and foul language as they tried to order request books for cons.

The Swan was also working in the library, the same Swan who used his nut to deflect the enemy at Liz Taylor's in Englefield Green twenty-five years earlier when he told them, 'I'm from the *Jewish Chronicle.*'

They got a bridge four together, until midget Jock told them in best Spenlow and Jorkins style, 'Can't do that, lad. I don't mind, but you know what the screw's like.'

When Peter appeared at Marlborough Street to be committed for the attempt on the Marylebone furrier's, a strange cameo was played out. Roger turned up at half-time. He'd prised a visit out of the local Old Bill. They had a five-minute chat.

'You had a result,' he simpered, bunging Peter a copy of the *Daily Telegraph.* 'How will you go on this one?'

How indeed?

'Probably get eighteen months on top,' he said as laconically as he could. But as he spoke, he saw two dangerous-looking law eyeing them from behind the glass partition. They had that hawk-like, predatory look. Peter drew Roger's attention to them.

'I don't fancy the look of that mob,' he whispered.

Roger glanced at them.

'Never seen them before.'

But he had. Coming back up from the cells ten minutes later to sign for some cash, Peter saw Roger in a chummy pow-wow with the pair of them. None of them noticed Peter, but it was no surprise when the two hawks appeared at his cell door.

'Police here to see you. Want to see them?' asked the jailer who was with them. 'I'll dwell if you want.'

There was never any love lost between screws and the élitist spivs of the force. Peter was curious.

'OK, I'll see them. No need to stay.'

They were a DI and a skipper from the Central Robbery Squad, and they got straight to the point.

'Since when did you take up armed robbery?' one of them asked, holding up a building society book in a sealed plastic bag. Peter knew its significance. His chum Arthur had lodged seven thousand in the Abbey National for Peter to await his signature, just before he himself was busted. The mob who busted him had a warrant for stolen jewellery.

'Armed robbery? Not my style,' Peter laughed, friendly-like. But he was telling the absolute truth.

'Not your style?' Hawkeye growled. 'So who put the money in your name in this building society book and why?'

'You know who put it there. It was Arthur. He sold some furniture he had stored for me, and put the money there for safe-keeping to stop me spieling it.'

The truthful answer did not suit.

'Furniture, eh? Not tom?' Hawkeye snapped. 'Do you know Bentley's in Bond Street?'

'Yes, I know it.'

'Ever been in it?'

'No, never.'

'Well, we think you have. You and some joker waving a gun held the staff up and cleared out the window with half a million in gems.'

'Not my scene, chaps. I left shooters behind forty years ago.'

'Not your scene? Listen, Scotty. An old prat is clearing out the window in Bond Street, the bells are going, our mob arrive and find they are locked out. Wonder of wonders, the door's wedged, so they bang on the window at Chummy, who waves to them as they shout, "Open the door! There's a robbery taking place!" And Chummy comes back, "I know, I'm doing it," then vanishes up the stairs and over the roofs. Now what do you make of that?'

'You think that was me? I'm fifty-five years of age, for Christ's sake.'

'You play tennis, you cunt, you're as fit as a thirty-year-old. Do you know what our governor said back at Finchley Central Robbery HQ? "Go and find Peter Gulston, he's the only man in England who'd get up to scarpering over roofs." And what do you think? When we go to Paddington Tennis Club, where you are virtually living, you've been on the missing list for a couple of weeks. That's why we fancy you.'

Peter allowed himself a smile: was everything in Mayfair down to him?

'I was on bail for a job in Bond Street. The area was off limits.'

'Really? Well, I think you popped Bentley's.'

Peter continued to smile. He saw the DI's point. Popping a tommer's on the same manor had the virtue of some sort of rough justice.

'I get your drift, but you're barking up the wrong tree.' Then Peter gave them a sharp shot. 'Have you asked Roger about it?'

'Roger who? We don't know any Roger.'

They went off the boil after that and settled for asking if he might know who did it? Did he know anyone else grafting on the manor?

Et cetera, et cetera. All in all, it ended quite friendly. Back in court, better was to follow.

When he appeared at the County of London Sessions, a diamond of a judge mused, 'If this matter was taken into consideration at the Old Bailey I must ask myself whether or not it would have added to your four-year sentence. On balance I think not. You are not a young man. I think eighteen months to run concurrently will satisfy justice. Good luck to you.'

So Peter went back to Wandsworth with not a day extra to serve. Trevor Davis, his young co-defendant, got community service. It was a blinding day all round, and back at Wandsworth Peter was met by congratulations from all, only excepting the screw.

'I was hoping you'd get a lagging on top. With seven on your plate I could have had you out of the library. Pity, really.'

The library war had forced them to develop a grudging respect for each other, Peter circumventing the screw's mandate whenever possible, the screw wearied, his retirement in sight.

On his final shift he gave Peter best.

'You fucked me, Scotty. I'm finished and you're still here. I thought I was just the same horrible cunt, but it looks a bit like I've mellowed and you haven't. Good luck anyway.'

He gave Peter a friendly dig in the ribs leaving the old dungeon after a thirty stretch serving Her Majesty the Queen.

Wifey Elaine visited Peter just twice in Wandsworth. The first time was to deliver an Oxford Paperback Dictionary, inscribed 'To Peter with love Elaine' on the cover leaf. (He has it still. At the top of the same leaf, a scribble indicates that it was for L42929 Scott, Library.) It was a sombre visit, with little to talk about. But there was one thing on Peter's mind. Elaine had her young life to lead and so he, not mindful of clinging to her future, canvassed divorce. She rejected the idea. It was the only reality broached that day in Wandsworth's enormous, impersonal visiting room.

She came once again, embarrassed, to ask, 'Did you mean it when you said you would give me a divorce?'

Peter adopted a false bonhomie, but he was sad at heart.

'If that's what you want. It's easy for you to get a quickie. All you have to say on your petition, Mrs Gulston, is that I had another name, unbeknownst to you. I was also a Peter Scott with a long criminal record. Tell them that and you'll be free in four or five months to get on with your life.'

'Will I qualify for Legal Aid?' the ever-pragmatic Elaine asked. 'I've never been divorced, never even been to a solicitor. You'll have to help me.'

She spoke hurriedly, making no attempt to conceal the elation in her voice. Peter felt not unlike those Orientals who, on encountering good fortune, purchase and release doves from the market-place.

And so it came about that a petition arrived from a solicitor's in Westbourne Grove alleging mental cruelty, deception, violence . . . the usual shit solicitors dig up once you consult them. A pox on them.

After he had done a mandatory year in Wandsworth, a friendly library screw gave him a leg-up.

'Fancy an open nick, Scotty? You've done your stint here. I'll have a word with Allocations. Don't see a problem.'

The Swan, who had driven Allocations mad, got an early transfer to Liverpool, a veritable pisshole, while one or two others (after rucking in the library) were hijacked to Durham. But Peter's patience paid off, and in the early autumn of '86 he was off to Spring Hill open nick near Aylesbury.

He was mildly surprised. A theft as large as he had committed could easily have disqualified him from open conditions.

A last pleasureless charade was to be played out before Peter left for the Butlins of the prison service. A production order was served on him to appear at Bloomsbury County Court. The freeholders of the Sutherland Avenue flat were anxious to evict Elaine, and not unnaturally they had to attack Peter to do so. There was some justice in their malice. Peter had obtained the tenancy through a back door, but before Elaine appeared they had offered to regularise it by offering him another flat. Peter indicated that he was staying put – foolishly in retrospect. In any case, the freeholders had no sympathy or benevolence now for the defenceless Elaine and were seeking possession.

Peter arrived at court in a prison van, handcuffed to two amiable North Country screws.

'We're playing the game with you. Don't let us down,' one of them said, uncuffing him.

A Legal Aid barrister was dismayed that a senior county court judge was sitting.

'Odd having him. Augurs badly. Got to tell you straight off, Mr Gulston, it looks like we're pissing into the wind. It's an application from a charity, and I see you have been made a criminal bankrupt at the Old Bailey for a sum of no less than four hundred and forty thousand. So even if you do succeed, the Official Receiver will pounce. But we'll give it a run.'

Elaine turned up in an ankle-length red fox coat and a wide-brimmed straw hat.

'I bought myself something to cheer myself up,' she said, but Peter knew it for the fanny it was. There was a new provider on the firm.

The Geordie screws were impressed when they saw his wife.

'Where did an old con like you find that?' they wanted to know.

She charmed everyone. She had a magnificent lunch complete with vino delivered at half-time for screws, counsel, Peter, and herself, and they quaffed and chatted in an ordinary third-floor room, there being no secure facility at the court. It was quite like Henley, with Elaine in her panama and fox.

But the writing was on the wall. Judgie was asking all the wrong questions and prompting the stumbling opposition when they got themselves anywhere near deep water. His Honour, the hearing completed, decided to give an extempore judgement as opposed to the (hopefully more considered) reserved one.

'I propose to read my judgement now. I am mindful that the defendant may have to be transported and accompanied over long distances from prison, so it is in everyone's interests I do so.'

With minimum ado he gave the charity possession, considering Elaine's position only so far as to say, 'It is never a pleasant task to deprive a young wife of her home, more so when her husband is in prison. But the law must be followed. I dare say Social Services may help.'

Looking at the elegant Elaine with scant sympathy, the prat assuaged his conscience in the legal prattle of English common law – the refuge of every well-heeled scoundrel in the land, and propagated by hordes of well-bred, ill-informed zealots who sit on the bench round the country. No wonder they are currently in such disarray.

When the court rose at ten minutes to four, the Geordie screws, winking, permitted another perk.

'You can have a visit with your wife upstairs till our transport arrives, if you like.'

But an alarmed Elaine shook her head. As far as she was concerned, conjugal rights were not on the agenda.

'No, no, I'm on a meter. It runs out at four o'clock.'

She gave the prisoner a quick peck and was gone. It was to be forever.

Transport was either late or had difficulty finding the court, though its front door was not hard to spot, on the Marylebone Road at the corner of Park Crescent. Eventually the court closed and Sirs and the handcuffed prisoner were let out of a side door onto Park Crescent to wait awkwardly on the pavement. The early-evening traffic was percolating out of the West End up from Portland Place into the Crescent and on to north London. The lights at Marylebone Road allowed impatient commuters a glimpse of the handcuffed Peter with Sirs, loitering forlornly, still looking for their transport. The thief was awesomely embarrassed, but an even worse experience was to follow.

As he anxiously searched the tailed-back traffic for the transport, a showy Range Rover came into view twenty yards or so away down the crescent. Its passenger seat contained the red-foxed Elaine, her arm draped around the shoulder of the driver. Both Sirs caught on as Peter prayed they would clear the lights at the next shunt opposite his perch on the Marylebone Road and vanish.

But the Range Rover was halted by the changing lights directly opposite the trio. Immediately the screws did a sharp about-face in unison to defeat Peter's inquisitive stare as he wondered who the driver was. Elaine did not move a muscle. She must have seen them, but she behaved as if she hadn't, staring straight ahead and completely ignoring the pathetic scene. It was the last time he ever saw or heard from her.

The transfer to Spring Hill went through in the autumn of '86. On the labour board he asked for and got a job on the gardening party.

He was now grafting at his second passion, gardening – something he'd developed in Dartmoor. He eventually schemed and worked himself into the position of being responsible for the housing estate that abutted the prison.

It was a bloody wilderness, all the more surprising when one considers that there were a couple of hundred work-shy prisoners in the camp above. Peter set about refurbishing the depressing demesne. He became a law unto himself, and though he planted out the common land with willow and Siberian cherry he finally had his come-uppance one Sunday, 'borrowing' a tractor-load of plants without authority. The effete governor had no option but to return him to the camp area and put him to work in the tomato tunnels. He commented prior to standing him down, 'I realise you have bucked the place up no end, but when you're gone it will be left unattended, I'm afraid. That's how it is here.'

Irked by the unrewarding exchange, Peter reflected, 'And whose bloody fault would that be? You're the governor.'

'Oh, by the by, Scott, you're forbidden to prune the roses. The garden party can take care of that,' the governor murmured gently.

Since his banishment from the estate, Peter had taken to attending to the two hundred-odd roses that languished unpruned and unmulched around the administration building himself. Tomato tunnels are a poor substitute for roses, and with 'borrowed' shears Peter prowled, out of bounds in the dusk, pruning the roses. Word got out about his nocturnal passion, and staff hid in the copse at twilight to catch him. Such is the vacuum of prison life. The War of the Roses epitomises the boredom endured by both staff and inmates in the custodial system.

47

The Death of Passion

On 1 February 1988 Peter was released from Spring Hill prison. No one picked him up as in days gone by, so it was bus and train to London, calling in at Sheila's jerry to pick up the keys to his temporary abode.

It was a very temporary abode. Madam returned from Spain unexpectedly and found that she had scant use for a freebie lodger under her feet. They gelled for about three weeks, but when Peter started to write this autobiography his typing in her back bedroom irked her. Meanwhile her chap found 'the fucking old lag' not to his liking, and this was used as the excuse when Peter finally got his marching orders.

'Peter, I know you'll understand. It was a favour for Diana, a temporary arrangement to get you out. But, you know, my chap feels inhibited with you here. Can you find somewhere else?'

A target criminal on parole is closely monitored by his probation officer and his permission alone permits a change of address. Peter tubed it to the Elephant and Castle to give the bad news to Mike Baker, whom he had initially regarded as a total arsehole when he saw him at Spring Hill prior to release.

The lift in Borough High Street was out of order, so he trudged up the stairs.

'Asked you to leave, has she? You haven't been a nuisance? When I saw that luxury flat I knew it wasn't for you. Well, we'll have to find you lodgings, or else you'll have to go back to Wandsworth in all probability. You have a week to look for something. I'll phone one or two contacts.'

Baker seemed genuinely concerned; he was even friendly. Perhaps he had started respecting Peter for reporting faithfully and keeping him informed. Five days' banging on landlords' doors in Kilburn and Cricklewood taught Peter that that ilk wanted no DHSS lodgers. So now he had two days in which to move out, with Madam getting more irritable daily. It was fucking undignified.

Baker could seemingly find nothing either until, on his penultimate day in Maida Vale, Peter had a phone call from him.

'Peter? Good news of a sort. A charity, Penrose, is willing to put you up in their hostel in Bonnington Square. That's Vauxhall. Know the area? It's a bit rough, but a friend of mine, Sue Livett, runs the hostel. If you could be there tomorrow at twelve she'll meet you. It's the best I can do, I'm afraid.'

There was great excitement in the opulent lounge in Maida Vale and Madam trilled brightly as she got out the *A to Z* to locate the almost indiscernible square.

'Vauxhall is an up-and-coming area. So central, too. You're a lucky boy.'

Up-and-coming? You could have fooled Peter. To him, Bonnington Square looked like the end of the world. It was grimy, with the appearance of Dickensian England, and the oddity of some gracious trees standing at each narrow corner of the mini-square. The houses, huddled together like Monopoly buildings, had provided refuge for a whole variety of ethnic groups during their long history.

Sue Livett rolled up to meet him in a Dormobile at ten past twelve – a pert, pretty angel, who took the suited and booted Peter in with a single glance, a sceptical look that said, 'You won't last very long here.'

He set out to charm Sue, and succeeded sufficiently well to persuade her to let him squat in a first-floor rear annexe room, one with the luxury of a wash basin and a cooker point. The room, though empty, had some of the previous lodger's bundled clothing, abandoned in the wardrobe. It was to be the essence of misfortune for Peter later on.

'That's John's stuff,' said Ms Livett. 'He's a black chap, gone to the USA. It doesn't look like he'll return, but if he does you'll have to move upstairs. I have a new duvet and some bedding in the van for you.'

So Penrose's angel ministered to the once-elegant Peter, now a sorry sight as he came to his eventual reward: charity!

With the exception of a lone Scots lifer enduring his parole, the cast at Bonnington Square were scumbags to a man – winos, petty thieves who vandalised the phone in the house to get a few pence, drug abusers, none apparently grateful to Sue Livett or the Penrose organisation for providing their refuge. Peter had to ask himself the question, was he too just another scumbag?

'They're all a load of shit, Peter,' the Scot advised him. 'Get a better lock put on your door.'

Peter never bothered. He had nothing they could steal. Elaine had lost or dumped most of his things. It was a bloody undignified time . . . but things were to get worse, much worse.

Settling in, his first port of call was the Paddington Tennis Club. He cannot now decide if it was bold of him or merely crass.

It was morning and few of the resident eunuchs were in evidence, though one old face pumped his hand: Ray Gibb.

'Lovely to see you, old boy. Home is the sailor, home from the sea, eh? Fancy a hit?'

They had just got started when a secretary Peter did not know came to Court Ten, called Ray to the fence, and whispered earnestly to him in emphatic fashion. Then she scooted off.

'Peter, I'm awfully sorry, some mix-up. You're no longer a member. Nor, I'm afraid, are you welcome. Shall we pop up to the office, try and sort it out?'

Peter knew that was not on, so the gracious Ray crossed Elgin Avenue and had a hit with him in nearby Paddington Recreation Ground. His only bake had vanished. The thief felt shattered.

There was a protest group in his favour, led by Larry Adler. An EGM was scheduled to lobby support. But no one turned up. He dropped in to his former friend Alan Waller's bookshop in Hammersmith, where Waller explained in sheepish fashion, 'The tennis committee met. They asked me what I could tell them about you because none of them knew you. I'm afraid I had to tell them the truth. It was not so much you they objected to, but the people who had visited you there in the past. You'll find another club.'

And so it was that the thief – skint, alone, unloved, and probably unlovable – came to the tennis courts at Regent's Park where he was to find the comfort of the odd kindly face sheltering, not unlike Oscar Wilde ostracised in Paris (where even the wallpaper punished him).

One true friend, Steve Reardon, played the game. Steve still had his tennis shop outside the club in Castellain Road, and was to provide racquets, balls, and eventually an old Mini banger, with little regard for the fact that he was struggling himself. Another player that was still shaping up well was Mike Baker, the once-despised probation officer from Borough High Street. They had the odd beer in Vauxhall and a healthy respect developed.

'Stick with Penrose and you'll probably get housed,' Mike advised him.

'I started to write an autobiography in Wandsworth in eighty-six,' Peter told him. 'I mean to change my way of life. The writing will help. I don't think I'll be back at it.'

Mike Baker examined his important charge with a sceptical eye. He'd heard it all before.

'One step at a time. Keep writing, stick to the park and your tennis. It'll pay dividends sooner or later.'

In March 1988 Mike Baker asked him on short notice to address some members of the Parole Board, to include a Secretary of State and a sitting judge. Peter performed well and R. N. Adair, Mike Baker's boss, wrote a letter of thanks, grateful that the Parole Board had the benefit of the 'consumer's' point of view.

So Baker became a pal and a crutch. The thief was fragile in his loneliness. In the past his passion for larceny had enabled him to buy friends and lovers, and he realised that most of his life had been spent buying company. What had he got for the hundreds of thousands squandered? A charity hostel in Vauxhall, and lucky to get it too! He discharged the bile of an ill-used lifetime pounding out his typescript on his Smith Corona, and slowly finding himself.

Meanwhile Mike Baker filled the vacuum left by his lost pals. He was an uncomplicated, sincere man, whose constant rubbing shoulders with liars and scumbags had not deprived him of his faith in human nature.

In time, they got to trust one another, so it came as a shock of disappointment to Mike when police from Wiltshire called on him at Borough High Street.

'We're from Chippenham, Wilts. We believe one of your parolees may have been involved in a robbery on our patch. Peter Scott, born Peter Craig Gulston.'

'Are you certain? I was sure he was keeping out of trouble.'

'Yes, we're sure. We propose searching his home – I assume you know where Peter is living?'

Baker nodded. He was gutted. He asked about the burglary and they told him.

On 29 April 1988, just under three months after Peter's release from Spring Hill, Bowood, the Earl of Sherborne's home at Calne in Wiltshire, was burgled and a large quantity of gems stolen. The Wiltshire officers had decided to arrest Scott as a result of information supplied by Detective Sergeant Wilkins, based at Vine Street police station, close by Mayfair. Wilkins had a reliable informant, who had told him of Scott's involvement and disposal of the property.

At 6 a.m. on 7 June, his bedroom door at 63 Bonnington Square was kicked in and he was invaded by eight or so officers. His room was searched, during which he was asked to account for a bloodstained bit of crêpe bandage.

'I recently started to play tennis again seriously. My thumb's been bleeding almost daily.'

Another apparently bloodstained article was found among the ex-lodger's effects. It appeared that some of his clothing had significance to the searching officers. Peter was arrested and taken to Chippenham.

Three days of interrogation, ID parades, and medicals followed. Peter appeared on seven ID parades, and was not picked out on any of them. But constant extended remands in custody, two before magistrates, made him so anxious and fearful that he began to have heart palpitations. It was of no importance that he knew he'd done nothing. The arresting officer, DI McKeaveney, an Ulsterman, was convinced he was guilty, for no better reason than that the computer and a Sergeant Wilkins at Vine Street said so. Blood samples were taken and eliminated, but still McKeaveney was reluctant to release Peter. Of course, in the end he had to.

Now Peter was concerned for his standing with Mike Baker and Penrose. He should not have feared. They both supported the shattered parolee.

It was not until August that he was told he would not be required to return. The experience had a plus, though: it scared the shit out of him. He realised how very easy it was to be in jeopardy on account of the past. Regent's Park became more tolerable. Then there was another plus. Solicitors acting for him at Chippenham thought he had a case of wrongful arrest. A summons was issued on his behalf.

Two years later, Mrs Laura Cox advised him at her chambers that, considering the defence the Wiltshire police had entered, his claim could not succeed. It probably cost the taxpayer five thousand pounds (Peter was legally aided) to arrive at that conclusion.

The year 1988 was a bloody one. Living on fifty-five pounds a week – his income support – cannot be done. He often walked to Regent's Park to save tube fares, until he eventually found an attractive young lady solicitor who would give him a fiver for a hit. Bless you, Harriet.

It was a life-saver. His typescript, some of which had been in the hands of the Wiltshire police, was returned, and a friend from Spring Hill, Tony S., interested a motor-trader chum of his in the book. Ray Thackwell put up a much-needed initial thousand pounds for the pair of them. But times were difficult for him and he bailed out, although his largesse allowed Peter to stay on the straight and narrow and continue to write.

Otherwise he imprisoned himself at the tennis courts, looking on it as his penance for his past sins. In his last six years of freedom he has spent at least two thousand of his days at the courts – quite his most protracted bit of bird.

Taters is now eighty-one, and he is still prowling about Mayfair, slowed down but still with the heart of a lion.

Outside the now seemingly passionless thief's criminal bankruptcy (£440,000), the only creditors are the likes of Mike Baker, Sue Livett, and Penrose, for putting a roof over his head when there was nowhere else to go, and of course Islington Council for giving him a tenancy in October 1988. They were the real players in a thief's resurrection. No one from his past wins any medals in this department, a ghastly indictment for the 'friends' of a man who sprayed thousands about to buy respect and company. In reality, he was being 'that flash prat', fostering jealousy and making enemies.

Learning to live on sixty quid in 'bad' weeks takes a bit of doing. Then again, thousands of blameless pensioners have struggled with that cross for decades in our caring society. It took the flash prat a little time to acquire their skill. Poverty, to his former acquaintances an unattractive feature in anyone, eventually became a privilege. He actually found who he was and where he was at, finally revealing to himself the parasitical, predatory motives of all the garlic crotches he had spent his life chasing, realising they had nothing to offer at all.

Peter Scott, as he is on the rent book today, has not re-offended. The temptation to do so diminishes yearly, and he recognises that his final purgatory is to live, in modest circumstances, with the absolute conviction that he was a 'mug cunt' for most of his life. His vanity had seen to that.

So what is he like today? He cycles around Islington on his collapsible Raleigh cycle, looks marvellous with his suntan, is not unhappy, envious, bitter, or even sad. He is above all mentally alert, having found himself beyond a thousand scars.

This bloody tome keeps him going. He writes often in vanity, frequently in penance, but not for gain (though a few quid would not come amiss). It is a cautionary tale for others who might think the V & A roof is their stage. Think carefully, assuming you have a choice and are not, like the author, the victim of a master passion.

But now the passion for larceny in Peter is finally culled, or so it seems, if only for the most elementary of reasons. He has no more time to give them.

GLOSSARY OF SLANG
TERMINOLOGY

Back (verb)	To go round the back
Bake	Place to hide; a good place to stay
Bin	Trouser pocket; (verb) to pocket
Boat race	Face (rhyming slang)
Bock	Bad luck
Bogie	Drawback; minus point (e.g. when calculating the risks attached to a prospective burglary)
Bone	Tediously repeated topic of conversation (from the image of a dog biting on the same old bone)
Bottle	Courage; nerve (rhyming slang: bottle and glass/arse)
Bottle off	Follow
Bream	Brilliant
Burnt	Window (rhyming slang: burnt grass/glass)
Cane	Jemmy; (verb) to prise open with a jemmy
Charkhams	A reputable firm of West End tailors, no longer trading
Charlie	Cocaine
Chavvy	Child
Cotch (verb)	To capture
Cotterell	Large package (e.g. of jewellery)
Cox and Coles	A firm of safe-makers; hence the safe itself
Cozzer	Policeman
Crank	Masturbator; (verb) to masturbate
Dolly mixtures	Pictures (rhyming slang)
Drum	House
Drummer	Burglar who first knocks on the door of a house to ascertain if anyone is home
Dwell the box (verb)	To wait (from greyhound racing)
Ecret	Value; price
Fanny	Lie

Flimp (verb)	To thieve; hustle; commit robbery
Gam (verb)	To suck; lick
Glamma	Brand name of mink
Glim	Torch
Grass	Criminal who betrays an accomplice; (verb) to inform on accomplices to the police
Hoister	Shoplifter
Hoot	Scream; press outcry
Hoppo	Mate; colleague; criminal partner
Hurry-up	Smash-and-grab raid
Jelly-baby	Weak person, unable to withstand interrogation
Jerry	Public house
Kettle	Watch
Kite	Cheque
Layer	Bookmaker
Minces	Eyes (rhyming slang: mince pies)
Monkey	Five hundred pounds
Nevis	Seven (backwards slang)
Odd lot	Police car
On top	Time to go
Pikey	Gypsy
Polar Ammul	Trade name of an ice-cold form of plastic explosive (often called Polar Ammo)
Pony	Twenty-five pounds
Punkah	Fan
Purdeys	A make of firearms
Pussy	Furs
Rabbit	Talk; conversation (rhyming slang: rabbit and pork)
Rasher	Trouble
Screwer	Burglary
Seconds	Second thoughts
Shiddock	'Marriage' or partnership between criminals (from Yiddish for a Jewish marriage-broker)
Slammer	Prison
Slaughter	Place where stolen goods are hidden until they can be disposed of
Spieler	Gambling club; gambler
Staveley	Trade name of a make of drainpipe, much loved by cat burglars because it never breaks or gives way
Stilson	Trade name of a make of bolt-cutter

Stipe	Stipendiary magistrate
Sweeney	Metropolitan Police Flying Squad (rhyming slang: Sweeney Todd)
Sweet out	Good escape route
Tank	Wad of cash
Tom	Jewellery (rhyming slang: tomfoolery)
Trembler	Burglar alarm
Turtles	Gloves (rhyming slang: turtle doves)
Up for none	All duck and no dinner
Verbal (verb)	To state (often falsely) that someone has made self-incriminating remarks
Verbals	Self-incriminating remarks attributed to criminal suspects in the written statements of police officers, often denied by the suspects who claim the police have maliciously concocted them